Three Came to Ville Marie

by

Alan Sullivan

Front cover: 'Les filles du Roi' by Eleanor Fortescue
Brickdale

Back cover: Map of Montréal (Ville Marie) in 1760

CONTENTS

In Old France

Castellon

— I —

The long arrowy street of Castellon lay baking under a hot Breton sun when the Abbé Callot stood at his gate talking with a young man whose formidable bulk towered a foot higher than his own head; nor did the contrast end here; in conversation the Abbé was prone to smiles, quick little communicative twinkles as though practically everything one said suggested its humorous angle; his face was rosy, with quick blue eyes and good-natured lips that were always in motion, his skull bald and pinkish, and a comfortable paunch revealed a suave curve beneath his accommodating cassock.

Beside this genial personality loomed Paul de Lorimier of less than half his years, with a large raw-boned body and wide shoulders supporting a head whose delicate modelling seemed at variance with his powerful frame: the head was small, the eyes sombre, the expression grave. Paul looked very substantial, very determined, and he smiled hardly at all.

Fronting the village street with its square white wooden-shuttered cube, the Abbé's house sat a little back in a small, formal garden with rectangular patterns of pebble-bordered beds, and from the gate one might follow whatever life moved in Castellon on a summer afternoon. To the south over gabled roofs rose a low ridge where the Château Marbeau lifted a cluster of conical topped turrets that exactly resembled candle extinguishers, and one could see the line of trimmed junipers marking its wide flagged terrace. East and west ran the street, sliding presently away from the houses into a dwindling ribbon of dust between two endless lines of Lombardy poplars; east to Vitré, west along the calm Vilaine to Rennes and its dark granite walls. This was a view of peace and plenitude, well loved by Abbé Callot, but now he was looking at Paul.

"My son, I have been thinking much of you of late; you have finished our course of reading, you have worked faithfully and know the classics as do but few of your age, yet I'm not quite content."

"No?"

"Not quite. I think perhaps there has been too much Plato, too little Horace, which without question is my fault, and for a comfortable view of life--one which brings a social poise--Horace is not to be overlooked."

"You may be right, father, but I do not know-- yet."

"Ah! that one little word--yet. What promise it offers, while I, alas, have no use for it. Now listen, my son, for I am going to surprise you. The time has come when I can offer nothing more, and what you acquire after this must be of your own taking and making; it will be a matter of feeling, of experience and emotion,

2

but first, Paul, there is around you that wall which you must knock down. This is why I commend Horace to you."

"But, father,----"

"Permit me! you have a comfortable income, you're young, strong and free, so what will you do first?"

"Travel, mon père, I desire to travel--there is Spain and Italy and Greece--then I shall write books."

"About those countries?"

"Why not?"

The Abbé's blue eyes fixed on the Château Marbeau. "You have discussed this with Jacqueline?"

"Not much as yet, but when affairs are settled between us I shall tell her more."

"So they are not settled--yet?"

Paul frowned a little. "I wish I could say they were; she is as wayward as she is beautiful, she is capricious, she changes like the wind."

"Yet you still think she is the right one for you?"

"With all my heart. Last week I thought it was arranged, this week I do not know."

"What does the Comte say to all this?" The Abbé knew very well how the Comte felt about it.

"He neither consents nor opposes; he simply says nothing, but Jacqueline's mother is on my side."

"Have you considered whether this future of a writer would be acceptable to her, because, frankly, I doubt it?"

"Why not? She is too young to know her own mind."

"While you, Paul, for your years, are the oldest man I know. It is curious that I, who am of an age to be your father, should yet feel myself younger than you. Now about this writing I suppose you will make the attempt, but I do not advise classical subjects--enough has been said there for the present--so as an experiment why not write about your own country? why not go to Paris, live there, make your friends there, study what you see, wait till King Louis is dead, and then if you still feel you must write, do so about him? If you have the gift, there is your opportunity."

"And all his mistresses?" said the young man, dryly.

"Undoubtedly--all of them--but keep space to tell about one who was not a mistress."

"De Maintenon?"

"Yes, de Maintenon. What a woman! and the greatest of them all." The Curé's eyes were very bright now, and he made a gesture of enthusiasm. "Today a humble daughter of the Church, though once a Protestant, yet she drew the king from how many white arms to be servant of the true God. And when you go to Paris you should be able to kick down that wall of which I spoke."

4

Paul appeared unconvinced; his huge body--he came of a long line of Breton farmers--looked almost monumental with its heavy moulding; such a frame might have been hewn in one of the quarries of Rennes, and seemed suited to battle with the elements; it was difficult to imagine a pen in the great muscular hand that now capped the Curé's gatepost. There was, too, a certain adamantine quality about him so that his power suggested stubborn resistance rather than effort. The Abbé Callot had laboured hard over this pupil of his, and he loved the young man.

"I understand what you mean," rumbled Paul in his deep voice. "I have often seen it in your eyes, but what is natural in you is not so in me. Nature has made us different. I would give much to be able to join my friends with a laugh, I would be glad if they smiled at the sight of me, instead of shrugging, but when I try to be at ease there is something in me that tightens and I become silent. One by one I lose these friends who know nothing of my hunger for their companionship. It is not them I dislike but myself, and today," he added desperately, "there is just yourself and Jacqueline."

"Then marry her, my son, marry her as quickly as is permitted. Be less of a rebel against a society that you do not understand. These are modern days we live in, so for a time forget your classics which are useful only so far as they may help you to understand the present. Wisdom may be learned in the arms of a good woman, while experience lies in the embrace of those who are not so good." The Abbé's eyes twinkled and his lips took on a curve. "Come, come, you are not in the confessional now. There is much in Paris that will attract Jacqueline, so why not go there? and I would be happier if in your expression there was less expectation of, shall we say, suffering. That wall, Paul, that wall, certainly you must kick it down."

The young man smiled a little. "With Jacqueline perhaps, I hope so; at any rate, I'll try."

"Be patient when she is yours; leave the door of the cage open, a small flight will do her no harm; if there is true love she will return. Remember that the woman is always more conscious of what she has given than the man who receives it. Also if she be one of spirit and imagination, such as Jacqueline, she will not be content with the attentions of one man only. Do not forget that. There is indeed," here the Abbé gave another twinkle, "a certain kind of heavy, stolid devotion that most women find stifling. I have often observed it--also has Horace."

With this he gave the big shoulder a friendly thump. "Enough of my celibate conclusions, which no doubt are quite misleading. Who comes now from Vitré, soldiers?"

He had sharp eyes and, a mile to the east, Paul caught sight of mounted men through a slowly drifting feather of dust. They approached at a trot, the sharp clang of iron sounded over the steeply arched bridge that spanned the Vilaine, and presently came a clatter up the cobbled street. There were four men; in advance a long-curled officer of the Musketeers in scarlet uniform with blue facings and plumed hat; at his heels a grizzled corporal and two troopers. The sun smote on glossy flanks, on a scarlet saddle-cloth with gold fringe, on soft russet leather boots with loose flopping legs, on silver spurs and silvered curb-chains. The sharp sound of this arrival and passage along the narrow street opened rows of shutters that till then had been closed against the noonday glare, a perspective of heads was thrust out, a troop of shouting children raced after the cavalcade, then stood sucking small fingers, staring at these gay visitors from another world.

6

Approaching the Abbé's gate, the officer pulled up with a jingle of polished chain; young, dark, smiling, his slim legs moulded in their tight-fitting breeches, his body lithe, agile, cat-like, he sat his charger as though he had grown there and, thus poised, made a wide salute.

"Mon père, I desire to find the mairie of Castellon; perhaps you will have the goodness...."

He broke off, eyes suddenly fastened on Paul. He hesitated a moment, then leaned forward with a quick laugh. "Mon Dieu! can this be? yes, it must be! Old Sobersides; is it you in the flesh?" He slid to the ground all in one motion, grasped Paul's hand and wrung it with enthusiasm.

Paul was now smiling. "Yes, Jules, it is I, and I knew you at once. I would know you anywhere; you have hardly changed at all."

"I'm sorry for that, but you, at least, are one foot wider. What luck this is! Mon père," he turned swiftly, "forgive my rudeness. I am Lieutenant Jules Vicotte of the Musketeers, at your service, also on present duty to establish certain billeting accommodation in this Breton country. And this solemn old Paul--Paul, you tell his Reverence what a model pupil you were at the seminary, and how bad myself."

There was an infectious warmth about him, a brightness that Abbé Callot found very welcome; he looked like a good soldier and bubbled with natural joyousness, so that sleepy old Castellon seemed rejuvenated by his coming, and the priest, watching Paul's reserve crumble under his friend's gaiety, thought that nothing could be more opportune. The habitual sombreness had given place to an unaccustomed grin, the whole great bulk of him looked far more human.

"You will be in Castellon for how long, Jules?"

"Perhaps a day, perhaps only a few hours, it does not really matter, my Colonel is a man of consideration."

"You will stay with me ... yes, you must."

"I will be enchanted; you live in Castellon?"

"Always; my property is here."

"Property! that sounds impressive. Not married yet, eh?"

"How did you know that?"

"You are still, shall we say, unmodified," laughed Jules. "You agree, mon père?"

"I grasp your meaning, lieutenant," smiled Callot.

"But I shall be ... soon," countered Paul.

"Alors! there is nothing else to do here, so you must present me," he turned to his corporal, "Henri, I lodge tonight with Monsieur de Lorimier. Take my horse. Mon père, my salutations. Now, Sobersides, let us inspect this domain of yours."

With Paul he strode off, a slight gay figure beside a soberly attired man mountain, walking lightly, like a dancer, eyes full of smiles, thinking that here was an experience, but just for a night and no more. Paul, he decided, had not altered a fraction, merely enlarged;

there was the same half stubborn, half wistful expression in the small, harshly modelled face balanced so oddly on the elephantine body, the same suggestion of something locked within and trying to get out. One remembered the face, and hardly knew why.

The house was like its master, square, solidly planted, a bare exterior, thick walled, with small windows; inside, a sort of semi-darkness peopled with heavy furniture; the walls were bare save for a few prints, the floors naked and polished; books stood in stiff, methodical rows; nowhere showed any touch of lightness, and Jules began to regret a too prompt acceptance. Picturing the Paul of other days, he might have known better. He found the dining salon gloomy ... it had not altered in a century, but just outside spread a fruited apple orchard, where birds sang and bees were busy.

"Mon vieux! you live here alone?"

"With Joseph, my cook and servant."

"Your parents are dead?"

"Five years ago, Jules; then the land came to me."

"Independent now, eh?"

"Yes, but there is little need for money."

"But Paul, what an absurd philosophy. Tchk-- tchk! do you mean it?"

"Why not? the farm has been in the family for hundreds of years; they were all farmers, all my people; they saved, they did not spend. I buy books and clothes, little else."

Jules, noting the clothes, drained his glass; it was not the wine he had hoped for; he dabbed his lips with a lace-edged kerchief, looked puzzled.

"My friend, you are a strange creature; do you never go to Paris?"

"I do not care for Paris."

"Come, Sobersides, that is incredible! it is not healthy, it is hardly sane: Paris is life, motion, colour, everything: you hear the heart of France beating in Paris, while in Castellon you catch the thump of the carthorse, the grunt of the pig. One might as well be in Canada, from which God protect us. Tell me, what friends have you in this Breton cemetery? You look satisfied, but I cannot believe you are. How do you amuse yourself, or is it possible you do not ask to be amused? Speak up, Paul, speak up; unburden that hairy bosom of yours."

He got this out, brows wrinkling, smiling in a way that Paul remembered well, and regarding his gigantic host as though he were some new kind of human exhibit: then----

"Come Paul, something is the matter ... tell me."

"Nothing, Jules, nothing at all; you ask about my friends here; well, they are few, I admit, but I have my books; I know where to find them, they do not change."

"What is life without change? but you seem to have provided for that; when do you marry?"

"Perhaps very soon."

10

"And the lady?"

"The only daughter of the Comte Marbeau; their château is close by ... that one with the turrets--you passed below it coming from Rennes."

Jules tossed up his head and laughed. "She has your agricultural instincts, I hope."

"Not exactly--not as yet--but we have known each other all our lives."

"Yet she hesitates?" Jules had become restless, his tone held a shade of unnoted mockery, "is there nothing more to tell me? honestly Paul, you do not suggest a joyous lover."

"You must see her and judge for yourself: she is twenty; her father served under Turenne in Holland; she is gay, like you, and...." he paused with a sudden softening of expression that gave his sternly moulded features a sort of pathos, "Jules, will you tell me something, and not laugh at me?"

"Certainly, if I can."

"You are perhaps in love yourself?"

"At the moment, no: I am what you call convalescent from the last attack, split between regret and anticipation. Today I am actually interested in the billeting of troops."

"Well, I am deeply in love, yet make little progress. Jacqueline's mother is on my side, but I am not sure of her father. My resources are sufficient, indeed for a Breton I am a rich man, and Jacqueline's dot is provided. For me there can be no other woman,

11

but, but...."

"You feel at a loss when with her, eh?"

Paul blinked at him. "How did you know that?"

"It is very simple; you lack practice."

"But my heart speaks."

"Perhaps her hearing is not of the best," said Jules, wickedly. "Listen, my friend! one does not question your heart, but obviously your intelligence is at fault. Has she no other admirers?"

"I hope not."

"Tchk--tchk! Sobersides, you are blind. Now, have I your leave to speak?"

"But, of course, why not?"

Paul, leaning forward on his big arms, looked very serious. "Your visit today may mean much. As for Jacqueline, I'm conscious I do not please her as I would, and when you have seen her you will tell me why. The Abbé advises me to forget the classics and read Horace, he suggests that I go to Paris and...."

"That priest strikes me as a wise man and a bonhomme," chuckled Jules. "For myself I am a stranger to both classics and Horace, but already I perceive in you and this Jacqueline of yours a pair of Castellon cabbages who...."

"She is nothing like a cabbage," grunted Jacqueline's lover.

12

"Well, we shall see, but, till then, a pair of cabbages that have grown up beside each other unaware of what goes on beyond the vegetable wall. The garden is well tended, and the life comfortable though undoubtedly dull. You, it seems, are content to go on living like this, but it may seem that in her composition--which is more young and tender than yours, Paul--is a certain something that makes her unwilling to end her days in a Breton soup pot. And this, Sobersides, will certainly happen if she marries you and you do not change. There I think you have the situation."

Paul gulped back his protest unvoiced; Jules was absurd, perhaps insulting, but his casual assurance had a quality about it that got under one's skin, and now it would be difficult ever to think of Jacqueline and himself without visualising a pair of cabbages. That vexed him, though oddly not as much as he might have expected, and this rediscovered friend of his seemed so immune and experienced in affairs of the heart that it would be foolish not to pick up what one could. He saw something in Jules' personality that he envied, though little in his point of view that one could admire, but there did remain an odd, unexplainable respect for a sagacity that caused him to accept life with such polished and careless grace. It would be a wonderful thing, thought Paul, if he could ever achieve anything like that for himself.

But Jules, glancing restlessly about the depressing apartment so solidly shut off from light and motion outside, had begun to lose all further interest in this old acquaintance of his. Sobersides he would remain to the end of his days, nothing one said could really have any effect here, and the ponderous lover simply could not understand. The girl he wanted, well-- she didn't matter, they were both doubtless but half alive, and nothing could matter much in a hole like this. It all made one hungry for the open road and the wind in one's face.

"Jules, I have been thinking that there is perhaps something in your view. I am not unwilling to change if it will help matters, but how is that done?"

"You cannot do it of yourself."

"Then by whom or what?"

"A woman, mon vieux, or better still, several women: that never fails, and I myself have achieved several transformations. Let us go into your orchard, it is brighter there."

— II —

Château Marbeau, le 15 Juin, 1688.

To Mdlle Clothilde Desfraines, 17, rue St. Honoré, Paris.

Clothilde, Clothilde, I am too much excited to write clearly but a coach goes through Castellon tomorrow for Paris, so I will try. It is now midnight on the most wonderful day of my life, and no sleep for me.

I must begin with Paul of whom you know. This afternoon he visited us and brought me some prints of old temples in Greece, and I could not help thinking how much those temples were like himself, big and enormously strong, and tremendously heavy; also there were some books, old books, with not a single Molière, Racine or Fontaine. Mother had been talking about him before he came, how worthy and sensible he was--I've told you all that part of it before--and there he stood more than ever worthy in his so severely cut clothes and a look in his eyes that made me sorry for him. You will understand that I had promised my answer in four days, and there were three still unspent, so I had not expected him. Mama is much in his favour, while Papa, though much urged by Mama, says that though it is very unusual he will not decide the matter himself, and often sends me a sly look, so I am convinced he understands my real sentiments about Paul.

When mother left us, Paul began not in the way he usually does by telling me of his devotion, and what young people like ourselves can do with their lives if they are just sensible, but something quite different as though he were actually trying to amuse me. Think of that from old Paul! And it was amusing, but not in the way he meant. Then he said that a friend of his, a Lieutenant Jules Vicotte of the Musketeers, had begged to present himself that evening.

Clothilde, can you imagine the whole world changing in the short period of six hours? Jules--I think of him like that--was superb in his ravishing uniform. He is just twenty-five years of age. He came, he kissed Mama's hand, he looked at me very quickly, and for some reason he seemed surprised. I looked at him, something passed between us, and it was all over. I found myself with a palpitation. Wondering not a little what he would be like, I had put on my new skirt of flowered satin, with bodice cut low and Venice lace. I wore an open ruff, my hair was powdered, and Mama thought the bodice much too low. I thought not. Paul had not seen me just like that before and looked surprised, but I wanted to show the officer of the Musketeers that Castellon is not so far from Paris after all.

15

The evening cannot be described. How can two people who have never met before completely understand each other all in a second, without any preparation? When Jules was not looking at me he conveyed somehow that he was thinking about me. His eyes are very dark and quick, and full of light. His stature is medium, his shape of excellent proportion. He has fought in Holland and Spain. His linen is very fine, and he wears one emerald ring.

To Mama he was most polite, though I thought her a little cold and disapproving, but between him and Papa there was at once a striking cordiality, for they knew some of the same people and houses in Paris, whose names Papa had not mentioned before. This was of vast interest to me, and while they talked I noticed that Mama was quite silent, for Papa never tells us what happens when he goes to Paris.

And Paul. Paul just sat with an expression of bewilderment, as though this was not at all what he had expected. He tried to talk to Mama because he had nothing in common with Papa's and Jules' conversation, but she found little to say, being too busy listening. Now--it is just past midnight--I am convinced that Papa has been summoned to her boudoir to hear something quite different. Poor Papa! Also I am persuaded that in his youth he must have been not unlike what Jules is now.

Clothilde, I know so much more than I did this morning; I know a lot about the King's balls and assemblies, and St. Germain and Versailles, and how de Maintenon got rid of Madame Montespan, and the new dances, and the salon of old Ninon d'Enclos where they say the most terrible things about everyone, and did you know that when de Maintenon was married to Scarron, that very wicked poet, her house used to be

16

called l'hôtel de l'Impecuniosité, where her friends sent baskets of food. It would take hours to relate all the things Jules and Papa talked about, and on which Papa was so surprisingly informed.

But the one important thing is that I'm in love, love, love, for the very first time. I am, of course, not a little sorry for Paul, but it is pleasing to reflect that in that business, and in spite of all his book reading, I have been right and he wrong. This gives one more confidence in one's own judgment; but while I think I can expect support from Papa, it is certain that Mama will be difficult. After dinner Mama made Jules sit beside her, and asked me to play the clavichord, which I did very badly, while Paul waited like a mountain of rock, with no expression at all, and Papa stood with his hands behind his back, looking amused about something. Then Jules asked me to play a composition I had never even heard of, and when I said so, Papa asked Jules if he could play it, and Jules said yes, and looked at Mama in the oddest way, so she had to beg him to do it, and he played superbly, and sang, and Clothilde, it was a Spanish love-song. I didn't understand a word, but it was certainly love, and his eyes told me all I wanted to know.

After that something else happened. The air being very mild, the salon windows were open to the terrace. Papa, Mama and Paul were talking and I with Jules, and then somehow we two were out on the terrace and out of the light, with his arms around me, and he was kissing me and calling me his little Castellon cabbage. Clothilde, it was like heaven. I had once been kissed by Paul, when life was stupid and nothing else to do, but that was just an experiment, nothing like this. Paul's kiss is like a cartload of something on one's face, and not at all pleasant, and when it was over he looked very ashamed, though it was my fault, not his, but

Jules' kiss is like the warm wing of a butterfly on one's lips, and I liked being called a little Castellon cabbage, it was so disrespectful, and after that I knew I would love him always. Then he whispered something about tomorrow, and we were in the salon again, and I am sure the others had not noticed.

After that the evening came to an end all too soon. Jules' adieux were very correct and formal. Papa said that, should he come this way again, he might present himself at the château, but Mama made no mention of this. Then Jules' hand touched mine, transferring to me a little piece of folded paper. I've been reading and reading it; 'At noon, below the terrace.' That's all, but it means no sleep tonight for Jacqueline.

I am so frightened and happy, and breathless. Now, while I write, he is in that old tomb of a house of Paul's--you can see it from here--and I wonder what those two are saying to each other and what persuaded Paul to bring him to the château. Paul might have known, but evidently he has not that kind of imagination. And to think if he had not brought him I would probably be Madame de Lorimier within the next few months. Don't you like Madame Jules Vicotte better? doesn't it sound more chic?

Alors, there it remains for just twelve hours longer; my feet do not touch the earth, my head is in the clouds, but I must take some rest or else look a fright. This letter is all about myself, but you will forgive your most devoted,

J. de M.

Le lendemain après-midi.

18

Clothilde, the most terrible thing has transpired, and I am able to tell you of it because the Paris coach is delayed in arriving from Rennes. How shall I begin?

This morning Mama reproved me for unmaidenly behaviour last night, accusing me of inflicting wounds on Paul that he did not deserve, and she, seeing the two men together, and presuming Lieutenant Vicotte of being representative of his class in Paris, was the more convinced of the desirability of Paul as my husband. Also it was not customary for parents to humour a young girl as mine had humoured me, and that if within three days, I did not say yes to Paul of my own accord, she herself would announce that we were affianced. Then she went away, with her keys in more of a jingle than ever.

A little later Papa asked me to join him in his library. It was then eleven o'clock, so picture the condition of my nerves. But he was restful, his manner so shrewd and kind, unlike Mama's, that I nearly told him everything, but did not do this in case it be unfair to Jules. Paul never entered my head. Papa seemed to be aware of what had happened to me, indeed his attitude suggested that at some time or other the same thing had happened to himself, when Mama was not involved; and he gave me to understand that if in the affairs of the heart I found myself in need of counsel he would regret it were my confidence withheld from him. Also he hinted that perhaps in such matters his experience was wider than that of Mama. It was nearly noon when we embraced with affection, and I left him.

You will remember the parterre below the terrace and beyond the junipers, also the shrubbery below that again in which is the pool with the lilies, where you used to feed the golden carp. Alors, I was in the shrubbery beside the pool, when I heard a low whistle and Jules came out of the bushes, with his eyes shining. One instant, and I was in his arms, and never before has your Jacqueline been so happy. Instead of going on to Rennes as he said last night, he had come to me. I asked about Paul and he only laughed, swearing he would marry none but myself, that I was nothing like what he had expected from what Paul had told him, and he had loved me from the instant he saw me. I swore the same and assured him that I felt Papa would not oppose us, whatever Mama might say, and, Clothilde, we were in each other's embrace, his face against mine, when there was a crashing in the shrubbery and Paul plunged out, just like the red bull that got loose in Castellon in the breeding season last year.

I could not stir. Jules was so astonished that he only held me more tightly, and gazed at his friend. Paul's face was inflamed, his expression wild. He made one strange, thick sound in his throat, and plucked us apart--we might have been children against such anger and strength. Then, very quickly, he stooped, took Jules by one arm and one leg, swung him round once in the air, and threw him far into the pond. There was a splash like a great fountain, with the carp darting in all directions; the lily-pads rolled over on edge, while the water mingled with disturbed mud, for the pond has not been cleaned in several years.

Of course my breath stopped. Paul stood glaring at me and Jules was now climbing back on his hands and knees, the footing being too insecure to stand upright, till he got out with water and mud running from his pockets. His face was white like paper, his eyes black like ink, with murder in them. I could not speak. He walked up to Paul, struck him hard in the face, and walked away. Paul shook his head like a great dog, waited one instant, then marched off in the other direction, not even looking at me.

I was most frightened, and remembering what Papa had said, went straight to him and told everything. He listened, asking not one question till I had finished, then threw back his head in a great river of laughter; it was so funny that I had to laugh also--we would stop and look at each other, and then laugh again--till in the middle of this he gave a sudden little frown and said of course now there will be a duel, and he did not think Paul would exhibit much dexterity against an officer of the Musketeers. Also he warned me against doing anything to interfere, for Jules had lost his honour in the lily-pond, and must recover it as he himself decided, so----

Marie has just come in to say that the post-chaise is in sight from Rennes, so I must end this letter. I will of course inform you what next takes place. Now farewell, and you will easily imagine the conflicting emotions that possess your devoted

J. de M.

Picture it, Clothilde, a duel about ME!

— III —

Paul sat in his library trying to re-arrange a disordered mind: opposite him Monsieur Raoul Fouquette, Notaire of Castellon, in whose judgment as a man of experience he had entire confidence. The family of Fouquette had looked after the business affairs of the family de Lorimier for over a hundred years.

"You will understand, mon vieux," said the notaire, in a smooth, silky tone, "that in this business you have nothing to retract, nothing to regret: such occurrences are not unusual and always between men of some position they take the same course."

Paul gave a shrug. The point might be sound and well meant, but he found no comfort in it. Three days previously he had for just a moment gone mad. This was unquestionable. On the evening before that, when walking back from the château with his guest, there was an undoubted coolness, with only a few words from Jules, and himself practically silent. Next morning the same coolness, but in the case of Jules it was graced by an extreme, if formal, courtesy that made his host feel like a peasant. Jules had vastly enjoyed his visit, he begged Paul to be assured of that, and perhaps they would next meet in Paris. No mention of Jacqueline. Then a springy vault into the saddle, a creak of leather, a silvery jingle of chains above the hollow resonance of beating hooves, and he dwindled in the direction of Rennes. That was about eleven o'clock, and a few minutes after midday Paul felt irresistibly drawn to the château. He remembered questioning his own judgment in going, he knew that he was not expected, nor could he explain why, instead of following the winding road, he had taken a short cut across the orchards that led to a wicket gate near the shrubbery.

Then revelation and disaster.

Next morning there arrived a smart cavalry officer from Rennes, with Jules' challenge. Paul, bewildered, took it to Raoul Fouquette, who formulated the acceptance, fixing day and hour, then borrowed a pair of rapiers and masks from a retired maître d'armes near Castellon, and gave his friend such practice as the interval allowed. His verdict was hardly reassuring.

"Paul," he would expostulate under the apple trees, "listen to what I tell you. When you look at me think of me, and what I am doing, not of someone else.

22

And your wrist! mon Dieu! it is of iron and too stiff. In your hand is an épée, not a battle-axe. Why will you not use this new riposte by which defence becomes attack without a pause? Believe me, an officer in the Musketeers will give your thoughts no opportunity to wander. You understand that the engagement continues till one or the other is incapacitated?"

To this Paul would nod, and immediately forget. The épée, its hilt engulfed in his huge palm, felt no more deadly than a feather, and resembled a skewer projecting from his bulk. Also it suited the agile Jules far better than himself. As for proficiency, had not Jules attended the military academy where the science of these slim ribbons of steel was part of one's education, so Jules would very probably kill him without wasting time. How queer and unexpected, he thought, to be killed by Jules so soon after they had rediscovered each other. On the other hand, and since this clash was of his own making, he had quite determined not to injure Jules if he could help it. But fortunately Raoul had not guessed that.

In the past three days he had seen none but Raoul and his own servants; he shunned Abbé Callot, and it seemed ages since they last parted, but this matter was not of priestly concern. He thought of calling on the Comte, putting the whole affair before him and asking advice, but something warned him that the Comte's views might be distasteful, so here he was, with his learning and property and education all of no present value whatever, and already feeling the biting point of Jules' rapier.

He was simple enough to believe that the matter had been kept secret. How foolish! A large, sedate young farmer of intellectual interests could not of a sudden begin rapier practice in his orchard without exciting domestic curiosity. Joseph Pardou, his manservant, knew all about it, knew even the time, place and date; from Joseph the news leaped to Marie Dufaut, once foster-mother of Jacqueline, now her worshipping attendant, who straight-way ran to her mistress. Jacqueline, with a flutter in her breast, passed it on to the Comte, whereat the Comte, with an approving nod, whistled to his dogs and strolled down the narrow hillside road for a chat with Abbé Callot. In his view a priest should be within call in case extreme unction proved necessary. And since Monsieur Raoul Fouquette had already engaged the services of Monsieur la Vallière, the surgeon, it will be seen that on the whole the leading citizens of Castellon were not ill-informed of what was about to take place in a secluded glade on the banks of the Vilaine just a half-mile beyond the bridge.

Raoul glanced at his watch. "Paul, are you ready?"

"Yes."

"Allons."

Paul sat in the high-wheeled gig beside Joseph who drove, with Raoul behind, back to back.

Something unreal and absurd about it all, he thought, absently noticing that the Abbé's shutters were closed against the sun. Of Jacqueline he did not think at all, but of Jules a great deal, because now, although he loved Jacqueline more than ever, he felt convinced she would have no regret, while later on Jules would bitterly repent of having taken the life of a friend on account of something that men called honour. How strange it all was.

Over the bridge, along the poplar-lined highway, then by a side lane through rustling beeches to a stretch of smooth turf, forest fringed. Here they got down. Joseph tethered the horse. The two men came forward. Jules and the young cavalry officer were waiting, and they saluted gravely. Paul and Raoul bowed. Jules' young face was a mask, it had a sort of static impersonal composure. He did not look directly at Paul, but beyond him. The seconds conferred. In the background, shrouded by foliage, Paul saw figures, but could not distinguish who was there.

The cavalry officer lifted two épées from a long case, and held them out towards Raoul, side by side, hilts forward. Raoul examined them, took one and gave it to Paul, saying in a low voice, "Remember what I told you." Paul nodded. There was only one important thing to be remembered, and this Raoul had not told him.

Now he found himself opposite Jules, who wore silk stockings, silk breeches with silver buckles at the knees, and a white silk shirt open at the neck, while Paul stood in his everyday clothes. The cavalry officer standing at Jules' right, looked at Raoul on Paul's right. One of them said "En garde," and Jules began the salute with extreme grace, Paul imitating as best he could. When they reached the final position, the other second said "Engagez," and Jules, crouching a shade lower, led his blade into intricate little figures that for Paul were impossible to follow, but some kind of sixth sense was bestowed on him for a few moments and he found himself automatically making passes and parries.

Nothing in view except Jules' face, neither young nor old, but ageless, Jules' eyes smouldering with a kind of cold, black fire, Jules' full lips pressed tight, Jules' body finely moulded as though it had just emerged from a sheath, and that flickering ribbon of steel now darting close to his own body, tracing a tireless pattern against his breast, only to withdraw, leaving him untouched, and weave again its deadly tapestry.

Of course Jules was playing with him. It was all strangely beautiful, thought Paul, but how long would it last? Then a lightning flicker of metal, searing pain in his right arm, his fingers slackened, his épée dropped. The seconds stepped between, Jules drew back, his point down, and Surgeon la Vallière, suddenly presenting himself, rolled back Paul's sleeve. A slight wound. The blade had ripped open the white flesh for a few inches, though not deeply, and bright drops were springing like a row of rubies in the sun. La Vallière looked at the cavalry officer, who shook his head.

"En garde! Engagez."

There was Jules again, lips now a little lifted, but Paul thought nothing of that for in his own body had set up a great tidal confusion in which waves of slowly awakened primitive force and fury made tumult against a rising flood of repulsion. Jules, wearying of the game, would presently run him through, that was certain, but even as the thrust went home he now knew that he would kill Jules. Jules had shed the blood of a friend, but it was even more horrible that he himself should extinguish the buoyant spark in that gay young breast. His own blood reddened his sleeve. Did he then propose as the last act of his own life to obliterate that of another? Would murder brighten a tarnished honour?

Suddenly, with an exclamation, heedless of the menacing steel, he flung aside his rapier, turned and walked away.

A moment of silence--one might hear the Vilaine,

whispering on its pebbled shore--then Raoul's hand clutching his shoulder.

"Paul! Paul! Stop! are you mad? what do you do?"

He did stop. Raoul was panting, incredulous, he might have been smitten in the face. He conveyed a sort of horror.

"Paul, Paul, you cannot do this. I implore you."

Paul sighed. The storm had passed, and he knew quite clearly what he must do. Figures had advanced from the wood, and stood gazing at him and each other. Jules had not moved; he remained, mouth open, eyes staring, staring till a second later he gave a shrill, high-pitched laugh of unspeakable contempt.

"Let him go," he yelped, "this coward, this poltroon, let him go."

It cut; it cleft the silence; to the rest it sounded dreadful, the death sentence on the honour of a man. It was like the whine of a guillotine that mutilated but did not kill. The Comte, his dry fingers biting into clenched palms, winced as he heard it; the lips of Abbé Callot moved and he felt for his rosary; Raoul had clapped his hand over his mouth to stifle a groan; Surgeon la Vallière, to whom a duel meant nothing new, though never before had he seen one finish like this, was putting his instruments back into a bag, cynically silent.

But Paul only fixed his sombre eyes on his adversary in one long, beseeching look, then climbed into the high-wheeled gig, and drove away--alone.

— IV —

"It is unfortunate, my son, that this should have happened," said Abbé Callot, gently, "more unfortunate than I can express. One could not dream that so happy a meeting could precede such a parting, but it is over now, and for you to decide what you will do, so why not commence your travels? It is advisable to go somewhere."

To this came no immediate answer, and the Abbé gave a gusty sigh. They were in Paul's book-lined retreat, the house very quiet, with no sound from the dining-room across the hall where Joseph, setting the table for lunch, murmured inaudibly and stepped as though his feet hurt him. He had been like that since yesterday when he walked blindly back from the Vilaine, head down, feeling very queer and ancient. The horse, reins trailing, had drawn the gig into the orchard and grazed beneath the apple trees. The library windows were open, and Paul sat motionless at his desk, face between his hands; Joseph's throat contracted at the sight. When the other servants begged for details, he had cursed them, and now the place was like a tomb.

Then arrived Abbé Callot, wondering not a little what comfort he had for this strange disciple of his. He probed about, trying this angle and that, till Paul, saying nothing, put before him a curt letter received that day from the château.

"The Comte de Marbeau informs Monsieur Paul de Lorimier that in view of what has taken place, no further association is possible."

When the priest read this he looked very hard at Paul. "It could not be otherwise, but presently you will

28

cease to love. It will pass."

Paul shook his weary head, "That is not possible, I shall never cease to love."

"An unprofitable pursuit, my son. I speak with knowledge, for Jacqueline herself is with her father in this affair. She approves the letter. So I urge you to start on your travels now."

"I cannot go alone," said Paul, dully, "I fear being alone."

"On the other hand, you cannot stay here in solitude. Listen! I must not conceal from you the fact that already Lieutenant Vicotte has permission to pay his addresses; such things do transpire, and we cannot prevent them."

"She will marry Jules?"

"I have talked with her father, and it is most probable."

"Jules is a traitor!"

"I doubt whether the world would call him that," said the priest, candidly, "and apparently he has something more acceptable to offer."

"His honour?" croaked Paul.

"Perhaps--and while it is not for me to adjudicate in such matters, it seems that this lieutenant has struck a spark that you, my friend, did not ignite, though you tried hard."

"Then you do not understand how it happened, or

why it happened?"

"For just a moment I did not, but now I do. You were brave, my son; but here in France such bravery is not popular, though certainly if one could find a way for its use the world has need of it. The dear Christ could have slain His captors with a word, yet He refrained."

The drawn face softened a little, "I am glad you remembered."

"It is curious, my son, but almost since you were a small boy, I felt your future held something not easily foreseen, that it had a purpose to be made clear at the right time. When you spoke of writing, I remained unconvinced, being assured that not in words would the story of your life be told. But here in Castellon there is small room for deeds, and now a wider wisdom than mine is required; therefore," here the Abbé's blue eyes were highly sagacious, "I beg you to go to Paris, taking...."

"But Paris does not attract me."

"The Paris I have in mind is not the one in yours. You will take a letter to my good friend, Godet des Marais, who retains, in spite of years of separation, some regard for the undistinguished Abbé of Castellon. I will tell him, if you permit, certain things you may find it difficult to relate; you will tell him so much as you desire, and what he then tells you will be worth hearing. He has a wide influence and a most keen perception."

"Who is this man?"

"The spiritual director to Madame de Maintenon, also Bishop designate of Chartres."

"Would one in his position have any concern for me?"

"There would be no letter were I not sure of it. Paul, you must go; there is nothing to prevent it, and your affairs will be safe in the hands of Raoul Fouquette."

"I doubt whether Raoul desires any more of me; he is too offended. I have not seen him since."

"What matter? His nose for business is not offended, and I have yet to meet a notary who frowns on a commission of five per cent. Also...." he added affectionately, "if it is God's will, I shall be in Castellon a few years longer, my work lies here, but with you it is different. Well, Paul?"

"You are right, father, I must go."

"I hope you will earn an honour higher than that some men think you have lost. Should you be in doubt, write to me, and the bald old priest, by whose knee you spent so many companionable hours, may be able to help a little."

"I will come and see you often."

Abbé Callot shook his head. "I doubt it, though you will be very welcome. Our paths divide now, but my prayers will follow you. God go with you, my son."

At Versailles

— I —

Over the road from Chartres to Versailles rocked and pitched a travel-stained coach, its body suspended on broad straining straps of leather between high, thick-spoked wheels; for miles the road was but a dusty track deeply rutted between lines of sentinel poplars, till, passing through villages, there were found stretches of pavé where the horses' hooves struck sparks and there was a rumbling rattle that made conversation inside the vehicle impossible. But, as it happened, Monseigneur Godet des Marais did not wish to talk, his mind was too full of his recent appointment to the ancient See of Chartres. Being of a naturally ascetic nature he much preferred a straw pallet to the crusted dignity that had lately come his way, but under the circumstances of its bestowal it was a preferment that one could not decline.

Now he leaned back against the black leather cushion, balanced his slight frame with the jolting motion, and glanced at the young man who sat opposite to him in mountainous silence. A strange, and not over-attractive creature, reflected the prelate, and certainly not of any immediate importance, so his thoughts travelled back to a certain unforgettable night associated with his recent dignity. It was the night when, sworn to secrecy, he had in the private salon of the King of France, witnessed the marriage of that monarch to Madame de Maintenon, widow of a deformed and disreputable versifier called Scarron.

That scene always remained printed very sharply on his mind. Midnight at the great sprawling château with snow falling and a roaring wind; the arrival of the frankly astonished de Marley, Archbishop of Paris, called imperatively from his bed: the unreadable expression of Bontemps, the King's valet, confidant and supervisor of Versailles, standing at the foot of the great fan-tailed stairway with a flaming torch, the rest of the sleeping palace being in pitch darkness. At the head of the stairs stood the King with the royal dignity that sat on him so naturally, more than ever the proudest aristocrat in all Europe, with his arched bushy brows, well-formed mouth twitching a little, and the marks of past dissipation on his finely modelled face. De Maintenon, the widow Scarron, calm as always she was calm, her large dark eyes holding no light of triumph, but pregnant with experience and a mingled cast of dignity, shrewdness and humility that for years past had baffled the court of Louis XIV. Then with the widow's large white hand in the King's a soundless procession over velvet carpets to the royal chapel, while Bontemps stepped ahead, a sort of ghostly guide, and his torch flung a passing gleam on successive portraits of the monarch's ancestors who seemed to look down and regard this secret midnight affair with cold disdain. One could not forget the face of Louvois, the Minister of War, who had always suspected and detested the widow. What did Louvois think of all this? Then the mass of Père de la Chaise. How that astute ecclesiastic must have muttered to himself as he watched Louis move so readily into the hands of the marble-faced woman, for was not the widow resolved to save the soul of this royal captive and make him a true son of the Church? Next, the giving of the marriage ring by de Marley, and the noncommittal expression of de

Montchevreuil who had sworn like all the rest to let no whisper of this dumbfounding union pass his lips. Then a pause, while all of them wondered if the thing really had happened, and the final return to the great courtyard, whence Louis, the remarried man, rolled off with his mature bride to a nuptial night at the Château Maintenon.

An extra lurch shattered the picture: the Bishop yawned, rubbed his eyes. Where was he?--oh yes--this uncouth giant and the letter of Callot. He remembered Callot at St. Sulpice, then the Sorbonne, with his round face always laughing; he had no fancy for doctrine, so made for Brittany when he got his priesthood, and had seemingly remained there ever since. Now this mournful young man, with a long screed from Callot explaining in detail all that had happened, and what could an old, an influential friend do to help? Suddenly the Bishop had an idea.

"Monsieur, you have doubtless heard of Madame de Maintenon?"

Paul sat up. "I have, sir."

"What?"

"An abandoned woman, latest mistress of the King."

"Hmph! What else?"

"But little else, sir."

"I thought so. Well, my friend, today I feel experimental. Would you like to be presented?"

Paul choked. He felt lost. Gaping at des Marais,

he reddened in his corner; he wanted to jump out and walk. His silence lengthened until the Bishop gave a chuckle.

"Presently I hope you will meet the most remarkable woman in France; if you do, the rest lies with her--and yourself."

Now St. Cyr--how well he knew every foot of that ground--and at long last to the plateau where Versailles overlooked the river: through great gates he rumbled across the vast courtyard to the Cour de Marbre. The big doors of the palace opened, and at sight of the Bishop a lackey ran for Bontemps. Bontemps arrived a little out of breath.

"Madame la Marquise is here?" said des Marais.

"In her apartments, Monseigneur; you will proceed there?"

"Yes, if you will have the kindness to care for Monsieur de Lorimier who will await my return. I shall not be long."

Mounting the great staircase he proceeded through salon after salon where opulence was reflected in a hundred glittering gold mirrors, past groups of bowing footmen, along interminable corridors, through the fronded aisles of the orangery with its yellow fruit, finally reaching the apartments of Madame which looked out on the terrace gardens.

At once admitted, he found his spiritual charge sitting very erect in a high-backed chair that had projecting upholstered ears to fend off draughts that wandered freely past the noble doors and windows of Versailles. She wore a plainly cut dress of grey damask, a lace scarf over her dark hair. A tapestry frame rested across her knees, no lady-in-waiting was visible.

De Maintenon rose, knelt and kissed his hand. "Monseigneur, you are very welcome; also you look cold."

He bowed, standing by the log fire to warm his bones. "The road from Chartres is in poor condition, and the wind strong. Well, my daughter, I had meant to come to you last week, but was unable. You are in good health--and His Majesty?"

"I am always in good health, it seems, but His Majesty has a migraine from loitering too long in the gardens discussing new projects with his architects."

The Bishop nodded. "Fortunes must be spent here."

"Too many, I fear, but the King has his fancies, and will listen to none; also I think it is the need of distraction that drives him. Louvois and Seignelay are always at his heels with affairs of State till at the end of the day he escapes them to spend an hour or two here. He is becoming oppressed, Monseigneur. Already he begins to tire of Versailles and spends other fortunes at Marly."

"There can be little rest for him."

"No; but when I urge him to do less he replies that this would be ingratitude to God and injustice to man. Outside of troubles at home there are England and Canada, which both weigh on him."

"I, too, have letters from Canada, describing it as a land of hardship and danger. Internally there is friction; the Jesuits resent their lessening authority."

"You will not expect one who was once a Huguenot to regard the order of Loyola with admiration," she said candidly. "The King holds that they have had too much authority in new France, and his Governor too little. I should not be surprised if the Marquis de Denonville is recalled from Quebec before long."

This news--and it was news--had significance: coming from such a source it came practically from the King, and the Bishop, as spiritual Director to the King's wife, might be trusted to keep it to himself.

"And his successor--who must have a strong hand in a country of savages?"

"When the time comes I think it will be old Comte Frontenac, if his age permits."

This was equally important, and would make a stir at court where the Count had been fretting in idleness for six long years, hoping in vain for re-establishment in Quebec, turning leaner, more hawk-like, eating out his soldier's heart as the months passed.

"It is not yet decided," she added, "but I feel it will be."

Des Marais knew enough of this strange woman to accept that: so strange a woman, he reflected, who in her fifty-five years had played so many parts. A prison-born Huguenot--relict of a wastrel poet--guardian of Louis' illegitimate children--confidante of Louis' dead wife,--and now herself the power behind his throne, the placid centre round which revolved both court and state. What pattern of fate, what rare infusion of body, brain and spirit had brought her to this? Here she sat, smooth-faced and black-haired; unmarked, unvexed, and unvarying, whatever storms might harry the land of France.

"Canada," she went on, "is that wilderness worth what it costs France in blood and money?"

"The soul of the savage, the skin of the beaver, those are its products. But you, my daughter, you are at peace?"

"The peace is not unbroken," she said, gravely, "I ask myself too many questions."

"You serve God, you love your husband."

"Perhaps it is more that I love God and serve my husband. Can any woman love one on whom she has been passing judgment for so many years? Monseigneur, to you I can say that I know him too well to love. For how long did I not care for his bastard offspring?" she added, with a slow warmth suggestive of deeper fibres within, "he is a great monarch but not, I think, a great man: he is feared and admired, but not loved, while it is better to be loved than admired. No, I have known too much to be able to feel more than a little. His Majesty has respect for my opinion, sometimes still a desire for my body: I am wife, but not Queen--an agreeable cushion for the crown of France-- that is all."

"Not quite all, my daughter."

She shrugged. "At any rate I have more than enough for one woman to carry. Now the king will be here in two hours, so let us talk less seriously."

"Would it interest you to see a letter that is something of a puzzle, with no mention of Church or State or army?"

"What letter?"

Smiling a little, he handed her the screed of Callot, explaining who the Abbé was. Using no glasses, she read it carefully.

"What sort of a person is this Monsieur de Lorimier?"

"A very large young man with an honest heart but no tongue, who waited on me in Chartres. His convictions in certain matters are deep, and as you see brought about his present disgrace. I have talked a little with him. Behind his silence there is something that may be moulded into usefulness, so I take him to Paris to see what can be done there. At present he is too dejected to be reasonable."

"He is in the palace now?"

"I left him in care of Bontemps."

"Then I will see this Breton of yours," she said, "it will be a change."

The Bishop went to the door; presently Paul's bulk loomed up; he stood confused till Madame held out her hand on which blazed one great diamond, gift of the dead Maria Theresa. Paul hesitated, then kissed it awkwardly, and glanced dubiously at des Marais, while that prelate stroked his chin. De Maintenon fingered the letter.

"Monsieur, I have this from Monseigneur and

know its contents. He desires to serve you if possible, and as one who deplores the shedding of blood, I too am ready. What is in your mind?"

This, exactly, was what Paul could not tell. His mind was blank; he had been perched stiffly on a lacquered gilt chair with fragile spindle legs in a gilded salon whose richness oppressed him. Innumerable lackeys passed and repassed on a polished floor so slippery that he felt afraid to stir, but none even looked at him. An hour went by. From where he sat he could see the twin grey stone wings of the palace and a huge equestrian statue of the monarch. In the great forecourt were soldiers--Musketeers, for they wore the uniform of Jules--parading, drilling and dismissing. Once he thought he saw Jules, which made him the more uncomfortable. Lumbering top-heavy coaches with yellow wheels drove up from Paris with a clatter, deposited men and women in fine clothes, and drove off again, so the King must be having a reception. But none of these people came his way, and he watched them disappear with a sort of self-conscious curiosity, a gay flock in gay plumage, suggesting Jules with their poise and casual assurance. He grew more moodish and lonely. Why had he ever left Castellon?

Finally, one of the lackeys, who walked with a sort of mincing step that resembled a peacock's, stopped in front of him and said that he would be received by Madame la Marquise de Maintenon. That had been almost too much.

Now, at sight of this mysterious woman, he turned red and felt lost. Why had the Bishop brought him here to the very heart of France, when he had nothing to say for himself? He avoided those large calm eyes, and stood twisting his big fingers, feeling like a fool, while the Bishop's smile broadened.

"It has occurred to me, monsieur," went on the even voice, "that a new country gives more opportunity for activity than an old one. Today His Majesty is building a new kingdom across the sea, where there is much to be done. Had you considered this?"

Clever, thought the Bishop; how little escaped the woman!

"Madame," rumbled Paul, "I had not thought of that, but since you speak I do."

"You are not averse from leaving France?"

"I do not see that there is any place for me here amongst those of good birth," he said, bitterly. "It seems that in obeying my conscience...." he paused, wondering if he spoke too freely, then with smouldering resentment finding voice, "in obeying my conscience, I am unfitted to mix with my equals."

"My son, we are all equal in the sight of God," murmured the Bishop.

"That is to be remembered," de Maintenon crossed herself, "but let me have your thoughts. What interests you most?"

"I had meant to write books," Paul was calmer now. "But the Abbé Callot thinks little of my powers. Had I not thrown a Lieutenant of the Musketeers into a lily-pond it might...."

"Canada is an inclement country with no lily-ponds," she laughed, "and savages instead of Musketeers, so the strength of your body should serve well. Monseigneur, who is there now in France to tell Monsieur de Lorimier more than we can?"

"Comte Frontenac."

"Yes, but the Comte is a soldier, whose first desire would be to fit a uniform to these wide shoulders."

"There is also Father Poncet from a Mission in the western seas: he is collecting money for proselytes in Martinique; a Jesuit, Madame, a man of action and experience, who once suffered torture in Canada and lives to tell of it."

How strange, thought Paul, composure now regained, to be hearing of torture and savages in the most guarded salon of all France and under the scrutiny of the woman of whom one had heard so much and knew so little. In Castellon and Rennes the talk was that she had put into the King the fear of God, demanded matrimony, and attained it; but there was no official announcement of marriage, and never had she assumed the position of Queen. Certainly she had discomfited Madame de Montespan whose wayward beauty once dominated Louis' heart: apparently she had reformed the monarch, made pleasant the path of repentance, and spread an unnatural calm over his chattering Court. Now, one heard, the King was never far off, and his apartments lay close by across the Salle d'Oeil de Boeuf. The dead Maria Theresa, it was also said, had been a weak fool and known all about it.

But Paul, nevertheless, had a feeling that de Maintenon understood him, and in his present mood any semblance of understanding was welcome.

"Father Poncet is this afternoon in the palace closeted with Père de la Chaise," she said, seeming to know everything, "seeking help from the King's purse for his converts. I will send for him. Monsieur de

42

Lorimier, are you inclined to serve the Church?"

Paul did not commit himself. The Abbé Callot had hinted at priesthood more than once, but only hinted, and it went no further. He had talked of the Canadian martyrs, of Father Jogues, of Lalement, Brébeuf and others who met their end in flame and agony, but it sounded rather unreal, too far removed from Breton orchards and fields, and not yet had Paul met a man who could speak first hand of what lay across the sea. Now, oddly, its very distance lent attraction. In depressed mood he had pictured himself as a martyr of conscience, but the forests of New France were sprinkled with the life-blood of true martyrs.

"I think," said the Bishop, "I will go in search of this Jesuit."

Paul was alone with the most powerful woman of her day, and she began to talk in a manner he could never have expected. It was all simple and sincere. She said that she approved of what he had done, she realised what it must have cost him, she understood what must be the condition of his mind, a condition to which she herself was no stranger. She too had been misunderstood, but the whispering that still went on behind her back no longer disturbed her.

"Monsieur, you are young, you are not a courtier, you have not learnt to glaze a lie with smiles and compliments, and I am glad of it. With you comes a breath of Breton air that is very welcome. Breathing it, I am assured of your honesty, and I would say this: From what I have learned, France is not the place for you any longer ... there you are right; now tell me how you occupied yourself in Castellon."

"With my books and my land, Madame; I

43

cultivated the soil and tended my orchards; I studied the sowing of grain and the breeding of beasts."

"Ah! there is something definite, so were you to continue...."

A knock, a door opened, and des Marais returned followed by a priest of striking appearance, tall, angular, with hair like snow; his face, burned almost black, was ascetic and finely moulded; across his cheek a blue weal ran diagonally from ear to chin.

"Madame, this is Father Poncet."

Her gaze widening a little, she kissed the newcomer's hand, while Paul observed that the index finger of the other hand was missing.

"Mon père, you are welcome, and I present Monsieur de Lorimier of Castellon."

Paul met a pair of burning eyes, bowed, and there followed a moment in which the air seemed tense. He wondered how much the Bishop had divulged of the affair of Castellon, if anything. Then de Maintenon told the Jesuit that here was a young man who contemplated leaving France, and if for Canada what counsel had he to offer? Now a pause. Des Marais, relieved that the matter was past himself, again stood by the fire and watched the living martyr whose body bore witness to the fortitude of his spirit. Poncet seemed to differ from any man he had seen before, for while France read of her sacred heroes she seldom viewed them, and this revisitor from the edge of death was not one to demand recognition. His manner was quiet, confident, almost proud, but had nevertheless a sort of modesty, and here at a glance stood one who held any bodily comfort but lightly.

"Madame, I can tell only the story of a servant of God in that land, and much of it is not for gentle ears. At first I was in Quebec, then went further west to Ville Marie; after that my journeys took me to the great waters and forests among savage tribes that know no law, whose gods are in the sky--storm and thunder."

"Are they then so savage?"

"I have seen them drink the blood of living captives and devour their flesh after torture," said the Jesuit, calmly.

She gave a little shiver. "Your picture will not attract Monsieur de Lorimier."

"Yet these heathen are nevertheless the children of God."

He made a gesture seemingly dismissing the savages, but his eyes held a rapt, haunted expression, as though viewing mysterious things, beheld by him alone: he exercised a kind of enchantment, and Paul felt his body tingle.

"Monsieur, I can tell you this of New France, if you serve either its Church or its Governor. Under the Governor you will make war against naked enemies and perhaps die from the arrow that flies without sound, but you will not die alone. Under the Church you will go far inland through dark forests without end, and may die, most likely alone. In any case the bullet of the arquebus will protect you no more than the Cross of Christ. If, however, you go there to trade and acquire beaver skins, you will be safer than if you desire to save heathen souls. Whichever it be you are not likely to return here, so it is not wise to dwell on what you have left behind. For myself I have voyaged far, I was taken captive, I suffered...."

"You yourself were tortured?" said de Maintenon, horrified.

He lifted his left hand. "The savages make no distinction and the story would not sound well here."

"But you will tell it."

"It was at Cap Rouge, a few miles from the cannon of Fort St. Louis at Quebec, that a poor woman grew a little corn beside her cabin, with no man to harvest it. I came that way when the grain was ripe, and found one man for her--that was Mathurin Franchetot--and we were making for the field when the Iroquois descended and carried us off. Through the forest we were driven to an Indian village on the Mohawk River, where we were stripped, and the savages amused themselves while the child of a chief cut off my finger to please his father; but," smiled the aged priest, "there were still nine left with which to serve God."

"And then?" asked the Bishop.

"Twenty years more in Canada, after which my superiors sent me back to France, whence I sailed to Martinique to proselytise the blacks. I had preferred to return and finish my work among the red men, and under the palms of the south I cannot forget this. That is all I can tell you."

The voice ceased, the man stood with his maimed hand hidden under the loose sleeve of his cassock; not a fold of the cassock quivered, and a flicker warmed the golden cross on his breast so that it glowed. Nor had the others moved; de Maintenon's eyes were large, her hands locked as though in prayer, her lips compressed; while des Marais' thin intellectual face had a glow of exaltation.

"I fear," added the priest, gently, "that the colour of my picture is not bright, but you have heard only the truth, and it is all a matter whether you desire to give or take. If it is the latter you should communicate with Monsieur Champigny, the King's intendant in Quebec; if it is to give, I will write a letter to Bishop St. Vallier, who is a great man but not a Jesuit. I will be at the college in Paris for another month--you will find me there."

Paul nodded in his curt, Breton fashion, aware that de Maintenon and the Bishop were watching closely; all he felt was that something seemed to have been settled--or had it settled itself?--and he was glad of it. Poncet had turned to the others, talking as an equal, quite unimpressed that he was in Versailles. Now de Maintenon opened a drawer, lifted a silk purse. A gleam shone through its mesh as the maimed paw closed over it.

"For your proselytes, Father."

The Jesuit bowed to her and the Bishop, then sent the young man one burning look. It challenged.

"In considering the matter, monsieur will remember that New France is a country for those without fear."

— II —

In her salon on the first floor of a tall, narrow-windowed house in the rue St. Charles, Jacqueline sat halfway through a letter to the Comtesse: she wrote with a long quill pen, head tilted, a little pucker in her lips.

*   *   *   *   *

....and that encounter is the only interesting thing of late. I keep wondering if anything will come of it. Six months married now, and the time has gone quickly. Also since my last to you I have seen much of Clothilde, recently returned from Dijon. I have met some of her friends, they are kind, but they speak so fast and are so well acquainted with things of which I know nothing, that often I feel foolish, and like the little Castellon Cabbage Jules calls me.

I have not made any debut, not till I am presented at Court. The advent of a Castellon bride means nothing here, unless she is distinguished by some scandal in noble families. That is the way to social success.

You ask me to assure you that I am entirely happy, and say that I write less of Jules than at first. I expect him back today from his duties in Picardy. Well, Mama, being a married woman, I am now less impulsive. Will you understand when I confess to a few disappointments. I am happy--yes, but not always so. Jules is affectionate, always complimentary, and, so far as I know, faithful, but I see much less of him than I hoped. When he goes out alone and returns late, I know he has lost money at lansquenet. It is in his face. He loves me in his ardent fashion, I am sure of that, and a nature like his must have some woman to love. He is so popular that he will never lack in that way, and I am convinced that he is ready at any moment to tell a woman what she would be most flattered to hear. Perhaps that is true of most Parisian men. Also he does

48

not desire a child, while I long for one. It would make such a difference when I am alone....

                *   *   *   *   *

Thus far, she paused; steps sounded outside, a latch clicked, the door opened.

"Jules!" She sprang up, ran and kissed him. "Oh, I'm so glad! it's been lonely without you. You look tired."

He put his arms round her, lifted her, held her close. "I was tired, mon âme, but not now: 'twas a long ride for one day from Meaux." He took off his plumed hat, gave his sleek head a shake, "And billeting in Picardy lacks something I found in the Breton country, eh?"

"You found no other girl in another château? am I to believe that?"

"Nothing but sour cider. You are well? You look well."

"The better for having you back."

"And that letter you write ... I suppose it tells the Comtesse what a failure I am, and how you dislike Paris."

"Exactly," she smiled, her pulse jumping.

"Alors, you cannot get rid of me, but you need not put up with Paris any longer."

"Be serious, Jules; I am very happy here."

49

"Then summon your courage, chèrie. I have news for you. On arrival I went to the administration to lodge my report and learned something unexpected. It sounds deplorable, but we are about to pack up and leave Paris."

"But ... but why?" she stammered, eyes round.

"I don't know, I cannot fathom it; on my way here I ask why ... why? and simply I do not know why."

"You are ordered to duty elsewhere?" she said, dully, "Jules, it isn't fair ... we've just settled ... we've...."

"And being a soldier I obey: but it isn't far, only eight kilometres."

"What are you talking about?"

Jules' eyes began to twinkle; he drew himself up stiffly, inflated his chest, assumed a most martial air.

"Madame Vicotte," he said loftily, "I am appointed to the King's Bodyguard at Versailles."

"Don't joke with me, Jules, I don't like it."

"This time I am not joking." He gave a great laugh, and began to bombard her with kisses. "This is exactly what happened. I gave my colonel my report; he put it aside, looked at me sternly, and said: 'what have you been doing with yourself of late?' I saluted. 'My Colonel,' I answered, 'nothing much worse than usual; what is the complaint and by whom?' then he said: 'No complaint, and I am sorry to lose you.' At that my heart sank: I thought I was being sent to Marseilles, or worse, to Dijon to the new squadron there. Then he

50

began to laugh, shook my hand warmly, and said: 'Captain Vicotte, you are appointed to the King's Bodyguard at Versailles, and your promotion is here on my table. Captain, I wish you success!' That's what he said--'Captain' my pigeon. Well, what do you make of it?"

"You a captain at Versailles," she breathed.

"Yes, my Cabbage, just that."

"Not in the palace?"

"Very much in the palace ... in the apartments for married officers. Are you going to be more respectful than in the past?"

She gazed at him, still incredulous, her heart in a riot, while a thought stirred in her, strange, wild, disturbing; she thrust it away as fantastic, but it came back, establishing a sort of secret lodgement.

"I can hardly believe it yet," she faltered.

"My sensations are the same. I had hoped for something like this in time, but certainly not so soon. It's a miracle!"

"When do we move?"

"As soon as you and Marie are ready. Also," he went on, eyes suddenly sombre, "there is something else not so pleasant. I have a confession to make. The time dragged in Picardy, and one night I joined a table at lansquenet, and ... well ... the play was high ... and...."

"Oh, Jules, how often have you promised?"

"Yes, you're right, how often?" he looked at her like a guilty child; "Chèrie, I do blame myself, but I hoped this other news would make you just a little forgiving."

"It's you, not myself, I think of. How is it all going to end?"

"Again you're right. I asked myself that, too ... how will this end? So I did put an end to it, and on the way here went into Egare's, and ... well...." he pushed a packet into her hand, "this might be suitable for Versailles."

She could not open it at once; she felt divided, disappointed and touched. Would he never grow up, would he always remain weakly impulsive, always lack stability? She loved him, could not help loving him. Was she weak to love him just for being gay, gallant, handsome, attractive? Had it all been a mistake from the start?

"You are very generous," she said, trying to speak evenly, "but, Jules, you can't afford it. Don't you see?"

"Open it."

She did open it, to find a bangle of filigree gold, daintily worked in the latest fashion, with small pearls set in still smaller diamonds. There was a lump in her throat as she slipped it on.

"It is quite beautiful. But, Jules, why do you lose money, then spend more that you have not got?"

"Who said I lost money?"

"You did."

"My little Cabbage," he chuckled, "you must be more attentive. I did confess to gaming, but said nothing about losing. On the contrary, I won three hundred louis d'or, of which only one half has gone into that bracelet. I await your apolo...."

She stopped him with her cheek against his, half laughing, half crying, calling him ridiculous names. "Jules, forgive me, it is lovely.... I have nothing like it."

"I'm glad, and Egare said it was the newest design on his shelves. Now, as to this move of ours?"

"Yes, it'll be strange to go to Versailles, not for a few hours, but to stay there."

"Why do you say that?"

"I have already been with Clothilde's aunt, the Baronne. That was to be my news to you. We went a week ago. She had permission to visit the gardens, and there we saw the King."

"You saw the King!"

"Yes: we had walked along the grand canal with its gondoliers from Venice, and near the shrubbery we heard voices, and two men came out. At once the Baronne gave an exclamation, made a very low curtsey, and hissed at me to do the same, so I did, much puzzled. One of the men was the monarch, himself!"

"You are sure?"

"Listen! At first I did not realise it was he on account of his simple dress. The other, the Baronne afterwards told me, was André le Nôtre, who designed the gardens. Well, when I curtsied the King lifted his lorgnettes, and glanced at me, saying nothing, but presently he smiled and bowed, and looked a great deal harder, and I felt myself blushing. He had a very distinguished manner, and his shoes were muddy. Then, to be polite, I ventured just a small smile in return, and this time he really did stare and asked me who I was, so I told him about you being a lieutenant in the Musketeers. We talked for some moments and ... Jules, what expressive eyes he has ... and he wanted to know where I came from. I spoke about Castellon and Papa, and he remembered Papa being under Turenne in the Flanders wars. He enquired if I liked Paris better than Brittany, and where we lodged, and took no notice at all of the Baronne, which made her very angry afterwards. When they passed on she was very agitated."

"That was all?"

"Was it not enough? Already I know the King and he knows me. When we are at Versailles, shall I be free to walk in those gardens?"

"Certainly, chèrie, but walk not too much without your husband."

"Why?"

"There is a small yellow devil called jealousy."

She laughed at him. She felt not a little excited; life had provided a new taste, and she relished it.

"Jules, don't be foolish. Shall I be presented now?"

"Perhaps at the next assembly. Have you seen the Baronne since?"

"No."

"After that meeting did she talk about His Majesty?"

"Without stopping till we reached Paris. She said that from being a libertine he is now reformed, against his will."

"Which is no secret. What else?"

"About la Vallière and de Montespan: she says that de Montespan plundered the King's purse for her losses at cards, and cast a spell over Vallière with a talisman of dry toads and pigeons' blood. Did you ever hear that?"

"I have; but, well, what more of this terrible woman?"

"That she sold herself to the demon, partook of the Black Mass, and complained to her friends that she had suffered the great misfortune of becoming the King's mistress. Is that true?"

"The Baronne seems to have enjoyed herself. Anything about de Maintenon?"

"Yes, quite a lot; how with the aid of the Church she has gained such power over the King that she, not he, is the real ruler of France. Have you ever seen her?"

"Once in the little gallery above the royal chapel in Versailles ... she is not easily seen."

"The Baronne says the nobility hates her, but she is too high and strong for them. Is that true?"

"True enough to remember. Go on."

"Jules, is she a good woman?"

"What a question-mark you are! You might ask her director, the Bishop of Chartres, about that. Anyway, good or not, the King gave her two hundred thousand francs to buy the estate of Maintenon."

"Then she is just like the others: also the Baronne says that through her the Court is gloomy and sanctimonious, and different from what it was, but this won't last."

"Really! Did she explain why?"

"Because the King is only forty-five, and de Maintenon years older and lacking charm and passion. He loves gaiety, while she has no art in love, and obeys Godet des Marais who was made a Bishop because he told her to become the King's mistress in order to aid the Church in his conversion. That's what everyone says, and he is becoming an old man much too soon. What do you think?"

"I think my Castellon Cabbage is too full of dangerous gossip: here in Paris, more so at Versailles, one cannot tell to whom one is speaking."

"But Jules, you can trust me."

"Naturally I do, but were de Montespan to learn that you repeated what you heard, and had she seen your meeting with the King, she would immediately spread the report that you yourself aspired to become his mistress."

"Do not talk like that," she flamed.

"It's for your guidance; you are young, beautiful, you go to Versailles, you join the Court circle ... therefore beware!"

"Jules, for just a minute that sounded exactly like old Paul, it was so funny."

"Paul," he shrugged, "I wonder what happened there?"

"All I know is that soon after that affair he left Castellon and his house was closed. It's a mystery there; Abbé Callot says nothing, but Papa thinks he's not in ignorance."

"Are you interested?"

"No, it's just as though it never happened. I could never have been content with Paul ... never. I wonder what good angel sent you there that day ... I think of it so often ... that first night at the château."

"And next day by the lily-pond," said he, acidly. "It doesn't matter now, and in some ways I'm sorry for him as for any man without courage. It's a strange breed."

"I don't think of him like that: he was afraid of something ... yes, but not you."

"He turned his back on my sword and pretended not to hear when I called him a coward," said Jules, grandiloquently.

"I believe there was something else that he did hear, but we'll never know. It's hard to explain but, as you say, perhaps it doesn't matter. Why do you look so sober?"

"Thinking about Versailles. Listen! de Maintenon's cold hand is visible everywhere, but men and women do not change on that account, nor their loves and desires and jealousies. She has many ears in the palace, nothing escapes her, she won't be thwarted and cloaks her ambitions under the screen of religion. The King calls her La Solidité."

"She is so large?"

"No, but because she does not vary, speaks hardly at all, is a mountain of determination. That's enough of her. As for you, my love, I hope I won't have to send out more challenges on your account. Be careful."

"Jules, you don't doubt me?"

"No," he said, looking serious, twisting the bracelet round her arm, "you have done nothing to cause that, but now I see the reason for my surprising appointment to Versailles; and a captain in the Bodyguard is at a certain disadvantage against his King."

— III —

Marie Dufaut, squatting on bulging haunches, laid her hands on her hips and frowned at a pile of clothing:

"Madame, it is no use at all, they won't go in, these portmanteaux are too small; let me go to the

58

market for some panniers, they're cheap and hold a lot."

"Perhaps that's best; I've more dresses than I thought, and more to come."

"Mon Dieu! We shall flatten them."

"For a few hours it does not matter," said Jacqueline, with a sigh of content. "What do you think of all this?"

Marie shrugged: to her the past few months had brought so stupendous a change, such an uprooting, that it was hard to imagine anything further. Castellon began to seem like a dream, and here in Paris, where at first she was frightened, she was now only puzzled. She said little, but thought much; she thought the Seine dirty and far less pleasing than the Vilaine; the streets endless, narrow and foul; the houses small, airless and mean. They stifled her. The crowds that jostled her were thrusting and lacked manners, they had no dignity, the argot and speed of their talk made her long for the more deliberate tongue of Brittany. But she kept this to herself, gave nothing away, and absorbed her new setting as a sponge absorbs moisture. Paris had not softened the wintry ruddiness of her cheeks, or feminised her sturdy peasant stride.

Jacqueline was her idol. Twenty years ago when the dry body of the Comtesse failed of nourishment, the child sucked life from Marie's deep warm breast, so some part of the babe was her own, never to be surrendered, and she made her claim good. Once in the Château Marbeau she stayed there; the Comtesse made no protest, the Comte welcomed it, and it went on year after year until the child flowered into young womanhood, and when that came it was impossible to contemplate life without Marie Dufaut.

"It is always changing, is it not? Is there a place in this new house to hang out the wash?"

"I do not think so," laughed Jacqueline, "it is not a house, but a palace where hundreds of people live."

"But you say there is a great garden, two kilometres long, is it the largest in the world?"

"Perhaps."

"Then there is a place for clothes."

"It is the King's garden, Marie."

"I know that, but his wife must have washing done, perhaps a great deal."

"Wait and see; and he hasn't a wife, she died five years ago."

"He lives alone?"

"Not altogether, he has a mistress, the Marquise de Maintenon."

"Then he sets the fashion."

"Why do you say that?"

Marie clasped her strong fingers, frowning. "From the talk I hear, it seems the ordinary thing in Paris."

"Perhaps; and you'll probably hear much more at Versailles. How many panniers shall we need?"

"Two is enough--I go now."

She got to her feet, and was at the door when steps sounded outside, then a knock. A plainly dressed man stood there carrying a small parcel. His face was smooth and shrewd, he gave her one swift searching glance.

"This is the apartment of Madame Vicotte?"

"Till tomorrow she lives here."

"She is within now?"

"Yes, m'sieu."

"The Captain Vicotte also?"

"No, he is not here."

"Then I would see her; I have something to deliver."

"Shall I take it?"

"Thank you, no."

"Your name, m'sieu?" demanded Marie, suspiciously.

"That does not matter."

His manner, though suave, carried a touch of authority and Marie went straight to her mistress: "There is a man here who gives no name, but desires to see you: he is not gentil, but seems of some importance, also he brings a parcel."

"If he gives no name, I will not see him. Do you get the parcel."

Marie disappeared; at once came voices, hers dogged and a little insolent, the other politely unruffled, but firm. Jacqueline put aside the lace she was packing and went to the door. At sight of her, the man drew himself up, set his heels together, and bowed very formally:

"I have the honour to address Madame Vicotte?"

"Yes."

"I am commanded to deliver this to you in person."

He laid the package in her hand; sent her a penetrating look, bowed again; they heard him pass quickly down one flight of stairs, and the outer door closed.

"Mon Dieu, but that is a strange person," creaked Marie, "now I go for those panniers."

Her mistress said nothing, waited a moment, went slowly back to her disordered boudoir. She examined the packet; it was oval, thin, heavy for its size, and bore a large crimson seal. In a wave of curiosity she ripped it open, exposing a case of morocco leather with a gold clasp. At this she hesitated, breath coming faster, then pressed a spring.

Inside a diamond necklet supporting a great pear-shaped pearl nestling against a fold of blue velvet; the chain from which it hung made a rivulet of stones in which each scintillating drop was secured by threads of gold so fine as to be almost invisible. There was no card, no name, no message.

She stood transfixed; the boudoir had a strange stillness, she could feel the rapid beat of her heart while she stared and stared. Never before had she seen so perfect a jewel; the creamy skin of the great pearl was fascinating; tall candles on her dressing-table lit the diamonds to white, restless flame.

Now she was living fast, her breath in tumult, her brain in a daze. It had not been possible to tell Jules all that passed between her and the King, for part of it was not in words but lay in the King's eyes. Quickly dawning, less quickly fading, there had been an instant in which his desire suddenly awakened from the torpor of advancing years, flooded up and out at the sight of this hitherto unknown girl. It was spontaneous, he made no attempt at concealment; nor could any woman misread it. What had been said after that was only camouflage on his part, and she knew it, and now with this flashing thing before her of a sudden she understood Jules' appointment to the Bodyguard with quarters in the palace. The perception slowed her pulse, she saw quite clearly where she stood, realised what the monarch expected. In his own well-proved fashion he had done his part. So what of hers?

She felt caught in a sort of vortex where there existed an ominous calm while around her swirled all the centrifugal force and glittering surge of the Court of the proudest ruler on earth. Great names came to her of soft-breasted women who queened it over the Court, the name of Maintenon whose price was two hundred thousand francs, and still held her own, Maintenon against whose cold dominance came this treasure of Louis' kingly protest, by which with one regal gesture he had put himself in the hands of the young wife of Jules Vicotte, and these cold but fiery stones were touchstones that made all things possible. Swept out of the vortex into its seething circling tide, she shut her eyes, squeezed them tight, as in a dream she hung the pendant round her white throat, lifted her tingling lids and stared again. Then came a sharp little cry. In the mirror beside her own face was another--Jules' face-- white like death.

"Jacqueline!"

She could not stir, her lips quivered, her heart faltered.

"Jacqueline," he was beside her, eyes level with her own, and alive with a queer distant flicker in them she had never seen before though Paul de Lorimier had caught it one summer noon in Brittany. "What is this?"

"It was brought by--some man--a few moments ago, but he gave no name. Jules, don't look at me like that, I know nothing. Don't! Don't!"

"You know nothing?" his tone was icy.

"On my soul, no."

He glanced strangely at the jewel, at the case, picked up the wrapping, examined its red seal; his fingers were unsteady. "This is the King's signet!"

"It may be, but I tell you I know nothing; take it, I don't want it--I would never see it again. Jules ... you ... you don't trust me?"

"How often have you met the King?"

"Once--only once--with the Baronne."

Suddenly he laid hands on her shoulders, swung her round, set his face close to hers; his eyes blazed, he looked a little mad:

"You swear it?"

"On my soul I do." In a storm of revulsion she flung her arms round his neck and held him with all her strength: "Jules, don't you understand.... I'm frightened ... frightened ... what shall I do...? what shall we both do?"

At this he drew a long breath; she felt his breast heave, pause, relax; his hand crept up to rest on the tumbled flaxen hair.

"Chèrie," he said softly, "when you say you are frightened, I do believe you, but just for a moment I was in hell. I, too, am afraid. First, take that thing off."

Fingers shaking, she put the jewel in its case, closed it and laid it aside, then told him exactly what had happened.

"This man ... his appearance?"

That, too, she gave.

"He called me Captain, not Lieutenant?"

"Yes.... Captain."

"My promotion is not yet published, so he could only know this from one source. That man was Bontemps himself, the King's valet, who has every royal secret and betrays none. You say he was commanded to bring this ... only one person commands Bontemps, and to his master I swore allegiance today for the

second time. I'm a member of his Bodyguard, his man
... his wish is my law, my duty to the death. Now do
you grasp this appointment of mine? I swear to defend
the monarch, while he plans to betray me. That is the
King I serve!"

"Jules," she faltered, "what can we do? what is
there to do?"

"Resign my commission and take you away."

"But ... but the army is your life."

"The army is less important than something else.
Can you protect yourself against the King of France?"

Again she faltered; she was now conscious of a
sort of wild confusion, and appalled to find it not
entirely unpleasant; she was secretly horrified to
confess that to have the king of all France a petitioner
for her beauty was not altogether unwelcome: it
alarmed, but equally it fascinated. She had no intention
of betraying the man of her heart, nothing there would
ever change, but was there not in this dilemma all the
opportunity for art and artifice that any woman could
desire? Her youth had risen to the challenge, and under
the sharp spur of the moment she put aside thoughts of
what the end might be.

"Well, Jacqueline, can you find any other
solution? Before you speak, remember that you must
never wear this thing ... never; if you do, you have said
'yes' to his Majesty. It is not his habit to accept any
evasion."

"You said you trusted me," her voice was low.

"I do."

"How much?"

"My heart and honour are yours; I have little else."

"You do not imagine I want this ... this distinction?"

"If I did, I think I would kill you," said he, harshly.

"And you'd be right! I'm not wise, Jules, but I'm not a fool. Sometimes the thing a woman is most sure of is the most difficult to explain, but I won't wear this, and I don't fear the King. Is that enough for my husband?"

— IV —

Louis XIV was sitting at a small table placed near the fire in the apartment of de Maintenon; he wore a high peruque whose masses of loosely curled hair added inches to his stature, square-toed shoes with pegtop heels effected the same purpose; his stockings were of silk, his wrists shrouded in lace, the embroidered coat was cut long and square and littered with orders; the lace at his throat overflowed a waistcoat of flowered silk, and jewels blazed on his finely-shaped hands. Shortly the monarch would attend an assembly in State, but first came an hour devoted to the affairs of his kingdom.

On stools near by were two men, Louvois, Minister of War, and the Marquis de Seignelay, Minister of the Colonies; beside them on the floor lay dispatch cases stuffed with papers. A few feet away in an alcove, where damask curtains were drawn back, sat de

Maintenon, busy with her tapestry frame, and so placed that she could catch the King's glance without observation by the others; her large white hands moved over the frame with the dexterity of long custom, and she did not speak.

"And that, Sire," murmured Louvois, pushing a document back into his bag, "is the state of affairs in England, where William of Orange sits ever more firmly on his captured throne."

Louis looked ruffled, as well he might. Imperious and despotic, he had finally succeeded in stirring up all Protestant and most of Catholic Europe against him, when moderation might well have meant peace, and today his armies were fighting in Bavaria over ground long stained with French blood.

"I am tired of hearing of England, Louvois, and recognise no English King but James, my guest. Produce something different, not that old story."

"The accounts for the month's expenditure here at Versailles, your Majesty, also at Marly."

"What of them? I am greatly intrigued by the possibilities at Marly."

"Also must be added the six hundred thousand livres a year you commanded to be paid."

"Eh ... what ... to whom?"

"To your guest, Sire, the fugitive King of England."

"Oh, that; I had forgotten, but he would have done the same for me."

"I do not doubt it, Sire, but these amounts are formidable, and I am at a loss to meet them without further taxation--from which I shrink."

"Then the less do I wish to review them. As to Versailles, my architect, Monsard, is bringing his new plans tomorrow, while le Nôtre has fine ideas for garden pavilions; I commanded them weeks ago."

Louvois, sighing, choked back what he greatly wished to reply: always he felt uncomfortable in these womanish surroundings, under the eyes of the one he styled in private "Old Widow Scarron." He knew she disliked him, had always disliked him since he protested against the royal marriage being made public, while he experienced for her what almost amounted to hatred. She loathed war, and he loved it, had built his reputation on wars and made the French army his life's work, and it was infuriating to sit here knowing that every word of his was weighed and pondered and would later be discussed by Louis with this large, stubborn, passionless woman. But the King would not have it otherwise.

"Affairs in Canada again call for grave consideration," ventured de Seignelay.

"Ah, Canada." The bushy brows gave a twitch, "that business is always grave; we shall have to do something there. What is the latest wail?"

"It seems that Governor de Denonville grows weaker and weaker, and the Iroquois more bold. You remember, Sire, that a year ago, the Marquis sent over some Indian captives to serve in your galleys?"

"I do remember--where are they now?"

"In the Mediterranean, but by the last ship Denonville asked for their return in order to placate the tribes from which they were taken."

"Return!" Louis swore a hot oath. "Who am I to swallow that? what else does he dream?"

"He is full of complaints, Sire; he has fourteen hundred soldiers, also the militia, at his disposal, yet he strikes no blow, and asks for four thousand more."

"Is he not aware that we are fighting half Europe?" snapped Louvois.

"His dispatches are full of nothing but his own anxieties ... also...." here de Seignelay sent an oblique glance toward the silent woman in the background, "the intendant in Quebec informs me that the Governor yields too much to Bishop St. Vallier. It is worth noting that the Bishop backs his appeal for more troops by urging that the Iroquois are the only tribe to defy the power and glory of God."

"And since when has this Bishop concerned himself in military affairs?" growled Louis, while he too glanced in the direction of de Maintenon; but she gave no sign, spoke no word, and he went on more confidently, "de Seignelay, I have poured money and men into New France, and there is no end to it. All I get in return is a few beaver skins. When my ships come back, it is always with a tale of trouble; either the Governor and the Church are opposed, or the English to the south have incited their Iroquois allies to new butchery. What is your view?"

"Sire, is it permitted to say that there was formerly a strong man in Canada, and you cancelled his service seven years ago, though of them all he best knew how to deal with the Iroquois."

"The Comte Frontenac?" Louis had had this from de Maintenon the night before.

"Yes, the Comte. Your Majesty has often rebuked him for extreme arrogance, for disobedience of orders, for continuous friction with the Council and the Jesuit fathers. Finally you thought best to recall him."

Louis made an uncertain gesture. "Recall?--yes. It seems that too much of my time is occupied in recalling those I sent to New France. Bigot, that plunderer, the Comte de Bouade and Laval--Seignelay, I often wondered how those two got along on their way back--Duchesneau, La Barre, now de Denonville--the list is endless. My navy has devoted too many leagues to this kind of transport when, God knows, it has other work."

"Am I permitted to remind your majesty of the last report from Chevalier de la Mothe Cadillac?"

"You do not propose his recall!"

De Seignelay, smiling, shook his head. "No, Sire, he is far too valuable."

"I agree. You have it with you?"

"Here, Sire."

Louis glanced at it with a sense of relief. Cadillac's very confidential despatches, sent independently of any authority in New France, were bold, unreserved and curt, but, somehow, had a strengthening effect. Here at any rate was one man who asked nothing for himself. He was the King's private scout in New France. A restless soul, this young Cadillac, no writer or formalist, a poor man of noble birth, blunt, explosive, direct, hating the English.

"On my soul! but this Gascon Hawk of ours speaks out," murmured the King, crossing his legs and fondling a silk-clad ankle of which he was excessively vain. "I had forgotten the thrust about the Jesuits--he says they smell of sedition! h'm--h'm--too many young officers strutting about Château St. Louis! h'm--h'm--Seignelay, did you see this? he writes that in his opinion France will never build a kingdom in America! Now why is that? have I left anything undone--anything?"

De Seignelay, who had his own doubts on this point, evaded an answer. France, he felt, was having too anxious a time at home to build kingdoms three thousand miles away. He stole a look at the marble-faced woman in the alcove; her hands moved smoothly, her expression betrayed nothing. How did she feel about this kingdom business? He would have given much to be able to read her thoughts, but not one soul in Versailles, not even the monarch himself, could penetrate that impassive front.

"Is there not something also from de la Mothe concerning the Comte Frontenac?" he ventured.

"I had not missed it. He was opposed to Frontenac's recall, and perhaps was right. Do you know, Seignelay, what it was about that young man that made me send him to New France?"

"You never told me, Sire."

"His nose! that enormous, thrusting, predatory beak of his: something about that beak made me feel I could trust him. I wish there were more such noses at my disposal," he tapped the papers on his knee, "you have nothing more recent than this?"

"There is a short report from Champigny--that is short compared to most of them."

"And the sense of it?"

"The old story over again. Your majesty, my conviction is that intendant Champigny of himself is devoted to your service."

"Of himself, you say--well?"

The Minister was on thin ice, and he knew it, so he went on carefully:

"Also he is devoted to the Marquis de Denonville, who in his turn is devoted to the bishop, while the bishop is under the influence of, shall we say, clerics loath to surrender the civil authority acquired when their position in New France was otherwise than at present."

"Quite neat, Seignelay, quite neat, but why not come out with it? You mean the Jesuits."

"I do, Sire."

Louis paused, frowned: he had no desire to antagonise the Jesuits, but the thought of them made his head ache. They were a breed of their own. Champlain brought them to New France, where they followed the Recollets, who had not done much in the way of heathen conversion; then the Jesuits dribbled over in every ship, kept dribbling. They feared nothing; men of steely courage, they travelled, outfooting even the coureurs des bois, penetrating where those reckless adventurers dared not venture, stationing themselves in remote pagan villages, preaching, baptising, suffering, dying at the stake to the glory of God. But before they died they knew the Indian as did no other white man, fathomed the dark corners of his mind, unravelled his motives, and gathered all that went on his barkroofed council chambers. No, the Jesuits were far too valuable to be antagonised.

Louis was well aware of this, had no intention to lose what meant so much to New France--and yet--! But would the fiery if half-crippled old Count for whom the folk of New France were clamouring, that high-tempered, arrogant old man of seventy years--the only Onontio whom the Iroquois trusted and feared, be ready now, in this extremity, to be a little less arrogant towards the Jesuits?

"Well, Seignelay, matters could not be much worse, so perhaps it would be wise to----" here he hesitated, turned his eyes to the quiet woman in the alcove, and caught her almost imperceptible nod "--yes, we will withdraw the present weakling, and send the Comte de Bouade back to his post. You will cancel de Denonville's commission and prepare the new one."

"Your Majesty is always right," murmured the minister, "do you care to speak to the Comte now?"

"Where is he?"

"Here in Versailles; one can say that he has been eating his own heart during years of inactivity."

The King turned in his chair. There sat the woman behind the throne, and he knew as well as did the others that this business had not escaped the close-meshed net she stretched over and around the affairs of State. So skilfully had it been extended, so fine yet strong its texture, so imponderable its weight, that the brightly-coloured human fish of Versailles were not aware of its presence till suddenly they found themselves directed or influenced to a course from which there was no escape. De Maintenon, herself invisible to all but a few intimates, was wise, deliberate and of cool judgment: she had mesmerised the King in hours when he was in a mèlange of religious fear and physical desire. Realising how vulnerable a target she offered, she made no mistakes, and, being without passion, her virtues were negative. Shrewdly, lest her hypnosis weaken, she had first through the Abbé Gobelin, and now through Godet des Marais, opened a channel that ran by way of Père de la Chaise, the King's confessor, to the throne. There she sat, uncrowned, so far as the world knew unwedded, yet more dominant than any Queen of France.

"What does La Solidité think?" asked Louis.

"If it please you, Sire, you have no more loyal servant."

Frontenac wasted no time in coming--de Maintenon having seen to it that he was on hand--tall, lean, with hawk-like features, a man of high ambition, of perverse and fiery temper. For seven long years he had haunted St. Germain and now Versailles hoping against hope, while his fortune dwindled and his clothes grew shabby. La Barre had taken his place as Governor in Quebec, and La Barre failed. Next, Denonville. Now, after two years of Denonville, it seemed that New France must inevitably be over-run by the Iroquois, then absorbed by the solid Dutch farmers of New England. Frontenac knew all about this, knew that his own work was being undone, just as the pitiful clearings around Quebec and Montreal were reverting to the forest, and he groaned in spirit. Then through some source that he could never trace, he learned that skies were brightening.

Now, designedly without notice of the woman in the shadows, he bowed profoundly to the King.

"Comte Frontenac, what is your view of the situation in New France, and how can it be strengthened?"

"First, Sire, the dissensions between Church and the military have much to account for: to secure the country these must end."

"My memory is that you yourself have been prominent in such disputes," said Louis, stiffly.

"That is true, Sire, but the Church--I speak of the followers of Loyola and not the Recollet Friars or Sulpitians--have their own spiritual domain on which I do not intrude, while too often I found their fingers meddling in secular matters."

"You speak boldly of the Church, Comte."

"Is it not possible that for fear of offence to your Majesty, and in ignorance of your royal understanding, some of your subjects have not been bold enough?"

"More than possible," smiled Louis. "Well, Comte, I am not forgetful of various charges against you, but am now inclined to think that the rancour of your critics led them too far. Today in Quebec there is Bishop St. Vallier, whom I know well, for he was once my almoner. Were you to return to Canada would you clash with him as you did with Laval, the Vicar General, and my intendant Duchesneau, who accused you of mastering the trade in beaver skins to your own advantage? Also it seems that invariably before starting a new quarrel you waited until my ships had sailed for Quebec for the last time that year, which put you beyond my intervention for a twelve month. In that," concluded the King, a trifle caustically, "I compliment your shrewdness."

"Did I make a fortune, Sire, I were more suitably dressed in the presence of your Majesty," replied Frontenac with a certain dignity. "Also I could not work with Duchesneau, of whose loyalty I am in doubt, but if the Bishop and the Church change their ways and are content with their proper position in the Colony, there will be no friction."

"Again the Church?"

"It is unwilling to surrender the power it once held. Your Majesty, unless New France has one supreme head in the person of your Governor, it will be dismembered."

"Then the Church does not make the savages into good subjects?"

"Sire, I have never known a savage to become French, but many a Frenchman has been transformed into a savage. We call them Coureurs des Bois; they are renegade soldiers or adventurers who have taken savage wives; they live for the most part in the forest, coming to Ville Marie and Quebec only to sell their furs and buy drink. They are wild men, fearless fighters, wise in the woods, but they know no law. I have hanged more than one already, but that made no difference."

"Then why not hang them all?"

"Because, Sire, I had not the means to catch them; they are more audacious than savages, and move like quicksilver; they are in Ville Marie today, and, in a week, two hundred miles distant. Had I had more troops...."

"Comte, I have nursed Canada like a child, and got nothing but trouble and expense, nor can I send more troops this year."

"Authority, your Majesty, is needed as much as troops."

He spoke sharply, confidently; Louis looked puzzled and glanced over his shoulder.

"Certainly the Comte is without reserve! Did your Solidité hear that?"

De Maintenon inclined her head: she was attracted by Frontenac's boldness, and his views about the Jesuits secretly pleased her, but she said nothing.

"Comte, how old are you?"

"I had to wait twenty-five long years after my birth for that of your Majesty."

"Here is a seasoned soldier who has not ceased to be a courtier," chuckled Louis. "Now why has Denonville begged me to send grain to feed my people in a land of plenty, when no corn goes from England to New York?"

"Because, Sire, his own softness has made the Iroquois so reckless that your people dare not venture out to till their fields such as they are."

"Then you shall go back and put an end to all this," exclaimed the King. "Louvois, you will confer with the Comte and arrange for a frigate from Rochelle when the rest of the matter has been attended to, and due notice given to Denonville. We will find something else for him here. De Seignelay, your department will do the rest. Comte Frontenac, I wish you well, but counsel you to wear gloves when you deal with the servants of His Holiness the Pope. I speak from experience. Now, gentlemen, you may go."

The ministers rose from their folding chairs and picked up their portfolios; with Frontenac they bowed, walked backward to the door and disappeared; Louis, stretching himself, warmed his hands.

"Well, what does La Solidité make of it?"

Laying aside the tapestry frame she joined him on the hearth; she stood just as tall, and were it not for his absurd heels and towering peruque would have overtopped him.

"As always, Sire, you did well."

"It was convenient that Frontenac be on hand so quickly, eh; how did it happen?"

"I thought it might save your Majesty's time. Do you return here after the assembly?"

"No, Solidité, not tonight, the assembly bores me, and I shall be tired."

"You look tired; there is still a quarter hour, and here is the couch."

He nodded, and lay on his back, the great

peruque carefully spread to save its opulent curls, while he looked at her with contemplative eyes. It was quiet here, one could forget that one was a King, no questions to answer and all conducive to thought. She had resumed the eternal tapestry, her large chalky hands looking ghostly in the half-light; she would not speak again, except in reply, and presently he found his mind running free and slack in a reverie of fair women.

Years back his mind travelled--was it really twenty-five years?--to Louise de la Vallière, that frail mistress of how many a moonlit night, and remembered love in the woods of Fontainebleau? Poor Louise, whom he had made a duchess, then found that she could love, but not glitter. And Montespan-Athenais!--there was a witch, dark-haired, dark-eyed, and wildly extravagant. It was Père Gobelin who said that when this lady confessed her sins each one was an epigram, or did that describe Madame Coulanges, one beauty whom Louis had never conquered? Back went his thoughts to the days when Montespan like Louise measured herself against the Widow Scarron who cared for the bastard children of both, and met defeat. Maria Theresa, Queen, wife and mother, had known all, but dared not protest, and instead leaned on the Widow. That death-bed scene, it was very clear, with Maria weakly drawing off her nuptial ring, flashing its great diamond, and putting it on the finger of the Widow, her trusted confidante. Strange, ruminated Louis, how through all those years the Widow had had her hand in everything nearest the King of France.

Now again marriage, five incredibly long years of wedlock made nearly unendurable by his own chastened fidelity. He gave a grimace when he reflected how that came about. He was lonely, Louise dead, Montespan no longer his, Maria dead, and Bossuet, the court preacher, thundering fulminations against immorality that sounded personal till presently it began to seem that the only permanent thing remaining in life, the only thing on which he could count in the emptiness of increasing years, was that same Widow Scarron herself. Her large, smooth, passionless body gradually acquired an unnatural fascination, her poise brought him calm, she was the only woman he had ever known who asked for nothing, so finally desire made him crave that body and he demanded it.

But to his astonishment the Widow was adamant. As he implored, so she hardened. Daughter of the Church, she leaned on the power that Church had through her acquired over her royal lover, and sturdily denied him. So the siege went on till one day with a fine gesture she tossed at his feet the nuptial ring of Maria Theresa. That was her answer.

Now he looked at her beneath languid lids, and his mouth curved into a smile. How undisturbed she was, how elemental, his Solidité. She knew a lot, certainly more than any woman should know, but she was his wife, though only four other men in the world were in that secret. And what, he wondered, would she say or do if she could read his mind at this moment, could picture what he did--the image of a girl of twenty, married but not yet a mother, with blue eyes, a flower-like mouth and a body that compassed man's desire? Soon--soon--he whispered to himself, while the old sweet tantalising hunger stirred in him anew. Bontemps--he could trust Bontemps--and presently would see his jewels lying warm on a sweet white throat. Good old Solidité! she didn't know everything after all.

De Maintenon glanced at the clock, rose, and stood beside him.

"Your Majesty, it is time."

"Yes, yes," he sighed, "I know. You will not for once come to look on, in private?" he knew well that she would not come.

"My thanks, Sire, but no."

"Why are you so determined in such matters?"

"My only determination is to serve your Majesty."

"Ah, my Majesty! I wonder if it is more difficult to save the soul of a King than of a subject?"

"The value to God in either case is the same, Sire."

"Possibly, yes." He felt a little flattened. "Though I had not been told so before. Goodnight, Solidité."

— V —

Jacqueline, her heart in tumult, stood by herself in a corner of the great Salon de Mars watching a gilded procession of courtiers, statesmen, soldiers and diplomats make reverence to the King of France, and of them all two figures stood out most clearly--Louis seated in a throne-like chair, with a cordon of orders on his breast and golden Fleur de Lys at his back, and to either side and behind, the members of the Bodyguard amongst whom was her husband. The King's face expressed a certain courtly boredom, but that of Jules was tense.

A few minutes previously she had been in that procession, her eyes bright, her pulse clamouring.

Approaching the throne, she curtsied profoundly and met the royal gaze, when Louis, his eyes rounding a shade, lifted a jewelled hand to his throat with an unmistakeable gesture. At this the blood flew to her cheeks; she dared not look at him again, and moved blindly on, aware that Jules had missed nothing. Now a moment alone--as yet she knew but few persons at Versailles--she was filled with fear, for on her breast but down out of sight below filmy lace lay the diamond necklet. Impulsively, at the last moment, she had snatched up the precious thing to carry with her.

The procession ended; Louis, motioning to his Bodyguard not to follow, stepped down: wherever he turned a way opened for him through the most glittering throng in all Europe; he walked very erect, placing his small feet with the careful precision of a dancing master. His part of the assembly was over, and it seemed that something had not pleased him for he vanished into one of the smaller adjoining salons.

Three minutes later Jacqueline heard a suave voice, "Will madame have the kindness to follow me?"

She recognised the man with a start. It was Bontemps who stood bowing, dressed very plainly in a sort of civil uniform with black silk breeches and buckled shoes. Her agitation increased, and she looked about for Jules.

"Presently, monsieur, when I have found my husband."

"Perhaps madame will wait for that later; her presence is desired now."

There could be no mistake about this; she bit her lip, felt a sudden weight of fear, and knew she must obey. Bontemps' face as before told her nothing, but today she needed no telling, and with a quick rush of loyalty and love for her husband she nodded.

How Bontemps got her away from that assembly so smoothly she could not understand, but it was not without attracting some attention, for too many sharp eyes caught Louis' gesture, turned to see what manner of woman had caused it. This stranger was young, lovely and unknown. Then came covert smiles and exchange of significant glances. Men stared at her, murmuring questions to each other, but none had an answer: seasoned beauties of the Court appraised her charms with shrewdness and cynical hazard whether Louis at long last meant to escape the deadening influence of his sanctimonious mistress and be young again. That was just for a moment, then the procession diverted them again and Jacqueline escaped, though not forgotten, particularly by a dark-haired handsome woman of some forty years, exquisitely dressed and wearing quantities of pearls. It was de Montespan.

She found the King waiting in a small alcove: as she approached he nodded, and Bontemps vanished.

"Well, madame," he said, "what make you of the Court of Versailles?"

"I have no word, Sire," she answered, trembling.

His blood warmed at the sight of her, and he smiled. "Your dress is elegant, but not complete; how is that?"

Her hand crept to her throat, and she turned scarlet: "Sire, my husband!"

"And what of him?"

"He knows of your Majesty's gift, and forbids me to wear it."

"You informed him?"

"He arrived while I was admiring its beauty: he insisted, and I promised."

"And since when has a member of my Bodyguard frowned on royal gifts? Do you despise it?"

She was stricken with fear, and all at once pictured Jules without rank or position, exiled from Paris, and perhaps the army; the King looked not furious, as she had dreaded, but rather puzzled, even slightly amused. So perhaps after all she had misjudged him.

"Your Majesty, I am more honoured than I can describe."

"Ah, that is better; you do not then return the gift?"

"I have it here," she touched her film of lace, "but to humour my husband I did not wear it."

She said this with so fearless a look in her blue eyes that the King felt captivated. Here was something different, young, fresh, infinitely attractive; she was not unlike Louise, with the same seductive transparency, and nothing like de Montespan whose undeniable beauty was too much aided by art. Also, reflected Louis, when a mistress has borne a lover eight children she should rest content, while in these soft white arms one might recapture youth.

"The King of France is not accustomed to have

his remembrances disregarded, and that neck of yours would look even fairer with a few diamonds," said he, in a sudden flood of desire, "permit me to assist you."

— VI —

Jules was in a quandary; around him swirled the Court with talk and laughter, groups were dispersing to the Salon de Venus and its regal abundance of gold plate, the Court musicians on a platform were giving Cesti's ballet composition from Pomo d'Oro, but nowhere could he get sight of Jacqueline, and he wandered about, ever more anxious, till the light tap of a fan came on his arm, and he met the mischievous eyes of de Montespan.

"Captain Vicotte, is it not?"

He bowed.

"Madame, your wife, has made some sensation on her first appearance; my congratulations."

"My thanks," he said, curtly.

"It is not possible you are just a little piqued, monsieur?"

"Madame interprets me--I am delighted."

"Then it is pleasant to meet a husband of so broad understanding."

"I do not follow you."

"Yet I do not think you lack intelligence. Your wife is very young."

"She is but twenty."

"You are now established in the palace?"

"His Majesty has so provided for my military duty."

"How convenient for all concerned," she laughed, "and agreeable to meet one so devoted to His Majesty."

He bowed again but made no answer for was he not in the presence of the most dangerous woman in all France, one who, defying the years, retained her beauty and held a high head in spite of the monarch's dismissal. She had not forgiven, and would never forgive de Maintenon; she had, it was believed, poisoned the young and lovely Mademoiselle Fontanges, who expired in agony after one short year of royal favour, and even today she watched with sharp and jealous eyes for the least sign of weakening on the part of her former kingly lover. Outwardly gay, amusing and carefree, she was nevertheless consumed by vindictive, undying resentment.

The pause lengthened till she sent him a mocking smile: "Our conversation is not what I had expected; your thoughts wander, Captain."

"I was looking for my wife." He spoke brusquely.

"Then perhaps I know the byways of the palace better than yourself." She put her arm in his, "Come!"

Through corridor after corridor they passed, Jules the more angry and confused, aware of sharp glances that followed them: the strains of Pomo d'Oro grew fainter and fainter, his heart beat the more violently, his lips became the more dry, till she stopped abreast the smallest salon of all.

"Well, monsieur, there is your wife."

Jules was transfixed: in a tapestried alcove stood the King with Jacqueline, one arm round her waist holding her close, while the other hand, after searching in her breast, drew out a jewel. It glittered in the candlelight.

"That," murmured de Montespan, "is a finer necklet than he ever gave me: our monarch's taste in diamonds has improved."

Something snapped in Jules' brain, a red cloud drifted over his eyes, he quivered, felt for his sword and was about to plunge forward, when a small hand caught his wrist in a grip of steel.

"Monsieur, are you mad? That is the King!"

He stiffened; breathed slowly, deeply, his heart suddenly felt cold.

"I must ... I must...."

"You must, if you are wise, do nothing," said she, coolly, "not yet has a member of the King's Bodyguard threatened the King's person. Remember the Bastille, Captain, and I doubt if we are wanted here. Also, monsieur," she added, looking up into his handsome face, "I suggest that you might seek consolation elsewhere--it is not so far off."

He heard a musical little laugh, and was alone. Now Louis and Jacqueline walked slowly from him, their heads close together: he stood for a moment, helpless, then with a gesture of despair turned blindly away.

Jacqueline was false and frail! Incredible! A brother officer passed, glanced quickly at his drawn face, and spoke. Jules did not reply, but wandered on in a sort of bewilderment, through a succession of lofty chambers, till he heard excited voices and entered a salon brilliantly lit with silver sconces against the wall. Down the middle of this apartment stretched a long table, where an absorbed group was playing lansquenet. Jules nodded to a few he knew, dropped into an empty chair and took some gold from his pocket.

The next half hour passed like a dream; he saw his money dwindle to a single piece, then swell as by a miracle, and at this he became possessed by a sort of fever. As he played he heard exclamations and someone clapped his shoulder, but all was in a daze-- the King--Jacqueline--Jacqueline--the King! He saw little else while gilded cards bearing the King's face settled lightly before him like leaves in autumn, and his recklessness increased. Now came a good-natured suggestion that if Captain Vicotte's pocket was short of cash, his signature was acceptable. This made Jules feel drunk, and he played on--500 pistoles--1,000 pistoles-- his pencil moved quickly over successive bits of paper.

By this time the room was quiet while a deepening ring of men and women, all of them gamblers at heart, observed this young fool undoing himself. A whisper went round carrying Jacqueline's name, and smiles broadened. The thing was at its height when an elderly officer of distinguished bearing came through the salon, and he too stayed to watch. Looking hard at Jules' flushed face, he inquired this young man's name; the information seemed to interest him and he leaned silently against the wall, a tall impressive figure, no gambler, a strange visitor to this careless circle.

Presently the dealer--the cards were now with young de Roquelaure--ceased to play them, and addressed Jules in a low voice:

"Captain, you have lost five thousand louis d'or. Can you afford it? As a friend in arms I advise you to retire." Then, in a voice still lower, "Jules, stop it, you have gone mad!"

Jules blinked at him. "That is my affair. I have not finished."

"Alors," said de Roquelaure, frigidly, "I am compelled to advise these gentlemen not to accept your signature any further."

Jules' blood was up, his veins on fire, around the table he saw eyes once friendly now regarding him with suspicion, and he shook his handsome, stubborn head.

"Gentlemen, here I stay and here I will play so long as a single one of you will take my note of hand."

"In that case, Captain, you will play only with yourself," announced de Roquelaure. "Tomorrow no doubt you will make your debts good; if not," he added significantly, "you know the alternative."

A woman laughed; there was a pushing back of chairs, a rustle of silk, the tap-tap of high heels, the heavier tread of men, and Jules was alone save for one individual only. He gazed dully for a moment at the tall stranger who remained silent, then of a sudden flung out his arms and hid his face between them.

Presently came another voice, dry but not unkind: "You are Captain Vicotte?"

Jules lifted a haggard face: "I am."

"Son of the late General Vicotte?"

"That is true, Sir; if you will excuse me...."

"One moment, please. I knew your father well, we fought together in Crete to assist the Venetians against the Turks. I am the Comte Frontenac, and would like to assist you if that is possible."

Jules got to his feet, put his heels together, and bowed: "Sir, I ask your pardon, but fear that tonight I am not ... not...."

"Come, come!" said the older man. "I am of an age to be your grandfather, so let us talk frankly, also I have seen what has happened. Have you five thousand louis d'or at your disposal?"

"It is impossible, unless...." Jules glanced at him with a wild hope.

"Nor have I, my young friend," said Frontenac, soberly, "or I would certainly offer them. What do you think you will do now?"

"I cannot say; I am ruined, more ruined, Sir, than you can imagine."

"Then listen: for seven empty years I have observed this Court, and at the end of them I return with relief to New France, to which His Majesty has just reappointed me. I shall leave within the next few months. Captain Vicotte, will you serve under me, and exchange the old France for the new?"

This was revolutionary; Jules gazed at him in

confusion. Canada! That land of savages and hardship! Men went to Canada and never came back; he heard that they lived--so long as they did live--with less comfort than peasants in France, marooned half the year in bottomless snows, while wine froze in the casks and the rivers turned solid. Such a prospect was appalling. Then, when he racked his brains where to find five thousand louis d'or, there flashed into it one startling idea that might save him from Canada.

"I thank you, sir, but might I consider the matter further?"

"Yes, but I advise you to lose no time. You are married?"

Jules nodded, biting his lip.

"Well, Captain Vicotte, there is no Versailles in that country, but room and a good welcome for men and women who are not afraid, and I remember your father as a man without fear. I bid you goodnight."

— VII —

Jacqueline roused herself; it was toward morning after a night of troubled dreams from which the figure of the King was never absent.

"Jules, is that you?"

"Yes."

"You are very late--or early; what has kept you? I have waited for hours."

"Many things kept me."

In the dim light of a candle burning beside her bed, she could just distinguish his features; they were wild, unnatural, and suddenly she was afraid.

"Come now and sleep."

At this he turned on her savagely. "My felicitations on your success, and I do not sleep with an unfaithful wife."

She gave a sharp little cry, and started up: the gown slid from one white shoulder, and at sight of this he choked, on the edge of murder.

"Jules! what are you saying?"

"Only the truth." The world whirled round him; he was aware of his voice, hoarse, cracked, the voice of another man. "I was a fool, a soft fool. There is nothing you can say ... I believe my own eyes, not you.... I saw you with the King, his arm round you, his hand in your breast. Well, he had paid the price, so why not?"

He got this out in a flood, transformed by fury, while she, seeing violence in his hot eyes, shrank further and further.

"It is not true, not true," she whispered. "I gave nothing ... I could not help what happened. After I passed the throne Bontemps followed me, took me to the King in another small salon. I was wearing your gift. I had his jewel hidden in my corsage for safety, out of sight. The King chided me for not displaying it. I told him why ... that you forbade it ... and he laughed, asking where it was. Then he felt in my breast, and...."

"And what?" rasped Jules.

"Suddenly he wasn't a King any longer, just a man with his hand there, and I slapped his face."

Jules' mouth opened wide, he tried to speak, made only an odd sound.

"You ... you...?"

"I just slapped his face." Her tone quickened, pitching higher, "and he turned first red, then he gave a funny little laugh, not at all angry, almost as though he liked it. Then I was terribly frightened, and ran and ran. I didn't know my way, but ran till I found our apartment. I got here just at midnight, one half-hour after I was presented; that was four hours ago. Ask Marie!"

It all came out in a quick, nervous rush, her eyes bright and hard but still with a shadow of fear, and it left him without a word to answer. His wife had struck the King! He could not believe it ... at the same time he did, for truth rang in every accent.

"Well, Jules?"

She was gazing at him, her pride still in arms, but her lips trembled, and in a flash he seemed to pierce into her very soul. Then she turned quickly from him, hid her face in the pillow and began to sob, long, tired, innocent sobs that utterly silenced his last doubt.

"Jacqueline. Listen." He bent close, put his arms around her. "Forget what I said.... I was crazed.... I didn't know all. I trust you, I love you ... always. All I knew was what I saw. That was through de Montespan who took me there. You met, you went away together. I would have followed to kill him, but she stopped me. Now! What shall we do now?"

"Go away somewhere, anywhere."

"We'll talk of that, but not tonight. You must sleep."

"Sleep?"

"You must. Tomorrow we will put our heads together."

"Yes, Jules, yes, that's best ... tomorrow. But I can't sleep now. Lie here beside me, talk about something else."

This hit him hard: he lay still for a while till her breathing slowed, steadied; then, when he thought she had fallen asleep, she said suddenly:

"What have you done since midnight? Where have you been?"

He was cornered; having heard truth he could not repay it with a lie, and it punished him the more to make his confession here and now. But he could not help it.

"I ... I have been foolish again, Jacqueline, very foolish."

This sounded genuine; it meant gambling, and tonight no play-acting about it, but she was too distraught to feel much more.

"Lansquenet?"

"Yes. I saw what I said of you and the King, then nothing seemed to matter any more. I found myself in the gaming salon and sat down, not knowing or caring what happened. I had lost you. Jacqueline, I signed paper for five thousand louis d'or."

At this he felt her recoil; she sat up, horrified.

"Jules, are you mad? you have not that sum, nor have I."

"I know ... I know ... but it must be found by noon tomorrow ... no today ... or I am disgraced."

"Then we share disgrace," said she, brokenly. "I can run from the King, but you cannot escape a debt of honour. With whom did you play?

"Ensign de Roquelaure holds my signature," he groaned, "and I cannot raise the money."

"Do you know anyone who will find it?"

"No."

"Then why not live in Canada? What else is there out of France?"

"That barbarism!" his brain was twisting and contriving all to no purpose, but he could not contemplate so harsh an exile, "it is no place for you."

"I'm not afraid: I'll never desert you."

"You are an angel."

"Jules, that money ... it must be today?"

"By midday."

"That necklet, the King's, is it mine?"

"Unfortunately."

"No, not unfortunately: I give it to you; do what you like with it, and then ... then we'll see about other things."

This came in a drowsy murmur--she was sleepy now--but it made his blood tingle.

"Sell it!" he exclaimed.

"I ... I said do what you like. I want never to see it again. I'm tired, Jules; goodnight, Jules. I love you."

The hours dragged on with no sleep for him; sometimes she murmured his name, he being in her dreams and not the King, and he found himself thinking of her as never before, for not till now had he sensed the high quality of her candour and courage. He had never been quite like that, not so candid, not so courageous: he was too much of an opportunist; he felt deeply, but there was little sequence about him; he was too much in love with life to reflect how he lived it.

For the first time the future frightened him. The King might laugh in amazement at the daring stroke of a girl's hand, but that would soon pass; he would never forget, never forgive. It was beyond belief that Jules would much longer wear the uniform of the Bodyguard.

The more he pondered and groped, the more bleak grew the outlook. He revolted at the idea of Canada. Jacqueline might not fear it, but that was the courage of ignorance. She knew not of what she spoke. Yet so dear and vivid had she suddenly become that, lacking her, he lacked resolution to decide anything.

She was still asleep when he rose at daybreak, and a wave of recklessness swept over him at the sight of her unconscious beauty. He dressed hurriedly, put the jewel-case in his pocket, went to the guardroom and ordered his horse. Clattering across the great courtyard, he struck along the route de Moulineaux, tree-bordered and fringed with green farms, passed the ramparts at the new Porte de Versailles, and followed the new narrow paved road that ran abreast the Palais du Luxembourg. Thence across the river by the Pont du Change, and a short distance brought him to the shop of Egare on the right bank. He tossed his bridle to a loafer, and strode in.

Egare, a small, wizened, bright-eyed man who slept in his wooden box of a place stuffed with treasures, knew him at once, smiled and bowed. Officers of the Bodyguard were likely to prove good customers, and this one seemed no exception. Evidently he had money.

"It is a pleasure to serve you again, monsieur." Then noting the rank badge, "my felicitations, Captain. The bracelet was acceptable?"

"Most acceptable."

"What more can I do for you?"

"Egare, I am on another mission this morning. I do not buy, but sell."

"That, Captain, is very different: I am not in the market."

"Listen, Egare! this matter is private; can you keep a secret?"

"If monsieur knew how much I do not repeat it would surprise him."

"Very well. You remember that within the last few days you disposed of a necklet of diamonds with a large pendant pearl shaped like a pear?"

The jeweller's brows went up, his delicate fingertips came together; he gave one sharp glance, and nodded:

"That is true; has monsieur seen it already?"

"Much more." Jules took out the case, opened it; "Can you now understand the privacy of this business?"

"Certainly; but you do not bring that here to sell?"

"You're wrong, Egare."

"Then take it elsewhere, I beg you."

"It returns to the only atelier in Paris that could have produced it. To assure you, let me say that it was ordered by one whose name had best not be repeated."

"That is correct." Egare's eyes had opened wide.

"And delivered by you to the personal valet of the unnamed."

"Yes."

"So you see I am not in ignorance of this affair."

The man hesitated; here stood an officer of the

Bodyguard and therefore no doubt in the royal confidence: also it was more than possible that though in the first place Bontemps acted for his master, the King had now changed his mind and desired that his valet be kept in ignorance. Furthermore, reflected Egare, the varied and often tragic history of other royal gifts fabricated in his atelier warned its owner not to pry too deeply into their destination. At the same time he was not entirely satisfied.

"This business, monsieur ... I would like to oblige, but...."

"Very well." Jules picked up the case. "I report accordingly, so the rest lies between you and ... and Versailles."

He was at the door when Egare caught his arm: "No, monsieur, not that, anything but that ... what is it you wish?"

"What is this thing worth?"

"It is charged at seven thousand louis d'or--a fair price."

Jules stifled a sigh of relief. "Then five thousand will be taken for it."

"As a credit to the account?"

"No, Egare, you will understand that there are occasions when cash is needed in high places, so I will take that sum in notes. Your silence would be to your advantage. In due course your account will be paid by the Treasury as usual."

The jeweller bowed, vanished for a few moments,

then returned with a fat, sealed package.

"Five thousand louis d'or, monsieur. Do we not exchange receipts in this affair?"

Jules shook his head: "There are occasions when a signed paper has had deplorable results for him who held it. I fancy your experience will agree with that. Good-day, Egare."

Riding off, he drove his horse hard. The die was cast, honour saved by means that, now that the thing was done, took his breath away. He had no conception of what lay ahead for either of them, and as Paris changed to an open country road that eased his horse's feet, a hundred possibilities stirred in his tense brain. Banishment--the Bastille--discharge with ignominy-- flight before the blow fell--anything was possible. On one point only was he sure; he had come out of this business with no credit. That remained with his wife.

It was just before noon when he found de Roquelaure, and that young nobleman regarded him with grave interest.

"I am sorry about last night," he began, "but you made a bad mistake; I talked with the others after we left the salon and they all feel the same--that you were too stubborn in flouting friendly advice. As a matter of fact, Jules, I fear we do not trust you any longer, and unless the cash is paid today your notes of hand will be sold to the moneylenders for whatever they fetch. I fancy that won't be much."

"God's death!" laughed Jules, "but you look morose."

"I deplore your misfortune."

"Then take this, and cease to deplore." He clapped the package into an unready hand. "Here are five thousand louis in exchange for certain bits of paper with my signature. At our next game I beg that you take these small matters less seriously."

— VIII —

At noon on the next day de Maintenon was examining the nearly completed design on her frame when her lady-in-waiting, Madame de Brinon, announced that Madame de Montespan craved audience.

"You may admit her, then leave us."

The visitor curtsied, de Maintenon inclined her dignified head and motioned to the fauteuil usually occupied by the King. She could afford to be generous and, with a placidity that many had found disconcerting, she waited.

De Montespan regarded her with well-concealed aversion: here sat her conqueror, her supplanter, fortified in a fashion that defied attack, strong because she asked nothing. Here she sat, this invulnerable woman, the unflurried centre of a Court from which de Montespan had for years purposed to remove herself but always weakened, and year after year haunted the scene of her former triumphs, still beautiful, still seductive, with bitterness in her heart.

"Madame desired to speak with me?"

"It is concerning the King, and I would do you both a service."

"From one who once understood His Majesty so well, any service is welcome," said de Maintenon, blandly.

"Then I have observed with interest," began the late favourite, in a faintly insolent tone, "how the occupations of His Majesty have changed of late: the pleasures of life seem to offer him no attraction; he devotes himself only to affairs of State, and does it not occur to you that this change is too taxing for one of such naturally social inclinations? It lacks any diversion."

"No, I have not observed it."

"But others, who are devoted to His Majesty, have not missed it, and the Court is without its former gaiety; it moves but stiffly."

"The diversions of the Court do not concern me, madame."

"I will speak more frankly. His Majesty grows restless, and I need not explain that myself having enjoyed his favours in the past I now recognise the symptoms."

"If madame suggests that the King can not find here all he desires she is mistaken."

"Are you so sure of that?" asked de Montespan, impudently.

Something in her voice drew a quick glance that was just a shade uncertain: "It would be better to speak still more frankly."

"That is agreed, so were I to tell you that His

Majesty proposes to take a new favourite, would you believe me?"

De Maintenon felt a shiver of apprehension; nothing disturbed her pale serenity; her eyes remained blank, but her brain became very busy. This woman had held Louis in willing if disastrous bondage for years; she had borne him eight children of whom those living were legitimised: she was fearless, daring, charged with the rancour of a discarded favourite, and much too clever to allow her resentment to make statements that were without foundation. A woman to be reckoned with.

"Madame has not told me yet, and I am sure she comes here with the highest of motives."

"My motives are those which inspired me to add to His Majesty's family, and perhaps difficult of understanding by one who has not done the same," answered de Montespan, her eyes hard. "At any rate there was recently presented at the assembly a certain Madame Vicotte whose husband is in the King's Guard. She is young and beautiful."

Vicotte? Vicotte? That had a faintly familiar sound, and automatically de Maintenon sent her shrewd prehensile brain in pursuit. Vicotte? Somewhere-- somehow--was it not here in this room, and not so long ago? Vicotte? Ah! now it was coming--coming and--yes- -Godet des Marais, he was involved, and did there not also loom near the door the phantom figure of a large uncouth young man, a Breton, who--who--then all in a rush it came back, and again she fingered the letter of the Abbé Callot with its fine priestly script. That recaptured everything, and she felt a faint glow at her own powers.

"And comes from Castellon in Brittany," she put

in, dryly.

"Then you know her?" stammered the other woman.

"I supposed you came to give information, not to receive it; proceed madame."

"Alors!" went on de Montespan with a toss of her curled locks, "as she approached I was near the throne and observed her agitation, also a peculiar interest on the part of the King. When she made reverence, he touched his neck as though indicating something I did not then grasp. Then she turned crimson and passed on. Shortly afterwards I observed them alone, and His Majesty, embracing her, put his hand in her breast--*her* breast madame, not his own--and took out a diamond necklet which he placed round her throat. Still in his embrace she disappeared, and I was too wise to follow. Should you require proof of this, madame is no doubt in the palace where her husband has quarters. That is all I came to tell you."

De Maintenon, with no change of expression, felt her heart grow cold, but was far too astute to allow this disgruntled tale-bearer the slightest satisfaction. That was her first care. At the same time instinct warned her not to discredit what she had heard, though not once in five years of intimacy and secret marriage had Louis betrayed himself by sign or look. Now she was deeply disturbed. Louis, however, could be dealt with later, and in the meantime here sat his former favourite in palpable enjoyment of the moment, so one must attend to that first.

"Madame," she said, coolly, "I thank you for performing what must have been a distasteful duty to one who once shared His Majesty's confidence. How you must have disciplined yourself to come here; so I am the more glad to be able to relieve your anxiety."

"Relieve it?"

"Yes, madame, relieve it. I have known for some time past that His Majesty was interested in this person."

"Oh!"

"You are surprised, but a little more reflection might have assured you that here, though secluded from the Court, I am not without information in any matter that concerns His Majesty."

"Madame already knew?" exclaimed de Montespan, in a thin voice.

The other woman, rising, looked her full in the face. "I have always known far more than I thought prudent to convey, so as to this business you can draw your own conclusions. Should I advise you that you tell me nothing new, you will have time to think about that in the leisure which I anticipate you will shortly enjoy free from any strain of life at the Court of Versailles. You will find the country air a benefit, and be less burdened with that sense of responsibility you now feel in the private affairs of the King. Madame, you may take your leave."

De Montespan waited one instant, dismayed and shaken, her mouth open, then she disappeared, and de Maintenon moved to the great fireplace. Her calm had given way to agitation and she looked strangely older; this news--for it was news--had struck hard, but now as always in the hour of stress her brain was clear for action. Of a sudden she gave an exclamation expressing both relief and determination, and rang the bell.

"Madame de Brinon, you will please inform the Minister Louvois that I desire to see him here as soon as possible."

— IX —

Three weeks later, the King, just recovered from a bout of rheumatism, sat in his own cabinet at council with Louvois: invisible to the Court during that time, he had admitted none but de Maintenon and Bontemps; his temper had been vile. Ridiculous that a man of only forty-five should be so plagued! Another factor that angered him--one he did not voice--was the interruption to a conquest he had anticipated with satisfaction, but to make love when one's joints creaked like an ungreased axle was out of the question.

He felt oddly about the insolent slip of a girl; it piqued him to be defied, sharpened his appetite; none other had seen that well directed slap--he could still sense its hot tingle--that seemed to startle into activity a craving he had deplored as gone forever, so for that he was grateful. But once was enough. She would be sweet, this young Breton flower, more refreshing than the dark shrewd beauty of de Montespan or the soft compliance of la Vallière.

Such his royal thoughts as he sat half attentive to Louvois, who watched his master with ill-concealed impatience, for, absent from the Widow Scarron, Louis seemed unable to make his mind up about anything, especially the war in Bavaria. Mannheim had been sacked, the city of Worms was in ashes, and as a finishing stroke the Minister urged the destruction of Trèves. But Louis demurred: enough blood, he objected, had been shed already.

"Then, Sire, it will be fortified, while one good blow would end the matter in our favour."

"Louvois, I am tired of this war which takes us nowhere."

"The honour of our armies is at stake, your Majesty."

"These campaigns cost too many thousands that are needed at home. Did I tell you about the new chapel Hardouin-Mansart is designing for me? There's Marly--that's swallowing a lot, far more than I reckoned. De Seignelay reports that his last impost of taxes has failed of its purpose; the response is miserable, citizens are grumbling. No, Trèves must not be attacked; we cannot fight without more money. Canada, too, draws on our funds. Is there any further word from de Denonville?"

"Nothing, your Majesty."

"For which we are thankful. When does Comte Frontenac leave?"

"In a few weeks more, Sire."

"Have any more troops been sent out?"

"A small company by the first ship two weeks ago."

"And officers?"

Louvois' lips took on a peculiar smile: "Here is the list, your Majesty."

The King ran his eye down a row of names, then gave a chuckle of surprise: "I see here Captain Vicotte, but what does it mean? I approved the others, but not him."

"That is true, Sire, but his name was added at the last moment before the ship sailed."

"But who--who arranged it without my order?"

"Your Majesty, it was at the wish of one I am not in a position to disregard. I asked if it was also your wish, and was told it might be left to her."

"Louvois," the King was smiling now. "This is incredible, but as it happens it suits me, on my faith it does; there are reasons why it suits me well."

He nodded, rubbing his palms and the minister secretly relished a moment that was yet to come. Squeezed tight for years between de Maintenon and the King, he resented the interference of one, the weakness of the other; congenitally a man of war, he had vitalised the armies of France into the finest fighting machine of their time, but de Maintenon just as steadily opposed his campaigns, so when three weeks previously he had waited on her and heard what she desired should be done he jumped at it. The affair with Madame Vicotte was no secret; de Montespan had seen to that; and here was opportunity to open a breach that might serve him well.

"I hope you approve, Sire."

"Undoubtedly; madame's judgment has not failed her."

"Here also is the list of female passengers."

"We are not interested."

"There is one name, Sire, that...."

Something in his voice aroused the King's suspicion: he snatched the list, gaped at it, spluttering a great oath.

"Louvois, was this also by order of madame?"

"The same order, your Majesty."

"God's death!" snapped Louis, white with rage, "Am I or am I not King? When did you say the ship sailed?"

"Two weeks ago from Rochelle, Sire."

Louis muttered something under his breath, thrust the papers aside and strode out. Traversing salon after salon he frowned at the long perspective lined with portraits of former rulers of France, all those other Louis whose intemperate blood ran in his own veins, and wondered if any one of them had ever been so flouted. Groups of lackeys saw him, stiffened, bowed, and dared not raise their eyes; he encountered Père de la Chaise who, with one swift look, thought best not to speak; he brushed by Seignelay and left that Minister, who was also in the secret, quite bemused; then, approaching the narrow ante-room that guarded the salle of his wife, his pace slackened, he frowned, gave his chin a thoughtful caress, and became a shade uncertain. Finally he marched in.

De Maintenon rose, curtsied, read his mood at a glance and was instantly aware of its cause. She did not speak, but offered her marble cheek for his kiss. He pecked at it, and she resumed her hypnotic tapestry.

Louis, still caressing his chin, already felt himself yielding to the well-known atmosphere of this room, he sensed it closing round him, the very air had a familiar taste; this chamber was a factor in his life, its passionless occupant his self-chosen arbiter. Part of him longed to escape, while the other part admitted that it could not stand alone. There she sat, his Solidité, quiet as a windless lake, with depths he had never yet been able to plumb.

But certainly he had something to say in this present affair, so he pulled himself together.

"Madame, I am on a business that has disturbed me and requires explanation. Louvois reports that on your demand a certain officer, one of my Bodyguard, has been suddenly transferred to New France, and is already on the high seas. Does Louvois speak truly?"

She inclined her Olympian head, and how like him, she thought, not to mention the woman.

"Then, as my wife and subject, you will answer three questions. First, to what ministry do you belong?"

"To none, Sire."

"Or what office do you hold under the Crown?"

"None, Sire."

"Then madame, in God's name on what authority have you acted?"

She looked at him quite without fear, her dignity was superb, and in those steady dark eyes he caught the expression of forces that deep in his heart he knew to be unconquerable. To oppose them was something like opposing nature, and brought the inevitable result, while compliance meant security. Then came a spasm of rebellion, and he wished he did not feel quite so old.

"I have asked a question, madame, and await your answer."

The answer came, but not in speech; she only sent him the ghost of a smile and fingered the great diamond in the nuptial ring she always wore.

This was so significant, so pointed, in a word so inescapable, that Louis bit his lip and frowned, but gradually the frown faded into a sort of unwilling exasperated grin. Her subtlety appealed to his wit no less than did her courage to his respect. What other woman, he wondered, would have confronted him thus, and even in defeat recognised the working of a brain superior to his own. He had blown off steam, the affair was ended, Maintenon had spoken only five words, but they left him with a dull conviction that he, the King of all France, was merely an elderly married man for whom the days of amorous escapades had long since passed.

"My Solidité," he said, with a grimace of sulky admiration, "to your knowledge I have had dealings with many women, all of them beautiful, all willing, but found none half as clever as yourself. How do you do it?"

In New France

Spade and Musket

— I —

It was on the last ship of the year that Paul de Lorimier sailed up the gulf of St. Lawrence and caught first sight of the high battlements of Quebec: he stood watching them for a long time but unfavourable winds kept the vessel tacking criss-cross over the narrowing river, and it was not till evening that she dropped anchor a hundred yards from the huddle of timber houses known as the Lower Town. The passage from Brest had taken seven weeks.

His luggage was lowered into a small boat, and as his foot touched the soil of Canada there came the profound conviction that at this moment he was taking an irrevocable step. He smiled at this, somehow it raised in him no doubts, and walked on, his eyes busy. Inquiring where he might lodge for the night, he was directed to the tavern of Jacques Boisdon on the edge of the Upper Town, and here found accommodation rough but acceptable.

The last weeks of his voyage had enthralled him. Under the flanks of mountain ranges whose foothills reached the northern shore of the Gulf, he came to Tadousac, a trading station where the Montagnais savages brought their furs to market: it was his first view of any wild tribe, and their tall athletic bodies, copper-brown skins, feathered heads and suspicious eyes, black like onyx, filled the young Breton with romantic interest. Then on by Mal Baie and Cap Tourmente, all deep in shaggy forest, to the seigneury of Beaupré with numbers of log houses, and here Paul saw stubble fields recently yellow with wheat, grazing cattle, young orchards burdened with apples. Next the tall, white cataract of Montmorency, the seigneury of Beauport, the flat extremity of the Île d'Orléans, and finally the great hummock of Quebec itself.

Now the sun plunged into the western reaches of the St. Lawrence, and the wild scene moved his fancy. From the shore came a babble of voices in a familiar tongue; narrow streets climbed crookedly to the lofty plateau overlooking the river, crowned by groups of ecclesiastical buildings. Here the Château of St. Louis, the home of the Governor; Fort St. Louis on whose high stockade were groups of men in uniform looking down at the *Ville Marie* as she swung at anchor; here too rose the great stone Church of Notre Dame from which came the clangour of bells, whose chimes drifting far out over river and forest sent the voice of the known to the unknown. The soldiers with their epaulettes, trim uniforms and white breeches, the muzzles of cannon that could just be distinguished pouting iron lips from timber bastions, all announced that here at the gateway of a new world both Church and State were on the alert.

That night Paul felt restless; there was no sleep in him, and under high stars he walked along the parapet guarding the abrupt edge of the Upper Town. From where he stood a stone might be dropped on the sloping medley of roofs below, where there were still lights and laughter and song in scattered taverns, while between the *Ville Marie* and the shore moved a constant

114

procession of boats unloading cargo and loading beaver skins. The boats swam with oars extended like the legs of water-beetles on the unruffled river. Far to the south beyond Point Levis stretched a dense forest which Paul had been told was the country of the Iroquois, while beyond that again lay distant settlements of the Dutch and English. From this wilderness a light breeze came sweet and clean, scented with, the aromatic odour of cedar and hemlock.

Paul was standing lost in contemplation, when he heard a voice:

"A fair view, sir, is it not?"

Turning, he saw a middle-aged man in a leather shirt, breech clout, moccasins and a sort of leather cap; he was smoking a short pipe.

"Yes, I have found nothing like it before."

"Nor will you in any land but this."

"You know the country?"

"Not so well hereabouts: I have come down from the upper reaches with timber, you see it lying there on that raft; and presently I go back."

"How do you go back?"

"By a canoe or batteau, m'sieu, there is no other way. One cannot walk, it is not safe."

Something familiar in his accent drew Paul's attention: "Are you a Breton?"

"From Vitré, m'sieu, five years ago from Vitré; I

115

came out with other settlers."

"And I come from Castellon."

The man wheeled, smiled broadly and put out a muscular hand: "It is good to meet a fellow-Breton. You have arrived, when?"

"By the *Ville Marie*, this is my first day in Canada. What is your name?"

"Jean Prud'homme, m'sieu, at your service. You stay in Quebec, yes?"

Paul did not answer that: he had in his pocket a letter to Bishop St. Vallier from Father Poncet, and thought of presenting it on the morrow, but now he decided first to gather what he could concerning Canada from some unofficial and unprejudiced source. This man's face was honest, and he carried an attractive air of independence.

"What do you do when you return, my friend?"

"I suppose the same thing unless fortune changes, which I trust it may."

"Then you are not a farmer?"

"But, yes, in Vitré I worked on my father's land whom God blessed with too many hungry sons and too small a farm to feed them all, so I came away. I am unmarried and free."

"And after that?"

"Here in Canada it is the same as elsewhere--if you have money it is one thing--if not, another. I had no money left, my passage took it all. I worked in the forest in several seigneuries, also on a farm near Ville Marie. Had I a little money, I should have bought a farm of my own, but for a single man to reduce a piece of forest to fields without help or oxen is too much. This will not interest you."

"On the contrary it does. Where is the best land to be had?"

"At the settlement of Lachine, almost within sight of the stockade of Ville Marie. The timber is not too heavy, the soil black, rich, and even better than that yonder at Beaupré, while elevations to the north fend off the worst of winter winds."

"How far is it?"

"Not far, m'sieu, about seventy leagues."

Paul, eyes measuring the *Ville Marie*, was thinking hard and he cast back to that last talk with Father Poncet at the College of the Jesuits in Paris when the priest had seemed to assume that the young man was going to Canada in order to enter the Church, but Paul, thanking him for the letter, had come away unconvinced. Long association with Abbé Callot had not drawn him to the Church, his fore-runners were farmers, a feeling for the soil was in his blood, and though Father Poncet had not mentioned farming in Canada, he had nevertheless brought with him a good supply of seed grain, field tools, and equipment for a small house such as might serve an unmarried man. It seemed only natural to take these things with him, he could not imagine anything else half as suitable, and they contributed a certain promise of direction and actuality to a purpose that was still unformed. With this and much more in his mind he remained silent so long that Prud'homme became uncomfortable.

"Alors, m'sieu, goodnight; it is good to have met someone from so near home."

He was moving off when Paul stopped him.

"Wait, I have more to say about this farming business--you tell me that it is too heavy for a man alone, but what labour is to be had in a land like this?"

"There are slaves, m'sieu; Iroquois prisoners that can be secured by small payment to the Governor; they do not like work but are better than nothing."

"Do they not run away?"

"At any sign of that they are shot."

"I see. You are free, Prud'homme, to do what you please?"

"My friends tell me that I am too free for my own good," said he with a laugh. "I have no woman, therefore I save no money. I had thought of taking a savage woman and becoming a coureur des bois, but that life has only one end."

"Have you here in Quebec any friend who will speak for you?"

Prud'homme jerked his thumb at a large stone building. "There is Father Morel in the house of the Jesuits who knows me and took my confession yesterday. He is a missionary with no parish, but all parishes are the same to him."

118

"Let us leave it at that; I will speak to him of you in the morning, so tomorrow perhaps you will meet me here at noon when we can talk further. I bid you goodnight."

In the tavern he lay awake hour after hour: there came from the *Ville Marie* a constant whine of blocks as her cargo was hoisted up and out, there were midnight bells from the Ursuline Convent, a great clock struck the hours in the belfry of Notre Dame, shouting rose from the Lower Town where sailors and woodsmen drank brandy in the log-walled bothys, while in rare intervals of silence something mystical and compelling reached him from the great lone land to the west, and Castellon seemed a million leagues away.

In a bare, white-washed room, Father Morel received him next morning, a spare, active, grey-haired man of about fifty with warm, brown eyes and large, kindly mouth. His hands and face bore signs of hardship.

"Jean Prud'homme," he said, "is a son of the Church, honest, capable, an excellent woodsman, also considered too good-natured for his own advantage. He can speak a little of the Iroquois tongue and has a pleasant sense of humour, which attribute," smiled the priest, "is sometimes worth a good deal." Then he looked with interest at Paul. "You will not stay in Quebec?"

"No, I go further west."

"I should have liked to see more of you, for our news from France is but scanty. What is happening there, and does the King continue to lead a reformed life under the influence of de Maintenon?"

119

"I believe so, Father; I had the privilege of meeting her not long before I sailed."

"Is she what they say, proud, calm, dignified?"

"So it seemed to me; I was there but a short time, with Monseigneur Godet des Marais."

"The new Bishop of Chartres! My son, you seem to move in high circles."

"It was not of my own seeking. There was also Father Poncet. Those three I met at Versailles."

"Versailles! for the sake of which the King is ruining France. It is strange that with such persons behind you, you do not turn to the Church."

Paul shook his head: "First I will turn to the land; I am of a family of farmers."

"Well, perhaps you are right, but it will be a new kind of farming so keep your musket primed across the nearest stump--you will learn that from Prud'homme. Where will you farm?"

"Perhaps at Lachine."

"In which case I will see you early next summer. God go with you, my son."

When Paul met Prud'homme at noon leaning against the parapet, he touched his leather cap.

"Well, m'sieu, the good father has no doubt said terrible things about me."

"Enough to satisfy my mind. Are you ready to

engage as my servant?"

Prud'homme gave him a straight look, noting the strength in his body, the quietness of his eyes; then he grinned: "We are Bretons, you and I; had m'sieu been a Parisian I would have said no, for I cannot stand their ways, but as it is--yes--very well."

"And your wage?"

Jean gave a shrug: "M'sieu will take up land at Lachine?"

"I think it will be Lachine."

"Then please listen to me. You know nothing of this country or the people in it, so I say let us wait till you reach Ville Marie and have your land, which I will help you to select; then you can talk to people there, learn what wage is usual and with that I am content."

"Jean, you and I should get on together."

"M'sieu is unmarried?"

"Yes."

"That is better, much better to begin with. But the implements for the farm, they are cheaper here than at Ville Marie."

"I have them, all of them, straight from France."

Jean gave his thigh a great slap: "Nom de Dieu! but you are wise, and the merchants in this country are all thieves, so now leave the rest to me. There are some batteaux starting in a few days, for the west."

"How long will that journey take?"

"Perhaps ten days, it depends on the wind. They will transport the implements--and an ox--we shall certainly need an ox, but that can be bought at Ville Marie."

"Why not two oxen?" smiled Paul.

"Tant mieux--that farm will grow quickly. You have of course an arquebus?"

"No."

"We shall need two of those, also four pistols with powder and balls. You see, m'sieu, at Lachine, which is six miles outside the stockade of Ville Marie a man works with one eye on the ground, the other on the forest. Now I go to arrange for the batteaux."

With this he drew himself up, made a rough salute in which there was a good deal of dignity, and marched off, singing, towards the Lower Town.

— II —

That ten-day journey to Ville Marie gave Paul his first conception of the new world; the size of the river, the massive forests that covered its banks, other rivers that fed from north and south, all were such as he could not have imagined. Along these shores he noticed the ragged clearings of various seigneuries, each with its cluster of log cabins inside a stockade that had one large gate opening to the banks, and behind stretched the home and hunting ground of hostile savages.

Nearing Ville Marie, he saw a village of friendly

Hurons, then in the distance the great mill of the Sulpitians, strongly fortified against attack, built of rough stone and pierced with loopholes. Now the land was more open, the clearings more continuous, another high conical windmill came in sight, a seminary, the Hôtel Dieu, and a straggling line of substantial houses with wooden walls, stone gables and cedar shingled roofs. To the north lifted a thickly wooded elevation of several hundred feet with an outline like that of a stranded whale; further west a jagged rampart of white lay across the great stream, the rapids of St. Louis. Here the river was more than a mile wide, and in seventy leagues seemed not to have shrunk at all.

On the shore savages were camped, and smoke trailed from their wigwam fires; a crowd had gathered to watch the incoming batteaux; there were soldiers in uniform, priests, nuns, Indian slaves carrying water in buckets slung from a yoke across their shoulders, frontier traders, coureurs des bois, wild-looking men with knives in their belts, and a few women who were not dressed with the care he had observed in Quebec where many of the wives and daughters of the military wore costumes just received from Paris, here they were more roughly clad, their hair neglected, some with bare legs, feet in Indian moccasins.

"Alors, m'sieu, we arrive," said Jean at Paul's elbow, "it does not resemble Vitré or Castellon, but all things have a beginning. Already in your journey you have seen nearly all the houses in Canada."

Paul agreed with him: the aspect of this outpost was striking, its uncouthness suggested courage, here was the furthest settlement of Church and State, thus far had reached the daring fringe of the human tide, and here it paused for breath ere the next irresistible pulsation carried it still further into the unknown.

"Those men with knives and arms are bushrangers who obey only the Governor here, being his particular children. They are dangerous and it is well to let them alone. As for the Chevalier, it is wise to make a friend of him. Voilà, there he is!"

Near the shore stood a swarthy middle-aged man in a blue coat with brass buttons, an old cocked hat and military boots; his tanned face had a commanding look, his eyes were black and very sharp, his mouth indicated temper and assurance.

"This," said Paul, saluting, "is the Governor?"

"I am, sir,--and you?"

Paul explained.

"You desire to farm at Lachine and not trade in fur?"

"I am a farmer, not a trader."

"In which you are wise," his expression softened a shade, "we have too many of those cursed speculators already, and not enough farmers."

"I am glad to hear it; and as to the land?"

"For that you will wait on the Abbé Belmont of the Sulpitians here: they own the island of Mount Royal, and can settle you at Lachine. Twenty years ago the seigneury belonged to the Chevalier La Salle, but he was too much of a wanderer, and now the priests have it. By God! sir, they will soon own the whole country. You were a farmer in France?"

"In Brittany, Chevalier."

124

"You will find richer soil here, but will need one additional implement at hand."

"What is that?"

"A musket."

He spoke like a man of strong will, was in love with the wild life he lived, well fitted by nature and energy to play his part, and in constant restlessness over de Denonville's ineffectual policies. Never had the Chevalier Rigaud de Callières lined his own pockets by trading in beaver-skins as did Perrot, his predecessor, who later spent weeks in the Bastille as a reminder of Louis' authority. He was too wise to quarrel with the Sulpitians, and held the bushrangers, most experienced of all in forest warfare, in the hollow of his hand.

Paul, studying him with interest, asked what labour was to be had.

"I can find you a pair of captives. Are you married?"

"No."

"Then you will want a woman."

When Paul shook his head, de Callières laughed at him: "You say that now, but winter nights are frigid here, and that big body of yours will feel cold alone. They are not so bad, these savages, when tamed. Well, when you have your land we shall see; now go to the Abbé, you will find him in the seminary. When did you leave France?"

"Two months ago, sir; I came by the last ship."

"What word from there?"

"There is war in the low countries, and William of Orange firmly on the throne of England; also James of England is in France, living at the expense of King Louis."

De Callières gave a great oath: "The Protestant William!--which means much to us here in Montreal; now we will have a war of religion as well as trade with those English to the south. Even when James had England it was bad enough but--did more troops come with you?"

"No, sir."

"I suppose the King still argues that he needs them all at home. Did you hear anything of Comte Frontenac over there?"

Paul shook his head.

"I wish he were back in Canada: we had differences he and I, but, by God! he knows what is needed in this country. Did you see the Governor in Quebec--no--well you didn't miss much. The Marquis de Denonville is too busy with that Bishop St. Vallier, a soft man without force, who thinks by flattery and stroking the back of an Iroquois he becomes the friend of France." Here he paused, chewing his resentment. "Monsieur, take it from me that to sit in the Château St. Louis and receive the benediction of the Church is no way to administer Canada. Denonville is afraid of the savages, and clips their wings. Come back when you have secured your land. I wish you well."

Three days later Paul, accompanied by Jean, set out for Lachine with permission from Belmont to select such uncultivated land as he desired, with only the stipulation that his grain be ground in the big stone mill at Ville Marie. Prud'homme was in high spirits, full of talk, and at times would pull a flute from inside his leather shirt and play a few gay notes.

The year had drawn on to the Indian summer when the earth, yielding to a nostalgic weariness of incessant heat, stretches its tired limbs in preparation for sleep; but first in gay defiance of coming snows it dons a garment of incredible colour. Bewitched by the first transitory touch of nightly frost, the maples festoon themselves in a vesture of living crimson; birch, alder and poplar are clothed in brightest colours, the dark-branched sumach is a burning bush, and each vagrant wind brings down a rain of ruined glory. There is still caressing warmth in the sun, while a penultimate hush pervades the air for this is a suave interval preceding change; the voices of men carry far, the atmosphere seems charged with lingering farewell.

The road, only a rutted trail, followed the bank of the St. Lawrence westwards along the edge of tumbling rapids whose roar distributed a muffled thunder; here the ground was broken and rocky, but on reaching the extremity of Lake St. Louis, a broadening of the great stream, they came on clearings extending some three miles further west, where battalions of blackened stumps were scattered through roughly fenced fields, and the short stubble populated by flocks of wild pigeons. The settlers' houses, strongly built of logs, some with shingle roofs, all fronted the river where canoes and small boats had been drawn up, and nets hung out to dry. Men and women worked in the fields waging peaceful war on the wilderness, oxen moved stolidly in front of lurching ploughs, the sound of axes echoed softly from the nearby wall of forest, and smoke climbed from half a hundred roofs into still air that carried a touch of frost. Paul saw farms first broken in when Chevalier La Salle passed that way some twenty years past, taking it as the gateway to the route for China; some were fertile, comfortable and well cultivated, evidencing what could be done by grace of labour and intervals of peace with the Iroquois, but more were neglected, half-tilled and ragged with weeds. Placed so as best to guard the settlement, were the three stockaded forts of Remy, Roland and La Présentation with their heavily weighted gates, while still further upstream a garrison of two hundred regulars made their camp. These with his band of nomad bushrangers constituted de Callières' strength against the five hostile tribes known as the Confederation of the Iroquois.

Paul looked about, vastly interested; he had come it seemed to the end of all known roads, must now make one for himself, and his spirits mounted at the thought.

"Whose farm is that?"

"Pierre Barbarin, dit Grandmaison; he is married with a Lebrun: there is Pierre himself."

Paul crossed a field, spoke to the man: he had a very fair skin, reddened with the sun, black hair and merry eyes.

"Good-day; my name is de Lorimier; I am just arrived from France, and look for land in Lachine. Perhaps you can advise me."

Barbarin leaned on his spade: "Just arrived, eh?"

"Yes."

"Yet you did not take the same ship back?" he waved a hand at New France, "As for land, m'sieu, help yourself; there is no one to stop you except the Iroquois."

"So I am told. How long have you been here?"

"Ten years--long enough; but there is nowhere else to go."

Ten years, thought Paul, and so little to show for it: the land had been neglected, half of it uncultivated though the whole grant was cleared in order to leave no cover for marauding savages, fences half down, behind the house an untidy patch where a small boy played with a dog: a woman came out to inspect the stranger; she had a wide mouth and looked good-natured, but her hair was unkempt and slovenly, so for the Barbarin family life must be a hand-to-mouth affair. It occurred to him that he might buy this place as it stood and turn it into something worth while, but that didn't attract him.

"My advice is to settle not too far from a fort," smiled Barbarin, flashing his white teeth, "if that is secured the rest does not matter."

Paul pointed to the north edge of the farm. "There, for instance? But if I built there could I cross your property to reach road and lake?"

"This country is different--no permission is needed--we are glad to see our neighbours cross anywhere. Also here you are but six miles from market in Ville Marie--that is worth remembering."

"Jean, what do you think?"

"To secure frontage on the lake, m'sieu, one must go another three miles west past Fort La Présentation, which would be on the boundary of nowhere. To take new land here means more work, but you remain in sight of Fort Remy, also we are amongst neighbours. It depends on the land itself."

"He's right," nodded Barbarin, "from here one can make a dash for Remy."

"Is labour to be hired in Lachine?"

"Except at harvest time, when you may get some regulars from the forts if you are friends with the Governor."

"Well, we shall meet again. I thank you."

Climbing snake-like fences built of split logs, they reached the unbroken forest wall, where with a sudden desire to be alone he motioned Jean not to follow and advanced a few hundred yards. What destiny, he wondered, had brought him to this wild spot so undreamed of but five short months ago. Around him towered a noble assemblage of tall trunks, walnut and birch, beech, poplar and hickory, maple and butternut, all branching half naked to the grey skies, their colonnades enclosing islands of dark green hemlock, pine and spruce whose warm depth would oppose the winter wind. His feet sank into a carpet of dead leaves that still retained some of their glory. The sound of axes did not reach here, but a faint murmur stirred overhead with the call of partridges and chatter of busy squirrels storing nuts against the bitter weather. How long he stood silent he could not tell till steps approached, and, turning, he saw Jean with a spade over his shoulder.

"M'sieu will excuse me but...."

"But what?"

"I waited one half-hour and thought that perhaps you were lost; it is easy to get lost when there is no sun."

"I was a little," agreed Paul, "but not far. What about this place?"

Jean spat on his palms, struck in the spade and began to dig; he dug a small trench five feet deep, working fast till his shoulders came level with the ground; the soil remained the same, dark, light and rich, with a top layer of vegetable mould, the leafy rain of centuries past.

"Regardez, m'sieu; what more do you want?"

Paul took a handful, put it to his nose, rubbed it between his palms, while the farmer in him felt a thrill. He knew good soil when he saw it, and this moist handful had a voice which spoke of fruitage, of seed-time and harvest and changing seasons of green and gold; it seemed that this secret corner of New France was giving him the ancient promise of nature to those who labour and love and understand their land, so that the elemental man in him went out to meet it; then and there the pact was made, and from that moment he knew what his future must be.

"M'sieu, I have seen Indian corn here eight feet high, and potatoes--mon Dieu! what potatoes,--and tobacco, le tabac Canadien--whatever one puts in the ground it is the same."

"It is better than the Breton land," grinned Paul, "but does one find water by sinking a well?"

"Wait--wait! I have a little idea that perhaps...." He darted off moving in a sort of widening spiral like a questing hound and disappeared amongst the tall trunks till there came a whistle and Paul found him looking pleased.

"You hear it, yes?"

Water was chuckling almost at his feet; it escaped white and sparkling from a circular sanded patch between two great pines from which it gurgled, bubbled and twisted into a deep runnel. Jean put his face into it, drank deeply, and laughed up at his master.

"There is no need of a well," said he, shaking his dripping beard like a dog, "this spring is born far down, it will run all winter under the snows, and we can build the house beside it. Mon Dieu! but we have luck today! wood--water--good soil and good neighbours. Is there anything more you desire?"

Paul gave no answer to that; what more he desired was not to be put into words, for here and now he was giving hostages to fortune, and with the planting of new seed in new soil must come the last uprooting of another growth that had struck more deeply than he suspected. The image of Jacqueline still shone clear though she had moved for ever out of reach, and it would be lonely work here at the best. From the little he had seen of Ville Marie it offered no promise of any real companionship; he was not drawn to the Church, there having been too much talk on the voyage from Quebec of how the Jesuits permitted the torture of savage captives that in the agony of death their souls might find salvation. Jean Prud'homme was acceptable with limitations, and the lightness of his heart might while away a dull hour, but he was uneducated and could not even read. The personality of

132

the Governor did not attract. Therefore, decided Paul, one must depend entirely on oneself, which probably was a man's first duty in a country like this.

He gave Jean an unreadable smile, and began to talk about the price of oxen.

— III —

Storms blew, snow came, but before it lay a foot deep Paul's house had its roof of split hollow cedar logs and a plume of pearl grey smoke joined the others that climbed from Lachine. So soon as the land had been measured and the grant made--it was a quarter-mile wide, half a mile long--he applied to de Callières in the matter of labour, and the Governor acted promptly.

"There is Onato, the Watersnake, a man of sixty but strong and active, also Eri, the Cherry Tree, his granddaughter of seventeen, they are unhappy when separated so take them both."

"Who are these people?"

"Onato is the father of Oguntwae, the Hairy One, an Iroquois chief with whom we have fought and will fight again. These two of his family I hold as hostages. If they escape, there are others whom I will put to death, and they know it. They have both learned a little French, and you must always remember that they understand far more than they admit, so do not talk too openly before them."

"I do not want a girl," objected Paul, "the man yes, but not the girl."

"Monsieur de Lorimier," cackled the Governor,

"you are new to this country and I hope for your success, also as master of these two of the family of Oguntwae, you become a person of some importance with the Iroquois who are well aware of all that goes on here. If you treat them favourably, and especially should you father a child to the girl--for which you will find her not unwilling--it may mean your salvation in the next war. For myself I have no care whether you do this or not, but believe me that someone to cook, wash and tend your house is worth having, and she will not attempt escape."

"Is she now a Christian?"

"She has been baptised--the Jesuits saw to that at once--but certainly it made more difference to them than to her, and I think that Cherry Tree suits her better than Thérèse which they called her."

"And the man?"

"They christened Christophe, though he suggests nothing of that kind to me, but suit yourself what you call him. Wait--they will go with you now."

He barked an order; presently the two appeared and stood watching him with onyx black eyes. Onato's body was short for an Iroquois, his features not unpleasant, he stood very straight and had a certain dignity of bearing; the girl was slight, lithe, smooth faced and moved with a panther-like grace. Their gaze shifted to Paul with a fixed, incurious stare.

"This man is now your master," said the Governor, harshly, "go with him."

Paul never forgot the return to Lachine; no words were spoken, the two walked behind in single file with

Eri last carrying the small bundle of their joint possessions; their moccasined feet made no sound, and when he looked round he met only that stony unaltered gaze. It was impossible to guess what they thought, whether they were in any way affected by this sudden change of mastership, so he concluded that they had secrets of their own which he would never fathom. The sensation of those ebony eyes boring into his back finally became uncomfortable, and he was glad to reach his own house.

He had thought best to settle this affair without first consulting Jean, and was relieved when the man, approving, spoke a few words of Indian to Onato and gave the girl a swift searching glance.

"You want her, m'sieu? she is not bad and cleaner than most of them."

"As a servant, yes, as a concubine, no."

"She will be disappointed. Alors, they must not sleep in the house but make first a shelter of bark, then build their own house close by."

"Sleep outside in the winter?"

Jean jerked a thumb at the forest: "Not so far from here there are perhaps five thousand Iroquois that do nothing else. M'sieu, let me advise you, do not consult with them about anything, give them blankets, an axe, flint and steel, food, and no more. If there is thievery, you must report to the Governor, when they will certainly be whipped, also they must never go out of sight of this house."

He spoke with experience: Paul de Lorimier, late farmer of Castellon in Brittany, now slave-owner in New

France, could but agree, and it seemed that this must be right for the two standing motionless, arms hanging straight, received it with no change in their impassive faces. Once Eri's black eyes turned slowly to Paul, remote and mysterious as ever, but that was all: man and girl, they struck him as human automata whose inner workings must always defeat him.

Months passed: four feet of snow lay in the forest; out in the clearings were piled eight-foot drifts, Lake St. Louis stretched a blinding plain of white, snow was heaped round the settlers' houses so that it had to be shovelled to clear the windows, and a high-sided trench cut to the doors. The nights were very still, illuminated by stars diamond-bright and hard white opalescent moons, while sometimes a great aurora flamed in the north like a vast iridescent curtain palpitating with glowing colour: the frost was so intense that far back through the woods one heard trees splitting with rifle-like reports as it reached their frigid hearts. During all this period there were no Indian raids, and bushrangers sent in word that Oguntwae seemed to have lost his former thirst for French blood.

Paul was comfortable. He had laid in a supply of eels with which the St. Lawrence abounded, fish were caught through the ice on Lake St. Louis and brought to his door stiff like marble, on the slopes of Mont Royal were fat red deer, in lower land further north one found the great tufted moose, while partridge could be killed with a stick.

Day after day they toiled, with muskets at hand ready for immediate action, but still there were no alarms. The constant sound of axes was heard on Paul's land, trees toppled, thudding into the snow blanket with a soft muffled crash, the clearing enlarged steadily till what had been dense forest was now a colony of naked stumps. The best of the timber he whipsawed into stout planking for future use, the rest he kept for firewood, which, warned Jean, must not be stacked too near the house lest the Iroquois set it ablaze and smoke them out. When spring came Paul was so impatient to plough and sow that he put charges of gunpowder under the stumps and blew them out, dragging thick, rope-like roots. This was the quick method, but expensive; no other settler in Lachine had been able to afford it, so he got the reputation of being a rich man, and Jean's position grew proportionately.

With changeable weather came intermittent frost and a fortnight of mixed water, ice and snow, through which it was hard to move, then of a sudden a warm sun with bright clear skies. The debris of winter was magically sucked up by beneficent southerly winds till almost overnight the rich land lay bare, moist but not wet, fat with the accumulated juices of centuries and ready for seeding. At first it was too rough to plough, stump holes had to be filled and levelled, so all four worked with spades in bare spaces around a huge pyramid to which the stumps were drawn and now blazed day and night over a great cone of glowing ash. When the fire cooled, the ash went back into the soil to fatten it still further.

Daring the possibility of late frost, Paul sowed early as soon as the snow had vanished, and got his reward. Carrots, peas, lettuce, their first green shoots appeared with May as though the earth responding to a knowing touch was anxious to show what it could do. Wheat, corn and barley were all in. Around the house he planted flower seeds from his own garden at Castellon, and vines along the log walls. These grew as though by witchcraft, and never before had he known such a soil. The farm--he now thought it began to look like a farm--promised to outshine any other in Lachine, and indeed he was the only real farmer there. The rest, disbanded soldiers they might be, or aging adventurers now too stiff for forest life, or unsuccessful merchants, had settled there, because from the soil might be had a sufficiency, and most were only half in earnest. In winter they took to the woods to do trapping, then spent what they got in trade brandy in Ville Marie; in summer they would fish, talk and smoke for hours, while their women did the work; some had Indian wives, some had slaves, both neglected and ill-fed.

With Paul it was different, a sort of elemental ambition possessed him so that with Jean and Onato he worked early and late, proud of his land and what he would make of it, talking to his neighbours hardly at all, and presently this isolation gave him in their minds a sort of dignity, so that in a country of equality they began to touch their hats and call him "m'sieu".

At night he would summon Eri and exchange French for her Iroquois, finding her intelligent and apt. The house she occupied stood fifty yards from his own. Now that the first heavy work was done she cooked for him and Jean, mended their clothes, made moccasins and leather shirts of tanned moose-hide and deer skins. She was industrious and very silent, speaking in monosyllables. During language lessons she would sit, hands on knees, eyes fixed on his, answering in a sort of throaty monotone that never varied, her slim body alert with a certain wild flexible grace that he found attractive, while Jean in a corner puffed at his short clay pipe with a smile on his lips that instantly vanished should Paul happen to turn his way. Jean was waiting for what always resulted in cases like this.

When the lakes and rivers were open there came to Montreal savages and coureurs des bois with their winter take of furs, and then began a fortnight's debauch of which Paul saw but little though enough. It was the great season for trade, and trade floated on French brandy. Thirsting for hard drink, the men of the forest, red and half-breed, voyaged upstream from the Richelieu, downstream from the country of the Eries in hundreds of canoes all laden with high-smelling bales of beaver skins. They camped on the north bank of the St. Lawrence just outside Ville Marie, and at night their fires gleamed red through the darkness. Inside the high stockades on a chair of state in the market place sat de Callières, Master of Ceremonies, in uniform with a sword and cocked hat to declare that wild emporium open. There were speeches, councils and smoking of acrid peace-pipes that passed formally from the Governor first, then from lip to lip, round a great circle of squatting, painted heathen. The merchants at their stalls drove hard bargains with these nomad clients, who came armed with clubs, bows, arrows and muskets, till gradually French brandy sold in quantities did its deadly work, while the black-robed priests of St. Sulpice looked on gravely, helpless. Soon with the potent poison in their blood the wild visitors from many a savage village sank into a stupor to wake with the dull knowledge that once again the white man had had his way. But for beaver skins and that alone did Louis XIV look to Canada.

It was after this affair that Paul, returned to Lachine full of useless protest, saw at the edge of his clearing a familiar figure in a rusty soutane: he dropped his spade and hastened.

"Father Morel, you are welcome!"

"It is good to see you again, my son. You have not been idle since we met last; this farm promises well."

"I have lost no time: there has been peace with the Iroquois and no alarms."

"Let us hope that will last, though I have my doubts; and Jean Prud'homme--you are satisfied?"

"Yes, he is a good man. Come into the house and rest and eat."

"I will do both," smiled the priest, "also I have a proposal to make."

Eri was in the small annex of the kitchen and at sight of her the priest's brows went up a shade.

"She is your slave?"

"Yes, with her grandfather, Onato. I had her from the Governor last year."

"Nothing else, I hope."

"Only a good servant that does much I do not even ask."

"That is well," he glanced about at the shelves of books, Paul's classics and prints from the library in Castellon, "yes--very good; but I might have known it. You are content with life?"

"So far as I will ever be."

The priest made a shrewd guess at the truth, wondering who and where the woman might be.

"My son, I wish there were in Canada more men such as yourself; your methods are those of the Dutch and English to the south who subdue each his own piece of the forest and make it yield food instead of running loose after fur like undisciplined children, so that little by little just a little more of this country becomes theirs. It is the only way. Our people are too restless, they waste their time in voyaging afar, and after a time each place is as though they had never come. That is enough of complaint; now I have an idea for you."

"It would be welcome."

"Candidly, it is not altogether unselfish; I have thought much about you since we parted and soon, next month, will arrive the first ship of the year from France with letters, and ours will go back with her. Would you not like to meet her?"

Letters! So nearly had they passed from Paul's thoughts that the word sounded strange. Before leaving Castellon he had conferred with the Abbé Callot and Raoul Fouquette, giving them his fixed decision, but stipulated they should keep that information to themselves. They had promised to write to Canada by the first ship of the next year, and since then he had forgotten about letters.

"There should be news for me on that vessel," said he, frowning a little.

"Then why not meet her in Quebec and write your answers there, for she will stay but a short time. I myself go down the river soon and shall be happy in your company, so think this over and tell me in the morning."

Paul, pondering many things, was very silent that night, while Morel, immersed in a volume of Molière, sat at the open door, his imagination far from Lachine and

New France: at times he would send the young man a pensive look, then turn his eyes to Eri who moved about efficiently noiseless: he noted the comfort of the place, the feminine touches of which its master seemed unaware, and it gave him the impression that here was established something permanent, and Paul had discovered the only way in which one like himself could be content in a land like this. Yet apparently he was not content.

As to Eri, now the priest remembered the girl; he had seen her just a year ago when, with the old man, she was brought in a prisoner after one of the punitive expeditions of Captain Subercase, the young officer in command at Fort Remy close by. Then she was wild, untamed, with matted hair flowing to her shoulders, legs bare, a child of the forest with hostile eyes furtive like a trapped animal. Today she had changed, all changed, and the priest caught the unmistakable look in those eyes when she glanced at her master, which she often did. Nor had the change come by the persuasion of anyone; Paul had done it without knowing, while the girl was striving to make herself acceptable and much more than a servant. Was it possible, wondered Morel, that the master remained blind to this? And how much the more desirable to lift him out of Lachine for a while.

Paul, too, had thoughts that kept him occupied. Pale green corn stood in rows a foot high. Jean and Onato were working late with the oxen, he heard the musical jingle of trace-chains, already his early vegetables brought good prices in Ville Marie where he could sell all he raised, raspberries reddened in bushy clumps, the captured spring had been led through hollowed cedar logs laid underground to a timber-lined, timber-covered tank near the door. It never failed, it never froze. Ten arpents of land had been cleared, stumped, ready for the plough, next year it would be under grain. This was all good, all of it, the virgin soil had responded to his touch and he was proud of his work, but the priest's news recalled visions that these months of labour only dimmed without obliterating, and above the blue plain of Lake St. Louis he now saw in a mirage the white red-roofed houses of Castellon, his own orchard and farm, Abbé Callot at his gate, Jules laughing down from his charger, and the conical turrets of Château Marbeau. This phantasm was real, poignant, compelling, and his heart went out in sudden hunger.

"I wonder," he said, half aloud.

The priest laid aside Molière: "Well?"

Something surged up in Paul and it all came out in a flood, all about himself. He told everything--of his boyhood, his love, the coming of Jules, the affair on the Vilaine and its sequel. Never before in his life had he talked so fast, the outburst ended with equal abruptness, and he sat looking at his friend with a sort of abashed regret. What a fool he must have sounded.

"I am glad you have spoken," Father Morel tapped his book with a brown finger, "and some of it I had assumed, though the rest is a surprise, but I doubt if you are in need of counsel from me. Always it is such chance happenings or meetings that decide the future of men. C'est toujours l'imprévu qui arrive, n'est ce pas? This love of which you speak, it still exists?"

"I tried to bury it under the soil but it won't stay down."

"Then, my son, you must accept it, it is your cross, you must bear it; I know many men in New France with heavier burdens and less strength to carry them."

"At night I am with her in my dreams, and wake in Lachine," said Paul, bitterly.

"There will not be any letter from her on this ship?"

"No."

"I think this, I think you have been too much alone. Jean is a good man you say--he is capable of being in charge here for two months?"

"He has earned my trust."

"Then come with me; you will be my lay-brother and carry the holy vessels, and we shall talk of many things because...." here the priest looked wistful, "even a servant of Christ hungers for a companionship he does not often find. We are apt to be lonely men, my son, and here one's intellect grows rusty from disuse. Also you will see other farms but not like this one: and while I sow the seed of the Church, you will teach those less experienced than yourself how best to care for their land; also," he added, with a touch of whimsy, "I hope my seed may flourish as certainly as yours. Is it a bargain?"

Paul laughed, and when the thing was arranged he felt happier, younger: then Jean joined them, and Eri came in with a platter of roast venison, hot corn pounded in flat cakes seasoned with young onions, a jar of tart cranberry sauce, a lump of brown sugar from the sap of the maple tree, a loaf of her own baking and a kettle of tea. She put these on the table, gave Paul a low-lidded glance that drew no response, and went back to the kitchen where she sat waiting, hands folded, her eyes like smouldering pits.

She had heard the two talking and understood everything: her master desired no woman here, but in the land he came from was a white one whom he loved.

— IV —

Along the shore of the St. Lawrence where some forty miles below Quebec it widens to an estuary, a bark canoe made its slow persistent way. Northward across the river lifted a silhouette of ragged summits naked of trees, but here the coast was flatter, heavily timbered with pine, balsam and maple, bordered by a wide shingled beach where flocks of crows fed on the mussels uncovered by a retreating tide. Westwards the extremity of the Île d'Orléans floated like a blue smear on the horizon, easterly the waters of the great gulf widened for hundreds of leagues till they met the open sea. There was no sound in all this immensity but a rhythmical dip of paddles and the muted voices of the crows.

"My son," said Father Morel, "don't exert yourself too much; take it more easily--employ the weight of your body; let your arms do little more than hold the paddle, and induce the water to retreat at your stroke. Persuasion is always better than force, and far less fatiguing."

Paul smiled, nodded, and slackened speed: the sun was high, he felt full of vigour, his spirit more at peace than in months past. This journey shaped well, he had made friends, and along the St. Lawrence his reputation as a skilled farmer was spreading. He was in touch with real things, Morel did not talk theology and now at any moment might appear the sails of the first ship from France.

"How much further?"

"Just round the next point a stream comes in through the seigneury of St. Denis where we shall find two houses and eleven persons, or perhaps twelve if all has gone well, of Felix Laflèche and Jacques Lafleur, good people all, and brave, my son, very brave. If their courage falters but a little, they are finished. It is different here from Lachine, where you have the forts and palisades of Ville Marie in case of need. These have but the forest or the river, where there is no refuge. The big Laflèche is a marvel with axe, adze and plane; you will admire the loom he built for his wife, who weaves the best étoffe du pays I have ever known. You will see her at that loom--she is so proud of it. Little Felix--he is lame of one leg from an arrow wound--can do anything with the scraps of iron he brings from Quebec once a year. The houses have even iron hinges, not leather, and nothing is there he has not wrought except the pots and pans. Next year they will grow flax, and Célestine begin weaving linen. There is no mill in St. Denis, so in late summer they take the wheat and rye to Point Levis to be ground--a great week for these good folk. Think what it means for these two women to have others to talk to!"

Here Morel paused, sighed, looked thoughtful. "But all their efforts will not take them far," he added "unless the preservation of life is in itself sufficient reward. They obey God, they work very hard, but--well--"

Paul, surprised at this despondency, asked the reason for it.

"Because, my son, the colony of New France exists only for two purposes: one, to satisfy the ambition of the King; the other, that it may profit the older land. The regard of His Majesty for this country is measured by the peltries it sends him. Also it is the haven for younger sons not wanted at home, and certain of the nobility that France is ready to part with. If Louis desired that Canada really should prosper, why have we not Huguenots here? The best artisans in the world, skilled in all trades, are not allowed to enter lest their doctrines corrupt the true sons of the Church. A few did arrive from Rochelle, only to be deported. The Minister Colbert had the right conception, as have the Dutch and English today. That was a merchant fleet for this service--fish, corn, pine lumber for our West Indies--sugar from the Indies to France--all the things we need from France to Canada--but the conception died with him."

"You would welcome the Huguenots, father?"

"But yes, why not! Their ideas of salvation are not ours, but in this land, of which you are beginning to learn a little, such differences should not be counted. Sometimes I try to picture what will happen here in the future. It always defeats me. I believe that the mother Church will still hold the souls of her people. I think that for hundreds of years the descendants of Felix Laflèche and Jacques Lafleur will till these shores we are passing now, and on holy days the bells will answer each other from Gaspé to Ville Marie. But of the rest of Canada, the larger part of which Chevalier Cadillac and les Sieurs le Moyne, and the Jesuit missionaries can best tell you, that I cannot see except that we are not enough to dominate so vast a country. So you see," he added with an affectionate smile, "this is a land where one like yourself should make his mark."

Paul paddled on for a silent moment: he felt that he would make his mark,--but what lonely work!

"Beyond this St. Denis, what is there?"

"Nothing much till you reach France. Tomorrow if the skies hold fair we will cross over to La Mal Baie and visit there, but it is all a matter of the weather, and I hope first we will meet the ship."

"Is it true the folk in Quebec have petitioned the King for Comte Frontenac's return?"

"Quite true."

"What do you say?"

"I should be content, though he would no doubt quarrel again with the Jesuits whom he accuses of profiting from trade in beaver skins, but he is a stronger man than the Marquis de Denonville. When he was here before there could be no peace between him and Laval the Vicar Apostolic, so the King recalled them both."

"Why no peace?"

"They were equally headstrong and imperious. The Comte always for the King, while the Bishop, well trained by the Jesuits though no Jesuit himself, held that the Church must rule the world, the Pope rule the Church, the Jesuits rule the Pope. There, my son, you have a key to the dissensions you find in Canada, and all else, even relations with the savages, comes afterwards. You see I speak freely, but we are fellow voyagers, so let our hearts be opened. Life here is sometimes too short for dissimulation. Do you smell smoke, or what is it? my faculties are not what they were."

Paul sniffed and stared ahead; the low point was now but a mile away and above its ragged tree-tops he could discern a faint vaporous wreath moving slowly northward.

"There is smoke, father, but...."

"Yes, and now something strange in that smell! I cannot tell, but...." he broke off, suddenly his blade began to swing with astonishing speed, "hasten, my son, paddle with all your strength."

Paul gripped the springy thwart between curving thighs and bent to his work, the canoe leaped forward with a hiss along its yellow sides, the ragged pine-tops drew nearer, they came abreast, the point lay abeam. He could hear nothing but a rush of water and Morel's hard quick breathing. Thus for a few moments, when on the right opened a shallow bay curved like a bent bow, fringed with a strip of white sand. Beyond lay a small clearing from the edge of which and close to the shore slow curling wreaths rose lazily from two charred and shapeless mounds. No life, no movement was here, and over this manmade gash in the forest hung a silence of death. With paddles arrested in mid-air the canoe floated on.

"My son, my son," groaned the Curé, "what have we here?"

Paul, unable to speak, crouched motionless: now for the first time he saw the grim work of the Iroquois, terrible children of the wilderness; he had read of it, heard much of it during the winter, talked with those to whom it was nothing new, but this stark reality surpassed all; it was as though demons gliding from the dark aisles had here celebrated a hideous orgy and retired to the fastness that shrouded them, and the young man transfixed with horror saw between the two blackened mounds something horribly human bound to an upright post.

"Is your spirit strong?" said the priest in an unnatural tone.

"I am not afraid."

"Then go on, gently, do not injure the canoe."

They touched shore and gazed at each other for a moment while hot stinging tears trickled down Morel's brown face, his lips trembled, and blindly he fingered his gold cross. Grasshoppers lifted a shrill cry amongst blistered stumps, a flight of crows sailed overhead, a noisy flock of wild pigeons, light blue and steel grey, settled on a pine tree nearby, but save for these wild things there was no life or motion where this hard-won clearing soaked in the hot breath of summer while the charred image of what had once been a man drooped its human head to survey his lost domain with remote and silent contemplation.

Paul's step sank in the beach: he went on as in a dream and stood in the midst of a piteous slaughter-house. Smoke curled lazily from the ruins of two cabins, stark corpses lay at his feet gazing to the sky, the adults' skulls with great crimson patches where the scalp had been lifted, a rag doll was still in the tiny grasp of a child of three years for the Iroquois spared none, a cradle new from France lay on its side, empty. All the bodies had been mutilated in a wild frenzy, and at sight of one woman disembowelled when about to become a mother, Paul covered his face. Eleven of all ages lay there, a foul odour trailing with the light wind made him sick. Father Morel was down on his knees beside the stake, commending the spirits of these stricken ones to God. Presently he got up, his face grey, and put a shaking hand on the young man's shoulder.

"This is the doing of the Mohawks, a tribe of the Iroquois federation: they came last night surprising these poor souls in their sleep; they are not long gone and at this moment are not far away. They have no canoes, so travelled under cover near the shore, and no doubt have observed us also. Now, my friend, if your heart is still strong there is work to do before other wild beasts arrive at sunset."

It was a slow, heartbreaking, speechless duty. Paul found a shovel standing upright amongst the young corn in the stumpy field, so they dug a trench in sand near the waterside and gently put these pioneers to rest, but when it came to the last horrific remnant of mortality at the stake, his spirit nearly failed. Then the priest gave him the small axe they always carried in the canoe and bade him hew a cross while he himself again searched the smoking ruins.

Paul glanced at the forest: between tall straight brown trunks rising like columns of a cathedral he could see narrow avenues and aisles into which light filtered from above, but for the most part it was dark and gloomy, carpeted with ground hemlock and a profusion of ferns. No sound came from it, and he approached a young sapling that offered the timber he needed. The odour of fire and burned flesh did not reach him here, the air came fresh and sweet, and he could see the father's dark-robed figure stooping in his desolate round. Now too he seemed to behold the ascetic face and maimed hand of Father Poncet as he stood in the apartment of Madame de Maintenon. In that setting the aged missionary had somehow seemed a little unreal, the hollow voice announcing that Canada was a land for those without fear had struck one as a little over dramatic. The Iroquois might be savages but were far too remote to be vivid. All that was in his mind, and he had raised the axe when a breath of wind kissed his face, and an arrow struck quivering into the sapling with its feathered shaft brushing his cheek.

He started and wheeled; there was nothing visible, but from the forest rose at a little distance in shrill clamour the first war-cry he had ever heard, pulsing with the lust for blood. The priest heard it, too, straightened his bent form, and stood for an instant petrified.

"To the canoe," he shouted, "quick! quick!"

Paul leaped forward still clutching the axe; the cries were now louder, more numerous, so it was clear that the Mohawks lying in ambush had seen Morel's canoe on its mission of mercy. Paul, racing over rough ground, neared the priest, and just in that moment a second arrow sank deep into Morel's throat. He gurgled and fell, hands clutching; Paul, panting, leaned over him.

"Run, my son," breathed the missionary, "this is the end for me. Save yourself!"

The young man's heart burst with rage, he shook his head: closing on him raced the first naked warrior, leading scout of the Mohawk riders, face painted with startling stripes, the bronze body tense, eyes alight with murder. Thus, thought Paul, might appear a fiend from hell. Then a wild fury surged through him, in a flash his arm swung up and the whistling axe descended on the raven crown.

The savage screamed once, toppled and died: in that instant the forest re-echoed with the chilling sound of Mohawk yells, and from its obscurity swept the rest of the war party insensate for revenge. But with death close at hand Paul did not hesitate. He twitched the barb from Morel's throat, picked him up in his great arms and dashed for the canoe. There were no seconds to spare, and the air sang with arrows, yet he felt no fear for something whispered that his time had not yet come.

Dropping the unconscious man between the thwarts, he pushed out and swung his paddle. A few yards from shore an arrow struck him, sinking between his shoulders, but he paddled on desperately praying that his strength might be maintained. The canoe leaped. More arrows whistled, but soon they fell short. Presently the wild cries dwindled, and, turning, he saw a row of naked men ranged like pigmies on the smooth beach.

Father Morel had not stirred, but his life-blood gushing out made narrow pools between the thin ribs of the canoe. Now he opened his eyes and they rested on Paul charged with the ineffable wisdom of one about to die. His lips moved but no sound came, while with failing powers he made the sign of the Cross. Then, with something like a smile, his eyes closed.

Paul, speechless, paddled on: the barb in his back was torture: he could not twist his body to tear it out, a warm stream trickled down his spine, a numbness crept into his arms. The gulf was now crisped with a light south wind before which the canoe even when he ceased to paddle drifted lightly further into the open. Presently he became dizzy, so instead of kneeling he sat in the bottom of the canoe. His strength began to run out, and he knew that, after all, the end could not be far off.

He had curiously few regrets, there being, it seemed, little to live for, since he had not come to New France to find God but escape from himself. That he now assuredly achieved, but he would have liked to see Jacqueline once more because she was still the only created thing he loved, and explain to Jules why he had refused to fight, and thank Abbé Callot for all those years of wise and friendly guidance. But none of them would ever know.

The dizziness increased, and making an absurd resolve not to upset the canoe if he could help it, he leaned forward bracing himself very carefully against either gun-whale, and laid down on his face beside the dead priest. So gently he did this that the canoe only rocked a little, then steadied and floated on.

$$-\text{V}-$$

His Majesty's forty gun frigate *La Perouse* had a bold horn-shaped beak, a deep fat belly below her narrowing waist, a high almost castellated poop that projected well beyond her creaking rudder. Fore and aft, she was heavily armed, and when she rolled the muzzles of her bullnosed midship battery nearly dipped in green seawater. Fast before the wind, she slid to leeward when she tacked.

In addition to her crew she carried some forty soldiers, these being the survivors of a full hundred that boarded her at Brest. Scurvy had taken its toll, and she marked her passage with milestones of shotted corpses. With her came a company of giggling, marriageable girls, all guaranteed virgin, under the care of two grey-cloaked nuns who were hard put to save their charges from the strategies of a group of fresh, young cadets posted to Cadillac's regiment of Carignan; Quebec merchants returning to Canada after a winter in France; a knot of grave-featured, earnest-eyed Jesuits who spent the voyage in prayer and study, seemingly unconscious of its tribulations; a pair of Recollet missionaries bound for Mackinac; masons from Brittany to work on the defences of Quebec; a sprinkling of adventurers of good family, who little knew what lay before them.

In all were some three hundred souls, chief attention being given to the women, who had their own section, with Jacqueline and Marie occupying a tiny cabin under the high poop, while Jules with other male passengers were compressed between decks that groaned complaint with every incontinent wind that blew.

In the frigate's strong box lay bags of gold louis for the pay of the king's troops: stacked tight were chests of gowns, laces and fripperies from Paris and Lyons for the belles of New France, ingots of copper and scrap iron for Canadian forges, glass beads, small hand mirrors, brass bangles and rings, dyed ostrich feathers, tomahawks, copper kettles, fish hooks--these being trade goods for savage tribes,--woven stroud for blankets, carpenter tools, guns, swords, powder, flints and shot.

This, with her human freight, set *La Perouse* deep in the water; from Brest it took her three long weeks to sight land, and at first glimpse of that faint blue line--the hills behind Chebucto--the hearts of her company rose with relief. It had been a turbulent passage. For a full week they were tossed by a westerly gale from one great bearded swell to another, while the groaning frigate used her human burden like shuttlecocks. Free of the storm, they encountered a noble procession of bergs marching majestically from Baffin Strait, and were becalmed in the midst of this ghostly Armada, rolling a stone-throw from lofty walls of moonlit ice, till Captain Leduc, sweating with fear, got the boats out and towed his ship free of danger.

But most of his passengers took the voyage well, some with indifference, and all but a few with a vague wonder of what the future might hold in store.

Jules for his part refused to regard his forced emigration with any composure: and as the weeks passed he became the more critical. As to the troops on board--they were Louis' grudging concession to Denonville's urgent petition of the previous year--he had little regard, they were but second-rate infantry, ill-trained, scant of discipline, and compared to Musketeers hardly worth attention. He made no effort to conceal his views, and in consequence soon became unpopular.

Jules, in short, was disgruntled: he thought this expedition was mad, its objective uncertain, its reward negligible. He missed his comforts and military servant, and saw little prospect of ever finding in Canada--if the officers there were like the ones on *La Perouse*--that companionship on which his naturally gay spirit so much depended for happiness. As the voyage lengthened he grew more and more out of sorts, and even sight of the Newfoundland coast failed to rouse his spirits.

Also during the voyage he had had time to think, and decided that he was abused by fortune, not of his own fault. That lay with Louis and Jacqueline! Day after day while *La Perouse's* masts traced crazy patterns against the sky, he brooded over this, convincing himself that this business was mostly the doing of his wife. On account of her he had ceased to be a Musketeer, the one thing of which he was inordinately proud. That was gone, little was left, he loathed the prospect of Canada with all it involved, and for his own temporary madness he found every excuse.

But on Jacqueline the affair had a different effect, and her first sensation was that of escape. Her nature was candid, it had congenital purity, and she had been thoroughly frightened. Also since she loved her husband with all her heart, she now resented the change in him. In spite of former protestations, he had not, it seemed, forgiven her: instead of the gallantry she prized he was curt and short-tempered, but not having quite forgiven herself, she tried to put that aside.

There was, too, something that seemed to be widening the rift between them. A month in *La Perouse* had done something to her, and within these booming timber walls her spirit was expanding. When, hesitantly, she spoke of it to Jules, he shrugged, saying that he envied her strong stomach, so it was no use trying to tell what she did feel, the sensation of having been caught up and absorbed in something far greater than themselves that was carrying them on a hitherto unknown tide towards some destiny vastly different from anything they could have imagined, and this destiny had a proportion and significance that made discomfort, uncertainty, and even danger, of secondary moment. It was far bigger than anything at the Court of Versailles; it had a purpose and--and----

She never got any further than that because Jules would not follow or even try to understand, but the conviction grew in her mind, and she never questioned her own courage or ability to meet whatever might lie ahead.

She hungered to know more of what awaited her, but there was no woman on board who had ever seen Canada before, so she spent hours on the poop-deck with Captain Leduc, wrapped in a great sea cloak, her flaxen hair loose, blue eyes intelligently bright. Leduc, who had never been beyond Quebec, knew more of nature and the face of the sea than anything else, and so far as concerned Canada he felt that King Louis had made a losing venture.

"Madame, I judge by what I carry in my ship from France, and what I take back in return. This is my sixth voyage to the west, with soldiers who have no say in what they do, or where, and others who cross the sea because there is no room for them at home. Look, madame." He pointed to the timbered shores a mile to the south. "On this deck you are safe, but there not at all. From those woods wild eyes are watching us now, and dark fingers itch for their bows. Why the King should desire this country I do not know. He will never hold it, and were he to empty half France into Canada they would be swallowed up. Always I thank God when my ship turns about, and I see the Château St. Louis over her stern."

"You are not very comforting," objected Jacqueline, "to one whose husband is a soldier and obeys orders."

"Perhaps not, yet to be a soldier in France is one thing, and another here, where the enemy that never sleeps lurks behind every tree. But you will doubtless live in Quebec?"

"I won't know till my husband has orders from the Governor."

"Then let us hope it is Quebec. Presently, if this wind does not die, we will sight St. Denis."

"What is that?"

158

"A settlement of two houses built a year ago, the most easterly in the Gulf. Brave people, madame! For a month in early winter while the ice forms, and another in spring while it disperses, they are marooned save for the forest trails, and truly I think they deserve more than they get out of life, especially the women."

"I was thinking of the women," said she.

"Yes, and while the story of men in this country will be written, there is little said of their women. No neighbours, madame, to visit and talk with, no meeting at the stream with the week's washing, no friendly voices in the cool of evening as in my home in Picardy. They bear children in loneliness, and if there be sickness or accident--well--doubtless I talk too much, so forgive me. You are young, you have no children, and in your eyes I see courage."

"Speak on, Captain."

"Well, it's not my affair, but if possible I would do you a service. It concerns your husband. Perhaps it is not for a merchant captain to advise an officer of the King, but you might put in a word. Here in Canada one does not speak to a soldier as in France: the discipline is of another kind, the understanding much greater. In forest warfare he who leads is the wisest and most skilled, so the fate of an expedition may turn on the judgment of men of low rank and perhaps mixed blood. An officer will be ready to sleep under the same blanket with a bushranger, and eat with his fingers from the same pot, for there must be brotherhood or else great danger."

Saying this Leduc looked a trifle apologetic, then waved a hand towards shore. "Alors, madame, I have letters for Jacques Lafleur at St. Denis where we should be within the hour. Doubtless in this weather he will row out to get them, and there you will see your first Canadian settler."

He went off to superintend the cleaning of the ship, opening of hatches, with other duties prior to arrival at Quebec, and left Jacqueline thinking hard. She had not misread the man's kind intentions, she felt grateful, she was determined to leave nothing undone to build success out of banishment, and loyally put aside the sense of slight that had weighed on her for weeks past. She remembered that Jules had urged her to live with her parents, at any rate for the first year, and they had favoured this, but she would not hear of it. She was in love, she was not afraid, she would take the bitter with the sweet.

Now she signalled to Jules who was on the main deck. He came, squatted on a coil of rope, and looked uncomfortable.

"The Captain expects to sight Quebec tonight. Jules, did you ever imagine how long the voyage would be?"

"I could imagine anything on a ship like this."

"But the ship is not so bad."

"I am glad you are so easily pleased; I think it is purgatory, and the food--pah! In another month we would all be dead of scurvy."

"I'm sorry," she said, "I've tried to think it a sort of holiday. The first week was bad, but the rest--well--I never felt so strong before."

"Then you should be content, though your

complexion--it has ceased to exist."

"I do not miss it," she laughed, "nor from what I learn am I likely to find it again." She paused with a sudden straight, earnest look, "Jules, why have you not really talked to me for so long?"

"Packed like currants in a loaf, the conditions are not favourable," said he, lightly, "but it seems to agree with you."

"You are not happy?"

"Do not expect me to be enthusiastic over this affair. And you?"

"I try to make the best of it," said she, gently, "and it were easier if I thought you blamed me less."

"It could not be helped, I suppose," the tone was grudging, he sensed that he played but a poor part, that he was indifferent and unfair, but the further he moved from the country he loved, the more unreasonable he grew.

"Is there nothing I can do--now, Jules?"

"It is too late--now. Two months ago I thought it better that you stay at Castellon at any rate for the first year."

"You still would have preferred that?" she asked, dully.

"I doubt whether you can withstand the life awaiting us here, and for me it certainly will not be easy, but we will only remain in Canada until my friends think it safe to return. Should Louis die, we would go back at once."

He spoke with no thought of anything save his own desires, and a cloud of sadness came over her. Here was her husband, her master, with him it lay to make their future, and so short a time past how proud she had been of him. Now a cold wind of reality had blown, stripped away all his gay infectious assurance, left but a shadow of the man she had taken him to be.

"But if you and I begin like that we are defeated at once. O, Jules, I have thought so much about it, and since others can be happy here why not us. I have talked with Marie, whose ears are full of queer stories about Canada, and she is only amused."

"Amused!"

"Yes, she laughs, and says all will be well, and never will she cross the ocean again. And you, Jules, if you are going to hate this country before you have seen it, if you continue to feel like that, then it is a pity that I ever left Castellon for Paris."

"Meaning it is a pity that you married me," he flashed.

"What is there in marriage without companionship?"

"Then you had preferred a certain Breton farmer who turned his back on my sword!" said Jules, sharply. "Do not hesitate to tell me."

"He might perhaps have thought less of himself."

At this he gave an exclamation, and turned away leaving her miserable. She had not meant to say it; this was their first real break, it wounded her deeply, but still she loved him so that love rose in her breast, obliterating all else, and she caught at his arm:

"Jules--no--no--I did not mean that--come back--there is so much I...."

She was interrupted by a cry from above where a man clung high in the rigging on the look out for shoals. He was shading his eyes from the sun. At the sound Captain Leduc mounted the poop deck, and began to search the western waters with a long telescope. He turned to Jacqueline, smiling.

"Madame, you can just see it, a canoe of birch bark made by the savages: the tide has carried it off empty, but no doubt the Iroquois are in these woods. Take the glass. This is your first canoe, but not the last. They are not so bad to travel in."

She saw it quite clearly, floating like a yellow leaf a half-mile distant. The ship drew on very slowly, moving before the last faint breath of southerly wind under which the river lay like a vast delicately wrinkled mirror. At a word from Leduc, *La Perouse's* course was slightly altered and imperceptibly they came nearer. A crowd had gathered amidships, hanging over the rail, staring at this first signal of human life since they left Chebucto in Nova Scotia three hundred leagues away. Leduc recaptured the telescope and examined the beach on his port bow. Thereabouts, he reckoned, was the clearing of St. Denis, and there certainly should be two log houses, but presently he made out the two blackened heaps, and caught that faint foul odour carried by an off-shore breeze. He glanced at Jacqueline, and was about to speak, but only tightened his lips and pushed through the ship's company toward her bows.

Now the sailor aloft gave another cry, again pointing, while *La Perouse* crawled forward broadside to the land, and the canoe worked out a little further into the river, so it became a sort of drifting match between ship and canoe till presently the two almost touched, and Jacqueline, breast thrust against the rail, looked down at a sight that lived vividly all her days.

The interior of the canoe seemed painted with blood. Two men were there, one a priest in a torn and rusty cassock. Both lay still, the priest on his back, the other face-down beside him. This man was much the taller, with big arms and legs and a broad back. Vertically from his body projected the feathered shaft of an arrow with the barb buried out of sight in a crimson patch between his shoulders. He lay almost flat, so the shaft stood up in the middle of the canoe like a tiny mast of which the stump was anchored in human flesh. The priest was obviously dead, his features grey, drawn tight over a bony framework, sharpened by the drainage of blood, and one could see a wide gash in his throat. His left hand touched the head of the other man as though in parting benediction. They rested very quietly, very close together, bodies cemented in a sanguinary bond, and the eggshell curve of canoe bark held them suspended over an abyss of cold green waters.

A great hush had fallen over *La Perouse*: one heard the creak of cordage as she rolled slightly, and the slow intermittent thump of her slanting rudder post, but this was all for a moment till along her populated rail stirred a low murmur of sympathy and horror. From stem to stern the very ship seemed to shudder as she floated beside this grim salute from New France to the new pilgrims from the old, while soldiers, sailors and settlers stared down at the inert bodies, at each other, then, slowly towards the uncommunicative shores whence these silent messengers had come.

"Jules!" whispered his wife, "these poor, poor souls! What has happened?"

He pressed her arm, but did not speak. *La Perouse* had lost way, the breeze was dead, the canoe seemed glued to her side. Leduc had a boat lowered in a hurry. It dropped with a wide splash, and two sailors leaned from it over the canoe from which they could not lift the upper man without danger of upsetting it. He was too big and heavy, nor could they turn him over on account of the arrow sunk in his back, so one of them broke off the shaft with a snap, and at this a gasp ran along the crowded rail. Then, at a word from Leduc, a boom swung out with a rope running through a block. A turn was taken round the big body, and the first man came up, dangling limply, to be swung gently inboard where ready hands eased him to the deck, and in those slack unstrung limbs, in the loose frame and short brown beard, was something that to Jacqueline suggested the descent from the Cross.

He lay motionless on his side, and now for the first time she saw his face.

"Jules!" she cried, "Jules! it is Paul!"

Jules gazed and nodded. Yes, certainly this was Paul, but how came he here? The drained face looked yellowish under its sunburn, the beard made him seem older, the big broad hands, now so slack, were scarred and blistered with work, but the rest was the same, and there could be no doubt. How small the world was!

Morel's body came up, and was laid beside the other, while all wondered who these men might be, till

165

the ship's surgeon, stooping over Paul, said that this one still lived, while his companion had been dead for an hour, and there was a chance of saving the big man if one could get at the arrow-head in his back and it had not gone too deep. So they covered the priest with a sailcloth, and carried Paul into the Captain's saloon. Now the blood-plastered canoe was also on deck with Morel's holy vessels wrapped in an altar cloth stuffed into its curving bows. A quarter hour later the surgeon came out carrying in his palm an Iroquois barb.

"It was very near the lung, but he is strong and will live." Then to Jacqueline he said: "It is true that you know this ma? did you not call his name?"

"Yes: he is Paul de Lorimier who once lived in Castellon in Brittany, but I did not know he was in Canada."

"And the other--the priest?"

But none on board had ever seen Father Morel before.

Then *La Perouse*, picking up a faint puff from the east, sailed on with her bloody freight past the holocaust of St. Denis towards the high battlements of Quebec.

In Quebec

— I —

Bishop St. Vallier in a black silk gown and wide-brimmed shovel hat stood on the parapet outside the cathedral of Notre Dame with the Marquis de Denonville. The evening was fair, the sun lowering in the upper river reaches. Below them in the Bay of Beauport and the roadstead over towards Point Levis small boats were plying, and rafts of timber lay moored like small yellow islands. On the opposite shore a cluster of wigwams ranged behind lighted fires, while smoke rose from huddled roofs of the Lower Town, and across the western horizon rested a wide band of gold. The scene was peaceful, inspiring, but while the Bishop's expression had its habitual calm, the Governor seemed ill at ease.

Now at any hour should arrive the first ship of the year from France--already she was a week overdue--and what she would bring from Seignelay, Minister of the Colonies, was of vital import to Denonville. By the last eastbound vessel of the previous autumn he had submitted a long, almost abject report, begging for further aid against the Iroquois, also urging that the savage captives, sent to the galleys of Louis on the Mediterranean, be returned forthwith. They were badly needed as a peace-offering to prevent further attacks. To such a humiliation he had felt forced to stoop by the demand of Dongan, the English Governor in Albany.

More and more did the Governor feel harassed and at bay. For two years the trade in beaver skins had dwindled, till today it was only a trickle. The Iroquois, intimidating the northern and western tribes, diverted the flow of fur to their allies in New England, and along the St. Lawrence the sprinkled population of French was hard put to it: they lived in dread, their fields lay uncultivated, while small parties of human wildcats made lightning forays, vanishing as swiftly and mysteriously as they came. Life in Canada outside the high stockades of Ville Marie was like living within a ring of wasps' nests. And what Denonville longed for by this first ship was more troops--troops he must have-- though even with these he contemplated the forced abandonment of western outposts like Forts Frontenac and Niagara.

He had never really understood the wild children of the forest, the scourge of New France: his attempts to patch up peace had failed: in one dramatic but futile effort he had assembled all his forces and led an expedition to stamp out the Senecas, burned their bark towns, destroyed their young corn, but the red men only scattered like pollen before a breeze, rebuilt their villages so soon as his back was turned and summoned again their councils of war. There had been a great gathering on Lake Ontario attended by chiefs of the Mohawks, Oneidas and Cayugas wearing horns on their heads, with painted faces and bodies, with fringes of scalps, and trailing tails of fur from their naked rumps, when belts of wampum were exchanged, the peace pipe passed from French to savage lips; and for a while things promised well. Then breaches of faith on both sides, and at Fort Frontenac the Christian converts, to whom Christianity was a temporary asset, tied Iroquois captives to stakes, charring their fingertips in hot bowls of glowing pipes.

168

So it went from worse to worse, till now there ensued a calm that was ominous, and Denonville waited and wondered where the next blow would fall. To fight these wildcats was like fighting the wind.

Beside him Bishop St. Vallier also searched the wide waters of the St. Lawrence, and between the two there was an understanding silence for these men were bound by strong ties of religious faith, and Denonville's real weakness was that he viewed affairs too much through clerical eyes. The Iroquois, argued St. Vallier, were the only enemies of the Cross in this new country, the servants of that Cross looked to the Governor for support, and every baptised savage, captive or free, increased the promised reward of the faithful. Such was the doctrine of Sulpitians, Recollets and Jesuits alike, men whose position in Canada did not turn on the whim of Louis XIV, men whose authority was secure whatever happened, and under their influence Denonville spent on his knees many an hour that had been better employed elsewhere. He was too devout for the harsh duties of his office.

Suddenly he gave an exclamation, and pointed: "There I think I see a three-master--she is hardly moving."

The Bishop stared hard, he nodded: simultaneously a cannon spoke from the stockade, and sent the gulls wheeling wildly. A moment later a puff of smoke was visible abreast of the Île d'Orléans, and presently came a soft distant thud, thrice repeated.

"At last, Monseigneur," smiled Denonville. "It has been a long wait, and I hope she is but the first of a squadron. A vessel of that size will not carry many troops."

Already from Upper and Lower Town people were swarming to the ramparts to view the most welcome sight in all the year, and what it meant could only be felt by those who had passed long winter months smothered in snow while northern gales harried the rocky nub of Quebec, heaping white drifts against windows and doors. That was a hard season, with the river solid like iron, the whole land blanketed in a sleep like death as far as the eye could see. In such months the savages were seldom troublesome, but life was nevertheless a thankless effort, and not a few would readily have changed places with the black bears and drowsed in darkness till south winds came again. But all this was forgotten in the relief of this moment.

La Perouse swam lazily, with hardly a ripple at her bows, sails were flapping, and carried by the last lift of tide she dropped anchor off Point Levis as the sun set. A swarm of canoes and small boats immediately encircled her when disembarkation began without delay. Denonville watched for a few minutes, till, stirred by some uncomfortable premonition he could not explain, he returned to the Château, and waited impatiently for news and dispatches. They were brought in by Champigny, the intendant.

The Governor nodded, glanced at the big wax seal of Seignelay, ripped one open. Suddenly his eyes widened; he made an odd sound of incredulity and dismay.

"The King," he read, "having come to the opinion that the burden of administration of New France was proving too heavy for the present incumbent informed His Excellency the Marquis de Denonville that the Comte Frontenac had been appointed Governor and Lieutenant General in his place. On his later arrival the Marquis would resign command to him, and embark for

France."

The parchment crackled between his fingers: hardly could he credit what he saw. True there had been warnings during the past year: true it was that La Barre, his predecessor, had been summarily recalled, but Lefebvre de la Barre had written himself down a boaster from the start, tried to ride two horses at once and turned out to be a speculator who lined his own pockets by poaching the King's monopoly; also he was flouted by the Iroquois, and made himself a laughing-stock in distant camps, so no parallel lay there, and Denonville racked his brain in vain.

Reviewing the situation with a sort of dull resentful hopelessness, it now seemed probable that Dongan, at Albany, was at the bottom of this, and since James of England, a sound Catholic, held close to Louis of France, it was doubtless at Dongan's insistence that he was being punished. But only a few months ago Dongan also had lost his post, so it must be that the two kings were paying each other the compliment of a mutual change in the governing of the new world.

He read Seignelay's document again: it was adroitly phrased, and an easier post was promised at home, but the real blow came with the re-appointment of Frontenac, that veteran of seventy years. He had always been envious of Frontenac's reputation, so there lay the sting. Seven years ago Frontenac had split with the Church, at the instance of the Church he had lost his post: Denonville clung to the Church, but that had not saved him; so it was clear that ecclesiastical influence in Canada was on the wane, further division of authority at an end, and the King's men would henceforth hold the reins.

That brought in St. Vallier, and he felt envious of

171

the bishop whose position did not depend on any king, but served one unchanging Master with the single ambition of saving savage souls, which was easy, if a sprinkle of water on the face of a tortured Iroquois meant salvation. Conscience gave a twinge that he, a son of the Church, should have a doubt on this score, but at the same time he began to wonder whether he himself had not been weak, too prone to follow the crook of a priestly finger.

He was still in this mood when St. Vallier was announced, and came in looking disturbed.

"Your Excellency," he said, "I have grave news."

"And I also, Monseigneur, read this. The King has no further need of my services."

St. Vallier frowned, though in one way he was hardly surprised. Five years ago now he and the Marquis had reached Quebec in the same ship of a squadron that carried five hundred soldiers of whom one-third never saw Canada, scurvy and fever claiming them on the way. This was an inauspicious start; since then things had not gone well for either Church or State, and the piety of the Governor did not compensate for his lack of force.

"It were more fair to those who carry the burden did de Seignelay come to Canada to see things for himself," said the prelate, soberly, "I am sorry for this. Always you have worked in accord with the Jesuits and myself, so doubtless some intrigue at Court has brought it about; but," he added, soothingly, "you will return knowing you have done your best. Who comes next to Canada?"

"Comte Frontenac!"

"Frontenac!"

"At seventy years of age!" creaked the Marquis, resentfully.

The bishop compressed his lips. He knew all about that bellicose Count, overbearing, imperious, short-tempered, who had quarrelled with Jesuits, Sulpitians and Duchesneau, the King's intendant, alike. Frontenac had small regard for any authority save his own, and his return to Canada would light old fires of dissensions that had sunk to ashes under the mild tractability of Denonville. At the same time he was the one man to put the Iroquois in their place.

"Well," he said, "one must hope for the best. Has your Excellency read any other dispatches?"

"I have seen enough for the moment."

"Then you do not know that the Protestant William of the Netherlands is on the throne of England, and King James the fugitive guest of Louis at St. Germain?"

"What?"

"It happened last winter."

"You tell me that England has turned Protestant?"

"Not turned, for she always was, and James' Italian wife proved no welcome visitor."

"So in this country we are faced with a war of religion!"

"I fear it is so, and wondered why of late the savages have been so inactive: it seems some bloody business is in preparation, for already small scouting parties are afoot. I have just learned that St. Denis is destroyed, with all killed. Captain Leduc of *La Perouse* has picked up a canoe with Father Morel in it, dead, and another man, one Paul de Lorimier, a farmer from Lachine, with little life left in him. He lies at the Hôtel Dieu."

"You know nothing more?"

"He is not strong enough to talk much."

A wave of depression settled over the Governor. The English were behind this, as always. They supplied the savages with guns and ammunition, were lavish with their rum, made no attempt to proselytise, stuck to business with stolid determination and left the fighting to the Iroquois. They did not weaken themselves by establishing far posts like Frontenac and Niagara, but were steadily pushing up the Hudson, up the Mohawk Valley, through the Oneida country, and where they settled there they took permanent root. And why, pondered Denonville, did the Iroquois hate the French so much more than they did the English?

In such an unprofitable mood, and once again alone, he opened a dispatch from Louvois. Louvois had sent but a few troops, all that could be spared, for the alliance with England was at an end, and war raged in the Low Countries. With them Captain Jules Vicotte, late of the Musketeers, and now posted for duty for Canada. For various reasons it was not desired that he return to France for several years, but no fault had been found with his military service. This, to Denonville, smelled of intrigue, but for the moment was unimportant, and he would attend to Captain Vicotte later.

174

There was more from Seignelay, written after a certain conference in the apartment of de Maintenon. The King, he said, could not understand why Canada needed corn from France, and considered it absurd that settlers on virgin soil should not feed themselves. Further, it was reported that speculators at Ville Marie had acquired whatever beaver fur reached that post by way of the Ottawa.

The Governor had stated that the shortage was due to Iroquois depredations, but it seemed that the trouble lay nearer home, and Denonville in what time was left to him might well use his authority there. Also what had got furthest under Louis' skin was the request for the return of the Iroquois galley slaves. Never had the King felt more affronted.

The Marquis was frowning over this when Champigny returned and from his expression it was obvious that he had the chief news from St. Vallier.

"Well, I see you know."

"Yes, your Excellency."

"I go, but it seems you remain."

"I don't understand it, sir," said Champigny, seriously, "and certainly I cannot work with Comte Frontenac as I have with you."

"From the tone of de Seignelay's letter, you are better off here than you would be in France."

"But why?"

"It is over the affair at Fort Kente. Champigny, we both went astray in that business."

175

"Oh, that!" Champigny felt uncomfortable, though apparently still secure in his post. Two years previously he arrived in Canada, civil representative of the King. It was a delicate duty. While he had no military authority, to him was deputed the fostering of trade, the preservation of the royal monopoly of fur, the care of settlers, the administration of civil law, and the holding so far as possible some balance between the Governor and the Church, but since he himself was subservient to the Jesuits, and no less devoutly religious than the Governor, the two only made a pliable team working in double harness, responsive to every twitch of the clerical reins. They were indeed little more than the instruments by which Sulpitians, Recollets and Jesuits alike went about the conversion of heathen souls.

Nor had the intendant any more than the Governor courage to grasp and crush the harsh Iroquois nettle. Approaching it gingerly, they were stung, and resentfully resorted to tricks. At Fort Kente, a Sulpitian mission on Lake Ontario, Champigny, feigning goodwill, invited a hundred Iroquois to a feast, then surrounded, made them prisoners, and at Denonville's suggestion sent his captives to France to serve on the galley benches of Louis. But amongst them were the brother and son of Big Mouth, chief of the Iroquois confederacy and for this faithless act there could be no forgiveness. As the affair stood, it was a legacy for Frontenac, under whom, as both men realised, there would be no such tactics.

"The King," said Denonville ruefully, "declines to return the slaves. You know what that means."

"What does the Bishop make of it?"

"Only a coming clash between the Church and

the Count."

"I think he is right. When does the Count arrive?"

"This does not say. Well, Champigny, I do not envy you what lies ahead, and for myself will be glad to leave a cursed wilderness where one's best efforts go unrequited."

— II —

Jacqueline, in her room at the tavern of Boisdon, looked up from a long letter to Clothilde, sharpened her quill pen, took a whimsical glance round the log walls, and bent to her work.

*   *   *   *   *

....so now you know all I can tell you of what happened to Paul, and how we found him, but I will be able to give you more by the next ship. I have asked that at present he be not told that we are in Quebec. *La Perouse* sails again very soon, so there is but little more opportunity at present.

We have been four days in Quebec, and Jules paid his respects to the Governor the morning after we arrived, but was received only coolly, the Marquis being in an unfortunate mood on account of his unexpected recall to France. The clergy are ill at ease in this matter, but the military set and people at large much pleased, believing that the security of the country will now be far better established. The Governor has not yet decided about Jules, but indicates we will probably go to Ville Marie, which I am told is a rough outpost about sixty leagues further west. My husband therefore is in anything but amiable temper, as he hoped to be

177

stationed here which is the only desirable also the safest place in Canada. Yet from my window one might for a moment think oneself in France. There is a square, and round it the headquarters of the Jesuits, the big church, the Château St. Louis, home of the Governor, such a strange sort of Château, and the Hôtel Dieu where Paul is now. These are all of grey stone and very substantial.

That much is like France, but only that much, and of course the people change the picture. There are the coureurs des bois, the bushrangers, strange-looking men with some French blood, in fur caps even in summer, and long black hair anointed with grease, and leather shirts, their eyes are quick and furtive like animals, and they walk with a smooth springy tread, also Indians and priests and nuns, those being the Ursulines who care for the sick in the Hôtel Dieu, and merchants, and officers in uniform, and their ladies often dressed as in Paris, amongst whom there is vast interest in the new modes that came out with us on *La Perouse*. No detail of toilette escapes attention, and there is much competition in the wearing of new and fashionable attire. It is surprising to see them walking in the Lower Town in high heels and silk frocks over the terrible roads, amongst the Indian women. Many of the savages and woodsmen carry guns, and knives in their belts, while some of the Indians wear a fringe which I am told is of human scalps, and very little else. Their bodies are active and finely formed, their eyes very black, their feet shod in soft shoes of tanned hide, their expression sullen. They sell their fur to buy brandy, and when drunk often go mad. All prisoners taken by us are baptised at once, and the Church loses no opportunity for this, especially when Iroquois captives are being tortured by the Hurons, a tribe living in this vicinity, friends to the French--but not as brave and warlike as their enemies.

Last night we were bid to an assembly in the Governor's house, about sixty ladies and their gentlemen. Bishop St. Vallier was there, head of the Sulpitian order in New France, but influenced of course by the Jesuits. The ladies were dressed just as in Paris, wearing many jewels, but their complexion has suffered from the rigour of winter winds, and exhibits a reddish frosty quality.

The evening was fine with many stars, and after being presented I walked with Paul on the promenade outside the Château, which overhangs a veritable precipice. Across the river one saw the lights of Point Levis where there is a settlement at the edge of the forest, and these with many more in the Lower Town of Quebec were reflected brightly in the water. The Governor's band from the regiment of Carignan was playing.

On the promenade strolled a multitude of people, with many smart, young Gascon cadets and lieutenants displaying their mouse-coloured leather uniforms, three cornered hats, flopping boots and silver spurs. Their colonel is a Chevalier de la Mothe Cadillac. He was presented to me, a tall man of about thirty years with a brown face and prodigious nose and eyes like a hawk. He is reputed the best swordsman in New France, and said to be in the very private service of the King--which seems strange for so young an officer--and I wondered if he knew about me. I have a feeling that he did, though he gave no evidence of it.

His conversation tends to satire rather than compliment. He has journeyed far into the interior, and told us much that to you would sound incredible. The freedom with which he talked surprised me not a little. When at one time we passed the intendant, Champigny, airing himself in company with the Governor, he laughed and said that the Marquis had thrown away in three years more than the Comte Frontenac had won from the Iroquois in ten.

He said, too, that many officers are over here to repair their fortunes but most of them seemed to get no further than Quebec.

Also he pointed out to us the le Moyne brothers, les Sieurs Bienville and Iberville, ashore from their frigates which lay anchored far below us. He admires them, and is perhaps a little jealous of their prowess for a few years ago they journeyed overland into the great Hudson's Bay in the country of northern savages, destroying the English trading forts, and gaining a splendid victory for France. It seems that Prince Rupert, brother to the King of England, was one of the proprietors of those forts.

I observed that Jules could not refrain from interest in our new friend, who disposed himself at our service in all things, but as so often happens when conversation turns on a subject with which Jules is unfamiliar he displayed an unfortunate aloofness. This is the more regrettable because we face an uncertain future in which the aid of such a man might be most opportune. I forgot to tell you that the Chevalier, having very black hair, is also called The Raven, or sometimes The Black Prince.

What I find here is all so diverse from anything one could have imagined that I can give you but a faulty picture. So much has happened to us in the last two months that it seems unreal, while at the same time I am assured of its reality. You too, my dear Clothilde, are, I confess, growing a little unsubstantial. In this strange new country I feel very small, much smaller than ever before. I think I shall make some discovery of myself as well as of others. There are new friends, a new position to be made. How this will come about I cannot anticipate, but somehow I do not fear the problem that lies before us, though we are so few persons in so great a wilderness. The Chevalier tells me that starting from Quebec in springtime westwards for the China Seas, one may travel till winter comes and yet not arrive at salt water.

Those I met were hungry for news from France, and I was kept busy. It seems that letters had arrived on the ship with me relating a much exaggerated story about me and the King and the diamond necklet, even going to the length of saying that our removal to Canada was due to jealousy and interposition of de Maintenon--which is of course absurd, so to some of these strangers my virtue must have been a matter of doubt judging by their mutual glances. That however did not affect their interest in me, especially with the gentlemen, but rather seemed to add to it, with the result that I held a small court of my own which I much enjoyed, and about which Jules expostulated later with not a little heat. He was divertingly jealous, and that was not unwelcome for several reasons.

Bishop St. Vallier must also have heard something, for when I was presented he gave me a cold look, and made no attempt to detain me. At these assemblies the formalities are in imitation of Versailles, so you can imagine in view of my late experience what a confusion of impressions I gathered. At any rate your Jacqueline seems to have made a successful debut in the social centre of New France.

Many of the persons I met expressed themselves without reserve about the attitude of the Jesuits in Canada, who follow every social affair with watchful eyes, and frown on the wearing of low-necked gowns that expose more than a fraction of bosom, considering these a device of the devil for snaring the souls of men. As my own gown was quite the newest and lowest there, I am doubtless already put down as a snarer. Also the Jesuits condemn the knots of ribbon, or fontages, much affected in their hair by the belles of the town. Is not that absurd? Even in private life they demand that one reads only books of religion selected by themselves. What would they say could they see the volumes of Rabelais on Jules' table beside me now. I am told too that they expect the Governor himself to attend no late suppers or sumptuous entertainment. They allow the dance, but an unmarried girl must do the gavotte only with one of her own sex, and in the presence of her mother. They forbid any private theatricals or playing of cards. Of course all this is what they demand, but though the Governor himself gives complete obedience, there is much going on that they never hear of, and one can be quite gay with the military set.

Just now and for some weeks to come everyone is reading copies of *Le Mercure* of last winter brought by our first ship. Can you picture that?

I am informed there is advantage in living here over Ville Marie, and this being the point of disembarkation from France, the young ladies get the first chance of picking husbands. In the warm weather they have a custom, the ones of highest rank, of dressing gaily and taking coffee at their windows at nine of the morning while they do needlework and converse with young men on the street, exchanging, I believe, many double entendres. On Sunday they wear their best with hair powdered, curled, bodkins and aigrettes. Many families have Indian slaves; these are prisoners acquired by purchase from the Government. I shall have one in Ville Marie.

182

Marie, whom you will remember in Castellon, seems not at all affected by where she now finds herself. She is vastly interested and comports herself as though in Castellon. She likes the appearance of the men in this country and says she would not be averse from matrimony, and since the men far outnumber the women she would have no difficulty in selecting a husband. Should this happen I would feel quite desperate.

It seems that the population here is in good heart in summer save when news comes of attacks by savages on the settlers at the seigneuries along the river--like St. Denis of which I have told you--but in winter when the last ship has sailed it is like being abandoned to fate. The harbour is frozen, and no occupation for the next six months save sleighing and skating when the breath is transformed to a white vapour as it leaves the lungs, and their extremities are attacked by the frost. The only way news can then arrive is by some trader from the English settlements to the south, and I think it will be even more lonely in Ville Marie.

We shall be transported there in a fleet of batteaux I think next week, and during the journey one sleeps still afloat, not on the land, on account of the Iroquois.

You may observe that in this letter I say but little about Jules. That is true, and there is little to tell you except that in moments of reflection I ask myself questions. A year ago I compared him favourably to Paul whom today I am allowed to visit, and how astonished he will be. You remember my first letter about Jules; so far away and long ago it seems that sometimes I doubt whether there be such a place as Castellon. But since Paul has made so strange a reappearance, I am not quite so sure about Jules. I still love him deeply, but would welcome in him something I see in other men that makes life possible and even happy here. Perhaps my fancy is misdirected, and the fault lies with me.

Now I must begin my letter to Mama, which will take not less than six weeks to reach her. The bells are ringing across the square, and again I might be in France except that just near my window is an Indian woman with her baby on her back, wrapped in moss and cloth, and fastened against a short board. I am not yet enceinte, which is fortunate.

When you receive this pray write to me fully, telling all you can think of. Put in everything of however little moment. What do you hear of de Montespan--is the King's docility under de Maintenon what it was--is the Bishop of Chartres still her director, is it possible she had anything to do with our coming here? You cannot imagine what every word of a letter will mean to

your ever devoted J. V.

— III —

In a lime-washed dormitory of the Hôtel Dieu, Paul watched the cowled noiseless figures of Ursuline nuns gliding over the bare floor between groups of wooden-framed cots. Outside sounded an hourly clang of bells with tongues so familiar that sometimes he too wondered if he were back in France; their tone was precisely that of the chimes of Castellon, the voices of the nuns had the accent of Normandy and Brittany, while coloured Crucifixion prints on the stone walls were duplicates of some he remembered in the library of Abbé Callot.

Hour after hour he lay, speaking hardly at all, his brain exploring a queer halfway house between past and present, with strength gradually flowing back into his great body, while laboriously he pieced together the fragments of what seemed to have been a bad dream. At first the thing was quite nebulous, almost a blank, then slowly became clearer up to the point when the arrow stuck into his shoulders and he paddled, it seemed for years, with a harsh shouting dwindling behind him. He faintly remembered gripping the thwarts and easing himself down towards Father Morel, but after that nothing till he woke up here and saw beside him a young nun with blue eyes who stood quite close with her finger on his wrist.

On the second day in the Hôtel Dieu, Bishop St. Vallier had come with his secretary, looking imposing and a shade severe as the secretary took down Paul's account of what had happened at St. Denis to be sent to Sulpitian headquarters in Paris. While this went on Paul studied the bishop, was not greatly impressed, and said nothing about the letter from Father Poncet he had brought to Canada the previous autumn. All he desired now was to get back to his farm as soon as possible. He mourned for Morel, wise, kindly, understanding and brave, the one man in Canada who might be counted a staunch friend. He would miss that priest.

The sisters were talkative; from them he learned that the arrow had grazed his lung, and the wound was healing, but his body had been nearly drained of blood, which accounted for his extreme weakness. Also from them he learned the manner of his rescue, but no more; they were too absorbed in the news concerning the Governor and Frontenac's coming for this certainly meant hot war with the Iroquois, and shrewdly anticipated a clash between Church and State when the old Count reoccupied the Château St. Louis. Paul would listen, and finger two letters that had arrived from Castellon by *La Perouse*, but somehow they did not interest him. Castellon seemed too far away, not quite real.

It was in one of these interminable silences that Soeur Roselle, youngest and gayest of the nuns--who reminded him uncomfortably of Jacqueline--stopped beside his cot, gave him a glance that she tried to make professional, then laughed.

"Bien, monsieur, you progress well, you will not be here much longer."

"That is good, but I shall leave in your debt."

"There is no debt: we are only thankful that you were found in time: just another hour or so, and...." she made a gesture, "now you must eat and sleep and not think too much."

"Father Morel?" he asked.

She crossed herself: "He was buried yesterday."

"I know, I heard the bells."

"We knew him so well here, that good man," she said gently, "and today his holy vessels are on the altar," she paused, sighed, then with her habitual cheerfulness, "of course monsieur has heard the news about the Marquis?"

"Yes, I heard it."

"And only half a hundred soldiers came out in this ship, which are far too few to be any use, also some settlers who go on to Ville Marie, also a young captain

186

and his lady from Paris about whom there is much talk already. You see there has been little to occupy us here for the last six months."

"What talk?" murmured Paul, little interested in Paris.

"It is said she was the new mistress of the King, which surprised everyone, considering his age: she is young and beautiful, but Madame de Maintenon--the King's old mistress, who still lives in Versailles--somehow heard of this and was very angry, and so--well--the lady and her husband are here in Quebec today. You can imagine the gossip that goes on."

"Is that all the news?"

"Your letters, monsieur, will you not read them? If I had one, the first after six months, I would not delay."

Paul fingered them with diffidence: one, he knew from the Abbé; the other, in a stiff script, would be the report of Notary Fouquette concerning his personal affairs during the past winter, but both seemed as from another plane that he would never revisit. Father Morel was real, and the smoking sacrifice of St. Denis, and his own farm, whither he greatly longed to return, and the new corn, where he now felt he had planted his soul with the oats and barley. They would be well up by this time.

"Would monsieur like me to read them to him?" suggested the young nun, who had become greatly interested in this prostrate Goliath, "and there is still opportunity to answer by the same ship. I could do that also if you wish."

"There is nothing that really matters over there, but I might send word of what has happened here. Yes, please, read this one first."

She nodded, smiled, opened the letter from Notary Fouquette. It contained a precise statement of receipts and expenses, to which was affixed a large notarial seal. The Breton farm had done well, apples and grain were sold at a profit, and Paul's house was leased for a period of three years. Certain repairs were advisable. This and little more except a brief note in Raoul's own hand, so phrased that the distinction between the writer's professional duties and his personal feelings was left in no doubt, but since this was what Paul had anticipated, it affected him not at all.

Soeur Roselle sent an enquiring look, but when he said nothing she laid the papers aside, and took up the other letter.

This was very different and Paul's heart warmed as she read: "....and you, my son, are constantly in my thoughts. Reviewing the business of last summer, which I now see in a light even more clear than before, I am convinced that it is to the credit of your conscience and devotion to true religion. Also in leaving Castellon as you did, you were quite right, for such things pass from people's minds, being rapidly replaced by others. In fact the only person who speaks of it now is Notary Fouquette which is no doubt due to the natural acidity of his disposition, but this, I can assure you does not affect others, and should you in a year or two decide to return to Castellon, you will encounter nothing here to disturb the serenity of life."

At this point she paused, regarding Paul with an expression so ingenuously curious that he gave a weak chuckle.

"You do not understand that, do you?"

"M'sieu, I do not ask to understand--it is your affair."

"Without question, yes, but you have been kind; there is no reason I should not explain--if it is to you alone."

"I would not speak of it to anyone. Alors, tell me."

"Well, that letter is from a good man, the Abbé Callott of Castellon, where I lived till last year. I have no parents, ma soeur, they died when I was young, and since then the Abbé has been like another father; he is fat and bald, his eyes twinkle, his heart is of gold. The matter he refers to is a duel."

"You fought in a duel?"

"To some extent, yes."

"And it was about--a woman?"

"Yes, ma soeur, a woman."

"And of course you killed him, then came away quickly to Canada."

"No," he smiled, "not like that: certainly I came away quickly to Canada, but that was because my friends thought me a coward."

"But ... but...." she gave her head a toss, then a quick little shake of protest, "that is not possible--it is ridiculous!"

"How do you know?"

"If you will tell me the rest, I will explain--it is easy."

"Well, the rest is that this other man had been my friend, the friend of my boyhood whom I had not seen for years, and he came between me and the girl I expected to marry. Finding them together, I threw him into a pond of lilies, so, naturally, there was a duel, and...."

"Mon Dieu, but I should have liked to witness that!" she breathed, "yes--yes--and then, please do not stop."

"And then," continued Paul, reflectively, "while we faced each other I knew I must not shed the blood of a friend, though he had already spilled some of mine, so I walked away while he shouted his insults. Therefore, I was a coward, there being no other word for it. Now I am a Canadian farmer with land at Lachine."

She doubled up her hands, compressed her lips, and looked full of protest.

"But that is absurd."

"No, it is not: I have always loved the land, and will make my farm the best in Canada."

"I did not mean the farm, but the rest of it."

"The first part of my life is done with, but I commence over again."

"And you had known her a long time?"

"We were children together when Abbé Callot came to Castellon, years ago."

"Where are those two now?"

"They are doubtless married, and in Paris."

"M'sieu, do you still...?"

"That is part of myself, and cannot change," said Paul, quietly, "but those two I shall not see again, which is much better."

The little nun--she was only twenty-three--took a long breath of complete satisfaction. Romance had lifted its alluring head in the lime-washed ward. Here in the Hôtel Dieu life was an exacting business, with little relief and often grim: the Ursulines, having offered their souls on the altar of self-sacrifice, were disciplinarians, they admitted no excuses, no shortcomings, and the bodies of their gentle devotees were but instruments for the performance of good works; but here and now Sister Roselle felt for a moment again a part of the living, breathing, hating, loving world that moved outside; and Paul's great stature, the compelling nature of his arrival, his remoteness, the scholarly features so oddly conjoined with the frame of Hercules, his atmosphere of strength in reserve--all these had invested him with a peculiar attraction. Yielding to this, for a moment she ceased to be a nun while imagination transported her to scenes far different.

"Well," he smiled, breaking in on her silence, "there is the story and not at all what you expected. Now what have you to explain?"

"M'sieu, you remember when monseigneur came here two days ago?"

"Yes."

"And what you told the secretary as he wrote it down?"

"There was but little to write."

"Yet you did not tell him all."

"No?"

"But certainly not, for only yesterday three men reached Quebec in a fishing boat from the lower river, and as they passed along the south shore they observed what had happened at St. Denis, and went to land to examine for themselves, and found what you had described, but more than that."

"What more?"

"The body of a dead savage with his head split open by one blow. Who killed that man?"

"I did."

"And said nothing of it to the Bishop?"

"It is only more evidence," smiled Paul, "that even in Canada I do not like shedding blood. What does it matter?"

"Yet you do this, then carry away a dying priest to save him from outrage, at the risk of your own life. Ma foi! but you are a strange person."

"Perhaps," he agreed, patiently, "I am peculiar in some ways. What else is in that letter?"

At this she sent him a look, quite baffled, then began: "....is sending you his report as instructed, and in my view your affairs have been well supervised. Certainly not one penny is spent without careful judgment. It has been a tempestuous winter here, but the grain is coming up well. Old Joseph has asked me to give you the assurance of his unchanged devotion. He is unwilling to leave the house, and has engaged himself to the new occupants. He is much affected with rheumatism."

"My land at Lachine is more fertile," interjected Paul, contentedly. "After the first three years there will be double the return: never before have I seen such soil."

"Then m'sieu does not love his land at home?"

"Not as I once did; it is old and tired compared to the other. What else?"

"Your letter written from Quebec before you started for the outpost of Ville Marie is of course my only news of you, and now five months old. I have read it many times and with satisfaction, remembering certain conversations when you impressed on me your ambition to write books, and I wonder if you recall my conviction that it was in deed, not words, that your nature would find its true office."

At this the little nun halted, regarding him with increasing interest.

"That is quite true. He is a wise man, that Abbé."

"What is true?"

"You were not meant to sit at a table with a pen like a monk."

"But the writer is no different from other men."

"I cannot say about that, m'sieu, but you are different."

"Which perhaps is unfortunate," smiled Paul. "What more from my friend?"

"I wait some description of your new farm, and am told that on account of the inclement season in New France it is not possible to work the land during six months of winter, yet the vegetation is of such hardiness that it survives under deep snow and ice, which seems incredible.

"Now as to the matter that doubtless pervades your thoughts as you read this, you will not desire me to dwell on it, but I pray that the pain it caused you has subsided, and you are not without interest in what took place in Castellon after your so abrupt departure. You should know, my son, that within one month they were married," here Soeur Roselle hesitated a little, but Paul's face remained tranquil, "married here by me, which was natural, and you will not object to learn that Jacqueline looked radiantly happy, so I am convinced that all is for the best, such affairs being in the hands of God. The Comte also was well pleased, but to my observation the Comtesse was not so gratified. Then they went to Paris, and I have heard nothing of them since, except that Captain Vicotte has...."

The nun gave an exclamation, stared again at the letter, then at Paul, her eyes rounding:

194

"But ... but ... no, it is not possible!"

"But what?"

"The name, it is the same, also he is a Captain."

"I don't understand."

"They came on *La Perouse*--this Captain Vicotte and his wife; they were on that ship when she found you--they are here in Quebec, and she it is said was the mistress...." she cut off, cheeks turning scarlet, regarding Paul with complete confusion, "they must have seen you in the canoe, think of that!"

"Give me the letter," he said, harshly.

He lay back, frowning at the Abbé's clear script, his heart in protest. Jacqueline the King's mistress! Jacqueline in Quebec! It was grotesque, preposterous; he wondered if he were quite sane, but there sat the little nun gazing at him tensely, visible, tangible, and the expression of that gentle face could not be misread, so presently he accepted the thing with a sort of dull surrender, while his very spirit felt chilled.

"Do not look like that," came the soft voice, "we are not in France now, and what happened there does not matter in Canada. It is all very strange, but nothing more, so you must get strong quickly, then go back to Lachine, and, m'sieu, what I said about her was only the gossip I heard, and perhaps all wrong, there being so little to talk of in Quebec. Also," she added with a wave of protection, "if you do not desire to see these people they will not enter the Hôtel Dieu, and...."

Paul lifted a hand; he had stiffened, he was now sitting up, big shoulders forward, chin sunk on the wide chest, his face a dead mask; he seemed to be looking through and past her, and Soeur Roselle, turning, observed the Superior of the hospital approaching down the central aisle with another woman, young and fair, whom she had never seen before. At this the nun's pulses halted while Paul, paler than ever, appeared carved in stone, and did not speak. Then Soeur Roselle rose quickly and met the two with a hurried whisper to her Superior at which the older woman stopped, while the younger moved on alone. She appeared agitated, and tried to smile, but the wounded man made no sign.

Jacqueline faltered; she had come full of sympathy and admiration, with many things in her heart she wanted to convey, and Jules would follow presently. She longed that Paul might realise that now she understood him better, and forgive what she perceived was a sort of blindness on her part in Castellon; she wanted him to know something of what she felt when he lay half dead on the deck of *La Perouse*. This and much more for which there were no words stirred in her breast as she entered the Hôtel Dieu praying that here in this wild country she might rediscover something of the old friendship of other days. But his expression sapped her courage, she saw him to be defensive and it was hard to find speech.

"Paul," she ventured shakily, "they said I might see you. Do you not want to talk?--shall I go away?"

He made a curious grimace that roused a thousand memories; he was struggling with himself, and it moved her deeply; here was the same Paul, clumsy as of old, whose thoughts she had learned to interpret; that part of him had not altered, in this setting his unbending nature seemed to have found its place and behind it all she saw that he still loved her.

"Only a few moments ago I heard you were here," he said, evenly.

"And we were on the same ship! how strange that was!"

"I did not know it till I was told later."

"Paul, that day I thought you were dead."

"Nearly--yes--but soon I shall be strong again. Let us not talk of it. You are well, Jacqueline, you look well."

"Yes, I am well and strong."

"And ... and Jules, I would like to hear about him."

"He too is in health but not overpleased at being in Canada; I fear this country may not suit him."

Paul, with a touch of satire, wondered if Jules would suit the country, but put that aside while his sombre eyes met those of the woman he still worshipped in his fixed uncompromising way, when, for some queer reason, he found a little comfort.

"You, Jacqueline, it suits you?"

"I cannot explain yet, but I like this New France where nothing is the same as before. Does that sound strange after what happened to you?"

"Nothing sounds strange out here; I think it will always be so."

"I begin to see that," she said, sagely, "perhaps

197

it is just ourselves, so one must change in order to fit the country."

This oddly matched what he too was feeling, then their eyes met and rested, exploring each other with unexpected composure for the difficult moment was now passed, and each knew with secret thankfulness that there had survived from other days something deep and real to which they could still turn with confidence, till Paul, searching the face still so dear, risked all in one straight question:

"What brought you to Canada, Jacqueline?"

"You did not hear--no--how could you?"

"I know nothing except this letter from the Abbé written three months ago. You were then in Paris."

"Paris, yes, with no thought of Canada, then everything came so quickly. You will think it a strange story, Paul. Am I to tell it here, now?"

He nodded: so she came closer and began to talk, locking her slim fingers, and gave it to him from beginning to end, for something assured her there would be no misunderstanding here. It was almost like being in a confessional with no sins to expose, and never a murmur from an invisible priest. While she spoke, Paul did not stir a muscle, so the more she felt it good to unburden herself like this, withholding nothing, and she talked on with so frank an expression, eyes so clear and candid, that gradually the weight that had oppressed his heart was lifted away, and he experienced a great calm.

"And that, Paul, is why we are in Canada today: for myself it is an escape, and Marie, who is with me, is

198

ready for anything and so amusing, but Jules...."

"You are not happy about Jules?"

"He is not reconciled."

"He will be busy here, far more active than in France. Is he on the Governor's staff?"

"That is what he hoped, but we go to Ville Marie where there is more need of the military."

"I have a farm but six miles from there," said Paul, holding his voice steady.

She smiled a little, then, meeting his gaze, was disturbed till a sort of glaze dropped over it as over the eyes of a hooded hawk, shrouding the hidden thing she had fleetingly glimpsed. It left her a little breathless, but with a queer, not unwelcome, sense of security that Jules had never created in her.

"You will live inside the stockade," he went on, evenly, "where there are few like yourself, and in a house built of logs."

"That is not so bad, is it?"

"Warm in winter, and cool in summer. Tell me more about Jules--what does he feel now--for me? It is better to know and not pretend anything."

"He has hardly ever spoken of you or that affair since it happened, and does not seem to care; he is outside waiting, if you desire to see him."

"Is he ready to be friends again, and forget?"

"Yes, I am sure of it," she answered, eagerly.

Paul made a gesture: "Well, I have put away all that business, it has no place in my thoughts. We are in New France together, and if we bring here that which divided us before, we are defeated and can make nothing of life. I feel, Jacqueline, that in this country one makes a fresh start, and for myself I would go back to the days when with Jules there was nothing but friendship. It may mean much in a land of savages."

"Paul, I know you are right," she said, eyes shining, "it makes me happy: I will bring him in."

Queer, thought the wounded man as he saw the familiar figure, to meet again like this when the last view he had was that lithe graceful body poised on quick feet behind the intricate weaving of his rapier point. Jules had changed a little, looked older, his face more set, and was there not a touch of furtiveness about him? Paul could not be sure of this, but there was only goodwill in his greeting, for on the deck of *La Perouse* Jules had been more impressed than he chose to admit by the bloody bulk of the man who had so lately dared not to fight. Paul, nearly dead, had a sobering, potent significance, and his corpse-like frame perhaps heralded what New France might have in store for Jules himself; Paul had faced the unsleeping savage and wore the scarlet badge of that encounter: a different Paul, no longer to be dismissed with contempt. Yet the essential man, as Jules saw at once, had not changed a fraction, his being the kind that never changed.

Their hands clasped, Jules smiled his old bright smile, Paul gave his old twisted grin, and the past fell away from them.

"Bien, mon vieux, you do not look so badly now-- much better than when I saw you last--certainly much cleaner."

"That was a bad dream, Jules; let us forget it."

"I am ready to try, but it will take time, being a strange welcome to Canada. You are better?"

"Nearly well; in a week I too start for Ville Marie."

"Then Jacqueline has told you?"

"Yes, we shall be six miles apart there."

"That is next door."

"Not in New France, especially in winter. You will serve under Governor de Callières."

"So I am told. What sort of a Governor? I hear odd tales of him."

"Something quite new to you; I think it will be better for us all when Comte Frontenac arrives."

"I have met that Comte once when he proposed that I offer for service in Canada, but in contrast to Paris it did not attract me."

"You never told me that," put in Jacqueline.

"I had almost forgotten, and at the time my attention was elsewhere, but now...." he added ruefully, "it has come about. Do we journey together to Ville Marie?"

Paul nodded, and there fell on all three a pregnant silence, crammed with reflections, all oddly alike, for which there were no words. Involuntarily they exchanged glances. Fate--destiny--had arranged this--they had nothing to do with it--they were puppets--marionettes twitched by invisible strings, snatched from all they had known, and now to dance to a new measure on a wild and foreign stage. Truly, thought Jacqueline, one needed to be born again for a venture like this.

It was a moment she never forgot. There was Paul in a coarse grey cotton shirt, his face a mixture of pallor and sunburn, the square chin brown-bearded, a giant in a drab robe, his bulk rising mountainously from the narrow cot, and even in that attire he seemed more a part of this new reality than did Jules in his uniform, speckless breeches and long shiny boots. Paul had served a grim apprenticeship, had paid to know much they must yet learn, nature fitted him for the contest: significantly he had freely chosen New France, while they were exiled. It all brought her a secret comfort.

"You are sure you can travel next week?"

"Quite sure; I must go then with the batteaux that carry you and the soldiers. You see, Jules, there are sixty leagues it is not well to traverse in small parties, only some twenty houses on the way, so the batteaux move in fleets for safety. But Ville Marie itself is secure."

"And you, at your farm, are you safe?"

"Near Lachine we have three forts with garrisons and small cannon; my house--you will visit me--is built like a small fort. Should the savages approach, our scouts--they are coureurs des bois--give warning, also

202

de Callières is a man of experience. Here is Soeur Roselle who has undoubtedly saved my life."

The little nun--she had been watching the three with growing fascination--now approached, put a warning hand on his shoulder.

"M'sieu has talked enough for one day, and must rest. Madame will understand."

They rose, Paul felt their friendly touch, there was a warmth in Jules' grasp, something strong and tender in Jacqueline's eyes as they left him that brought a strange glow to his heart, and he lay looking so long in their direction after they disappeared that Soeur Roselle grew anxious, felt for his pulse. It was bounding.

"I shall be scolded for this: it must not happen again."

"It cannot--ever," said he, and slid off into a slumber of exhaustion peopled with fantastic dreams.

Council with the Rat

Kondiaronk, The Rat, was holding council in a large, round-roofed, bark-covered lodge. Before him squatted forty warriors, naked like himself, their beady eyes fastened in unwinking stares on his commanding figure. His head was shaven save for the long dangling scalp lock that hung between his muscular shoulders, and about his neck was a fringe of dried human fingers whose shrivelled tips caressed a small brass crucifix bestowed at his recent christening by the Jesuits. He welcomed these sacerdotal gestures, and usually made them a means of profit.

Born a Huron, and therefore believed friendly by the French, his restless, resolute brain soon widened his boundaries; he achieved a position of importance, his sagacity was great, he had shone in battle, his name was repeated by many a camp fire, and behind all this moved the born trickster, the instigator of intrigues in which French, English and the five Iroquois nations became involved. This great savage child was the Machiavelli of the northern forests.

The lodge where he now presided stood in a glade on the south shore of Lake Erie, not exposed to nearby open waters, but with a belt of timber between. It occupied the centre of a hundred others, all much smaller, pointed, with a thread of pearl-grey smoke climbing from their conical tops. At open flap doors shapeless squaws with rusty teeth sat weaving rush mats and stitching moccasins, others tended smoking pots suspended over small fires: young warriors, stripped to the skin, were cleaning guns, moulding bullets, fitting trimmed feathers to the shafts of arrows and whetting their long curved scalping knives; blanketed old men lay drowsing and smoking; children played on the dusty earth; on one side the dead of the village, wrapped in skins, lay on platforms in trees, safe from the wolves; a patch of corn rustled softly in the breeze; pumpkins swelled, sunflowers nodded great golden heads, wild grapes, raspberries and blueberries grew in abundance, dozens of canoes lay in the shade lest the heat soften their gummed seams, and over it all poured the vivid rays of a midsummer sun.

From the council lodge where the elders sat in semi-darkness, came a deep guttural voice, punctuated by throaty grunts as some point was driven home, for now The Rat, warming to his work, began to unfold a long-considered plan. Wiser than most, he thoroughly understood those to whom he spoke, he knew where lay their strength and weakness, and that the flame of courage, though easily lit, was apt to subside at the first reverse. He had learned that his compatriots when dealing with the white man always lost in the end, and beneath his tawny skin burned the contempt that all Indians felt for the white intruder. Treaties might be signed, wampum belts exchanged, gifts bestowed and promises made, but enmity, however openly disavowed, did not die, and the hatchet so often buried rested in no permanent grave.

There was no haste about this council, for time did not exist in savage lodges: The Rat had prepared for it with considerable care, and the headmen now before him had travelled many a silent league to hear his words. Senecas were there from Irondequoit Bay, Cayugas from the gorges of the Niagara, Oneidas from Lake George, Mohawks, whose bloody forays spread

205

death around Lake Champlain and along the Richelieu. All were represented, all deep in their hearts hated both French and English; the ambuscade, the sudden descent on lonely settlements, fire, axe and the scalping knife were their instruments, and so far they had acted on impulse, mostly in scattered war parties. But now The Rat had a wider plan to put before them.

He spoke in a resonant tone, onyx-black eyes picking out man after man as though addressing him alone, producing belt after belt of wampum to fortify his arguments. He spoke of the strong water whose taste so maddened his people that to get more of it they sold their beaver-skins for a trifle, and already the beaver were scanty except on the Ottawa and north of the Great Lakes, which was not Iroquois ground; he scoffed at the black robes who permitted torture of captives taken by the French that they might divert them through flames to the worship of a strange god; he derided the peace that the present Onontio in Quebec desired to establish with the federation, urging that any talk of peace was a mistake and ill-betided those who made it. There was but one thing to do--wipe out both French and English, and since Onontio had proved a weakling, it was well to begin with the French.

"Seven summers ago the old Onontio, whose eyes were like those of a hawk, called us to Cataraqui, greeting us as his children, giving many presents, and speaking words we understood. Being men ourselves, we saw that he too was a man. He built there a storehouse so that we could trade without long journeys, there together we planted the peace tree, and all went well because he looked in our faces and spoke with a straight tongue. To the Algonquins of the Ottawa and the Senecas of Salmon River he was the same. Then he went away without bidding farewell, and we were sad at this, and since then there have come two more Onontios to Quebec, but not the same as before, and the last is the worst. Making too many promises, it was easy to see that not all would be met. Many blackrobes he sent to live amongst us and win our trust, trying at the same time to divide us so that he might first destroy you Senecas and Cayugas, while you Mohawks, Onondagas and Oneidas, being propitiated by his gifts, did nothing."

At this he paused, the first seed had been well sown, a rumbling murmur sounded through the lodge, and the naked men turned to each other, nodding gravely. Here certainly was plain talk.

"Now," continued The Rat, well content, "keep that in your hearts while I turn to something else. For many years the beaver has been dwindling in our midst, his houses are empty, and it is in the country of the Hurons, the Ojibwas and Ottawas that good fur may now be found. These tribes, who are not our friends, live under the protection of Onontio, so we ourselves look to the Dutch and English of Albany for our guns and powder. But without beaver skins they are hard to buy, so soon we shall be without weapons unless we take by force that which comes from the north!"

Again he paused, again his auditors grunted approval, for now he dealt with that which touched them all.

"Listen then to my words!" here his voice lifted as he approached the sharpest arguments in his quiver, "I am a Huron, I stand here before the enemies of my fathers and yours: like fools we have fought each other and we may fight again, but today we hold together, first of all against the French, and now I will tell you something not to be put aside. One year ago Onontio proposed peace to the Iroquois, inviting them to send ambassadors to talk with him. Then this man, saying nothing to me of the peace, told me that the ambassadors were a war party, and I should fall upon them, which I did, and killed some, making the rest captives. After this I learned the truth which you now hear, and sent the captives home again with gifts, and sorrow and anger in my heart. And after that this Onontio came to Irondequoit with many soldiers, and his allies from the Ottawa, and burned the towns of you Senecas, destroying your young corn, hoping thereby you would ask for peace out of fear. But...." here The Rat gave a harsh laugh, "not by this means are any of the Iroquois tribes subdued, and do you not now see that he aims to secure every beaver skin from the north by creating war between us so that we destroy each other?"

At this came a shout: it cushioned against the bark roof, rolled out over the silent village, and startled the wild pigeons till the sky was filled with innumerable wings. War was in the offing; these men smelled it as the ivory-beaked raven scents carrion afar, they visioned the lifted scalping knife, and their wild souls leaped at the prospect. Then with their gaze fixed on Kondiaronk's tense figure, they waited for the last and most important words of all.

"Now listen to me, and do not act quickly like children who have no sense. Go amongst the French, sleep beside their stockades and hear what they have to say. Let their corn ripen and their animals feed in tranquillity. When you encounter them on the lakes and rivers, hold up your weapons in friendship. Listen to what the blackrobes talk of in their villages, and when they desire to make a sign on your forehead let it be so and take what they give for that does not matter. If you do these things for a little while, soon Onontio, who offers gifts but to hide his fear, will decide that you are indeed his children. Then, when the time comes, I will send word amongst you that you will hear, and, gathering many fighting men, you will suddenly appear and run through those Frenchmen like fire through dry grass in a season of the year. Many captives will be taken, the old for torture and the pot, the young for adoption, the women to breed sons for your warriors. When this is done, we will deal with the English at Albany, so that soon this country will be as it was before they came to take what is not theirs. And till the word is given let no man whisper of this thing save to himself. I have spoken."

With a wide gesture, holding out his last belt of wampum, The Rat squatted, immobile as an image, while through his tawny audience ran a thrill of conviction. Here was great wisdom; it suited them exactly, it had the element of surprise and strategy that appealed to their furtive intelligence. For more than a hundred years now the forest tribes had marked the coming of the whites; save for the blackrobes all whites were to them a predatory race, the French more grasping than the English, and all under the taint of suspicion.

Now rose an ancient sachem of the Cayugas, grizzled and bent, his fleshless arms like withered branches, his voice hollow, cracked and dry.

"It is true what Kondiaronk has given us, but he has not given all. Two winters have passed since I was at the fort of Frontenac where the big lake moves into the great river. There I saw posts planted in the ground, to each of which was tied an Iroquois, and Christian followers were burning the fingers of those Iroquois in hot pipes, while the blackrobes pretended not to see. Then Onontio came with many soldiers, and professing peace set these men free, and, to show his sorrow, invited others from nearby villages to a feast within the stockade. Trusting him, they came unarmed, but in the midst of eating were surrounded and made prisoners. Now this would not have come about had there not lived amongst them a blackrobe who also professed goodwill, asking nothing for himself. For myself I think this man was honest, but now it will be seen that Onontio uses the blackrobes for his own purposes, so the sign they make on the forehead is but a trick to gain our trust, and we are not safe with any white man. Having done this thing, Onontio took the son and brother of Kondiaronk who sits before you, with many others, and sent them across the bitter water to labour in the ships of the French King, who nevertheless says he is our father and loves us. I have spoken."

The hoarse growl that followed was interrupted by The Rat, who raised a brown hand for attention.

"You have heard a true word," he said, smoothly, "and I am not one who in speaking to you puts first that part which most concerns himself. One year ago I sent a message to Onontio saying that till my son and father are returned there can be no peace with the French, but doubtless by this time they are dead, and I shall not see them again. It is well to remember such things when you encounter a Frenchman!"

Nothing more was needed to fructify the seed so deftly sown, but now there towered a bronze shape of a man who had sat for an hour without the twitch of a single muscle: he was broad and sinewy, his face scarred in battle, his body with a strange growth of coarse glossy hair so that back and loins had the silkiness of an otter. This was Oguntwae, chief of the Onondagas.

"I too have something to tell my brothers," he

began, harshly, "when Onontio by deceit took those prisoners there were also amongst them Onato, The Watersnake, my father, and Eri, The Cherry Tree, my daughter. Being old and his bones dry, my father was not sent across the bitter water, nor was my daughter sent, being only a young girl, but both taken to Ville Marie, and there sold as slaves, where they are today. Now it is in my mind that these two, who will hate their masters like ourselves, be told to observe all that goes on amongst the French, and when the time is ripe, and they think not at all of attack by us Iroquois, let us have a sign. Having those of our blood in that place, is it not wise to use them? and it would be easy when selling fur at Ville Marie to speak secretly with these two. I myself would do this were I not known to the French by the hair on my skin."

This plan was received with approval by all but The Rat.

"One does not try to sell fur to anyone late in summer-time," he objected, "it is not good; they will not trade, and the man be killed as a spy or put in chains."

Oguntwae took this with a hard smile: "Not that, but the man who offers it will act like a fool, have the loose tongue of a fool, and certainly be thought a fool: none will pay him any attention, and thus make him more free to talk with whom he will. The face that can look foolish when desired often hides a great wisdom. I have spoken."

The applause that greeted him was sufficient answer to The Rat, who for years past had been aware of Oguntwae's rising reputation. The Hairy One, being a true Iroquois, held the advantage; his tribe, the Onondagas, formed the central core of the federation, while Kondiaronk had often been hard put to it to make himself so useful to the enemies of the French that they forgave him his Huron blood. By nature a deceiver, by instinct double-faced, his was a dangerous trail, and it took brains to follow it. But now, and he saw this at once, came the opportunity finally to establish himself in Iroquois confidence by close co-operation with The Hairy One. Together, he reckoned, they were undefeatable.

"You have heard the speech of a wise man whose thoughts are very deep," he said, suavely, "and I too am glad to be guided by them, so Oguntwae and I will choose the one to be sent. It is well."

There was no dissension: the counsellors, blinking under the strong light, came out again under the sun to sit in circles round steaming pots while the squaws ladled stew into wooden bowls. There were partridge in it, moosemeat, wild pigeons, young corn and choice fragments of human flesh, for that day an Algonquin captive had been put to torture and death on the Irondequoit. Awestruck children watched these great men eat; grey-headed warriors and lanky youths, though hungry for news of the council's decision, pretended to be uninterested and asked no questions, while the women, fishing in the swirling stew, transfixing dainty morsels to offer their distinguished guests, were shrewd enough to keep silent.

Then when all was done, and the final pipe smoked, came grave salutations, deep-throated words of farewell, and significant glances. Now the die was cast. Brown hands lifted canoes into the shining waters of the lake and a small river that wound from the south, whereby many had travelled to the place of meeting. There was a flash of paddles, the canoes became living things moving without sound, a silver wrinkle widening from their birchen bows; they dwindled, one by one they disappeared, leaving Kondiaronk, The Rat, deep in thought with a light of crafty satisfaction in his slanting eyes.

In Ville Marie

— I —

The batteaux moved slowly upstream; thrusting blunt bows against a persistent current they resembled great pot-bellied spiders whose distended legs, swung in a rhythm, disturbed the placid surface with tireless uniformity. Each carried a packed burden of some twenty passengers and two tons of freight: there were raw soldiers--new recruits for the forts guarding Ville Marie, coureurs des bois bound westwards after selling their furs in Quebec, river drivers who had left their tawny rafts moored below the capital's high-crowned promontory, a merchant or two bent on forestalling rivals on the Lower River, Captain and Madame Vicotte, Marie Dufaut and Paul de Lorimier.

Liquid miles slid by, day after day died redly in the west, and for Jacqueline the changing panorama had a constant interest: at every thump of the long oars she moved further into the unknown, and would sit for hours scanning the rampart of dark green that marched massively to the shore. Its mysterious process matched the medley of her thoughts; she felt the ties of the old life slacken, things of yesterday began to lose their sharpness, obliteration and replacement were going on.

Aware of this, she welcomed it. Sometimes she found herself regarding Jules with an intensive stare as though he were something new; his face, now lacking its old good-natured smile, had an angry red from the blistering sun; he seemed uncomfortable, moving restlessly with every sign of impatience, pushing out full lips, giving his head little shakes of disapproval. His uniform with its bright colours and gay facings lent him the aspect of some tropical bird pausing here in migratory flight and foreign to the sombre aspect of the relentless river; she had a feeling that he did not fit into this setting, and never would fit. And when he looked at her his eyes were resentful.

Paul, for his part, spoke very little. His brain was kaleidoscopic, its pattern constantly changing: he was happy and unhappy; content yet ill at ease, telling himself that there must be some purpose behind all this, but could not get at it and doubted whether life so near Jacqueline, yet without her, was a bearable thing. In New France he had discovered himself to be a man differing from the former one; at his present angle he could see how and where old barriers and inhibitions had been surmounted till now he was a part of something more significant than himself, and the one thing that steadied him was the reflection that she too was part of it. The courage that shone in her eyes strengthened his own heart, and all he could do would be to offer such service as he might. This made him thankful for the farm and its comfort, glad that he was neither priest nor soldier, and called no man his master.

As to Jules, Paul felt uncertain. There had been no talk of the past between them, that ground being too dangerous, but he could see that Jules' ideas of military duty in New France needed revising, and the process might cost him and others dearly. Jules, it appeared, had a contempt for the savage, no conception of what it meant to face invisible death whistling from the unseen. But this was his affair. Also he would certainly be separated from his wife, perhaps for long periods, when on duty beyond Ville Marie; he might be sent on expeditions to Fort Frontenac or even the inland post of Michilimacinac, and if that happened it would be a different Jules who returned--if he did return. This thought gave Paul a revulsion, made him want to take Jules by the arm, beg him in the name of God to forget old scores and accept guidance from one who knew more than himself, but his manner made any such venture unwise. Paul would meet his eyes to find small sign of friendship; he volunteered but little news from France, asked practically nothing about this wild country, and seemed occupied in regretting his lost distinction as a captain in the King's Bodyguard.

The batteaux laboured on with no diminishment of the great river as long leagues dropped behind. The north shore, which mostly they followed, was the ground of the friendly Hurons, but the possible presence of marauding Iroquois from further south made any encampment unsafe unless in the shelter of some welcome seigneury, so the travellers landed but seldom, often sleeping still afloat and anchored with strict watch kept on the dark line where still waters lipped the unbroken woods.

It was on one of these breathless nights that reality came home to Jacqueline.

All day the air had been charged with heat and a faint drift of opaque smoke from further west: it had an acrid savour, and came, explained Paul, from inland forest fires: it overlaid the glassy river like a veil, obscuring its upper reaches. There could be no question of landing, and the batteaux were moored in a long line well out of arrow shot.

At midnight, Paul went on guard, lying outstretched on his belly in the bows, only his head appearing above the gunwale; thus prone, he resembled some titanic, familiar spirit of the wilderness, breathing its air with deep inhalations while there came to him a thin chorus of tiny voices, all inarticulate, blending into what men call silence. Curled round bales from Lyons and Lille, wedged between boxes, coiled slackly on mounds of ropes, the others were lost to the world, inanimate, unconscious, save only Jacqueline, who could not sleep. Her bed was a pile of cedar-brush over which a blanket had been thrown, and she lay watching the motionless figure in the bows, her brain running riot. "It's not true," she said to herself, "it's only a dream," and just then Paul turned suddenly as though at a signal and gave her a long straight stare. A half-moon was riding in a cloudflecked sky, at one moment the world was shrouded, ghostly, in the next the forest wall stood revealed in solid purple.

How long this lasted she did not know, for things now seemed to have neither beginning nor end, when, without a sound, she saw Paul's body stiffen. He waited a moment, then turned, and again his eyes met hers. He was smiling grimly. Putting a finger to his lips, he beckoned, so she crawled forward to crouch beside him.

"Look!" he breathed.

A long lane of shadow paralleled the shore in which a phalanx of pine tops lay sharply mirrored, and presently she saw their tufted images distorted by a slowly spreading ripple, their symmetry was marred, and it seemed that this was produced by something small and dark that moved slowly towards them.

"Some animal?" she whispered.

"Certainly an animal--a Seneca--do not stir."

At the edge of the shadow lane the dark spot paused as though fearing the light; the ripple died; the pine-tops reassembled in a natural pattern, while Paul's arm stole towards a short-handled, wide-bitted axe that lay near him; it had a curved edge and was very sharp.

"When you see him, make no sound: no danger now."

She waited, her pulse slowing: now the dark spot neared a silver streak cast by the moon; again it paused, then swam out, and at the sight she was hard put to stifle a cry of terror. Breaking the silver, floated a human mask painted with streaks of vivid yellow and red; from its dark crown a rope of plaited black hair floated like an eel: she could see glistening eyes; across the wide gash of mouth glinted a long, curved knife, clenched between white teeth. Held just above the surface, the horrific thing swam downstream; she caught the play of brown, naked, muscular shoulders; like a lithe otter it came, and death swam with it. Her heart was in tumult when she felt a heavy hand.

"Again there is no danger. Put down your head."

She obeyed him, amazed that she could obey, nor did it occur to wonder why he had not roused Jules and the others; she felt content to leave it to him--that was the strange part of it--and buried her face till out of the silence came a thud of steel into wood, a yell of agony, and the night was full of commotion. A human hand, brown, chopped off clean, had fallen beside her, blood spurting from the severed wrist, while a flight of arrows whistled from the forest wall. All dropped short. Twenty drowsy men, snatched from sleep, set up a commotion that spread along the line of batteaux till the night was full of alarms; some of the coureurs des bois discharged their muskets at hazard, bullets rattled amongst the pine trunks, but the only reply was a high-pitched yelling that trailed off into silence when, somewhere downstream, a mutilated savage, dripping blood and water, climbed into cover. Paul picked up the gory hand, examined it closely, tossed it overboard.

The coureurs des bois were amused, nothing unusual to them in this affair; neatly managed, they thought; but Jules resented it; he, an officer, was allowed to sleep during danger. He blurted this out, eyes hot, while the Canadians glanced at each other and shrugged. They knew.

"Jules," said Paul, calmly, "you will understand better later on: had I given the alarm when I first saw him, he would have escaped. Also it is better not to kill him, for with one hand he will suffer more alive than dead. Now he is a mockery for the rest of his life. And...." he added evenly, "I have much still to repay the Iroquois."

Jules gave a sulky grunt: dignity would not allow of argument with a farmer, and for the rest of that day maintained an aloofness that even Jacqueline could not break, brooding over another angle of life in this detestable wilderness. In his pocket was a letter to the Chevalier de Vaudreuil, acting-Governor of Ville Marie, who would doubtless send him to one of the small forts guarding Lachine, where Paul's farm lay. The prospect of this duty was irritating. Jacqueline would live within the town's stockade, and he did not relish this either. What he now felt for her was satisfaction in a beauty the more striking in this crude setting, and a sense of ownership, though still in secret he blamed her for his banishment. Now he would be chained to an unwelcome post, leaving Paul, the farmer, free to come and go as he pleased, and this a different Paul from the coward of Castellon. He had no doubt of Jacqueline's loyalty, but the whole situation was disturbing.

The fur-trading hamlet of Trois Rivières was abreast: with a steady thrashing of oars the batteaux crept on into the shallow expanse of Lac St. Pierre; there were scattered clearings, recently abandoned, but already the untamable woods reclaimed their own; the wild grape climbed over empty door frames and tumbled roofs where the men of France had settled for a while, built a cabin, raised a patch of corn. Then, lured mysteriously from the old life, they had discarded the shackles of the past, taken Indian girls, gone deeper into the forest, fathering broods of half-wild children who played naked in the sun, and in their turn would be coureurs des bois leading the unfettered existence that sapped the strength of old France in these savage domains of hers.

Only three established habitations had the flotilla passed in fifty leagues above Quebec, but now, nearing Ville Marie, one saw where seigneuries had been granted to retired officers and public servants to make the town a little more secure, but only a little, and Jacqueline wondered what sort of life women led within their palisades. The same reflection was in the eyes of Marie. How distant were the conical turrets that overlooked Castellon! She nodded to the woman, smiling:

"I can nearly read your mind--what is in it?"

"Madame, I cannot tell myself. After what has happened I think none of this is true, and we shall wake up somewhere else."

"You want to wake up?"

"Yes--and no; I am not sure. Should I write to

Castellon what I have seen, they won't believe it."

"It may be to say you have found a husband in Ville Marie."

"Tchk! tchk! had I desired one he would be here now--or I not here."

"What?"

"But certainly; it happened before we had been a week in Quebec. You have heard of 'les filles du Roi'-- those shiploads of unwanted girls sent by the king as brides for his subjects in Canada?"

"You are not 'une fille de Roi'," laughed Jacqueline.

"Far from it." Marie gave her head a toss. "In the Lower Town lives a Mons Larivière who trades in beaver-skins when the Iroquois do not capture them all to sell to the English. Being an honest man unlike many others, he is under license from the Governor. Alors, for some years he met that ship, and watched those girls coming ashore in their best, but when they approached they would not look at him. It was younger men they sought, and of course his nose was against him. Finally, he became tired of that business and approached me with politeness when I was waiting for you outside the Hôtel Dieu. He was in great earnest, but much too lugubrious."

"What about his nose?"

"When he spoke, I said little, but enjoyed the sensation of being desired. He is a hairy man of considerable age, with a large nose on which is a bright red mound sprouting still more hair. It is, madame, like a bed of young asparagus, and I kept watching it, wondering what it would be like to be saluted thus every morning when I woke up. This was not attractive. Next day he met me again, renewed his suit, and swore that he much preferred a middle-aged, well-plumaged hen to any half-feathered chicken of a demoiselle."

"I take him for a wise man."

"For myself, I prefer wisdom in less need of a razor, but that, petite, is only half the truth; you have drunk at my breast and only the good God knows what you will find in this strange country. Very well--you shall not find it alone--of that I am determined." She took Jacqueline's hand in her own, strong, firm, still shapely. "Already I have forgotten that too hairy suitor."

"I have a husband," said the girl, gently, "but you...."

Marie, who had recently formed an unflattering opinion of the husband, said nothing, but glanced at the heavy boxes filling the bottom of the batteau; here were linen, silver, household goods, Jacqueline's wardrobe in Paris and Versailles, silks, ribbons, high-heeled slippers, powder, laces, gloves, Jules' uniforms, books, pictures, prints, all the precious freight that had decorated the old life, and much of it so little likely to serve in the new one. She gazed up the watery avenue that led to Ville Marie, and her heart went out in pity to the girl beside her. Finally she gave a faint chuckle.

"What is it?" asked Jacqueline.

"I was only thinking."

"Of what? I've been thinking too."

Marie's eyes roved to the great figure of Paul; he was sitting in the bows, smoking, had been there since sunrise, talking hardly at all: at times he would raise his big head and sniff the air as though scenting some invisible object, while his body expressed confidence and repose. Here was a man returning to things welcome and familiar.

"Perhaps," said the woman, in a low voice, "in spite of what happened in Castellon it is fortunate for us that m'sieu Paul came first to New France."

— II —

"But this is absurd! What shall we do?"

Marie, hands on hips, looked about, frowned, shrugged. The cabin in which they stood was of substantial stone for the first floor, low-roofed, then a shingled attic of "colombage", a roof mixture of wood and plaster; it had five rooms, the largest some twelve feet square, floored with hewn plank in which the adze marks were visible. A stone fireplace in each room. Through a trap-door in the largest, one descended to a small, stone-lined cellar that had the chill of death. The windows were small, square, heavily shuttered, frames lacking glass, and sealed with membrane from the stomach of a moose, stretched tight, scraped thin. Bright sun shone outside, but only a pale light filtered through.

"This," went on Jacqueline, chaotically, "must be the salon--that the salle à manger--there," she pointed to a smaller cube, "my room, the other the captain's, and the kitchen speaks for itself, but where will you sleep?"

"Naturally above in the attic; but do not distress yourself."

"Those boxes fill me with fear; there isn't space for half of what we brought. What a fool I was!"

"Perhaps, yes," said Marie, candidly, "you will remember that in Versailles I...."

"We had better forget Versailles."

"Undoubtedly that is best, and if again you ask the Chevalier he might...."

Jacqueline shook her head. The Chevalier had greeted their arrival with politeness, but his manner was cool. Just like de Denonville, he thought, to send him a young, inexperienced officer, and worse still with a wife hardly out of her teens, when what he needed was more troops under those who had a record of service; also he had viewed with certain diffidence some two tons of belongings little of which was likely to be suitable in an outpost like Ville Marie. But that was the affair of Madame Vicotte. As to Jules, that young man was told to wait the return of de Callières, expected any day, who would probably send him to Fort Remy, six miles out. Jules received this in silence, flushed a little, gave an automatic salute. He was in revolt.

"Perhaps," repeated Marie, "the Governor would build you a larger house."

"There is no chance of it; also I've a feeling I'm not very welcome here."

"Then Quebec, madame; you liked Quebec."

"Here we are, Marie; here we stay."

"You will not be vexed if I burn the dinner on an open fire? That red-nosed Larivière, he has a stove from France."

Jacqueline paid no attention: she was standing at the door, staring about at Ville Marie. In front of the house ran a narrow plank walk two feet off the ground, a shallow weed-grown ditch, a deeply rutted road, some scattered houses even smaller than her own. Across the "chemin de ronde", a beaten track that followed the river, she caught the glint of a great stream and a long low island, the Île Ste. Hélène. At the water's edge was camped a family of Hurons cleaning fish beside a small fire, its flame palely visible in the strong light.

South of the Rue St. Paul--how absurd a name, she thought, for a string of crazy habitations built mostly with an axe--was an open space, partially cobbled, the Place d'Armes, used twice a week for a market. Near it a corps de garde. In a neighbouring square rose the Church of Notre Dame adjoining the combined Sulpitian Seminary and Manor House. Further east lifted their massive stone mill, sails turning rhythmically in a light breeze. Here, Paul had told her, his wheat would be ground. Nearby, the house of the Governor, with water barrels on raised platforms for use in case of fire.

To the north a long, rounded, thickly-wooded hill dominated the settlement and sent a small stream trickling riverwards beneath the stockade, but to make sure of water in case of beleaguerment, two wells had been sunk; they had stone copings and heavy wooden covers on wide leather hinges that opened like trap doors. Roughly clothed men lounged in the Place d'Armes, voices of women called from cabin to cabin, lean dogs lay against the palisade scratching for fleas, brown-skinned children, some naked, others in short buckskin breeches, played in the afternoon sun, and over all rested an air of languor and lassitude.

Jacqueline, repressing a sigh of disillusionment, saw Jules coming towards her, trim and formal against this casual background. He had been away for hours.

"Well," she said, "what news?"

He mopped his brows. "Only what one might expect in this hole. I've just seen the acting Governor again; he feels uncertain, thinks the savages have been unnaturally quiet for too long, and is anxious about an order just in from Quebec."

"What order, Jules?"

"To destroy Fort Frontenac."

"Where is that?"

"Sixty leagues further west, built by Frontenac himself, who will be furious when he hears about it. Fort Niagara, still further on, is already deserted. Vaudreuil thinks that de Denonville is mad."

"But why destroy these places?"

"Exactly--that's what I asked; apparently Denonville reckons it will appease the Iroquois, while people here know it will only encourage them. Fort Frontenac commands the entrance to the great freshwater lakes, with Captain Vedrenne in charge. An officer is on his way there now with the order. What sort of a crazy country have we come to? The Governor talks as though it was ours--that is a joke."

"It all sounds rather ... rather uncomfortable."

"A good deal more than that. I am told that a year ago de Denonville might have given the savages a lesson they would not forget--they were spurred on by the English, of course--he had them practically beaten, then with two thousand soldiers and native allies at his back, he weakened. I have this from a Captain Valterie who was there. Afterwards, he said, our friendly Ottawas drank the blood of the slain, cut up the bodies, and put them into kettles. Faugh!"

Jacqueline shuddered: "Why tell me such things?"

"Better myself than anyone else, but that is forest warfare. Also I hear that Vaudreuil has asked de Denonville to come and see for himself how things stand in Montreal."

"You must be very careful," said she, shakily.

"I have no desire to have my throat cut, even by our Christian allies. Forget the rest of it." He put his head in at the door, stared about, made a grimace: "What a hovel!"

"I thought you'd say that."

"Well, isn't it?"

"It doesn't matter; much worse are here, and it's clean. What else did you do?"

"A look at Fort Remy, where I report later on; it's the second one out, built of logs of course, has a parapet with a sort of firing platform all round, and lies not far from Paul's farm. The officers' quarters are what you might imagine."

"Did you see Paul?"

"In the distance."

"You didn't go in?"

"Why should I? He was working his land, and didn't see me. That's a comfortable place, quite the best out there--flowers and all that. He had a musket on a stump beside him. I don't think we're likely to meet often from now on. There were two savages with him, a man and a young girl--the best looking native I've noticed yet."

"Oh!"

"Doubtless his concubine," added Jules, lightly, "in the custom of the country; think of that old Castellon cabbage with a concubine. Does it make any difference to you?"

"Why should it?"

"I had the idea you'd put our farmer friend on a much higher moral level."

"Jules."

"Something I want to say--walk with me a little."

"Well?"

He sent her a mocking glance. "By all means; to the terrace or--ah--the lily-pond?"

To this she made no answer, and they set out

along the Rue St. Paul, past straggling houses, past the sentry at the western double timbered gate that commanded the Lachine road. Jules was smiling a little, but her eyes were grave.

The clearings they crossed were continuous, flooded with light that struck slanting through the solid forest close by, from which came a constant drumming where redheaded woodpeckers hammered through the dry skin of dead trees. Blackened trunks lay prostrate in shrouds of flaunting pink fireweed, autumnal flowers, the blazing golden rod, wild asters and alabaster immortelles on long milky stems crowded together by road and ditch, and in shady nooks glowed ruby-red berries of the glossy-leaved wintergreen. Fences of split logs meandered between strips of fields now yellow with wheat and corn; oats were already garnered, partridges fed in the ragged stubble, black stumps thrust up at random, and between them bent men and women swinging their curved sickles. Harvest was on, but nothing suave or gracious pertained to this spectacle: it was raw, crude, uncompromising, a battlefield of men and forest where man, the temporarily triumphant pigmy, made haste to snatch his scanty gleaning ere the unexhausted forest close in and smother him again. It did not seem that in all the world were men enough to win permanent domination here. Men slept, but the forest--never.

"Well," said Jules, breaking a long silence, "I await the lecture--not the first in New France."

"It is not a lecture; I'm just puzzled--don't you mean to be happy here? I do."

"I ask nothing but your happiness, and to get back to France," he answered, stiffly.

"I think the last comes first; but, Jules, can't we start over again? It's not going to be easy for me, here: I don't mind that; I'm not afraid of the future. You have your duties, but I have little. This is a man's country, not a woman's, and we may often be separated, so is it again between us as it was at first, before we went to Paris? It would help to be sure of that, but you have changed and perhaps...." she admitted, "I too. Now I want everything changed back."

"Everything?"

"Yes, between you and me; we mustn't go on like this."

"Well," he conceded, "as for me enough has happened in the last few months to change any man," then, in a tone that sounded faintly curious, "you still love me?"

She took this not in the way he expected but with a sort of soberness as though it called for reflection, not impulse.

"I still love the old Jules, though of late he has been hard to find."

He nodded, slowly: "I can't altogether blame you: look at me--now--here; look about, see what you see, then ask yourself can any man remain unchanged. All I worked for, all the life I loved, is taken from me."

"It's no consolation that I remain?"

"You've just told me how hard it'll be here," he countered, evasively, "and when I wanted you to go back to Castellon you wouldn't hear of it, even if it had been permitted!"

"Why?"

"Perhaps the romance of New France called too loudly."

"Romance!" she recoiled a little, "you know why I came--you were glad then--now you feel the responsibility of my presence, is that it?"

"You've just said it's a man's country."

"Yet I wanted to try and make it a woman's as well, so it's better not to argue any more. Do you prefer that I go back to France? Shall I ask the Governor?"

"What!"

"The batteaux leave again soon, the boxes are unopened yet, I'm quite ready: I could just catch the last ship."

She said this with a kind of metallic brightness that made him stare: he had not dreamed of such a thing; she was too devoted, pliable, and anxious to please. Not unaware of his own stiffening attitude, he had been glad that hers was unchanged, and felt sure of her. But not today. She had never withheld anything, had shared his passions, his desires and ambitions. She was beautiful: in Quebec she had created a sensation: in this desolate spot would make the cabin habitable, even attractive, a good place for escape from winter duty at Fort Remy. It all came in a rush, and suddenly he was aghast at the thought of losing her.

"Jacqueline, are you crazy?"

"Probably, but I mean what I say; my parents would be delighted, Marie weep for joy, and my father perhaps take me to Paris after Noel. You see, Jules, you are not the only one who begged me to stay in Castellon if I could. Or I might go to Quebec for the winter."

"Why Quebec?"

"Thinking you might not be pleased I did not mention the invitations. They all assure me it will be gay there when the Marquis arrives; dinners, theatricals, the plays of Molière, receptions at the Château St. Louis, driving on the ice. The time goes fast enough, and I would like Quebec if ... if...."

"You little Castellon Cabbage," he blurted, "why all this nonsense? Forget such wild dreams; you are my wife and I want you here."

He put his arm round her, kissing her, but she could not misread that kiss, and her lips felt chilled: he had not lied to her, sworn that she was all wrong, and he loved her and was sorry, and secretly she was content that he hadn't. Now she knew. He wanted her in Ville Marie less for what she was than for his comfort; he was acting well, but not quite well enough, and she knew him too thoroughly. This talk had taken all her courage; she was terribly in earnest, and--and he would not see it.

"I stay here then," she said, dully.

"Of course you do; there's such a thing as duty."

"Three months ago if I'd been told it was my duty to stay in Castellon, I'd have been willing. Well, it is settled. Shall we walk on--I would like to see Paul's farm."

"Too late and too far; if you drive with me to Fort Remy we will pass it. And as to Paul there is...."

"What is there?"

"You realise he is still in love with you?"

"Absurd!" she parried, knowing it to be true, "he has talked very little, and never of the past: I haven't seen him except with you. Not jealous, are you?"

"It isn't necessary for him to tell you in words--I saw it in his eyes. As for jealousy, can you imagine it? The day after we met you said you had never really loved him--why should you begin now--this, apart from the fact that there is little for any woman to love. Paul, you see, knowing more of this detestable country than I do, thinks himself my superior. I couldn't miss that."

"You are wrong," she protested, "completely wrong."

"I wonder! You will find yourself much alone, Jacqueline, so be careful."

"You think I don't know my obligations," she flamed.

"There was a period not so long ago when you weren't so sure of them," he said acidly, "which had to do with what happened to both of us."

"Jules, that is impossible! I was foolish--yes--but tried to make amends, and the king...." here her cheeks grew scarlet, "would never have banished us together; you, perhaps, but not me, so that business had nothing to do with it."

"Then who banished us?" he asked in an odd tone. "You think it was some enemy of mine?"

"I don't know what to think. Perhaps Egare betrayed you."

"Shall I tell you something to open your eyes-- something you won't like?"

"That's not unusual of late."

"Till now I thought best to keep it to myself," said he, in the manner of a man who relishes the moment. "Before we sailed I tried to find out what I could--one had to be very careful with so many tongues and eyes in Versailles. Finally I got on the track from a confidential clerk in the Ministry of War--everyone has his price--and I'd given him a few louis. There I found the truth. It was not the king who banished us: he might well have disposed of me, but not you."

"Then who...?"

"Listen. This clerk was one of Louvois' secretaries. On the morning of the day I got my orders, the Minister sent for him and, smiling to himself, dictated a letter to my Colonel. This clerk wrote it himself, brought it back to be signed, and as Louvois took up the pen he burst into a great laugh, saying to himself: 'What a woman! What a woman!--Now do you understand?'"

"Did he mean me?"

"You were nothing to him; the woman was de Maintenon, from whose apartment he had just returned. She knew all about that business."

234

"But how--how could she?"

"How is it that everyone there knows of everyone else? That we shall never discover."

"But she could not banish us without the King's...."

"She can do and has done all that suits her plans; a formidable female whose one object in life is to hold the king in leading strings. You were long enough in Versailles to see that, so imagine the effect when she learned about you, as she must have. Well, there it is, and now that you know," he concluded, loftily, "perhaps you'll credit me with a certain delicacy in keeping the thing to myself. I did not want you to be--er-- embarrassed by it."

This revelation rang true, and it struck her dumb. De Maintenon, whom she had never seen! Shipped off by another woman, cold, childless, relentless, the power behind the throne, whose implacable touch was felt over a thousand leagues of sea; a flood of humiliated anger engulfed the girl. It was not Jules' gambling--not the sale of the necklet that had done this. She reproached her husband for having changed, yet she herself had ruined him!

"Jules, Jules, what shall I say?"

He was thrashing the tops of blueberry bushes bordering the rutted road; they were loaded with bunched clusters of dark, shining fruit that bled a pale purple juice. He made one casual sweep, drew his cane through the grass, and laughed.

"Say?--there is nothing more to be said; it is over--done--finished, can't be undone. We are here--we make the best of it, each of us; I will visit you as often as I can; you will make yourself as comfortable as possible. What else offers?"

They were back where they started from; it had all been for nothing except that she was left with a wound that would be slow to heal, while Jules seemed untouched, coolly polite, as distant as ever.

"Let us return; it's getting late," said she in a small voice.

— III —

Paul, straightening his back, gave a sigh of content. His last sacks of grain had trundled down the road behind a yoke of deliberate oxen on their seven-mile journey to the big Sulpitian mill, and through a shimmering haze of dust he could still make out the low-wheeled wagon with its golden freight. His fields were now bare, prickled, glistening in the sun. Behind the house lifted a natural mound where for shade he had left standing a great maple tree, and beneath it the ground began to glow with a rain of ruined leaves.

Into this mound Jean and Onato had dug a horizontal cavity, a root house, had lined it with timber, had set bins and shelves of whipsawn lumber. A small six-inch funnel to the surface gave ventilation. At the entrance a heavy door of double thickness.

In the dry coolness where frost could never penetrate were stored potatoes, beets, onions, piles and piles of them; two sides of salted pork hung from the roof; there was a keg of pickled eels from Lake St. Louis, fish smoked over a maple fire, blocks of hard, brown sugar from the same friendly tree. Some of

Paul's grain had been ground, the Sulpitian Fathers taking one-tenth. There was a bin of oats, another of maize, a sack of dried peas, a small pocket of dried lavender that gave out a faint essence. He had had lavender under the library window in Castellon.

Here was the work of one long arduous summer when to him and Jean the opulent earth had been mistress, wife and lover, thrilling with new life under their caress. This was what she gave. While Paul lay in the Hôtel Dieu at Quebec, and before the strange appearance of Jacqueline, his one thought was of the farm. There was no way of writing to Jean, no message would reach him, so one could but wait and trust. Father Morel, he reflected with a touch of fatalism, had followed the gory trail blazed by so many of his sacrificial brotherhood, but the farm was another thing. Men were mortal, while a farm should live for ever if treated with kindness and understanding. How much of this, he wondered, was Jean good for? Now he was answered.

It had been a good homecoming, with Jean nodding, smiling and obviously pleased with himself; he knew he had done well: he wanted this farm to shine beside a dozen others whose owners did a little trapping, worked when the mood took them, then reeled back under the stars from Ville Marie fuddled with strong brandy. True he had often felt lonely, ached for a woman of his own, but first he must save money.

"It is all nothing at all, m'sieu," he grinned, "and that pig grew fat feeding himself on roots. I wish we had land cleared for more corn. But you--you are not well--have you been sick?"

Paul told him in a few words, an unheroic tale, then went on to speak of the meeting in Quebec, saying nothing of what happened on the journey upriver. At mention of Jacqueline and Jules, he sounded diffident, but beneath the calm Jean sensed an undercurrent that puzzled him.

"That Father Morel was a good man--for a priest," he said, soberly, "and fond of you from the first. He told me so himself. How many were killed, m'sieu?"

"With the children, eleven."

"The Mohawks?"

"Yes, a war party from New England by way of the Richelieu--the old story again. I would like to be sure there are none within twenty leagues of us at this moment. Has all been quiet here?"

"That is just it--too quiet; at night I lie awake, listening, listening, imagining I hear something in the forest; but one doesn't hear till too late. Often I went out in the small hours to see if Onato and Eri were still here; they were, but, somehow I was glad to get back."

"There are Iroquois on the north shore below Lac St. Pierre, but I think not many," said Paul quietly, then went on to tell of the night attack.

"That is bad. They won't return to their own country till winter. Does it not seem strange that we and the English, both white, encourage the savage on this murderous business? Does the savage think at all? If so, what does he make of us?"

Paul sat down a shade heavily. "Ask Onato--or Eri."

"Ah--Eri! No use asking her."

238

"Why not?"

"May I speak without reserve?"

Paul laughed: "Why so mysterious?"

"Well, you are the reason, and at her age a brown-skinned girl is already a woman. From a child she has seen life given and taken; now her blood is hot, she desires her mate, it is you she desires. I have watched this grow since she came. Onato knows and approves; he spoke of it to me when you were away, saying there are many men about here ready to take her, but she will not look at them. Did you see nothing of this yourself?"

"Go on."

"You have done nothing, I see that, but it was bound to come. Onato does not much care what happens to him, but he loves that girl; he says if you take her as your woman you and this farm and all on it will always be safe. No savage will hurt you. More than that, you would learn what goes on in the Iroquois councils, which would mean much to New France. When he said that I asked if I would be acceptable instead, but no, it is only you. Also, m'sieu, there was an evening when you talked freely with that Father Morel about yourself. What it was I do not know, but Eri heard it and understood much, which made her desire you the more; and while you were away she worked like ten women, but that was for you, not me. There is the situation. Why not take her? There is nothing to lose by it."

This, quite the longest speech he had ever made, was got out in a burst: obviously, he felt better for it, stood looking at his patron with a deprecating smile,

239

then added:

"You are young, m'sieu, strong, it is against nature to live as you do. You observed her expression when you returned?"

"I did."

"Alors?"

"You expect me to raise a flock of half-breeds?" said Paul, with a great laugh.

"For the children I care nothing, but winter nights seem to be growing longer in this country, and pass more quickly with a woman beside one. Also a brown breast is as soft as any other--any man here will tell you that."

"Then take her yourself."

"Hien! with a knife between my ribs. M'sieu is too generous; that is what would happen, otherwise I would take her. Perhaps...." he added, daringly, "m'sieu does not understand women?"

"Apparently not." Paul was thinking how little he understood the one woman. "Where is she now?"

Jean pointed: "You have not been out of her sight since you arrived."

"There is only one thing to say."

"And one to remember. We are in peace till her people decide on the next war; she and Onato know this; when a savage is silent it is not because he has nothing to say--even more with a woman. I am not

240

without observation. Before you came that girl was not allowed outside the stockade at Ville Marie: since then she could have escaped at any time with no chance of recapture--one might as well pursue a young deer. What held her here, m'sieu?"

"Jean, I suspect you of being a philosopher."

With this, Paul walked slowly across the fields. In one corner was a patch where he had planted pumpkin seeds to test the ground for melons the following year: like everything else they had flourished; great spheres the colour of pale gold lay glowing under a thatch of enormous leaves, now wilting; a pile of them made a squat pyramid ready for the root house. Onato was collecting a heap of dry vines for burning; the girl stood near him, arms slack, legs bare beneath a short cotton skirt that shewed the smooth curve of pliant thighs; she wore moccasins and a sort of loose deerskin skirt, cut deeply open at the neck, revealing the pale bronze of a firm young breast. Her eyes were black onyx, unfathomable.

He greeted the old man in his usual friendly manner, getting only a grunt in return, but Onato was shrewdly alert. When he looked at the girl, smiling, saying something about her good work, she did not reply, just opened and closed her hands, slowly, slowly. They were slim hands, strong, well-formed, with no marks of toil; the narrow nails had the shape of filberts, her arms were smooth, her teeth small, regular, very white like the teeth of a forest creature; her black hair, tightly braided in a long pigtail, gave the oval head a neat sleekness.

"You have done well," he said. "I thank you both."

No answer to this: she did not stir and he felt a little confused. Ridiculous! but it had to be met. She had the grace of a young panther, and for an instant he was tempted to take her in his arms and subdue her.

"Eri."

She gave the slightest nod.

"Will you marry Jean?" he spoke in his own tongue, watching her closely.

She understood: two tiny points woke in the onyx eyes as though little lamps were lit behind them, the slim fingers crooked, the brown breast gave a stormy heave--that was all.

"She says no," mumbled Onato, "she tell me she marry you--your woman--good girl--plenty children."

Paul shook his head: "Let her go to Jean--a good man--he will make her happy--I'll build her a house."

He went on suggesting what else he would do for them: it was all chaotic; he knew he sounded apologetic--apologetic to this savage virgin!--and felt the intensity of her gaze, hungry, desperate. It shouted at him. Here stood the eternal woman, insensible to everything save what pulsed in her half-tamed blood. But she spoke no word. With his own defences weakening, he made a gesture.

"That is the best thing; I will always be your friend."

With this, and not daring to look at her again, he went back to Jean, lit his pipe, and sat giving out little volcanic puffs.

"Well," he said, with a short laugh, "I've done my best for you, but it's no good."

"She is a proud one, that girl: I fear you have made enemies out of friends."

"Then I send them both back to the Governor."

"Perhaps it is best; we need little help after the snow comes, and slaves are scarce in Ville Marie, too scarce."

"Shall I tell them?"

"Not yet: it is best not to tell a savage too much too quickly. You did not mention that?"

"No."

"If you had, they might not be here tomorrow."

"I see. There's one house, Jean, where she should be useful, that of Madame Vicotte."

"But you told me she had brought her own servant from France."

"She did: at the same time there is much to do-- everything," he paused, chuckling, "I have it now; there's the woman for you, Jean, that Marie Dufaut: I've known her since I was a child."

"Of what age, m'sieu?"

"Short of forty, but still a bonne femme; you and she...."

Jean sent him a sharp glance; if his master had known Marie all his life, he must also have known madame. Curious she should have followed him to New France! Would this have anything to do with his silence about women--all women--till his return from Quebec?

"It sounds possible, that. This captain and his wife, what brought them out here?"

"Military duty."

"M'sieu has known them also before?"

"Yes."

"It is fortunate to have old friends so near; we have cabbages to spare--will madame buy them?"

Paul said nothing to that: when was it and where that someone joked about a pair of Castellon cabbages? Again he saw Jules lunching in a great gloomy room, looking politely bored, twisting his glass and suggesting that if a man wanted to transform himself it might best be done through a woman, or, better still several women. And the process, he reflected, had actually begun with the first woman doubtless in Jules' arms a few miles away, while close by waited the second. The system seemed to have points.

"This Marie Dufaut, she is a widow?" asked Jean, thoughtfully.

"Of a sort, yes: she had a child, but no husband; the child died at birth, when she came to nurse the infant daughter of the Comtesse Marbeau, now Madame Vicotte."

"That château on the hill above Castellon, eh?"

244

"While my farm lies just below," Paul rumbled on about things he had so far avoided except to Father Morel; his coat was off, shirt sleeves rolled up, and Jean fixed curious eyes on the familiar fine blue scar, four inches long, that made a threadlike line on the right forearm. An accident, Paul had explained when a pitchfork slid from a loaded hay-cart.

"M'sieu will return there some day?"

"If so, you should have the farm, but, no, I stay here. Nothing to go back for now."

He said this last as though to himself, then looked disconcerted, while Jean stared blankly at the glint of Lake St. Louis. One began to understand.

"Bien, m'sieu, I should be enchanted to own this farm." He strode off, large, easy, dependable.

Two hours passed, shadows lengthened, muted voices came from a distance in the rough speech of Brittany and Picardy, all colouring a daydream from which Paul made no effort to escape. He heard the invisible bells of Ville Marie, their tongues also familiar, with exactly the same jangled tone one knew in Castellon, and visualised the shining skull of the Abbé Callot at his wicket gate, but these chimes were perhaps also caught by circles of naked men with painted faces who sat round small fires counselling when next to strike. Life, he reflected, was a curious affair in which things--inanimate things--seemed more satisfactory than people. The farm, for instance; one could depend on the farm, but even at that what did life amount to? If one could eliminate Jacqueline and that passionate slip of a heathen girl with her firm brown breast, then perhaps----

At sunset Eri came in to prepare the meal; he heard her almost noiseless step in the kitchen. Fire crackled in the open hearth. They smelled cooking. When she set the table her eyes were quite calm, they looked negative, and when the two sat down she did not speak. Then she vanished, and Jean, whose expression was a little sly, could contain himself no longer.

"M'sieu, do you know I have been in Ville Marie but once since you left, to draw a load of grain to the mill; even then I stayed but long enough to see that those priests took no more than their share."

"Meaning you have earned a holiday?"

"Something like that."

"I agree. How long--and you'll want money?"

"Not much for one night--a few francs."

"One night!"

"I will be back for supper tomorrow; all I need is a shirt or two, a pair of strong pantalons and some tabac."

"As you wish." Paul dropped two louis d'or into the hard cupped palm, and felt relieved; then, meeting quizzical eyes: "Out with it, Jean."

"I thought you might ask me to take something from the farm for those friends of yours, a good cabbage for instance; their ménage may be difficult at first."

Paul blinked at him: "Not a bad idea; by all

means a cabbage, with anything else you like."

"Alors, a bottle of maple syrup, some peas for the soup, a sprig of lavender, an eel or two and...."

"Enough to begin with, and my compliments to the captain and madame; they are in a small house on the Rue St. Paul near this end."

"And mine to that Marie Dufaut," grinned Jean. "I will see to it."

Shouldering his musket, he went off in the direction of the root house, whistling "À la claire fontaine". Now it was growing dark and Paul lit a shallow, iron lamp, shaped like a lidded spoon, the wick protruding from its pointed lip. At first it smoked, then steadied, casting a reddish glow that flickered over log walls of peeled bark, stained a yellow brown, chinked with moss and white-washed clay. Tanned deerskins lay on the floor; the central table, heavily framed, had a thick top and strong square legs; an iron arm to carry kettles swung across the stone fireplace; books were stacked on shelves, prints of classical scenes tacked up unframed. A long-barrelled short-stocked musket rested on wooden pins, below it a brace of pistols, powderhorn and bullet pouch. His seat was a great rocking chair Jean had made for him. In the next room two bunks mattressed with meadow hay, two cupboards and little else. Beyond that another room, unused, and the kitchen where the fire was dying. It had a back door that Eri always used, beside it a second water barrel.

Paul sat smoking, glad to be alone, for it had been a long tiring day. Coming through Ville Marie, he had reported to the Governor the attempted ambuscade and Vaudreuil was disconcerted, this being the first word of Iroquois crossing the river; so, doubling the town guard, he sent rangers scouting in the direction of Trois Rivières. Privately, he would have liked to bring in soldiers from the forts about Lachine, but dared not, for if the southern tribes were really on the move, they would come from the area of Lake Champlain. Fort Frontenac had, he reckoned, by now been abandoned. What a mistake! And de Denonville was expected in Ville Marie before long.

An hour passed, and Paul barred both doors. In the back one he had cut a small slot, and behind that a hole in the sliding bar, so that one having the secret could open it from the outside with the right sized pin, and Eri could enter at any time to do her work. Finally he took musket and lamp to the middle room, and lay down. A dull ache had set up in his back where the arrow was cut out, and sleep seemed far away. It was so quiet tonight that he could hear a loon's chaotic laughter through the soft voice of rapids where Lake St. Louis plunged over bellowing self-dug caverns towards the pointed palisade of Ville Marie, and these two, the wary, black-backed white-breasted bird and the ceaseless note of the great river, one unearthly, untameable, the other cosmic and deep-throated, expressed as could nothing else the essential soul of this wilderness. It was all so unreal that he got up to swing open the arrow-proof shutter sealing his window, and make sure the farm was still there. It lay washed in moonlight, and he waited a moment, sucking in the cool air.

Sleep still evaded him, the sense of unreality persisted, and presently it seemed there were assembling within these log walls pale images of the human links in the chain that led from Castellon to Lachine: he could make out old Abbé Callot, smiling, assuring him that some day he would assert himself in deeds, not words: Jules, white-cheeked with fury, climbing from the lily-pond: Bishop Godet des Marais stood there just as he had before a great fireplace, puckering ascetic lips: he could distinguish de Maintenon, large, smooth, marble-faced, saying that she too knew what it meant to be misunderstood, and Father Poncet's scarred visage while white fingers dropped silk-meshed gold into his maimed hands: there was a girl probationer in the Ursuline hood: Father Morel was in the group kneeling as he so lately knelt at St. Denis before a dangling corpse; and Jacqueline as she looked that night in the batteau. All were there and of them all only two had now any part in his life, one ignoring his advances, the other inaccessible by his love. Dear Christ! but life was a lonely thing.

The air quivered a little; the apparitions dissolved, leaving tiny motes dancing in a bar of moonlight that bridged his bed and slanted on the hewn floor, and marking its dilatory passage he heard the slightest sound. Instantly on the alert, he peered through the shutter. Silence everywhere, darkness in the cabin of Onato, and nothing stirred. Moving stocking-footed to the other shutter, he could see other farms, grazing cattle, the Ville Marie road winding empty under the starry sky. Never had there been a more slumbrous night. He shook his head and laid down again, musket within reach.

Presently again the same ghost of sound, but more definite, and he knew it to be the sliding bar of the back door; but only four people knew the trick of that opening, so this must be Jean who had forgotten something, or changed his mind, and tried not to wake his master. More risky than wise, thought Paul, also he doubted whether Jean ever moved as quietly as this, so he waited, fresh-primed musket at his shoulder. Then very slowly the door opened.

It was Eri!

She had on moccasins and the short skirt, nothing else: as she saw him she looked straight into the muzzle of the gun, and gave a faint smile. She came on. Something caught in his throat; he leaned back, wordless, musket across his knees, and her eyes did not leave him.

Now she moved closer, halting just where the bar of light fell full on her smooth bronze body, a daughter of the night, baring her young breast to the goddess moon; the faint smile remained, the slim arms hung straight from naked supple shoulders, palms outward as in petition, and not a muscle stirred beneath the gold brown skin. No need for any words.

Paul felt a thrill in his own body; his heart faltered, he put the musket aside, while there came a mocking whisper that he had been a fool, a fool from the start, always searching for things beyond him, and it took this pagan virgin to show him how much of a fool when he dug himself into this pit of loneliness.

Then his great arms went out.

— IV —

"This is M'selle Marie Dufaut of Castellon?"

She looked round with a start, sleeves up, strong white arms in a tub of hot water: at the back door stood a large man with brown face, smiling brown eyes; he carried an Indian basket of woven grass. It bulged.

"Mon Dieu! I wish it were still Castellon. Who are you--how do you know?"

"Jean Prud'homme, lately of Rennes, but now content with New France. Bon jour, m'selle."

A neat touch that, she thought, her mood relaxing.

"Bon jour, m'sieu; and what do you do in this--this hole?"

"That question I frequently ask myself, but there is no answer. M'sieu Paul de Lorimier, my patron, sends this cabbage with his compliments to the Captain and Madame Vicotte. I have added a few other trifles."

Marie dried her hands, poked into the basket, and laughed: "The cabbage might itself have come from Castellon: I remember a field that...."

"You are not far wrong: my patron brought the seed with him."

"Then he was more sensible than some others:" she jerked her chin at the stuffed confusion of the house, "look at that mixture--it drives me demented with no room for a third of it. What is in the bottle?"

"Syrup, m'selle, syrup of a tree: in the spring time just before the snow goes you bleed the tree and...."

"What sort of a place has your patron?" she interrupted.

Jean straightened his shoulders. "The best farm in Canada for a young one: he is shewing these Canadians something. We live in comfort, and have two slaves."

"I could do with a slave myself," she said, promptly.

"Obviously, m'selle, but they are scarce. You have known m'sieur Paul a long time?"

"All my life, and an odd one he was too, but I expect happier here than at home. He is happy, eh?"

"He should be, having all a man needs, but I am not so sure."

At this they exchanged a glance of understanding: Marie felt lonely that morning, and it was good to chat with a fellow Breton. He looked like a bonhomme this man, much preferable to that old Larivière of Quebec. She wondered if he might be single.

"Sit down a moment; the Captain and Madame are lunching with the Governor. Your m'sieu Paul, you say, has all he needs?"

"So he assures me, but between ourselves...." here Jean's tone dropped to a companionable pitch, "he has changed while away; certainly enough happened to change anyone, but there is something else too. Often I think he is two men, of whom I know but one."

"The first chops off the hand of a savage so it drops in a batteau, and thinks nothing of it, eh? I saw that myself."

"Exactly! and the other...."

Marie gave him a shrewd glance, was satisfied with what she saw, unsealed a flask of red wine from Bordeaux, and filled a glass. Six weeks now since she had had a real talk with one of her own sort, so this visitor was undoubtedly sent from heaven. She heard a gurgle, as Jean wiped his full lips.

"Ah! that taste brings many things back; were there more of it here and less brandy it would be better for New France. Now, as to m'sieu Paul, I am his man; he is good to me, very good; he loves his farm but visits none in Ville Marie; he does not talk of France, and never of any woman; he writes and receives no letters. Why is that--is it a woman?"

"Does he strike you as one who cares much for women?" she asked, cautiously.

"No sign of it, but if he ever loves one he will never forget her. The slave-girl on our farm desires to be his concubine, but for her he is a block of ice from Lake St. Louis."

"One of these savages!" sniffed Marie.

"Certainly one of these savages, but any man in Ville Marie will look at her more than once, and she knows it. She is not bad, that Eri, and for a country wife very good indeed."

"Alors, there is another woman, but not for him."

"In Castellon?"

"In Ville Marie, taking lunch with the Governor: it is no secret in Castellon, they all know it, so why not you?" she chattered on, realising she was saying too much, but stirred at the same time by an odd sensation that somehow her loyalty had been shifted from Jules to Paul--which was ridiculous. She had had keen eyes on Jules of late, resented an attitude he made no effort to modify, and only last night was wakened in the small hours by Jacqueline crying softly to herself, which angered her greatly. The new life in a new country was starting all wrong, and she had found comfort that in the background moved the speechless Paul. There was a real man!

Jean didn't wink once while she talked, then gave his thigh a mighty slap:

"M'selle, now I know all--and nothing--trust me for that. My patron still loves madame?"

"He has never ceased, however little use it is."

"And madame perhaps begins to love him, eh?"

"You go too far, m'sieu; extract that nose of yours from her affairs."

"Pardon, but I was thinking only of him; it is hard for a man--or woman at that rate--to live alone over here. I myself have had too much of it."

He was so contrite, the brown eyes so charged with regret, that she softened at once.

"Alors, you are unmarried?"

"It is not my fault, I am only unfortunate; yet certainly there were temptations."

"The subject is not without interest," she said, suavely.

"Certainly not; and amongst those filles du Roi who have skipped ashore at Quebec there were, you will understand, girls of all sizes, shapes and complexions, tall and short, wide and narrow. Those most plump were of course chosen first."

"And why?"

"It was considered their size would make them less active, more likely to stay at home, also they keep a man warmer in winter. One, m'selle, attracted me strongly, who might have been your sister, a shade younger; had the thing been arranged the Government would have given me an ox, a cow, a pair of swine, a pair of fowls, a barrel of salted meat and eleven crowns in money."

"You lost a fortune," murmured Marie, with conviction, "was there no other?"

"One that made it very plain that--well--you understand, but her nose was sharp, her lips thin, her tongue long. Why should any man go to bed with a wasp's nest?"

"Why indeed, m'sieu?"

"I am glad we see the thing as it stands; other available women have either been too old," he glanced at her thick, dark hair, "or too lean," he noted the firm moulded body, "or of uncertain temper," he welcomed the broadening smile, "and there you have it."

Marie's pulse quickened; she thanked God she was neither lean nor old and harboured nothing of the hornet.

"A little more wine, m'sieu?"

"You are too kind: my patron unfortunately brought none with him."

"So in New France there is a desirable age for marriage?" she hazarded.

"Let us say between thirty and forty when a woman may still be young in heart, yet mature in sense; when she can still experience love, and has learned how to cook." His eyes twinkled over his glass. "I drink to her now wherever she is!"

How delightfully flustering, she thought, and certainly a bonhomme, this visitor, with his clear healthy skin, his humour and touch of daring, a personable fellow with nothing clumsy about him, and so sure of himself in a country where it was hard to be sure of anything. Suddenly a twinge of remorse took her; she was not, as he must assume, a virgin.

"All kinds of people here, eh? I have seen some queer ones already."

"Every kind you can imagine; some glad to escape from France with their heads on, others whom France is glad to shake off, but...." he added shrewdly, "what of that?"

"Why, m'sieu?"

"Arriving here, everyone begins over again, putting away the past like an old shirt. Of what use, I ask, is an old shirt?"

How sensible, she thought, now quite cheerful.

"Of course," he continued, looking into the clear sky, head back so that she saw the muscular throat, "in this season we have fine weather, but there is always the winter."

"Naturally the winter--what of it?"

"You will understand later: snow piles above the windows, one digs a tunnel to enter one's house, at night the trees crack with frost under the stars like the report of a musket, wind cries in chimney, wolves prowl at the forest edge, one cannot walk without raquettes, and...."

"What are raquettes?"

"Your education will come, m'selle. However, even then it is not so bad beside the fire with someone to talk across the hearth, but without that, mon Dieu! one feels solitary."

"There is your patron," said she, wickedly.

"Exactly, my patron, but does one confide in him as in a--forgive my tongue, m'selle, it runs too fast--it is doubtless that Burgundy. When you need more Castellon cabbage we have plenty."

She gave him a straight provocative look; an hour had passed in a flash, bringing a pleasurable tingle, and the bulbous image of Larivière faded forever: it was encouraging that the most attractive man she had seen in New France made no secret of his interest, which never would have happened in Castellon, where women were not at a premium. And that fireside picture, with snow above the windows, got under one's skin.

"No, m'sieu, you have not talked too much, though perhaps I have, so pray come again, and madame's thanks for the Castellon cabbage. You think we shall have much snow this winter?"

"Everything indicates it will be prodigious: the squirrels are far busier than last year; ground hemlock, food of the moose and deer, is thicker; berries of the mountain ash are double in quantity. Yes, a hard winter is coming, and for unfortunates like myself a lonely one. Au'voir, m'selle."

He strode off along the undulating plank-walk leading to the Place d'Armes, not once looking back.

In Lachine

Jules cast a cynical look at the cart that was to take him and his luggage to Fort Remy, a long, deep-bodied affair on small broad-tyred wheels, drawn by a yoke of oxen: the driver, Henri Bastelle of Trois Rivières, a bareheaded half-breed in leather pants, woollen shirt and leather sandals. He had a pigtail. In his hand a goad. The body of the cart was cushioned with wild meadow hay, across it lay short planks.

"Jacqueline!"

"Yes."

"Are you not ready yet?"

She came out in a moment, followed by Marie who gazed at the conveyance with fascination:

"Mon Dieu! quel équipage! Madame, be careful."

Jacqueline laughed: her "pannier" skirt was very full, of flowered silk, with a low-cut, laced and pointed bodice, her mantle of blue reaching to the elbows: her hat black, jaunty, three-cornered, the latest thing from Paris: she carried gloves of thin leather, a small muff, stockings white, shoes square-toed and low-heeled. Dressed exactly as at Versailles, eyes suspiciously bright, she paused for a moment as though for approval, but Jules said nothing.

"You do not like it--no?"

"Is it suitable--what if it rains?"

"Sometimes a woman puts on her best even if it does rain."

Jules shrugged.

"My friends in Quebec," she went on with a sort of cold brightness, "were more complimentary: I hope some officer at the fort will approve--and there's Paul."

"No time for that today."

"But I want to thank him; things have been coming for a fortnight."

"And no doubt will continue to come," he snapped, in a vile temper.

She coloured faintly, making no answer; she climbed up, spread her skirt and perched on a plank.

"What about you, Marie? I rather like this."

Marie, trying the plank, subsided into the hay; the driver, beside whom Jules took his place, gave a throaty grunt, a poke with his goad, and the big beasts, necks swaying under a massive double yoke, moved forward with a creaking of dry wood. Two miles an hour, thought Jules, disgustedly, what a devil of a turnout for an officer!

He was in bad mood that morning: two weeks now in Ville Marie, and already the house transformed;

how this had come about he did not know, having seen nothing of the process, but felt no wish to leave such increasing comfort and Marie's cooking. Pictures were on the wall, he slept on one of the feather mattresses that Marie vowed must cross the sea if she did; rugs from the Château Marbeau cloaking the rough flooring; clocks from Versailles; brocade curtains, ruthlessly cut to the size of the small windows; even a chaise longue that Jacqueline refused to abandon. The house promised to be the most attractive in the settlement.

Suddenly Jacqueline laughed out: "Jules, oh Jules! Why so sombre when this is all so funny."

"You find it so?"

"But isn't it?--You and I in our best, bumping about in this chariot: I'll make a drawing to send home. I know one person who'd be satisfied could she see us now."

"Who is that?"

"La Solidité," she tittered, "can't you be just a little more gay? It may be our last drive for some time."

The tone was light, but tears not far off. Desperately unhappy, she was making one last effort at reconciliation, longing to feel that he still loved her. It was unwise to bring in de Maintenon, but in the night she had lain awake for hours, divided in herself, hoping for his touch, pushing back vague fears that lurked in the dark, assuring herself she was making much out of little, and that Jules would be his old self again before he left. But he gave no gesture of affection, no word of regret, and dawn brought with it a revolt sharper than anything she had before experienced.

While Jules played lansquenet with officers at the corps de garde, she had slaved till her back ached, moved the two single beds side by side, scrubbed elbow to elbow with Marie, gone marketing in the Place d'Armes, carried unusable things up a steep ladder to the dark gabled attic, played the smiling hostess when Jules brought de Vaudreuil back to dinner without warning, and listened absorbed while the guest unburdened himself over the distressing condition of New France.

He was something of a draughtsman, and that evening made a map: it showed the Richelieu flowing up from the Champlain country, land of the Mohawks, towards the military seigneuries of Sorel, Chambly, Varennes and Verchères; there was a crooked string of great lakes where one might as well be at sea; the River Ottawa, along whose banks dwelt the friendly Hurons. There were strange names on that map, like la Famine, not far from the unfortunate Fort Frontenac: Lac St. Sacrament, that had a story of its own; Nyagarsh, the great Mohawk falls, six hundred toises high, leaping so far clear of the black cliffs that one might drive four oxen abreast beneath them; Michilimacinac, the old mission of Father Marquette, furthest inland point from which King Louis drew beaver pelts if the Iroquois did not seize and take them to the English.

It was clear while he talked that Vaudreuil had little confidence in de Denonville, who would shortly arrive in Ville Marie, and longed for the return of Frontenac. There, he vowed, was a man who never asked approval from the Church on acts of State. As for the Church, he held the Sulpitians were good men, good landlords, who did not object to the torture of prisoners for sound reasons, while the Jesuits were political agents as much as missionaries. He was dubious about these Jesuits, but admitted that they alone had any influence amongst the five Iroquois nations, and were entirely without fear. It was generally suspected that the Recollets, mendicant Franciscans, had been sent to Canada to balance the Jesuits' growing power, but Vaudreuil doubted if that would make any difference. How could one influence a band of ascetics who welcomed their own crucifixion on the chance of making a few red-skinned converts?

That evening the Chevalier talked with a freedom he seldom used, addressing himself more and more to Jacqueline; she, he decided, was the responsive one, and in his pocket was a letter arrived that day from Quebec, making mention of Captain and Madame Vicotte. It told him that this girl, the most recent mistress of the King, had been banished as the result of a royal tiff, but certainly she was not what he had expected; something about her made him feel younger; mistress or not, the honesty in her eyes could not be misread, and there was room for more of her sort in New France.

With compliments on the best dinner he had tasted for months, he took a curious glance at Jules, wondering what impression was made on so indifferent a subordinate, then assured Jacqueline he would do his best for her comfort, and send her the first available slave-girl. The captain's comfort, he decided, did not matter.

She had felt stimulated, encouraged, that evening, but later came depression.

The road they now followed presently bordered the rapids of St. Louis where spruce, pine and aromatic cedar stood moist and glistening, but soon they were crossing meadows where wild hay had been cut, and the air had a sweet sharp odour that gave the girl a nostalgic longing for home. Now the clearings became continuous; for the breadth of a half-mile from the shore no standing timber was left, and a long line of houses fronted the lake, their concave roofs thrust out to cover narrow verandahs the length of each building. There was a vista of farms, only four arpents wide but forty deep, log barns, clusters of black stumps, men, women and children scattered through the fields with oxen and cows: the settlement suggested an adventure, a kind of hastily arranged sortie with axe and fire against the solid rampart of forest to the north.

Further on she recognised Paul moving in slow irresistible fashion behind a plough, leaving dark furrows that curved between the stumps; his posture and great stature suggested peace, security, and in her present mood the sight of him was comforting. Near him an Indian girl spreading seed on ground ready for it, and two men splitting fence rails.

"Les voilà!" exclaimed Marie, eyes on Jean.

"Paul and his country wife," said Jules, cynically, "he has more sense than I gave him credit for. Domestic scene, eh?"

Jacqueline said nothing; no affair of hers, but it hurt, and the girl's arm had a smooth, graceful sweep. In comparison with the rest, the house was strongly built; it resembled a small fortress softened by a surrounding riot of flowers. They had seen few flowers in Canada.

"They've done a lot of work in a short time," she hazarded.

"He has nothing else to think of: in a few years

the place will swarm with brown children, and Paul be the go-between for French and savages."

"Is that Fort Remy?"

"Yes--what's the matter?"

"Nothing."

She meant--everything, for this six-mile journey might be the most momentous they had ever taken together, with nothing afterwards quite the same again, and the picture of Paul with his plough was part of some change now taking place on the chessboard of life. But Jules, obviously, didn't dream of anything like that; he simply did not need her any more--though that did not hurt as before--while Paul had taken this copper-coloured girl--which did hurt. What a blind fool she was!

The cart trundled toward the new farm; Paul, turning, saw them, waved a hand, spoke to his oxen, while Jean signalled with an axe flashing over his head.

"Do we stop, m'sieu?" asked Henri.

"No--go on; it will be late before madame gets back."

"You are right: I think a storm is coming."

He spoke truly: the air was growing oppressive, with no life in it, Lake St. Louis a brazen shield, no cloud as yet but a sort of leaden murkiness through which the forest wall looked unreal, while the whole countryside seemed to breathe deeply, then fall silent so that a dog's bark was startling. The cart was in motion again, Paul had resumed ploughing, the two men were piling rails, and only Eri stood as before,

265

motionless, staring.

"Our friend's country wife is admiring your clothes, Jacqueline: better avoid her; these people will steal anything."

"She can have some I don't want."

"Paul wouldn't like that--don't think of it."

"Are no wedding presents given in New France?" said she, in an odd tone.

Jules made no answer: Marie glanced sharply at her mistress, whose lips were tremulous, small hands twisting her gloves.

"That other man, Marie, your visitor, he looks very strong."

"He is a Hercules--he told me so: that little hill with one big tree on top--he made a great cellar underneath when m'sieu Paul was away; it is filled with everything to eat, enough for an army, so we shall not lack this winter. Mon Dieu! I am glad there is someone else from Castellon in this formidable place."

Jules frowned, Jacqueline laughed, the cart rumbled on its dislocating way. The houses they passed were empty: in the fields behind laboured the whole community, even children: infants lay sucking thumbs, sentries were posted at intervals, and a guard of regulars from neighbouring forts ranged in a thin line along the forest wall. Thus toiled the folk of Lachine, swarming from field to field as each lay bare: even in daytime it seemed they were never safe, so what of the night, wondered Jacqueline. And what of Jules with the hour drawing out, leaving them still divided? What if

Jules went off to fight the savages, and did not return. At this all her defences toppled.

"Voilà! Fort Remy!" Henri lifted his goad.

They saw it, standing in its own clearing close to the shore with its high rectangular fence of brown logs over which lifted the roofs of some small buildings. Towards the forest the timber had been felled and burned for some two hundred yards, leaving a great patch where pink firewood spread a gay blanket and there was no cover for attack. The heavy gate hung on massive posts; at each corner were guerites, or watch-towers, looking like pigeon cots; they overhung the base, commanding a clear view in two directions. Along the palisade were heads and shoulders of men parading the narrow platform that ran all round, ten feet above the ground. A soldier lounged at the entrance; others played boules with three-inch cannon balls on a strip of bare earth, cursing the black flies that danced at their sunburned necks; the fort baked in the now oppressive heat.

The sentry straightened at sight of a uniform in the cart, gave a salute, and Jules jumped down:

"The commandant is here?"

"Within, Captain; he expects you."

Signing to Jacqueline to wait, he disappeared and presently returned with Jean Despérè, his senior officer, a man some fifteen years older than himself, with dark hair and eyes, a large humorous mouth and small pointed beard. He gave Jacqueline a look of frank admiration.

"Madame, I am bewildered; is this Lachine or

Paris?"

"I wish it were Paris," she smiled "my husband thinks I am overdressed for the occasion."

"When he has been in New France a little longer, he will welcome a touch of the old one."

"Then I am acquitted. May I see the fort?"

"Certainly, such as it is."

"Better next time, with the commandant's permission," put in Jules, stiffly. "Rain is coming soon and hard."

Despérè glanced at his new subordinate, did not seem attracted, and gave a shrug:

"Madame, I am desolated, but only a soldier, not a husband. Captain, she is very welcome: one can't reach Ville Marie before these clouds break."

"Think nothing of it, sir," Jacqueline gave her fair head a toss, "and a good wife always obeys. My clothes, they do not matter. Jules must bring you to lunch soon."

"I should like that, also to hear the last news from home. Is the king still under the thumb of de Maintenon?"

"So I am told."

"What is she like, that woman?"

"I ... I have never seen her."

"And the king--he begins to look old, eh?"

"He looks very well, Commandant."

"Madame de Montespan--is it possible she has no successor?"

"None," said Jacqueline, her cheeks a little pink, "and, sir, my husband knows more of Paris and Versailles than I do, so count on him. Well, Jules, it is au revoir till when?"

She spoke lightly, brightly, with a kind of forced gaiety, and searching his face for what even now there was time to discover, found only a formal politeness veneering a suggestion of boredom.

"Till when? Well, perhaps not long. Commandant, what do you say?"

"Almost any day that suits madame. The Iroquois seem to have lost interest for the present ... there's no sign of them. Say one week from today."

She nodded, the two saluted, the cart gave a creak: she saw Jules vanish, the sentry prop himself against the palisade, the boule players were at it again with dubious glances at the sky. Suddenly she felt very lonely, her eyes began to burn, and long suppressed tears came with a rush. Marie watched for a moment, till calm returned.

"Chèrie, men are often such strange creatures, many are born like that; they are not touched by what touches others, so it does not do to worry. The captain is like that, so let him taste the fare of Fort Remy for a while; he will be his old self when you see him. And there is no danger."

"It wasn't the danger."

"I know, but it is not easy for him to be buried in that pile of logs."

"The commandant seems happy enough."

"Being a bachelor, why not?"

Jacqueline, grasping at straws, admitted there might be something in this, but found scant comfort: not before had it occurred that she might fail to attract and hold her husband, but the thing had happened, and the doubt it cast on her own powers stung more sharply than did Jules' coldness. If that had gone, what had she left? Had he never really loved her?

Unmindful of the rocking cart, she besieged herself with questions. For so short a time had they known each other, and love could not be tested before that fateful order from the Minister of War, nor had she discovered that around every husband and wife should be a curious unsubstantial casing, a sort of transparent wall that each must keep in repair, for it guards against wounds involuntarily inflicted by the other. Now that the discovery was made, she asked herself whether this fragile protection was lost, whether she was weakened by her quick instinctive surrenders to Jules' least desires, had become a supersensitive creature who made much out of little. Queer, she reflected, to be arguing in such a fashion for the first time in her life, bumping over a bush road in New France. Perhaps it was the cart that shook it loose in her, and this made her smile.

"Marie," she said, crisply, "in the last mile I have discovered something. I am a fool, and there is nothing to worry about--nothing. Also you and I are going to be soaked to the skin. Look at that!"

From the south climbed a great bank of cloud, massively dark, its edges ripped and jagged; one saw irregular rifts like tears in a blanket, behind which at an immense distance a pale green light blinked intermittently. This aerial shroud appeared to carry with it and impose on the breathless land a silence even more intense than before in which the notes of terrified birds and slow deep inhalations of the oxen sounded preternaturally loud.

The bank climbed very slowly, they could not measure its speed, there was only an imperceptible darkening of the air like the creeping onset of night, new bottomless rifts opened and closed as though they had been patched, while very far off sighed a low turbulent murmur as of waves on a rockbound coast, the faintly born threat of forces somewhere let loose. Little puffs of hot wind picked up small flurries of dust along the road, but elsewhere was no motion at all.

Fields were empty save for lines of yellow stooks ready for threshing; the folks of Lachine had scuttled to shelter, were closing their heavy shutters, while some stood on verandahs and watched the slow passage of the cart. Sentries and regulars, shouldering muskets, made for their quarters, deserting the forest wall that looked more impenetrable than ever.

"Madame, we shall certainly be half-drowned in a moment."

Jacqueline wanted to laugh; something about all this suited her mood; she had repaired that recently discovered enclosure of hers, and felt happier. Clothes didn't matter, and Jules must certainly be anxious, which would do him good.

271

Just then she saw Paul standing in front of his house, beckoning and waving; he raced towards them, Jean close behind, and Henri, with an exclamation, goaded his oxen into the side road that led past the farm of Pierre Barbarin to Paul's land.

Funny, thought Jacqueline, to watch Paul plunging towards her, arms doubled up, head pushed out, and all the funnier as she had never seen him run before; she was on the ground when he reached her, picked her up as though she weighed nothing, and made for the house. Jean had possession of Marie, the race began, and just as they gained shelter the black cloud split open with a crashing report, and forked lightning traced a pattern of coruscating light.

Paul, fastening the door, gave a grin:

"In time and no more; why didn't you stop before?"

"I'm glad we didn't," panted Jacqueline, "nor did I know you could run so fast. How long will this go on?"

"For hours--I hope. You had to cross the sea to enter my house for the first time, eh?"

This pleased her. He had never said anything like it before; she found satisfaction in being with him, and again that odd sense of security in his presence. Certainly a different Paul from the old one, no trace of his former awkwardness, and strikingly well suited to this new setting he had carved for himself.

"Well, Marie, we did the right thing after all; we seem more welcome here than at Fort Remy."

Marie lacked breath to answer: Paul looked

puzzled.

"Jules made us push back to Ville Marie," she explained. "Paul, how comfortable you are."

"Not bad," he nodded, "and mostly due to my friend Jean. Let me present him; the adoption took place in Quebec thee day I landed."

Jean, wrenching his gaze from Marie, touched his forelock: "Madame, I hope you liked our Castellon cabbages: as for this place--well--it is because when my patron came to New France he brought what was needed, nothing that was not."

"It didn't happen in our case, eh, Marie?"

Marie's bosom was still heaving, her cheeks flushed, she felt convinced that this gathering was the direct intervention of Providence, and nothing could have suited her better. Now she telegraphed to Jean, spread her skirts, settled on a bench and looked completely at home.

"Ah, there it comes!"

At last the real storm burst, preceded by a sharp drumming that deepened as they listened; the surcharged skies emitted a deluge carried in the breast of a driving gale; the whole heavens were dark; the great black canopy ripped to tatters and at once rebuilt to another just as ominous, while rain mixed with hail pelted in gouts: nothing could be heard but a universal clamour in which the sun presently set to booming salutes, leaving Lachine plunged in sodden obscurity.

Paul opened a shutter, peered out, shook his head. He lit the iron lamp and put candles on the mantel.

"This thing is bad: Jacqueline, no Ville Marie for you tonight; and the crops--what isn't gathered is ruined."

"But ... but we must."

"Why must?"

"Jules will be anxious, and...."

"Onato can go and tell him you're here and safe. As to sleeping, you two can have the house, we'll take the barn."

"Oh, no! Don't leave us, not tonight."

"God forbid!" ejaculated Marie, fervently. "I should not sleep one wink. It is simple, madame, with room for all."

"And this is not Castellon," put in Paul, quietly. "In any case the road is flooded; that cart would founder on the way."

"While for myself," volunteered Henri, "I sleep in the barn with my oxen; that road is now a river of itself."

"So you see...." smiled Paul.

Something in his voice, gentle, calm, assuring, went straight to the girl's heart; it was as though the new Paul was speaking, one she hadn't met before, quite different from the old one who used to hesitate and flounder, and of whom one could predict what he would do or say under given circumstances. And he still loved her, no doubt of that, but would never embarrass her; and there was Jean watching Marie with eyes that told the same story, so that she felt that they were there, the four of them, not altogether by chance.

"All right, just as you...."

She cut off abruptly, and Paul wheeled to see Eri behind him: in the press of storm none had heard the back door open; her appearance was silent as that of a spirit, black eyes wide, shining drops like diamonds in her hair, slender arms hanging straight. She stood gazing, saying nothing.

"His country wife," whispered Jacqueline to herself, having forgotten all about that.

Paul had a wave of discomfort, caught the expression of the woman he loved, and hesitated. He too had forgotten about that.

"So this is Eri, of whom I have heard," Jacqueline's manner was casual. "Paul, you have very good taste--can she cook--I am hungry?"

Paul gulped; he did not know what to make of this, or whether she cared at all, but any diversion was welcome. Marie, at Jean's crooked finger, retreated to the kitchen, while Eri only stood and stared.

"We will have supper, all of us," he said, sharply.

She gave him one extraordinary look, and went out.

"She understands French, Paul?"

"Yes--enough."

"There is another slave?"

"Onato, her grandfather."

"How long have you had them?"

"Since I came."

"Life is different out here, isn't it? What is it like to ... to have slaves?"

"Useful, that's all. Do you want one?"

"The Governor promised the next suitable," she answered, coolly, "but I don't expect anything like that."

"Then take her," he blurted.

At this her heart gave a silly leap, and all at once she pitied his confusion. Poor Paul! he had always meant so well; there was no art about him, only the old familiar bluntness which now, for some reason, she welcomed.

"Forgive me for something."

"For what?"

"I'll tell you another time. You meant what you said just now?"

"Certainly I meant it."

"Can she come with me tomorrow?"

"Why not?" said he, vastly relieved.

"I wish we had a house like this."

Never before had she expressed interest in anything of his, and it was on his tongue to offer the house here and now, or he would build her another like it, but should he venture that far he would never stop, so, mastering the profound joy it gave to have her there, he showed her cupboards, lockers, the wide chimney where one could smoke hams over a hardwood fire, the covered cistern with running water at the door, slits in the log walls, narrow outside and widening inwardly so that a marksman commanded every approach--they were like the old fire slits in the turrets of Château Marbeau, the rocking chair fashioned by Jean with his drawknife, the arrow-proof shutters, the classics and prints from the library at Castellon. Here was both house and fortress where a man might rest and read or fight for life.

The storm seemed to be subsiding; rain was less persistent, but the cannonade continued reverberating in caves of hollow blackness as though its ammunition were inexhaustible. Paul opened the front door, standing on the lower step so that her head came level with his. The outer darkness had weight and substance; they could see nothing except when intermittent flashes lifted the curtain for a fraction of time, exposing a line of low-roofed houses, snaky fences, drenched fields where patches of hail lay glistening; the houses looked unreal, imaginary like those of a mirage, phantom houses from which came ghosts by moonlight to gather fairy sheaves, and the only actual house in the world seemed to be the one that gave her shelter, the only living, breathing people herself and Paul. In this moment she felt closer to him, put a hand on his great shoulder:

"Forgive me for something else: I understand so

much better."

"There is nothing to forgive."

"That day when you and Jules fought by the Vilaine."

"When I did not fight," said he, grimly.

"Now I know why, but then I was a fool--I thought you a coward."

"To what am I indebted for this conversion?"

It was meant to hurt, it did hurt, but she never flinched. Certain things had to be said:

"To yourself, to what happened at St. Denis--and afterwards. I had to tell you. I've changed, Paul; so has Jules--everything except yourself. I'm glad of that; you mustn't change--ever."

"I don't know how."

At this she leaned forward and kissed him--once. He did not move.

"In hospital at Quebec they told me what was said of you and the king. I said it was not true."

"How did you know?"

"I just knew."

"You were right, Paul; it was never true."

He drew a long involuntary breath: "I wanted to

hear that--from you."

"Then everything between us is...."

"As you would have it."

He had stepped back into the old shell she knew he would maintain as long as they both lived.

— II —

Marie, Jean and Henri Bastelle talked, laughed and ate in the kitchen: Jacqueline and Paul were by the fire in the living room where maple logs gave a comforting blaze. The hail had ceased, but rain still fell, and the night was pitch black with random mutterings of thunder. Paul had lit his pipe: he sat in a little haze of smoke, looking thoughtful and content: Jacqueline balanced in the rocking-chair, lost in it, only her toes reaching the floor.

Paul had been talking about St. Denis and Father Morel with a freedom he had not used before; of Kondiaronk, about The Rat whose treachery might some day cost the colony dear, and how the Iroquois could never make peace until the king sent back from France the slaves trapped and shipped by the Governor two years ago. Today they were chained with convicts and Huguenots to the long sweeps of royal galleys.

"These people," he explained, "are wild forest children with wolfish hearts, whose eyes meet yours, but their thoughts are always their own. They have no fear of death, their braves glory in torture; some are our allies, but the scalp of a Frenchman is as precious as any other. There is no difference in scalps."

"What a country to live in!"

"If the English had invaded Brittany, would I not have fought?"

"Yes, but...."

"We are not wanted here; our brandy lights fires we can't extinguish. The English know better. I have heard of one living on a river called the Delaware; his name is Penn: he does not believe in fighting or brandy, makes no slaves, and keeps treaty with these animals. He is a preacher who writes books, and the savages there--it is called Queen Mary Land--never attack. Now if we did something like...."

Eri was at the door, her eyes like black pools at midnight.

"Is that all?" She spoke in Mohawk to him, but was staring hard at Jacqueline.

"For me, yes, but tomorrow you go with this woman to Ville Marie; now you belong to her. Understand?"

Jacqueline's brows went up. She looked at him quickly with a swift enquiry, then at the girl who waited, voiceless; her full lips quivered very slightly; her ebony eyes seemed to expand, the tips of the long slender fingers came together slowly, tightly.

"You say I go from here--you?"

Paul flushed. He was secretly hating himself, and put on a magisterial manner. True, this girl had come to him by night, but only once, and now the moment of parting had arrived. She meant nothing more to him;

280

there was nothing else but that they must part, and Eri would never tell--he knew her well enough for that, she wasn't that kind, so one must be patient and cautious, and give her a parting present, and quite easily she would find some courier des bois who would make her welcome. That was the way such things went in New France.

"Paul, are you explaining to her about me?"

"Yes."

"She does not like it."

Eri got every word of that, understood perfectly, but still made no sign. For the moment she had put them both aside, and was considering only herself, and when the black eyes sought Paul out of her remoteness, they exhibited no urgent appeal, no quick reproach, only a sort of helpless astonishment, as a child who begins to realise it has been hurt. Nothing could have affected him quite so much.

"Tomorrow," he spoke more gently, and again in Mohawk, "you go to Ville Marie, where you will be happy with this woman: also I will give you a present."

At once he knew he had made a mistake; her uncertainty vanished. Her lips stiffened and closed tightly, the large obsidian eyes narrowed, and she became a brown statue of strange wild dignity. Then, with no word at all, she turned swiftly, and they heard the back door bar give its dry familiar creak.

"What an odd creature!" murmured Jacqueline. "I'm a little afraid of her. You really think she will come?"

"Why not?" said he, curtly.

"I doubt it."

"But why?" he asked, secretly doubting it himself.

"It was too unexpected: she didn't anticipate anything like that; she changed even while you talked, and I could see her change. When she went out she was thinking about something quite different. Are they always like that?"

"It is as I told you. No one without Indian blood can ever enter their thoughts, and more often what they are really thinking has little to do with what they say. Any savage will take some idea aside and brood over it for weeks in silence."

"If it is like that I don't think I want her at all."

"Well, as you please; you can send her back to the Governor."

Jacqueline considered this for a moment: "Tell me something more. She and her grandfather have been here for a year, haven't they, living by themselves?"

"Yes."

"Then couldn't they have escaped any night if they had wanted to?"

"Any night."

"Why didn't they?"

"Well," said Paul, warily, being far from ready for

282

this, "it's simple enough if you think of it; she likes life here better than the bark shelters of her own people, she is better fed, better clothed, better housed. The Governor told me there was a risk of her escape, so," he concluded, heavily, "the only answer is that she didn't want to escape."

"I see," she said, "Yes, I suppose it must be that. I am tired now Paul, so is Marie."

"All right." He knocked out his pipe; "you and she take that room. Jean and I sleep here."

"On the floor?"

The difficult moment had passed. He breathed more easily, then he laughed: "The floor, yes, why not? It wouldn't be the first time: on a night like this a dry floor is welcome. The wind is changing again, so the storm may return; we are not done with it yet."

Marie stretched herself between Jean's blankets, put her head on Jean's pillow, stuffed with meadow hay, and yielded to a series of pleasurable reflections. It had, she decided, been a good day, infinitely better than promised at the outset. The captain was safely out of the way for the present, and she thanked God for relief from his critical, dissatisfied personality. M'sieu Paul was unquestionably in love with her mistress, and determined to get rid of that Indian slut, who would certainly be handed back to the Governor the instant they reached Ville Marie; so here was a vitally interesting state of affairs that gave scope to one's imagination. Also she was vividly aware of the presence only a few feet away of Jean Prud'homme, for whom again she thanked God even more fervently.

On the whole a most satisfactory evening, with

everything developing far more quickly than she had ever dared to hope. Henri, after a knowing wink, went off to crawl into the hay and enjoy the warmth of his oxen, for always, winter and summer, he slept beside them. Then Jean had barred the door, smiled in unmistakable fashion, sat close to her on the bench, and at once began, not foolishly or clumsily as a boy in love, but like a practical man who knew exactly what he wanted. When he talked, his arm was around her, his method of love-making assured and possessive. It suited her exactly. The fire sputtered, they drank tea seasoned with maple sugar, she pictured the long winter together, snow piled above the window sill, and a grateful procession of other evenings much like this but even more intimate.

In the middle of it, while she was feeling more young and romantic than in the last twenty years, and glowed with response, and he was swearing that nothing would ever change his devotion, and they were still young enough to raise a family that would be a credit to New France, she realised with a shock that now before it was too late, she must tell him something which, if she did not disclose it, he would assuredly discover for himself later on.

"Jean," she began unsteadily, "wait a minute, I have a confession to make."

"Chèrie, I am no priest."

"Nor do you resemble any priest I ever knew, but I must tell you. It was...." she hesitated, and went on stubbornly, "it was just about twenty years ago in Castellon when--when something happened."

"To you?" he asked, smoothly.

"Yes, to me."

"I should be greatly surprised if nothing ever happened to you in Castellon."

"But this is different--it is not--well...."

"Was it that you met a certain young man whose name does not matter at all to me?" he interrupted, grinning, "and, shall I continue?"

"You know?" she stammered, quite bewildered.

"Certainly I know, and from one whose word is good enough for me, also I know the result, which was the process of nature, also what happened to that result, so do not distress yourself. Was there anything else, another young man later on?"

"Jean!" Her arms went round his neck. "No, never, only the one. Who told you?"

"My patron: he said that--well--what he said was exactly my own thought in the matter, also he said that should you and I marry I might count myself a fortunate man. My little pigeon, can you imagine that I am the sort to be disturbed by a small affair that took place twenty years ago, perhaps amongst the cabbages in Castellon?"

At this she had cried a little, very happily, kissed him with great heartiness, felt inexpressibly young, and an hour passed on wings before she hugged him goodnight, hoped he would not find the floor too hard, stretched herself in his bed. Now with all that settled, and the future shining bright, she wondered, as often before, how she could leave her mistress, and Jean his patron. This had harassed them both, and she lay thinking about it when Jacqueline spoke in a half-whisper across the darkness:

"Marie, are you asleep?"

"No, far from it."

"So am I. Comfortable?"

"These blankets tickle the skin a little, do they not?"

"So do mine. It's funny, isn't it, to be here like this?"

"Yes, but fortunate: we are better off than at Fort Remy."

"I think so too. That Jean Prud'homme is a fine man. I like him."

"Yes, madame."

"Do you?"

"Very much." Her voice was husky.

Jacqueline laughed: "So much that you will be married?"

"Mon Dieu! How did you guess that?"

"It was not difficult, and such matters seem to move fast in this country: I think it is just right."

"I am glad, but you--you could not do...."

"Without you perhaps?"

"That is what came to us both; we have talked of it, often."

"Twenty years is a long time in one's life, Marie: I have had that out of yours, and the rest must be your own, so don't let that part of it worry you. We'll think everything over when we get back. Been a hard day, hasn't it?"

"Very fatiguing for you."

"This afternoon you were quite right about the captain. I see it now. He was only upset over the change, he'll be his old self before long."

"Yes, madame; he was just a little dejected: it is all so strange to him."

"And I'm not taking that Indian girl. I don't trust her."

"For myself I would be sorry to see her in my kitchen with a knife preparing potatoes," said Marie, promptly.

"Did you say anything to Jean about her?"

"A little."

"What did Jean think?"

"He said she was enamoured of m'sieu Paul, which was ridiculous."

"Quite ridiculous."

"And when he explained that to his patron, m'sieu Paul only laughed and asked if he himself desired the girl, for if so he could have her, but he declined. He is like that, is Jean," she added, contentedly.

"So she isn't m'sieu Paul's country wife at all--is that what he meant?"

"No, madame, certainly she isn't."

"Did she say anything to you or Jean when she went out tonight?"

"Not one word, nor did she even look at us--we might not have been there."

"Isn't it strange?"

"What?"

"Everything."

"Yes, it is strange, but of interest."

"If the captain had not happened to ride through Castellon last year and found m'sieu Paul talking to the Abbé Callot, I should not be in his bed in New France tonight, talking to you about an Indian girl. That is what I call strange."

"Certainly it is curious, but that is how things happen, so why trouble about the future, ever? Some little thing transpires, some small thing of no importance; alors, everything is turned about from that moment."

"I think you're right. What would the Countess

say could she see us now?"

"She would have a prostration, madame, and say nothing."

"Again you are right--she would. What time is it?"

"About one hour before midnight."

"And four in the morning at Castellon. Marie, you understood about that duel?"

"No, not to this day. I talked about it with old Joseph Pardou. He told me how he had watched m'sieu Paul practising that very morning in the orchard with m'sieu Fouquette, the notary, and how clumsy he was, and how his friend scolded him, but it seems he didn't take the thing seriously at all, as though he thought it a bit of play acting. It was the same when the two met, with the captain very skilful, the other still very clumsy. So, seeing he had no chance, m'sieu Paul threw down his weapon and walked away, while old Joseph, who could not believe his eyes, stood under the trees with the tears running down his face."

"And if I told you it was because he would not shed the blood of his friend?"

"Is that possible?"

"More than possible--it is true."

"In that case there was no braver man in France."

"I agree, and you had better tell Jean; it may help him to understand his master. Open the shutter a little. Can you see anything outside?"

Marie stood up, felt about in the dark and gave a wrench. The shutter, a heavy affair with thick leather hinges, fitted flush with the outer wall as it was meant to fit, leaving hardly a crack, and she tugged in vain.

"It is too tight, and, mon Dieu! What is that? Listen, listen!"

Her voice melted to a quaver, and died; Jacqueline's heart faltered, and in the same instant she heard Paul: he had come in without knocking, stood at the open door.

"Are you awake?" His tone was harsh, imperative.

She sprang up, trembling; he had lighted the candle; his eyes were like steel, behind him Jean, musket in hand. Jean looked hard at Marie, but did not speak, while through the night, cutting sharp across the drone of the wind, came the wild note that spread terror in the wilderness--the war-cry of the Iroquois!

— III —

That first single yell, it came from the voice of Oguntwae, The Hairy One, was repeated near and far, flung savagely amongst naked warriors from painted mouth to mouth. The shriek ran along the shore of Lake St. Louis, cushioned against the forest wall, and came back hollow with horror to be maintained so long, so distantly, that at once Paul knew the Iroquois were here at last, and in force. But in what force who could tell?

Under cover of the storm they had crossed the lake, avoided the forts, moved eastward with the wind: travelling as it were in the dark belly of the gale, their movements were unseen, and they made no sound. Then with pre-arranged strategy each sleeping house was surrounded by a ring of mortal enemies, and now at Oguntwae's signal they let loose their terrible assault.

The folk of Lachine, snatched from slumbers in which there was no vision of attack, awoke too late, the hour of travail had begun, and of that night Jacqueline afterwards retained but a confused jumble.

"Listen," said Paul, stiffly, his bulk looming huge above the light of a pinpoint flame; "you two must help us. There is no other chance, and even with that not much. Jacqueline, you will load for me: Marie do the same for Jean. I take the front of the house, he the back. Don't stand up. Sit on the floor. Jacqueline, use this candle. Set it close against the wall, away from the powder. Don't talk, don't do anything but load. Do you understand?"

She nodded mutely: Jean and Marie were already at the back, and the thing began. They heard intermittent shots, muffled and irregular, but not many, so it seemed that save for this house, Lachine had been utterly unprepared, and soon, mingled with the fierce chorus of war-cries, sounded the pitiful shrieks of those dragged from sleep for torture and butchery. Through the slit where Paul was already firing, Jacqueline saw scattered flames spring up in a scrimmage of wild, naked, demoniac figures; she heard the screams of women, the fierce agony of men, the pitiful wail of children.

There was no light in Paul's house save for the two candles at front and back. Jacqueline crouched in semi-darkness, her fingers blistered with hot barrels of musket and pistols, shaking with a palsy as she tilted the powder horn. Bullets rolled on the floor, the candle spluttered, a sharp acrid smell gradually filled the dwelling. Muscular bronze bodies were thrust against the house, and their cries, now so near--shocked her brain; but Paul, shooting steadily, never wavered; his cheek cuddled down to the brown stock, his finger crooked, the hot weapon was pushed at her, another snatched, while Mohawk, Seneca and Onondaga halted beneath his leaden defence.

In this stupefying hour, with hand and eye in strange automatic obedience, she wondered in a dazed way what had happened at Fort Remy, and why no succour arrived from there, or from any other of the forts. Where was Jules? Did he still live? Were the forts all overwhelmed? Was Ville Marie also doomed and were they all to die? Dimly she made out Paul's face, his eyes sunken, upper lip lifted like a mastiff's. Here in action was still another Paul, one she had never seen before, the fighter, the killer. He was firing coolly, carefully, giving a grim little sniff at each explosion, so that his nostrils were white and rigid. He wasted no powder. Always when he fired came a groan or a shout. Once he stopped, saw to it that both musket and pistols were loaded, then of a sudden threw open the front shutter. Instantly were framed two horrific faces, streaked with paint. Blazing into the shouting mouths, they became grotesquely disfigured, whereat he laughed, banged the shutter and bolted it.

She heard Jean's voice calling encouragement from the back, a voice singing in the murk, and so cheery that she took a little heart. One could not gauge how long this thing had lasted, but she did note that in front and at the back of the house were writhing mounds of dead and dying, and nothing in the world mattered any more, not even life, for she was now much too tired to want to live. France was a dream,

292

only a dream. Doubtless it would be all finished soon, perhaps as well this way as any other since life seemed to promise so little, and somehow she felt content that when the end came it should be with Paul, not Jules.

At this moment, he darted to the back of the house, spoke into Jean's ear, returned, and bent over her.

"If we can hold out one more hour, it will be dawn, and they will go. The house won't burn from outside--it's too wet. Understand?"

"And if we cannot hold out?"

"Then," he said, with a strange look, "they must never take us alive. You understand that, too?"

So it would end thus! She accepted it dully; her lips, moved, but she could not speak. Who could have dreamed that life might run itself down and close in such a fashion. Paul would shoot her--then himself. No other way out.

"If that comes, we go together," he went on, hoarsely. "The same with the others. You trust me?"

"Yes," she whispered. "It was always you-- always, never anyone else."

He said nothing more; his face was grimed with burned powder, but his eyes were now like stars, his hands quite steady. He looked almost happy.

Another hour dragged on, with firing both here and in the settlement becoming more intermittent, and finally it ceased altogether, there being no Frenchmen left elsewhere to lift a musket. Pillaged brandy was doing its work amongst the wild spawn of the forest. In traders' houses kegs of it had been discovered. The potent liquor dissipated Oguntwae's first careful plan of assault; warriors drinking the stuff like water were reeling about, their blood on fire, lusting for cruelty and torture, but no longer as formidable to the four who had survived thus far. More fires were lit, more unspeakable scenes enacted, while round they staggered, a painted ring lost to all sense of discipline or obedience. Most of the killing and scalping had been done so that there came a sort of satiety of sudden death, and now the lingering agony of those bound to stakes furnished a more gratifying spectacle. The night filled with choking wails gradually sinking to the last shudder of dissolution.

Finally a slow broadening of light, a cessation of all wind, an instinctive turning toward the forest palisade with dangling scalps and speechless prisoners reserved for the death that comes by inches, then dawn with stark revelation broadened over the settlement of Lachine.

Jacqueline lay on the floor, one hand under her cheek, the other grasping an empty powder horn; her eyes were closed and she hardly seemed to breathe. When Paul picked her up she gave a sigh, nestling like a child in his great arms, and for just a moment he gazed on the face he loved, weary, brave, smudged with black stains, the flaxen hair loose. He could see the faint pulse in the white throat. Well, he thought, together they had lifted the cup of death, signalled each other over its bitter rim, and still lived. So with this he must be content.

He laid her on his bed, replaced the blankets and turned away.

In the kitchen Jean had his arms round Marie, who was sobbing brokenly on his shoulder. He did not stir, but looked at her with burning eyes.

"Alors, it is finished, and we are still alive."

Paul nodded: "So far, yes, and they have gone; you are not hurt?"

"Thanks to God, not one little scratch, and you m'sieu?"

"As you see me, but I fear there are not many of us left in Lachine. Are you all right, Marie?"

She put her hands to her breast, breathing and pressing hard.

"Yes, m'sieu."

"Your mistress is asleep, so let her sleep. What about you?"

"No, I couldn't sleep."

"Jean and I are going out, but only for a short time. Take this pistol and keep watch. If you are alarmed, shoot, and we'll return. There is no danger at present. When we go outside, bar the door and open it to none but us on any account. Light the fire and boil tea. Is that all clear?"

"Yes," she said, steadily, "quite clear, but what about those poor...?"

"I know nothing yet. Come Jean."

The sun was halfway over the horizon when Paul

opened his door and with Jean stared about in a sort of dumb confusion. Dead Iroquois lay round his house in contorted attitudes; two with their faces blown away were propped against the log wall. Hard by a wounded Mohawk, ferocious in his last gasp, and covered with blood, began to crawl towards him on hands and knees. Paul crooked a finger, and Jean, drawing a knife, leaped on the man's shoulders, straddling him like a horse. The knife lifted. It took but a second, and cost no powder.

The air was still, and Lachine lay plunged in appalling silence. Up and down the shore wraiths of smoke climbed straight into the clear windless sky from mounds of half-consumed logs that yesterday had been houses, but were now only formless funeral pyres, and Paul caught again the repellent odour he had first known at Saint Denis. He glanced mutely at Jean, who shook his head.

"How many?"

"Only God knows," said the man, crossing himself.

"Let us see to Henri and the oxen first."

With muskets ready they went across to the barn; no fire had been laid there, though the place was stuffed with hay; it stood unscathed like an unlit torch, and Paul wondered why. The double doors swung free. Just inside Henri lay on his back, arms outstretched as though crucified, with three arrows in his breast, scalp ripped off, his crown a gory patch. Behind in a great lake of blood sprawled the four oxen with gaping throats.

"Eri--Onato," creaked Jean in a queer voice.

Warily they advanced to the cabin.

Nothing touched here, all in order, no sign of man or girl, they might have just left to work in the fields: Eri had taken nothing which was not hers, and this was the habitation of ghosts.

"She knew?" asked Paul, "you think she knew what was coming?"

"I think not, but who can say? Of course, she was angry with you--you told her to go to Ville Marie, and instead she escaped. For myself I...."

Paul made a gesture: Eri didn't matter now, and they went on slowly, across the farm of Pierre Barbarin, whose land lay between them and the Montreal road. No sign of Pierre, but Mathilde Barbarin lay there with her children as the men of Oguntwae had left them. So often had Paul watched those children at their play. Then, dumbly, on again, passing horror after horror, headless half-roasted babies, women from whose gaping bellies unborn infants had been torn, mutilated men whose crazed posture proclaimed what manner of death they had died. No houses were left, only stinking heaps of smouldering fire, and eastern Lachine existed no longer.

"How many?" groaned Paul, swallowing his vomit.

"I do not know, but more than one hundred souls were here yesterday, and I see no dead Iroquois."

He spoke truly--the dead were all white: and Oguntwae had lost but a fraction of his company.

"I do not understand why...." he paused,

stumbled, and could not continue.

"Why understand anything?" rasped Paul, "or what has happened to the forts?"

"The women, m'sieu, they must not see this."

"No, you're right, we'll go back now: we'll wait till...."

"Les voilà!" A file of regulars was visible coming towards them from the west, led by Despérè and Jules: at sight of Paul, Jules ran forward, his face grey:

"Jacqueline! Did you see her, did she reach Ville Marie?"

"No. They are both alive and well."

"God be thanked. Where--with you?"

"In my house." Paul jerked a thumb. "They took shelter as the storm broke--they could get no further-- they are safe, Jules, quite safe." Then, pausing, with the blood rushing to his face, he stormed savagely: "How is it that you and your men were not here? By God! you soldiers sleep soundly."

Jules, flushing, bit his lip; it was Despérè who answered; he looked old, tired, shocked, desperate, hopeless, like a man whose honour is lost.

"You may well ask, but we knew nothing, heard nothing, till one hour ago a fugitive reached the fort."

Paul gaped at him. "Lachine butchered, and you heard nothing!"

"No sound," said the officer, brokenly, "not one sound. The sentries were alert, I saw to that myself." He gazed about, eyes moist. "Dear Christ, do you think that...." then at Paul as though he had arrived from another world, "you, how did you escape from the middle of it? Are there no others?"

"We were ready, we fought. I found no others."

Silence gripped them all. The regulars were fingering muskets, waiting for orders, their eyes fixed on the forest line, well aware that even now Oguntwae and his warriors were not far off; a few coureurs des bois and Huron scouts were hunting about like dogs, running from wreckage to wreckage lest breath should linger in some unfortunate. A cock crowed, saluting the sun. Hail still lay here and there in quickly dwindling patches, pillars of smoke climbed steadily from the altars of sacrifice. This was the price paid by His Majesty Louis XIV, resplendent monarch of the Old World, for a few beaver skins from the new.

The moment became unendurable and of a sudden Jules gave a strangled sob:

"By God!" he gasped, "by God! let's go and do some killing ourselves. I can't stand this."

"Leave that to those who know how, and go to your wife," said Paul, sternly. "Jean," he spoke to the man for a moment in a low tone, then austerely and louder, "go with the Captain. Don't let the women come out here. Get them back to Ville Marie somehow, and at once." He glanced at Despérè, "A small escort of your men--you can help me there."

Jules without a word went off, running, four regulars behind him.

Paul looked after him, eyes hard: "The end is not yet; shall we bury some dead while we have time?"

— IV —

Three hours later Jean sat with Marie in her kitchen: there was food on the table and a bottle of wine. He looked at her with a grin and, to relieve his pent feelings, began to whistle.

"No, Jean, no--thank God she is asleep."

"And why not you?" He patted her shoulder.

"Presently, not yet. Eat something, you must be starved."

"I could eat an Iroquois alive, with his paint on. Will you do something for me?"

"But certainly, what?"

"Alors, stop thinking."

"Is that possible?"

"Listen to me. This thing has happened, it cannot be undone, so we must try and look ahead, you and I, otherwise you will never sleep."

"I am thinking just of you," she said, gently.

"Well, my little pigeon, here I am, with an excellent appetite."

"But for how long, Jean, how long? When do you return to that terrible farm?"

"Ah, I will tell you. For the present I do not return, but stay here. That was the order m'sieu Paul gave me privately as we left him this morning. Also the Marquis himself, whom God reward for his heart of a chicken, has ordered that no man leave Ville Marie."

"You--you stay near us?" she breathed.

"Exactly; it is the patron's wish till these troubles are over." He emptied his glass, laughed, knelt on the floor, and put his arms round her. "You hear that, my small brown partridge, till these troubles are over, which will not be tomorrow nor the next day either. I shall sleep on your doorstep, and there is nothing more to fear for either of you."

"But will m'sieu Paul stay out there alone? Madame will not like that."

"So I asked myself, too, but the look on his face did not encourage questions: he is a man of few words, that. As to the farm, the work is practically done for the winter."

"It is bad for him to live alone."

"From today he may be happier like that: he knows how it is between us, and told me that now I must consider only you and myself. You see, we have both fought beside the ones we loved best, and he sounds content. He might indeed give me the farm and return to France himself."

Their eyes met in understanding. They would never part again--that was quite clear. "Beside the ones we love best", she nodded to herself. But how much did Jean really know about his master?

"You remember," she said thoughtfully, "that not long ago I told you to extricate your nose from my mistress's affairs?"

"And at once the extraction was made--yes?"

"Because you were not far wrong that time, Jean. Your patron has loved madame since she was a child; all Castellon knew it, and when they were affianced the Captain came along...."

"There was trouble, eh?"

"Like something on the stage. At once my mistress transferred her affections, and finding them together m'sieu Paul hurled the Captain into a lily-pond at the Château Marbeau, and after that there was a duel, all very formal with Surgeon Larivière and his black bag in attendance, but in the middle of that duel, m'sieu Paul suddenly refused to fight any more with his friend, and was branded a coward, and soon afterwards came to Canada, and...."

"Where he brained a Mohawk at St. Denis, cut off the hand of a Seneca on the Saint Lawrence, and fought all night to save your mistress. That kind of coward, eh?"

"Exactly, that kind, and he still loves her for he can't help it, and in the bottom of her heart she loves him but does not know it yet, and will never tell him. That is the story of those two, and now do you understand it better?"

"Mon âme, when first I saw that man I said to myself, here is one behind whose eyes moves something his tongue will never betray, and I would like to work for this person. I had no doubt about that. Well,

I have worked, it has been good, all of it, and once done needed no doing again. He is like that. When we sat in the evening talking, it was always of the farm, the country, the savages, of France, and never of a woman, so I said to myself that certainly one was hidden away somewhere, and when only yesterday he carried your mistress from the ox wagon to the house, I had it all. Now what can we who have each other do for those two? They love, yet cannot speak. It is very sad, that."

"At present, nothing."

"Where is the Captain?"

"Set out for Fort Remy an hour ago with the four soldiers."

"I am sorry for that young man," murmured Jean, "he doesn't seem quite made for this country."

— V —

Jules, mud-bespattered and weary, found Despérè and Ensign de Liesseline eating their hearts out.

"We have just had word from the Governor," said the Ensign, bitterly, "who forbids any present pursuit. God, if it were only Frontenac!"

Jules, pacing like a caged tiger, tossed his head. He had reached the fort sick with what he saw on the way. There had only been a strained moment or two with Jacqueline when they embraced, clung for a moment, then drew apart regarding each other with foreign eyes: she mindful that she owed her life to Paul, not her husband, he tortured because he had slept while Paul fought. That bit deep.

She had looked death in the face since they last parted. She seemed older, translated in a night from the former vivacious, responsive Jacqueline to a young-old woman, just as lovely, but quite distant, whose eyes were sombre, at times dilated by visions that chilled her blood. In spite of all Jean could do or say she had seen too much on the weary road from Lachine.

Jules waited for what his seniors should decide.

"You say the Marquis has arrived?" grunted Despérè.

"He got to Ville Marie two days ago with his family from Quebec: now he confers with Vaudreuil and others. From what I hear they are of different minds in this affair."

"It is hard to have a weakling for a Governor." De Liesseline hammered the table in anger. "He will only say what he always says--wait--wait--wait."

"What do you say?" snapped Jules.

"My friend, do you fear death?"

"No, if others pay for it first."

"Have they not already paid?" interjected Despérè, "also you know nothing of forest warfare, you are new to this game."

"I am willing to learn, sir."

"Captain, I believe that. Also, the probability is

you will not lack for lessons, and--yes," he turned, "what is it?"

"Monsieur de Lorimier," said a soldier at the door. "He desires to see you."

"Bring him in. Well, sir, we three meet again under different circumstances. God! was that only yesterday?"

Paul stood his musket against the wall, and gave a nod: he did not seem to notice Jules.

"Commandant, I am come for information, and to offer my services."

"You fight all night, I doubt if you have eaten, and are ready to begin again?"

Paul shrugged: "Also I speak Mohawk."

Despérè waved a hand: "You are very welcome; be seated. How many Iroquois descended last night? Have you any idea?" Then in a strained tone: "You are about the only man who saw them."

"I myself saw but few, and they mostly remain," said Paul, calmly, "but I heard many. On the way here I passed a man, wounded, making for Ville Marie, who told me he was taken captive and escaped before dawn. He says there are fifteen hundred warriors within three miles of here at this moment."

"Fifteen hundred!"

"That was his story: he heard the names of Oguntwae, of Kondiaronk, The Rat, of...."

"That Huron reptile whom Denonville is fool enough to trust! What more?"

"Their canoes are now hidden in the woods. They will shortly cross the lake with nearly one hundred captives to be distributed to villages in the south. You know why."

"And we stay here talking," blazed Jules. "By God! I start alone if...." He had reached the door when Despérè sprang up, eyes flinty.

"Captain, you will await my orders or go under arrest. De Lorimier, you know these animals better than most of us, though you may not know my position. Vaudreuil sends word that no man shall leave this fort until the Marquis makes up his mind, which doubtless," he went on, acidly, "will take some time. Now what is in your head? The number of men at my disposal is 50 regulars, thirty friendly Hurons who may be worth while. Do you consider Ville Marie in danger?"

"No," said Paul, "the surprise is over; the Iroquois know that, and will not attack. Also at this moment there is probably quarrelling over the division of captives--there always is. It is of them I'm thinking."

"We are all thinking," groaned Despérè, "well?"

"Fifteen hundred savages will soon swallow what brandy was found in Lachine; after that it will be more difficult."

"You're right! what else?"

"If you take some men and attempt rescue, while Captain Vicotte takes others, I will go with him. There is a debt I must repay," he added, grimly. "I have some volunteers--will you join us?"

"When?"

"Now, at once, later will be too late."

"With all my heart I would, but my orders--my commission."

"Women will be tortured tonight, Commandant; perhaps you will hear them! I did before dawn--their wails came straight out of hell."

On Despérè's jaw the muscles were twitching; he glanced at Jules who stood tense as a bowstring, and into the calm features of the giant beside him, then he rapped out an oath.

"De Lorimier, I'd give my soul to go, but...."

Something welled up in Jules; it gripped his heart. He felt a quick pulse in his veins. Something was dying in him, something else being reborn. He looked Paul in the face, smiled as he had not smiled since that first day in Castellon, and put out his hand:

"Allons, you old cabbage, allons! What is a commission worth in this hole? It's time we did something together, and I too have a debt to pay."

— VI —

At the door of the Governor of Ville Marie stood a sentry of the regiment of Carignan, now two years in New France: inside, at a long, hewn table a group of stern-faced men sat in council with the Marquis of Denonville, Governor-General of Canada, recently arrived from Quebec.

Rigaud de Callières was there, wondering if his new, three-sided, twelve-foot stockade would stand an assault by the Indians; he thanked God that their triple timbers were green and could burn but slowly: Champigny, the King's intendant was there, a shrewd man ever mindful of what had happened at Fort Frontenac, and steering a cautious path between Church and State: Vaudreuil, commanding the King's troops in New France, now secretly dubious of what might have befallen his private trading post at Île des Tourtes, twenty miles upriver--he had no right to trade anywhere, and knew it, but reflected that de Denonville, whose wife carried on the same illegal activity in a room in the Château St. Louis, was in no position to protest. Messire Dollier de Casson, land comptroller for the Sulpitians--they owned the island of Ville Marie--in his worn soutane and well-thumbed crucifix, shuffled his sandalled feet, pondering whether God had at last lost patience with those wildcats of coureur des bois, his renegade children of the new world. Gédéon de Cathalogne, ensign of marines, engineer and architect, quiet-eyed, broad of brow, stared silently at the heavy axe-marked ceiling, asking himself what was the purpose of palisades if weak spirits dwelt within. He had his own reasons for doubting the courage of the Marquis. Subercase, youngest of them all, was itching to get back to his men in camp only a few miles from the stricken village, cursing himself for dallying in Ville Marie that storm-swept night. Charles le Moyne, Sieur de Châteauguay just across the river, a stiff-necked, fearless pioneer wise in the ways of the forest and its savage populace, reckoned that his seigneury must be bathed in blood like Lachine.

These men and others waited the word of the

Governor.

The Marquis' smooth, well-tended fingertips drummed the table while he sat torn by indecision. Never before was he gripped in so sore a strait. His wife and family were here in the beleaguered outpost, and he deplored the impulse that allowed them to follow from the security of Quebec; but when he started the skies were clear, Canada lazed under a broiling sun with no warning whisper from the woods. And he knew full well that did Frontenac, the old Onontio, sit in his chair New France would not be in her present peril.

From the Place d'Armes, whose trampled earth lay sodden with tempestuous rains, came shouts of sadistic gaiety where a circle of dancing Algonquins tortured three painted Iroquois captured just outside the stockade. Slow fire consumed the shrinking flesh, splinters were forced under their finger nails, aged squaws had severed their genitals, but in this ultimate agony no groan escaped them, their bodies yielded, but not the untamed spirit, the proud black eyes signalled only defiance. Coureurs des bois, hastening by, long matchlock rifles over their shoulders, with bullet pouches and powder horns, gave but a passing glance, more serious business being afoot. Tonsured priests from the seminary averted their gaze. This was not a clerical affair. From the twin towers of Notre Dame clanged a jangling hollow-throated tocsin; on the bastion guarding the heavy gate, a small cannon boomed alarm. There was a running to and fro of women and children amongst the log houses bordering the rutted Rue St. Paul; painted Hurons sharpened tomahawks beside conical teepees on the river bank, while a flash of paddles glinting downstream told of inhabitants racing to refuge from the settlement of Point aux Trembles. A light breeze fretted the St. Lawrence breathing over Île Ste Hélène and the green

309

slopes of Châteauguay, the skies were very high, very blue, and westward beyond white-fanged rapids that furrowed the river's wide expanse lifted a tenuous veil of pale grey smoke. It overhung the crucified parish of Lachine.

"Gentlemen," said the Marquis, in a voice ragged with anxiety, "the situation is bad: I share your hunger for revenge, but everything is at stake. We must be prudent. If we scatter our forces we may lose Ville Marie, and should that happen we lose all between here and Quebec. Vaudreuil, what troops have you--and where?"

"Here two hundred regulars, and we shall not lack for volunteers. In the four forts the garrisons are intact so far as we know, and Subercase...." here he glanced at the young man, who nodded, "has not less than two hundred under tents near Fort Remy."

"All apparently asleep!" snapped le Moyne.

Subercase flushed, thrust out his chin--and said nothing. He must redeem himself first. Over in France he had flung a challenge at le Moyne, but here things were different, one drew sword only against the Iroquois, or the English further south. Now Denonville, sensing the undercurrent, turned to le Moyne:

"Whence come these savages?"

"Doubtless by the Châteauguay River from the Five Nations: amongst those killed--there are not many--are Senecas, Oneidas and Mohawks."

"Spurred on by the English?"

"It is possible--I know not what to think." Then,

with a straight look, "Their memories are long, like their knives."

De Denonville frowned: no question what this implied, and he could not miss the reproach, but he passed it over:

"In that case your seigneury will have suffered."

"Perhaps; if so, some of them are still there," said le Moyne, grimly. "My seigneury must take care of itself."

His speech conveyed no courtesy, little sign of respect, but again Denonville ignored that. It was borne on him with deadening conviction that this sanguinary reaping was the inevitable harvest of his own treachery of two years past when he stretched the ringed hand of seeming friendship to the Iroquois at Fort Frontenac. The tale of that day and the shame of it ran like a flame through unmeasured forests: on the Illinois and Mississippi it was told by countless campfires where naked men smoked the bark of the red willow in pipes of carven soapstone; it had reached the furthest Great Lake where the Sleeping Manitou rests by the Bay of Thunder and the Ojibway boils water in vessels of birch-bark. That stain would never fade.

There was a lengthened pause. Dollier de Casson, man of God, who feared only God, wondered about the outlying forts, and how Soeur Sommilard, Sister of the Congregation, fared with her brood of French orphans and Huron children in the old presbytery at Remy. What of his missionaries scattered out beyond Bout de l'Île? Vaudreuil--he shot a glance at Vaudreuil--there seemed a good soldier but not long enough here to discard what he learned in Flanders and learn a new warfare against an enemy mostly invisible. Now there came the strangling death cry of a tortured Iroquois, and automatically he made the sign of the Cross. No time to baptize these captives and save their souls after the Algonquins began their deadly sport.

"What number of these fighting men?" asked the Marquis, suddenly.

Le Moyne lifted his broad shoulders. "Some say one thousand, others twice as many. Striking quickly--very quickly--with three hundred men we will blot them out if they have not taken to the forest. There was much trade brandy in Lachine, many will still be drunk: that is our best chance. Ville Marie is safe enough--they won't attack here--not in twenty years have I known them face a cannon."

"Champigny, your thought on this?"

The intendant, his civilian garb sober amongst the uniforms, parried the question: he knew the Marquis too well; his personal reports to Minister Louvois in Paris contained much of which the Governor was unaware; not so long ago he was used to pull the Marquis' chestnuts out of the fire, and his fingers still stung.

"Le sieur le Moyne knows best," said he. "My experience is nothing to his."

De Casson listened keenly, disturbed but not desperate, having seen so much of the reckless life of this new country. Was it, he ruminated, only twenty years ago that in a twelve-foot canoe he started with Sieur de la Salle and de Galinée on a mad search for waters that ran to the Pacific and China? and when a year later he came back defeated New France had laughed and called his starting point Lachine. Since then his mind had grown orderly, methodical; already he was compiling a history of Ville Marie; each grant of Sulpitian land needed his authority, so he loved the fat leagues he knew so well, and a map of Lachine, with its ribbon-like farms all running to the river, hung in his retentive brain. He did not love the Jesuits, but respected their courage. How many of those gaunt, weather-beaten apostles were lost to sight in distant forests, sleeping beside savages, rearing their barkroofed altars amongst naked pagans whose most fancied dish was the boiled flesh of a slaughtered foe? Of all at that table in this tragic hour de Casson could see furthest ahead, but this was a council of war, so he said nothing till de Denonville looked at him pointedly:

"Messire, you have not spoken."

"Your Excellency, why am I here except at your order?"

"You know the parishes on this land better than any man."

"It is to my reproach if I do not."

"Between Forts Cuilleries and La Présentation how many souls are there?"

"They come and go, so it is hard to say: now harvest is near, and most are at home, so there will be not less than three hundred and fifty, one half of them children, and without those in the forts."

"One hundred have been slain or captured," said the Marquis, gravely, "and the others...."

"Then in the name of God why sit here and talk?" creaked le Moyne, "those others--what of them?"

313

The Governor flushed. "Monsieur, I understand your heat, but here in Ville Marie are more than a thousand souls. What if the Iroquois break through?"

"I agree with le Moyne," put in Vaudreuil, firmly, "and no savage will attack a guarded fort. To catch them is another matter, like catching mosquitoes, but at least we can strike one blow; otherwise, seeing our weakness, they will send for thousands more, we shall be trapped here--and starve. Your Excellency, we can fight, but not starve."

Came a murmur of approval, and Denonville, unwilling further to expose himself, made a gesture:

"Monsieur Vaudreuil, you will do this, you will take fifty regulars and...."

"Fifty!"

"I said fifty regulars, thirty Hurons, with such officers as you desire as far as the camp of Subercase, then with his company you will visit the forts and see that all is well there, but draw no strength from them. That is imperative. Do not expose your men, and attempt no pursuit whatever into the forest. Champigny, we will attend to the defence of the town. At this hour tomorrow we will meet again, all of us. Gentlemen, to your duties!"

The room emptied in a flash: Vaudreuil, le Moyne and Subercase raced to the Place, assembled the regulars; there came the tramp of trained feet, excited yells of friendly savages brandishing tomahawks, now forgetful of three bronze figures that hung motionless on planted stakes. Subercase was wound up, his blood in tumult. Of a sudden he gave a great oath, plunged ahead, tore along the Rue St. Paul through mud and water. At his shout the western gate swung open, and his flying figure dwindled up the road to Lachine.

"That young man is a fool, but I like him," grinned le Moyne. "I am sorry I said what I did. You noticed the cautious Champigny?"

"He has reason for it. Le Moyne, we are all in hard case today--there is no reason for secrecy between us."

"That is true."

"Then listen! Yesterday Champigny divulged to me that the Marquis is considering the destruction of our fort at Cataraqui on the Niagara River: he thinks this may placate the Iroquois."

"Has he gone mad...? and with Frontenac on his way to Canada!"

"You may well ask."

"But that fort, it--it commands the route to the west! Cathalogne, you made those plans?"

"I did, with Villeneuve; it is a strong post; thirty men could hold it safely."

"There will be no West for us unless the Count arrives soon. Why in God's name did the King ever send that weakling here?"

"Ask the Jesuits," grunted Vaudreuil, "they do what they like with him, but they can't handle the Count. I don't understand those fellows. If this is a general rising," he jerked his head at the nearby forest, "what about them?--they're everywhere--even beyond

Michilimacinac."

"Safe enough," said le Moyne, "they don't trade--
no brandy in their canoes--they ask nothing--carry no
arms--just talk and teach. There's something queer
about them; they'll watch a Seneca gnaw the boiled leg
of a Huron, then baptise him. You cannot say they are
not brave--they are--a kind of bravery I have not.
You've seen them at work, eh, Cathalogne?"

They tramped on, long hip boots squelching into
the mud, long scabbards slapping their muscular thighs,
pistols in their belts. Behind came the regulars'
measured tread, next a line of Algonquins and Hurons,
then a fringe of coureurs des bois--these men walked
lightly on the ball of the foot, knees always a little bent;
they wore moccasins, leather pants and deerskin shirts,
tomahawks and long knives in their belts; some
affected the Indian scalp lock, and the braided hair fell
like a pigtail; their bodies rippled with supple muscle,
their movement was a sort of shockless glide, their
black eyes oscillated as though filmed with oil.

One mile out--two miles--past log-walled cabins,
steep-roofed to spill the snow, empty cabins, doors
shut, clucking hens, pecking, industrious. The tall green
corn stood five feet high, tips of its slender leaves
drooping like bent bayonets, but alive to the very tip,
and so green against the now oversignificant wall of
solid timber that screened, somewhere, its wild, blood-
drunk children. Little gashes opened in this wall where
Jean, Pierre, or Philippe had hacked out some straight,
clean bole for their building, but that made no impress
on the majestic front. It remained, threatening,
mysterious, unconquerable.

Now the road was populous like market-day in
peace time, dotted with lurching ox-carts, small-bodied,

big-wheeled, driven by inhabitants with goads, sharpened, merciless, carts with women, children, hasty piles of household treasures: the women looked wan, stricken, their eyes had a sort of flat blankness stamped there by sight of too great a horror; they sat on the floor of the carts with babes close, very close, in their arms. Other children played with rag dolls, chattering, laughing, on this their first visit to Ville Marie. The skirts of death had brushed close and left them untouched.

Vaudreuil and his men stepped aside to let the carts pass, and the farmers stared in a stunned silence pregnant with reproach, signalling that they were too late, the thing had happened, and where were they when it happened. The officers felt this, they could not escape it, so over them also fell a silence while cabin after cabin dropped slowly behind, the steaming earth sweated its moisture back into the hot, bright air with a cushioned roar from the tumbling rapids nearby.

They had passed Fort Cuilleries and the stockade of Remy was in sight with the head of the column abreast of a still smoking farmhouse, when they reached the first victim lying on his back, naked, scalped, hairy chest gaping with wounds.

Cathalogne bent over him.

"Pierre Perusseau--I know him--he was married, there were children--I don't know how many. Where are they?" He looked up and round: there was a smell of death and charred wood; a drove of horned cattle rested in a sea of blood, throats slit; a child's flannel nightshirt, hung on a cord between two trees, swayed in the light wind; his eyes met le Moyne's, "Let us get on, there are others who...." he choked, stammered.

"God knows," groaned le Moyne, "but we can do

317

nothing here."

Vaudreuil barked an order; they pushed on.

Fort Remy stood an arrowshot from the river, its southeast bastion was a loopholed, stone windmill whose patched sail revolved laggardly with no corn for the grinding that day: its palisade of pointed boles overlooked Lake St. Louis towards Beauharnois swimming in summer haze. Smoke climbed from stone chimneys laid in clay.

As Vaudreuil came up he heard a warning shot, the heavy gate opened, two officers appeared, Commandant Jean Despérè with Jean de la Liesseline, his Ensign.

"Chevalier," said Despérè, saluting, "we are glad to see you. What orders from the Governor?"

"Is all well here?" Vaudreuil spoke stiffly.

"Within--yes--we have not been attacked, but over there," he waved a hand, "it is a sad business. We have made but one patrol, our instructions being not to lose sight of the fort."

"You found...?"

"Work only for a priest, and a gravedigger!" There was a pause, men met the eyes of men, shared their shame, were averted; Vaudreuil's fingers had clamped over his swordhilt. "You have new orders, sir?" Despérè was panting as he said this, he looked thwarted, dangerous, like a straining hound, while Liesseline searched le Moyne's face with a dull comprehension. But that couldn't be true!

Vaudreuil jerked up his chin; a knot of soldiers was edging nearer pretending they heard nothing.

"We will talk in private, sir."

The two Jeans stood aside to let the others precede them. Safe enough here, thought Vaudreuil, looking about with interest: as much a village as a fort with its convent, presbytery, guardhouse, stable, barn, magazine, church, even its own cemetery. Across the square stalked a tall woman in black with a white border edging her hood, at her heels a queue of gabbling children, French, Algonquin and Huron: she glided on, eyes lowered, vanished into the presbytery.

"Sister Sommilard?"

"Yes."

"Messire de Casson was anxious about her." Vaudreuil unbuckled his sword, laid it on the guardroom table, looked Despérè full in the face, and spoke in a brusque, apologetic fashion: "You asked for orders--well--they are the same--no pursuit...." he glanced at le Moyne as though inviting support, "we protested--le Moyne pointed out our advantage while these devils were drunk--'twas no use--no pursuit, at least into the forest."

Despérè moved to a small window, stood gazing out, saying nothing, then he wheeled:

"That, sir, is all you bring us?"

"Not my orders, Commandant, not my orders."

"Dear Christ!" groaned the other man, "It happened...." he went on, "between midnight and sunrise; we heard nothing, saw nothing, 'twas all drowned in thunder and hail; 'twas like the dark killing of cattle, sheep and ... and lambs."

"Where did they land?"

"Near La Présentation--a black night."

"Blackest of all for New France. Subercase--have you seen Subercase?"

"This half hour past, running alone towards his camp: he would not stay; it may be he never reached it."

"Those orders apply to him also, and he knows it; he must hold his men. Send a patrol with word to that effect: send quickly."

Despérè strode out on the square, gave an order, came back: it seemed he had found something alleviating, now he was smiling a little, a hard smile with no mirth in it but some secret satisfaction.

"Gentlemen, will you follow me?"

He led them up on the firing platform where their plumed hats projected over the sharpened palisade like roosting birds: this platform ran all round the fort square except over the great gate, wider where it curved at the four bastions. Sentries were posted every forty feet and stood back saluting as the officers passed, looking hardest at Vaudreuil. Halfway along the west side Despérè halted, pointed:

"There! General, there!"

Round the slow curve of bay with its fringe of

sand stretched only desolation: the long line of cabins had shrunk to a row of steaming heaps, beside each stood a naked chimney, and the south wind sucked the foul breath of the heaps into gaping throats that yesterday were friendly hearths where the folk of Lachine sat and worked and played and sang the chansons of Old France. Fire was still visible where heavier beams lay unconsumed; small gay flames, transparent under the bright sun, played like corpse lights in the sordid ruins, nothing stirred except the smoke wreaths. How amiably had those cabins so lately ranged themselves, back to the north wind, venturing further and yet a little further from Ville Marie so that the furthest was the home of the latest exiled pioneer.

Two miles west a belt of timber marching to the shore cut off view of Fort Rolland, and in all that axe-won clearing only a single house had survived, squat, square, nearest the forest wall.

"That," said Despérè, his smile broadening to a grin, "is the home of one Paul de Lorimier, a Breton, a great giant of a farmer. He was a breath of life when he defied me."

"Defied you?"

"I met him a few hours ago, with him a Madame Vicotte, his servant, one Jean Prud'homme, and a serving woman."

"That lady was the king's mistress."

"If so, his Majesty is a man of taste. Captain Vicotte reported here for duty but yesterday; she came thus far with him, was caught in the storm. The two women spent the night with de Lorimier, and he made a good fight, that farmer. Now they are back in Ville

321

Marie."

"I will speak with Captain Vicotte."

"Chevalier, he is not here. De Lorimier, having disposed of the women, came to Remy swearing vengeance on the Iroquois, and with the captain followed in pursuit: there were other volunteers, some forty in all, all mad with rage at what they had seen. I could not stop them, but warned Monsieur Vicotte that this would cost him his commission."

"Perhaps more than that: where are they now?" asked le Moyne.

"God knows: it is forty against fifteen hundred."

Vaudreuil stared hard at the cabin:

"How many men have you here?"

"Fifty regulars, some thirty habitants, thirty Hurons."

"Assemble one half of these and come with me; no others must leave the fort till our return. We will pick up Subercase and his regulars, a few more from Fort Rolland, and see what we can do."

Despérè brightened at that; he passed the order; a sudden swirl of excitement spilled in the square; in a flash he was besieged by volunteers; all wanted the chance, all of them: he pushed his way through to de Liesseline, who stood frowning, knowing he was out of it.

"Jean, you with Sergeant Beloncle will remain in charge: should you be attacked fire a cannon."

Vaudreuil moved on, noting that Pierre Remy, Curé of Lachine, had taken station at the church door and was blessing them as they passed. A good Sulpitian, that Remy, with money of his own all spent on his scattered flock. Vaudreuil saluted him.

Now west for Fort Rolland with one solitary, unscathed cabin standing clear against the dark belt of forest. De Lorimier? Vicotte? who was it told him of these two fighting over a girl in Brittany and how de Lorimier, though wounded, lost courage in the middle of it and ran from the field of honour? Now he was chasing savages! And the girl? was it not a Madame Vicotte that Champigny had recently pointed out to him in the Château St. Louis as the King's late mistress, saying that de Maintenon had disposed of her just as in the case of de Montespan, only banished this one much further? So that was her sort! How far these last names seemed to take one, setting up a nostalgia in this haunted land where so much of the best blood of France was marooned. As for himself, the part he had taken in Denonville's treachery at Fort Frontenac had shamed him ever since. He was obeying orders, but that did not sweeten it. Two years of this life warring against painted savages who wore horns and tails was more than enough. Such his thoughts as he stepped out on the road of suffering.

They did not endure. The rutted trail of road clung to the shore; a few feet away smouldered those heaps, stumpy chimneys lifted their wide throats where the wives of Pierre, Simon, Philippe had smoked legs of pigs and whitefish from the rapids of Lachine. There was a smell of death, of charred timber, charred flesh, small charred things lately handled and loved. He found himself gaping at the body of a woman, sliced open; beside it a stake, pendant from the stake the singed corpse of an infant wrenched from the womb before its time, small scorched bones protruding. Fire, axe and knife had done their work. He groaned. Beside him Cathalogne and Despérè were breathing hard, nostrils compressed: behind him rose cries of fury, hoarse oaths. A settler, volunteer from the Parish of Verdun near Ville Marie, knew these folk of Lachine, mostly friends of his: as each holocaust was reached he would jerk out the names in a strident, nerve-shaken voice:

"Mon Dieu! c'est--non--mais oui c'est Jean Fagueret, le dit Petitbois! Nom de bon Dieu! voilà Perinne Filastreau--elle était mariée avec Simon Daveaux. Où soit il, le gros Simon? Regardez le petit Jean Baptiste! Sainte Vierge, embrassez ces pauvres!"

The dirge ran on; corpse after mutilated corpse he addressed, weeping, features convulsed: his poignant accents ran along the line lighting a bloodlust in those who caught them; they would halt, choke, stare forestward, jerk up their flintlocks with a click of hammers, then lower them foolishly. Hurons and Algonquins took it with outward indifference, black eyes unflinching, tongues silent, for not so long ago had they themselves taken bloody toll of the palefaced intruder. Here too they caught a thousand signs that no Frenchman would ever discover, and this affair was to them significant of just one thing--the power of the Iroquois, their ancient enemy. Why fight with the French if the French were so quickly and easily destroyed?

Sickened by what he saw, Vaudreuil hastened on under the mocking benignity of the August sun, when Cathalogne gave an exclamation:

"Chevalier, there is our friend. He moves fast."

Half a mile ahead an open line of regulars

deployed across the abandoned farms, it opened, closed, curved, bulged, straightened; came a faint shouting with random shots and flash of swords; its right flank brushed the fringe of solid timber, its left held the Lachine road. At sight of it a murmur rippled the length of Vaudreuil's loose column, his own blood quickened. Then duty, obedience, took its grip:

"Trumpeter, sound the recall."

The order blared out, shrill, clear; the extended line slowed, halted, opened, scores of faces turned eastwards as a figure ran towards Vaudreuil stumbling as it ran. It was young Subercase, eyes flashing, his sword scarlet; he was excited, tingling, his cheeks had the colour of a rosy child. He pulled up, swept the other officers with a lightning glance, saluted.

"Chevalier, many of them are there ambushed in that belt, they swarm like bees, many are drunk. We have killed a few stragglers. Strike now and we have them."

Vaudreuil shook his head: "You heard the order."

"By God! we all heard it, but what of that? I have seen...."

"I also have seen, monsieur." The voice was leaden with regret, "but you...."

"General!" stormed the young man, "I resign my commission--here--now--this moment I am free."

"Your resignation is not accepted. France is at war."

Subercase's gorge rose, he stiffened defiantly;

again his bright eyes sought his friends--surely they were with him. Then the grave tones of Vaudreuil for whom speech was hard to find:

"Lieutenant, halt your men till they are joined by mine...." pausing, he laid a hand on the rigid sword arm, gave a comprehending look, "there is no alternative. I understand what you feel ... I share it ... but France needs you."

No alternative!--with Denonville safe in Ville Marie thinking first of his own skin! No alternative! with sprawling pagans infesting the woods, fit stuff for slaughter. Searching the strong features, he perceived only resolution and regret. The fire died in his eyes, he saluted, went back to his men, choked out the order, and they stood, muttering, disheartened, till the column drew ahead, then fell in at the rear. They could make nothing of it--there crouched the enemy--here was the commandant of the King's troops in all France! And yet...!

Now along the shore to Fort Rolland, eleven miles from Ville Marie; near one bastion a pile of bodies on the farm of André Lapin, but of André himself--nothing. Then César Marin, Sieur de la Massiere came out with Gabriel Dumont, his lieutenant, telling the same story of darkness, storm, hail and ignorance. The belly of that storm was charged with torment; they had known nothing. No attack on Rolland.

Marin pointed to La Présentation two miles away beyond more formless ruins: in the fitful wind some of these had recoalesced, shewing a red core of hot coals.

"My scouts say they are still moving in the woods close by the fort."

"You have no idea of their numbers?"

"Chevalier, none. My orders were to remain here."

"You have seen many?"

"Hardly one."

"Did a Captain Vicotte with others pass this way?"

"It may have been them I saw in midforenoon, some forty in all."

"Since then?"

"Chevalier, nothing."

"Exactly where did you see them?"

"They moved along the edge of the forest--there; some one, a big man not in uniform, seemed to be giving orders, which puzzled me. Then they went in. We heard no firing."

"Too small a company for that work," frowned le Moyne, "we may add forty to the missing."

Vaudreuil stood in hard case: nearly four hundred restive, vengeful men at his back, and orders against him! It was now mid-afternoon: three hours at the least to regain Ville Marie. Every drop of his soldier blood was shouting at him, and for a moment he wavered, his officers watching, wordless, straining like hounds. He thought of Châteauguay and Beauharnois across the lake. How did they fare? Of Bout de l'Île and Point aux Trembles down river. If he did attack now, and if night caught him in pursuit, what then? He could hear nothing but men breathing as they stared at the dark line where a copper-coloured, stinging hive lay shrouded in greenery.

"Commandant, La Présentation has not been attacked?"

"No, nor will it. All settlers who survive are within that stockade of mine. We can hold out for months."

That pushed Vaudreuil to decision: he turned his column about, faces to Ville Marie. It moved eastwards, loath to stir. Then, near Remy, it halted, mesmerised.

The church bell was tolling: on a stricken farm stood Pierre Remy in cassock, surplice and stole, on his breast glowed a golden cross. With book, candlesticks and holy water his acolytes were gathered round him. To the threatening forest wall, to the men at arms, he gave no attention. With tender care he had assembled torn bodies, the martyred children of his parish, was wrapping them in fair linen, laying them in shallow graves till the cemetery of Remy should later receive them. His weather-beaten face was upturned, his eyes burned with holy zeal, his voice, burdened with love and sorrow, sounded over the tenantless fields, over the standing corn:

"OSTENDE NOBIS DOMINE MISERICORDIAM TUAM."

Sortie

The forest was silent, empty, so empty that imagination could not picture an army of Iroquois sheltering nearby in its damp recesses: almost they must have incorporated themselves in its immortal growth, have relinquished their human shape and even now be listening, watching, waiting, in the guise of tree, bush and moss-grown stump.

The range of vision constantly varied; at one moment in groves of maple and birch the eye followed narrow avenues radiating like the spokes of a wheel where slanting beams fell athwart the vacant floor as cathedral aisles are vacated by departing worshippers; then would come patches where draperies of grey moss feathery and unsubstantial to the touch hung in stark funereal folds, while thickets of spruce and cedar, peopled with darkling shadow, looked deadly and imminent.

Carrying a musket, Paul walked at the head of the column, Jules next, armed with sword and pistols. Paul stepped lightly for all his bulk, leaning a little forward, he had the springy tread of a woodsman. Jules, lighter, more agile, tried to imitate this, and found it difficult. Often he would catch himself thinking not about Iroquois but the last time he had looked at that broad back on the banks of the Vilaine, and cursed it, screaming "Coward! poltroon!", and how Paul kept on walking just as he did now. At times he would raise a hand, halt, and the whole line stiffened, forty pairs of eyes running this way and that for some sign of what none desired to discover.

Coureurs des bois and a few Hurons were out scouting ahead and on either side; no sound came from them, but rarely was there sight of a lithe figure in fringed deerskin tunic and leather cap, while at intervals drifted the low flute-like hoot of the brown owl signalling that so far the Iroquois trail had not been found.

Jules had forty men, carrying, with their arms, three days' rations and small axes. Leaving Fort Remy he had taken his course parallel with Lake Saint Louis and a mile distant, with flanking scouts in constant touch.

The column progressed slowly with infinite caution: two hours out now, only two miles from Fort Rolland, and still no contact with the Iroquois.

The light began to fade; a marked withdrawal of day rather than the onset of night, so that imperceptibly the forest became blurred; it lost distinction; a sort of closure took place, an indrawing encasement that confined the column to the ground where it actually stood, while the surrounding timber merged and fluxed into an opaque wall that one almost touched. Simultaneously, the human owls ceased their hooting, the scouts drew in, and further advance was too perilous. At this moment a coureur des bois appeared immediately in front of Paul and pointed.

"They are not far off now," he whispered, "look at this--he still lives."

Ten feet away the naked body of a man gleamed palely in the half-light; like Henri, he was on his back, arms out, forming a cross, breast and belly mutilated, his eyelids severed, his crown scalped. The torn chest still stirred, but very faintly, the defenceless eyes had gathered a slight film. He rested speechless, dying, a bloody token from the Iroquois.

Paul bent over, stared, and shook his head: "Pierre Barbarin, farmer of Lachine," he said in a low voice. "The next house from me."

Even now the man caught it, his lips moved, the torn chest expanded, he heaved one last tremulous breath.

"Ma femme--mes enfants--les sauvez!" he murmured, then the breath escaped, he shivered and died.

Paul, crossing himself, turned to Jules, whose face was blanched.

"We can do nothing now, nothing but stay where we are till the moon comes up and there is some light. Let every man lie down where he stands. No talking."

Jules nodded with a dumb thankfulness that it did not fall to him to direct this hazardous enterprise, then the word went swiftly back, for already the soldiers were fingering muskets, peering about with sharpening uncertainty. At first they knew nothing of Pierre, but presently the news travelled from mouth to tense ear as the whole line stretched in rigid discomfort, and in the silence that enfolded them the pattering of small forest creatures was magnified to a tocsin of alarm.

"Unless we surprise them, we are lost," whispered Paul. "They must not surprise us, and are not half a mile off. If presently you hear sad sounds, it cannot be helped."

It was hard to wait, harder than the darkness. The cloak of night gathered and fell with no twilight, only a short, changeful interlude after the sun set; then the real night came down with a rush, while the file of French and Hurons lay motionless on a carpet of sodden leaves, priming the pans of long-barrelled muskets covered against the damp; there was a sense of exposure, of loneliness, a man would put out a hand in the gloom to make sure of his neighbour, and presently receive the same questing touch; they heard each other breathe, swallow rising spittle, the creak of a leather strap when stiff limbs were stretched, a faint stir of wind in branches overhead, the drip-drip from a saturated spruce.

Jules lay beside Paul, elbows in contact, with the dead man within reach, and the presence of this poor raw corpse lying so peacefully after the storm was almost vocal. It had done what it could in life and failed, and now wanted to know what these newcomers proposed; it suggested that it had time enough to await the answer, but its wounds proclaimed there was but little time for others.

Jules could not divert his eyes: whispering to Paul he would keep watching it, would wrench away, explore the phantom forest, strain his ears, and inevitably be drawn back like iron to a magnet.

For Paul he had now a certain envy, or perhaps rather for Paul's attitude in this business. The decision made, Paul automatically put all else out of his head, his brain was busy, his body alert; better than anyone he knew that survival hung on a hair, but he looked unruffled. Obviously he was made for moments like this, and only thus might be judged. Certainly he was no coward, this Castellon cabbage, and an apology was due him. But not here.

In the shadows a coureur des bois took form, squirming on his belly like a lizard, moving fractionally, almost in sections; one shoulder came forward, a pause, then the other. His head lifted so they could see his eyes glisten. Lying flat he put his mouth to Paul's ear, and Paul nodded.

"They are within a few hundred yards," he whispered again to Jules. "Their scouts are out too. This man nearly touched one. The woods are alive. They have prisoners but are suspicious of pursuit, so there may be no torturing tonight. That business is too noisy. Send back word that no man makes a sound, and they see to their priming. If you look more to the left, there is something."

The word went back, a soft shuffling took place down the line, while Jules, straining his eyes, caught a red blink from the very heart of the forest, a small focus of light like a tiny sanguinary eye, too red to be a firefly.

"One of their war parties," breathed Paul. "The others are near. They are too quiet for my taste, and will not move before dawn. The prisoners are gagged."

Jules pressed his arm with a chaotic feeling that there was something unreal and fantastic about this, and he would shortly wake up and smile. Ridiculous that he, late captain in the Bodyguard of his most puissant majesty Louis XIV, whom may God for ever blast, should be sprawled in the wet leaves on his stomach within touch of a butchered Frenchman till Paul de Lorimier, recently of Castellon, permitted him to stand up.

There was no sense in this. It didn't get one anywhere, but just at that point what was left of Pierre

Barbarin seemed to lift a white arm and signal that though there was little sense, there certainly existed a sound reason, and he himself was part of it, and presently there came to Jules for the very first time the novel conviction that in spite of affairs in general, he might not have long to live, whereat Pierre almost gave a definite nod of agreement. "No, not long now," he appeared to convey, "and I know what I'm talking about."

At this Jules' throat contracted, his lips felt dry and hot; he was licking them when in the rear a musket went off like a thunder-clap.

Then a paralysing silence, in which a regular gave a sort of puppy whimper. Jules' scalp prickled, and he heard Paul gasp.

The whimper did the rest. Down that recumbent line the tension snapped like an over-taut bowstring. There followed a confusion of hoarse whimpers, the lifting of flint-shod hammers; shadowy forms heaved up, creeping, kneeling, even standing, while shrill from all around rose the piercing yell of Iroquois scouts.

"Lie still! Lie still!" snarled Paul, crushing Jules to the earth.

It was useless. Taxed nature could endure no more; it broke under the tension of inaction. The line was dislocated, ceased to exist. Some crawled to trees, setting their backs against the bark, others tried the shelter of fallen logs, so that in a moment there was no line left, no order, no cohesion: the cries of naked scouts were repeated near and far, the woods rang with a yapping chorus that spread north to the edge of Oguntwae's invisible hordes.

"What next?" muttered Jules, in a strange voice.

The next was a pale gleam from the horned tip of a rising moon, and with an arrow singing through the dark; it rattled against a trunk and stood quivering in the ribs of Pierre Barbarin, three feet from Jules' face. Then scattered gunshots.

The light spread a little, the forest remarshalled its tenuous battalions. One could see fifty yards, soon a hundred: now along the boundaries of light the Iroquois appeared, a ring of them, always in motion; one would pause a second, a bow twanged, and as if magic were at work there again remained only a tree, and no man. The volunteers, confused, disconcerted, were firing at random. Sometimes shots stabbing the dark roused an answering scream of agony, but more often a flight of arrows sang back to bring a groan from a French throat with a futile plucking at winged death.

Slowly the ring contracted till standing timber and fallen logs gave no protection, but slender shafted barbs bit deep into backs and buttocks. Men pitched forward, curved fingers clawing, to be straddled by sinewy bronze figures with knives in their teeth. A circular sweep, a wrench, and a scalp came free.

"This is the end," whispered Jules, his pistols levelled.

"I think so--there--on the right, quick!"

Paul fired as he spoke. The pistols barked. Jules reloaded swiftly, hands quite steady. They were his pet pistols: Jacqueline had often polished them, admiring the delicate mechanism, the arabesque tracery on their barrels.

The tumult began to subside; only a spasmodic report split the night, the coureur des bois had scrambled off to be caught and killed twenty yards away, and excepting the two it seemed that not a man still lived, save where inarticulate sounds came from a few who could not stir.

Paul had lifted his arm to reload when a flying axe caught him in the head and he dropped limply.

Jules stooped over with no particular fear for himself; the moment had gone past all fear, but with the sudden recalling of a lot of things he had meant to say to Paul, things it was only fair to say, and now it was too late. Paul would never know, and the shock of it struck Jules with such a wave that he was filled with recklessness and did not wish to live any longer, so, standing straight, he shouted loudly, fired at two savages who raced at him, then threw the pistols away.

In the next moment one arrow went clean through his shoulder, another sank deep into his groin. He looked stupidly at this in a sort of surprise, gave it a dazed twitch, and remembered nothing more.

Hope

Father Dollier de Casson, Superior of Saint Sulpice, sat talking to Jacqueline. Three weeks now since the foolhardy sortie from Fort Remy set out, and no whisper came back from the silent forest that swallowed them till a Huron scout reported finding the mutilated bodies of forty men only three miles beyond Fort Rolland, but of Captain Vicotte, and Paul de Lorimier, farmer of Lachine, there was no trace. Ravens and timber wolves, said the scout, had been at work, and soon there would be little left to bury.

Ville Marie, still numbed with shock, stood on terrified tiptoe, though a little fortified since Vaudreuil's second patrol had killed a few Iroquois and returned in safety, while de Denonville, stunned by the deadly result of his own vacillating policy, marked time as before.

Thanks to the activities of Vaudreuil, the country in the immediate vicinity of Ville Marie was now clear, that much was certain, but men only ventured past the ghastly relics of Lachine in armed parties. What crops stood ungarnered on that fatal night were ruined by hail, the stored grain burnt with those who reaped it, hundreds of settlers from nearby and defenceless seigneuries had flocked within the town's palisade, hastily strengthened by Jacques Bizard. Little work was being done at Chambly, Sorel, or Trois Rivières, New France had lost courage, and men felt in their hearts that salvation lay in the return of one leader and one only. Frontenac!

A few in that frightened community had kept their heads, amongst them the giant Superior of Saint Sulpice. Through hazards many, when life hung on a hair, he had arrived in virtue of fortitude and knowledge of the country at his present post. With humour unfailing and infinite resource, he had served God in New France for more than thirty years, and loomed like a bulwark of strength in these days of travail. He knew about Jacqueline, there being few things concerning the folk of Ville Marie he did not know, had seen her in the market place, admired her distinctive beauty, and thought but little of the story that came with her. The tales of a gilded Court had no interest for him.

"My daughter," he said, in a deep voice full of sympathy, "there is always hope. They have not been found, we do not know they are dead, and I have seen men return from Iroquois camps as though from the grave years after they were captured."

"Were they soldiers?" she asked dully.

"No," he admitted, "mostly priests, but do not despair. I know it is hard at your age, but this country is one of sacrifice, which is seldom realised at home."

Home! A hard word, she thought, to use now: it recalled too much, nor was it imaginable that this huge priest with the enormous muscular body, bigger, more powerful even than Paul's, with his weather-tanned features and air of confidence, had ever longed for home as she did at that moment. But between her and home stood the woman who had sent Jules to his death. Was home, she wondered, only to be found in this land of fear?

338

"There is no peace here, father."

"You are too young to expect peace now," he said gently, "that comes only after life's storm, when we are too old to fight longer. I have not found it yet, except at the altar. My child, there is one woman here you must talk to--Marguerite Bourgeoys of Notre Dame--she is on her way to ultimate peace."

"You think I should become a nun?"

"No, but there is much to do--she will tell you. Believe me, I understand what you feel, I have been long enough in New France for that, but remember you are among friends here, so lean on them. We must all stand together always, otherwise life would be insupportable. Also the Governor desires to help you so far as he can, he has been speaking to me about you."

"Why?" said she.

"He has learnt, from what source I do not know, the reason of your husband's being sent to Canada."

"That lie!"

He nodded: "About you and the King."

"There is no truth in it," she protested, "I was foolish, yes, but never faithless. The King's only mistress decided I was in her way, and we were banished. You are a priest, shall I go on my knees and swear?"

At this he waved a big hand, gave a rich comforting laugh.

"No, my child, stay on your feet and listen. I

myself did not believe this story and now it seems absurd; also the squabbles of courtiers count little over here. The Governor says that if you desire it, he will ask that you be allowed to return to France, and after what has happened there can be but one answer. Authority, however, could not reach here till next summer. By that time we shall know if your husband still lives, so till then why not take my advice?"

"About Marguerite Bourgeoys?"

"Yes, you will find her companionship worth while; and try not to occupy yourself with emotions that can change nothing and only exhaust the spirit. Instead of that, do what you can for us here in New France, and have faith--not least in yourself."

With this he blessed her, and strode off, mountainous, confident, to talk to the ministering mother of Notre Dame.

In the Camp of the Hairy One

Oguntwae, The Hairy One, sat in seclusion, smoking a soapstone pipe with a long square wooden stem, and pondered his own success with incredulity. The result was breathtaking; not in any way could he have anticipated anything like it; at the cost of a dozen warriors he had struck the hardest blow ever aimed at the French; one hundred villagers lay dead, forty more corpses--the men of Fort Remy--had coughed out their lives in that fatal sortie, another eighty were distributed to confederation towns in the Mohawk and Seneca country. Onato and Eri were with him again, a French officer and a farmer of Lachine lay close by, waiting their doom, his fighting men were eager to resume the warpath.

Only one matter was undecided, that of Kondiaronk, The Rat, who had disappeared two days after the affair, taking with him a few other shifty Hurons, and this made The Hairy One suspicious. He knew himself to be already a marked man, while Kondiaronk could probably squirm his way out. There was also the probability that the English, when they heard of Lachine, would disavow any connection with such an excess, and might even join the French to put an end to the Five Nation terror. That thought filled The Hairy One with foreboding, and robbed his pipe of its taste.

A fortnight had passed since the attack. At noon of the second day after the massacre the Iroquois crossed Lake Saint Louis in a great fleet, camped on the south bank, and at nightfall the terrified folk of Ville Marie watched from their palisade the distant fires of torture, heard the last agonies of those they were unable to succour. Oguntwae's scouts reported that in two of the forts the garrisons had not dared to venture out, the third stood nearly empty, Ville Marie was shut tight like a trap, sentries with lighted fuses patrolled the stockade, and since then there had been no attempt at pursuit. The Frenchmen, a hundred miles away, were still staying at home.

Oguntwae was also at home. Here in the heart of his own country the warriors of his own party sat round a clear space, blankets across their knees, and in the centre two stakes had been planted.

Onato was there, squatting a little apart as became one of his age and position. Two hours before the assault on Lachine a native scout, armed only with knife and hatchet, had crawled into the village under cover of the storm, warned him what was about to happen, and bade the two follow. There was no chance to give warning, even had the old man desired it, and the girl made no protest. Her love had turned to anger.

Bound, under a bark shelter, lay Jules and Paul, guarded by a young man of fierce and aquiline aspect, his left hand missing, truncated bones projecting whitely from retreating flesh. In view of past events he had demanded this privilege, and his eyes kept fixed on Paul in a basilisk stare. The smaller captive, he concluded, being nearly dead already, might never reach the stake, but the big one, in whom he was directly interested, should last well.

By land and water they had travelled, Paul reckoned, a full hundred miles, and were now well down in the Champlain country, far south of the military seigneuries of Chambly and Sorel. Of the journey he remembered little, save that for the latter part of it he carried the unconscious Jules on his back. His temples hurt where the hatchet had caught him, knocking him senseless, but nothing more. With Jules it was different: weak from loss of blood, the bedded barb in his groin burned a hair-breadth away from an artery.

The flies were bad under the bark shelter, crawling in swarms over Jules' waxy face; he would lift bound hands in feeble efforts to dislodge them while his brain wandered and he gabbled for hours in a thin, high-pitched voice, of things long past and far away. It seemed he had meant to apologise for something, but now it was too late, and Paul lay wondering why he had transported that broken body to the fate so imminent, instead of letting merciful death come to it days ago. Much better to have allowed Jules to die as he begged. But Oguntwae ordered that he live for this. Here too was the savage whose painted face he had last seen at the head of a triangular ripple when a bar of moonlight silvered the sleeping river above Quebec.

"Paul." Of a sudden the voice was normal; it sounded as from a distance, weak, thin, but quite steady, with a sort of penultimate clarity; "How much longer?"

"Not much. I am sorry, Jules, all my fault, we should not have tried it. The Governor was right."

"What about Ville Marie?"

"Safe! All inside; they won't be attacked: I overheard that. The Iroquois are puzzled."

"About what?"

"There being no pursuit."

"No pursuit...." Jules knew what that meant, then quite calmly: "She will go home on the next ship, if it is permitted."

"I hope so, that is best."

"That talk about her and the King--you never heard it?"

"I did, Jules."

"Where? how?"

"A nurse in the hospital in Quebec, and from Jacqueline herself, before I saw you. Till then I didn't know you were in New France."

"So!" Jules was silent a moment, saving his strength, for the thing must be put right: "There was no truth in it, not a word, none, just Court gossip. Versailles," he went on with weak determination, "is like that: if a woman is beautiful and gay she has no chance."

"I knew it," said Paul, "is that why you came out?"

"Madame de Maintenon heard the slander and was jealous; she gave the order."

"She sent me, too. From the Abbé Callot I went to the Bishop of Chartres, who took me to Versailles. There I met her, and she said, 'Go to Canada.'"

"You at Versailles?"

"And felt like a fool; certainly I looked one." He went on talking about that meeting, of the drive from Chartres with Godet des Marais, of the gilded, spindle-legged chairs, of Father Poncet, and how de Maintenon told him that she too knew what it meant to be misunderstood, and when he spoke of farming she pitched on that at once as the best way out, in spite of the Father's suggestion about the priesthood. Paul rambled on, spinning the thing along, making such a story of it, and in a voice so natural, that Jules actually seemed interested, and from the wavering brain was displaced the horror that otherwise occupied every hopeless moment, which was just what Paul wanted, and all one could do for one's friend.

Jules took a long shaky breath; not much life left in him now, but enough to ponder on the web of fate that brought them both here. Paul at Versailles talking to La Solidité, while he himself, Captain in the King's Guard, had never even seen her. How typical of the marble-faced woman whose passionless will governed Louis of France.

"Paul--when you met her did you tell her the story of Castellon--yours and mine?"

"Yes, all of it."

"Then she intended that we come together again, you and I; it's just what she would do."

"Not like this."

"No, but here we are."

Presently it seemed there remained nothing much left to talk of, or perhaps it was the realisation that nothing which passed between them here could ever mean anything to anyone else, which produced an extraordinary sense of isolation, and at last they stood with each other where in their secret hearts they had always longed to stand, so each retired as it were to contemplate with what calm he could muster that which might be shared with none. Very privately Jules knew that if he could only get a hand free he would be able to find his own way out of this, for the barb in his groin was sending stabbing signals that it needed just one firm wrench to puncture the artery. But Paul in his surging strength had no chance of escape.

Two fighting men appeared, cut the thongs around their ankles, jerked them upright. Jules, swaying rested his bound arms on Paul's shoulder and fell. Again he was jerked up. This time the savage, seeing he could not stand unaided, slashed his wrists free. The numbed arms went up for the last time, one curving round Paul's neck, the other feeling blindly downward. His eyes met Paul's in unspoken farewell; he gave one desperate twist, the life-blood gushed from him, and with a weary sigh he pitched forward.

*   *   *   *   *

The slanting eyes of Oguntwae were troubled. Superstitious by nature, a pagan of violent passions and swift revulsions, of fanatic fury and profound depression, he was swayed by omens only to be read by the medicine men of his tribe; and now one had just come to him, fantastically clad, wearing a painted wooden mask, head-dress of black and white skunk skin, brandishing a rattle of serpents' bones, and bringing the interpretation of a dream that had disturbed The Hairy One the previous night. In it appeared a woman who looked like Eri, The Cherry Tree.

This dream, announced the necromancer, had been a message from the spirit world. It meant that the great Onontio, the one Oguntwae both respected and feared, was about to return to Canada after seven years' absence. He would be filled with wrath over the business of Lachine, and assemble an army of whites, half-breeds, Hurons and Ottawas such as had never been gathered before to repay the great killing with interest; so that the Iroquois would be slaughtered like beaver in their houses when the dam has been cut and the water runs away.

It remained, therefore, that Oguntwae must do certain things, or else his children's children would spit on his memory. He must release his own captives, returning them in security to Ville Marie with hostages for his future behaviour. Further, he must send dispatch runners to every village where the prisoners had been forwarded, carrying orders for their instant freedom. With gifts of very many beaver skins he must abase himself before the great Onontio, bury the hatchet deep and place above it a large stone, that it might never again be unearthed. Thus only could he himself survive.

The appearance of a woman in the dream was significant, though not yet quite clear, and Oguntwae would be well advised to consider carefully the next thing said to him by any woman, for much might turn on it. Women were all fools, but sometimes, without knowing it, they spoke words of wisdom.

Thus concluded the seer and, shaking his rattle, went off to the seclusion of his own lodge, where none, not even The Hairy One, might enter uninvited.

A second disconcerting fact was that one prisoner had died on his way to the stake, thus spoiling the double entertainment promised for the evening. The third was the unreasonable demand of Eri, who insisted that she alone do the torturing of the big farmer from Lachine.

In his own wild fashion Oguntwae loved the girl; he rejoiced when, in the heart of the storm, she appeared at the heels of his scout, and saw that, with Onato, she had been well-treated. Since then they had talked much together. She made no protest against the torture of prisoners on the shores of Lake Saint Louis, but did not look on. During the forced journey that followed she showed no interest in the two white men, and he observed with satisfaction that eighteen months with the French had not tamed her; she seemed to slide back into the old life as oil slides from a bottle, and save that she now understood another language, there was no difference at all.

Divided between the necromancer's warning and the knowledge that his fighting men grew impatient, The Hairy One argued that her demand was absurd. It would deprive others of undoubted privileges. Why did she make it?

Eri, sitting on her feet, gave him a straight stare: "Because I hate him."

"Again, why? He has not beaten you, or my father."

She shook her dark head.

"Also," he grunted, "you are a child, you know nothing of torture."

"Wait and see. I am less of a child than you think."

"You would go too quickly and kill him at once."

"No; tonight I will only play with him so that he survives till tomorrow, when the old women will help."

Oguntwae, secretly nervous, torn with indecision, watched her narrowly. His suspicions were aroused, this thing did not ring true, but her face remained unreadable. Setting his wits against hers, he was minded of what the necromancer said about women, and of a sudden a solution flashed on him. It was feasible, and attractive; it might mean pardon from the Onontio if he could manage it without detection by his own people, so, fingering his necklet of scalps, he put on a pleasant manner.

"You are sure about tomorrow?"

She nodded.

"Then we go together. Listen! They are impatient."

Now a stir ran through the ring of fighting men, lengthening shadows fell across the camp, and the sun's last rays illuminated their wild painted faces. They had waited and wondered; the chatter of grey-haired squaws, hungry for cruelty, grew more shrill, but there spread a hush as Oguntwae seated himself, relit his pipe and frowned on the extra stake. His warriors leaned tensely forward, black eyes shining, and a grunt of approval sounded when Paul appeared, stripped to the waist. Immediately he was lashed tight. The body of this man, so large, formidable, so sheathed in rippling muscle, met with approval; his skin looked very white; he carried himself without any sign of fear, a fact instantly noted, his head high, jaw set, while his eyes, grey, deep-sunk, showed only a remote indifference.

They rested a moment on Eri. Crouching beside The Hairy One she stared back with exactly the same expression, at which he gave the faintest possible smile. Nor was this missed and again the warriors felt content.

Many a Frenchman had they fought and captured, but none more acceptable than the giant who regarded them so coolly. In Lachine had he not defied them, piling his doorstep with their dead. At Saint Denis his arm had brained a Mohawk of repute, and on the river severed the wrist of a Seneca chief. Here indeed waited one worthy of attention.

Oguntwae lifted a hand, silence fell; Eri, moving like a panther, lit a small fire. The fire was not at his feet as Paul expected, and he turned his head to watch. Then a hot brand approached his face and his eyes closed.

He felt glowing wood scorch his skin, shrivelling his brows, but no fire actually touched him. Eri was playing. No aged virago this, lusting for human torture, but a raven-locked slip of youth, discovering her first sadistic satisfaction in holding the centre of the stage, a young wildcat, flexing her claws. Spots gathered on his breast and arms like hot coals, so that the skin became a stinging shroud, but nothing went deep, nothing to maim or cripple. Once he opened his eyes to find hers close, with the same basilisk stare she had given before--was that only three weeks ago--it told him no more than it did then, and slowly he became aware that what he now underwent was only a refinement, a preliminary, a delicate feminine infliction from the pagan girl who had once, only once, lain in his arms, and could not therefore steel herself to the stark horrors that were the special function of grey-haired hags. But the hags waited their turn.

His brain grew chaotic. One thing he was glad of, Jules had escaped, so he nerved himself to endure the coming night and the hour when dawn broadened over the camp of Oguntwae. For Eri he had no special anger. She was only like the rest, and could not help it. He felt a sharp sense of the uselessness of life that passed like the widening ripple from a flung stone. In a half-swoon his head drooped, he seemed to hear Oguntwae's voice, and knew they were leading him away. Then again thongs about his wrists and this time his feet, too.

He had stood at the gate of hell and walked on, but when night came he was quite conscious. Beside him a bark dish of pounded corn and deer meat. Ten feet off the young warrior with shortened arm. Paul lifted the dish, set his seared mouth to it, and the Seneca nodded approval. This meant strength for tomorrow.

Night came in front of the scattered teepees, small fires shrank to flattened pyramids of embers, and gave a reddish glint like the eyes of a lynx. A little wind stirred in naked tree tops. The young sentry drew a blanket over his shoulders, and became an image, but Paul could see the whites of his eyes. A dog whimpered, the moon spread a breathless milky light in which teepees and twin stakes looked phosphorescent. Jules' body had been removed to be dismembered and eaten. Tomorrow ... Jacqueline--Jean--Ville Marie--the farm-- all began to recede. Why had one not taken more out of life while one was part of it?

The wind increased till a sighing moan set up overhead, and the whole bark shelter creaked as it lifted a little. Now the moon was obscured; darkness increased, with only a concentration of gloom where the Seneca squatted, the whites of his eyes no longer visible. Paul tugged at his lashings till his temples throbbed. If only a man could fight--just once more.

Then something touched him, another hand that felt smooth and slim. This was incredible, so he lay very still. Again the light touch, groping, and his swollen fingers closed on the haft of a knife, his thumb crept up its edge. The other linked hand encountered something else, a small bundle, tied it seemed with babiche, or rawhide. There followed the faintest imaginable movement, the ghost of movement, then silence.

Still on his side he gripped the haft in his teeth, moving his head slowly with a sawing motion.

It was a full hour later that a great weight fell on the Seneca. A hand clapped over his mouth, another thrust against his forehead, a knee drove in between his shoulders. His head started back, and when his spine cracked he made no sound.

Resurrection

— I —

"Madame, Jean is about to go out to the farm."

"Is that safe?"

"Quite safe, the regulars are on patrol; the rangers say the Iroquois are back in their own country."

"Well, let him go; there is nothing to do here."

"He asks that I go too, it is for the day only."

"Why not? It will do you both good."

But Marie hesitated, then came forward, arms out. "I told him no, unless you came too, and, ma petite, why not? The day is fine, there is no danger, this town is full of gloom, and Jean has borrowed the best horse in Ville Marie."

"I think not, Marie, not just now."

"Please, madame, and it would help Jean. That poor man eats his heart out over what happened; he loved m'sieu Paul and says had he gone too, as he wished, it might have been different, though God knows it could not. He talks for hours about it, and some little sign that you do not think so too would mean much to him. Please come."

Jacqueline wavered: in the past dumb weeks these two had surrounded her with a sheltering wall of devotion; they had been completely understanding, their care infinitely deft, and in that isolation began a secret awakening that turned her thoughts to Paul rather than to Jules. To dwell on Jules was to realise that she had mistaken love for something else, and however she mourned his tragic end, however she admitted that she had not tried to understand him as she might, it became quite clear that had he lived there was little promise of happiness together. So long as the world saw him as he desired to be seen, he was gay, buoyant, fascinating. Then her youth moved, magnetized, towards his, but when the sun ceased to shine joy was at an end.

Poor Jules, who believed that life owed him so much. The last time they had said goodbye he only lifted an indifferent hand. She had not wanted to feel like this, but truth was in the very air now, and the rest of life had to be lived.

And Paul! That picture brought back much in which she herself appeared with little credit. It seemed she had never done anything for him, while her final most vivid impression was of Paul wreathed in acrid smoke, cheek jammed to a hot gun-barrel, finger crooking, left hand reaching to her for another weapon. That was his farewell, and nothing could have been more like him. He had never taken, always given, her own life was his latest offering, and since she felt it to be his last she saw his dumb worship as never before. One thing at a time for Paul; and never anything but herself.

"Allons, madame will come?"

Jacqueline nodded: of a sudden she wanted to

see Paul's house again, kneel where she knelt before, powder horn in a shaky hand, and signal to him in some secret way that she understood. It would be cowardly not to go.

Marie sprang up, rejoicing. "Your cloak, the heavy one, thick shoes--it will not rain today. You are wise to escape from this prison, and, petite, we need some more vegetables, one of those Castellon cabbages, eh?" She chattered on, trying not to look too happy, shooting little proprietary glances at Jean who, having now adopted Jacqueline as his patronne, gave her the salute he always gave Paul, handed her into a high-wheeled gig, and put a deerskin robe over her knees.

They had cleared the stockade and were well out on the road before she spoke:

"Jean?"

"Madame?"

"It is difficult to say what I want, but you will understand."

"Madame will please not inconvenience herself."

"It is about you and Marie--so much to thank you for and...."

"But no, nothing," he put in hastily, "nothing at all."

"Just what she told me yesterday; you two are very much alike."

"He is quite right," broke in Marie, who had her

back to them. "He has good sense, the old porcupine--that is for a man."

"You begin well, you two," smiled Jacqueline, "so why wait any longer?"

"Wait?" Jean drew his whip lightly across the horse's flanks, "wait," he asked innocently, "for what?"

"I think you need each other."

"Mon Dieu! But that is one great truth," he blurted.

"Then why wait--now?"

"Madame there is a certain little difficulty."

"Is it that Marie thinks she is necessary to me, like you did with your patron?"

Jean coughed, looked awkward. "That little partridge behind us will explain."

"It is like this, madame. We have talked it over, often, and think that till...." she hesitated, "till something is settled about you, I cannot leave you. As to Jean, he must soon go back to the farm--it is neglected. All the property of m'sieu Paul is there, and some drunken coureur des bois may set the place on fire. Also m'sieu Paul said that should he ever leave that farm Jean was to have it as a gift. I do not know whether he wrote it down or not, eh Jean?"

"He said nothing to me if he did, though m'sieu Bénigne Basset, the notary, may have it. Anyway, that makes no difference--you stay with madame."

"There will be no need of that," said Jacqueline, gently. "You know Marguerite Bourgeoys?"

"The angel of Notre Dame?"

"I am going to join her, work with her this winter, and perhaps go back to France next summer; it's all quite simple."

"To Castellon?" breathed Marie, "Think of it!"

"Eh bien," Jean gave a great sigh in which he seemed to unload a burden, "if that is settled my small pigeon will soon change her name, but is it settled?"

"Yes, Jean."

It was automatic. Queer, she thought, that decision should come so quickly with no uncertainty left. A straight question from a simple soul, a brief answer, the die was cast, and already it was shaping the lives of others. She who was so young envied the confidence of these two so much older. They had each other and no fears.

The reflection held her silent while miles dropped behind to the steady thud of hooves on the soft road. As they approached Lachine the air grew chill with a light wind, with a promise of later frost. Presently a low mist, only breast high, blanketed the flat soil; the horse ploughed steadily on as though swimming; fences on either side were half submerged, trees rose from it as from a feathery lake and like a shroud it overlaid the ruined homes of man where nature strove to hide her scars. Well-known landmarks had an aspect of unreality, seemed to have gone adrift, floated about, finally grounding in new positions.

All three were silent, with only an occasional cluck-cluck and jerk of the rein from Jean. They traversed grim reminders, faintly distinguishable except when the charred mass of burnt houses thrust up like battered sentinels that still held loyal to lonely posts. Jean's lips compressed, his roving eyes were hard: he would give exclamations, instantly choked off, at sight of something familiar, yet quite changed.

They passed groups of men carrying spades who regarded them blankly, and fatigue parties from the camp-volant, when the officer in charge would look wonderingly at Jacqueline, ask a question or two, and give a salute with a warning they must return to Ville Marie well before dark. No Iroquois about so far as one knew, he would assure them, but this promised to be a dark night.

"Voilà!" Jean lifted his whip, "it is like something in the middle of the sea."

Paul's house stood up intact, the only house left in all eastern Lachine; four-square, shouldering out of the clinging mist, it looked more solid than ever. Front door and shutters were closed; behind, just visible as though nearly sunk, the smaller cabin, the barn and rounded knoll with its great naked maple, all apparently unharmed. The silence was deathlike: Jacqueline felt her throat contract as Marie's arm slipped under her own.

"We do not stay long; it is just to see that all is safe; we will go in and light the fire. There is some tea left, eh Jean?"

"Certainly, if no thief has got here first. Also, chèrie, you will do some sweeping, that house is demoralised unless...."

"Unless what?"

"Nothing, my pigeon."

As they turned into the side road the house emerged more clearly; it had an air of silence, of mystery, being a monument as much as a farmhouse, the maker's name set out in big square timbers with neat dovetailed joints. Jacqueline could see the loophole through which Paul had fired, surrounded by a blackened patch, could also see the door open with the giant figure of a man standing there. Jean had jumped down, tossed his reins on the horse's neck, and held out a brown hand.

"Wait a moment, I will go in the back way."

Almost at once she heard his step within, the sliding bar pulled clear, and the door did open. Jean was standing gazing about, eyes round.

One glance told her there was nothing to be done in that house, nothing out of place, no least vestige of what had happened except the faintest smell of burnt powder. Apparently it had just been swept and garnished, the floor was clean, cups and dishes on their shelves, folded blankets neat on the two beds, every small thing where it had always been, except that Paul's muskets, pistols, powder horn and bullet pouch were missing, and it seemed suitable they should have vanished with their owner.

On the table, weighted with a book, a letter in Paul's big round script. "To Jean Prud'homme." It might have been left there a moment ago. She could almost see Paul put it down, then looking about in his deliberate way, and stalking out.

"For you, Jean," she said in a strained tone.

He picked it up with thumb and finger, turned it over, shook his head: "Madame, I cannot read: will you...."

She opened it: a note to Jean and three closed envelopes; Monsieur Bénigne Basset, Notary of Montreal; Monsieur Raoul Fouquette, Notary of Castellon, Brittany; the Abbé Callot of Castellon, Brittany.

"Dear Jean," she read:

I start on a venture from which I may not return. If you do   not hear from me within a fortnight, give the letter to   Monsieur Basset, who will attend to my instructions and put   the farm, with everything there, in your possession. You   have always served me faithfully. I wish you luck, and hope you will marry without delay. Also see that the other two   letters go to France on the next ship.

Your friend and patron,

Paul de Lorimier.

Her voice trailed out; Jean's mouth was twisted, sudden tears starting; Marie had caught his arm and squeezed hard. Jacqueline put down the sheet and turned away, her own eyes moist. No word left there for her, but she needed none, for had they not together looked death in the face? He had remembered that, and to the end was the same Paul, always giving, never taking, to the very last act of all, and in this moment she was very proud of him.

"Well, Jean, it is as you thought."

He took a long, long breath, touched the letter with a sort of reverence, made an odd grimace, frowned, and went out quickly. Marie stood, fingers locked, her expression puzzled.

"It is true, all that?"

"You heard it; he forgot nothing. You should be happy here, you two." Then, brain suddenly whirling, "I'm tired, Marie; make a fire, and tea if there is any."

The woman bustled out; she heard flints struck, crackling, and she dropped into the great rocking chair. The room felt chill. Outside Jean was talking to himself and the horse. Presently he put in his head:

"Madame, do not distress yourself, but we cannot move till the fog clears. It is very thick. There is plenty of time."

She looked out and saw nothing but a vapoury cloud obliterating the earth, hanging damp, motionless and cold: no sound save from the kitchen, the barn and smaller cabin now invisible, Jean's moustache dripping.

She went back, took a brand from Marie, and lighted the fire Paul had laid five weeks ago, Paul who was now dead. Again, how like him, and again she could see the big hands placing twists of birch bark, putting the smallest sticks in crosswise pattern to give a quick blaze, and over them solid logs, nodding as he turned away. Did he pause at the door? She felt he did, and glance back to make sure that all was right for whoever came next.

In the midst of this she blamed herself for thinking so much about him, so little of Jules, but something told her with startling force that she should have done so before, and though it was now too late she would continue to think of him for a long long time to come.

The bark curled, glowed, spitting hot little flames; a hollow sound set up in the chimney throat, and the room was soon warm. Presently Jean returned to join Marie in the kitchen, and she could hear them chatter.

"Bien, my partridge, that barn has not been touched, except there is much blood about. Poor Henri Bastelle--I told you how we found him that morning--must have been buried by the regulars with those Iroquois, also the oxen. There is a big pit close by, filled not long ago. It is all very depressing. Kiss me, you little woodchuck! Ah!"

"Jean, do we live here?"

"Why not? I am a farmer now, you can see how it came about."

"I see nothing yet," said she, sombrely.

"Then readjust yourself and think. I told you why I returned with you to Ville Marie five weeks ago."

"Yes, well?"

"Well, after dismissing me, Monsieur Paul came back here, wrote those letters, and put the house in order, caring nothing what lay outside. That done, he wasted no time over the dead, but went straight to Fort Remy, where the sortie was arranged. That is according to the message left at Fort Rolland as they passed. Evidently the man forgot nothing."

"The letter says if after two weeks, but is it not possible...?"

"He still lives, eh?"

"Isn't it?"

"Anything is possible in New France, but consider what has happened: forty-two men go in pursuit of fifteen hundred, and, chèrie, not one, not a single one, comes back with the story. The Huron scouts have accounted for all except two...." He paused, shaking his head with a vision of fires across Lake Saint Louis seen at night from the stockade at Montreal.

"God help us to forget it. About that girl and the old man, did they know it was coming?"

"Who can tell?"

"Did Monsieur Paul never possess her?"

"If so, only once--let me explain. The evening I came to you with cabbage--you remember--before that he had been lonely, unhappy, so I advised him to take the girl, but he would not, and offered her to me."

"Don't boast of what you told me before, you disreputable old crow!" exploded Marie.

At this came the sound of a struggle, pans dropped with a clatter, smothered protests, a smacking kiss, Jean's voice in masculine triumph.

"You see what happens when you forget yourself, eh? Well, I assured my patron I had intentions elsewhere. Also I knew the girl desired him, so to efface myself I asked for a holiday and came to Ville Marie.

When I got back I felt something in the air. Later m'sieu Paul seemingly changed his mind, and offered the girl to madame, and I am convinced it was the sight of her in this house that did it."

"That would be like him," she agreed, "but it is all over now. Does the fog disperse?"

"No, much thicker. My pigeon, we may have to spend another unexpected night in this house."

"Madame will not fancy that."

"Tchk! tchk! it cannot be helped. Otherwise we are lost in five minutes. This place is not haunted."

"Are you sure, Jean?"

"For a woman of some sense you surprise me; am I to build another?"

At this Jacqueline heard a chuckle, then Marie came in looking rosy, lit the lamp, and was setting the table when she shot a quick glance at her mistress.

"Madame, are you ill?"

"No, just tired."

"Then eat."

"Not until you two join me."

"Jean," her voice lifted, "go wash yourself, and come here."

A strange meal, thought Jacqueline, at Paul's table with Paul's food before her: his invisible presence seemed close by, watching, waiting, listening, seeing to it that nothing lacked, a sort of ghostly host with no desire save that his guests be satisfied, so that she found herself waiting and listening with an extraordinary expectancy. The others made no effort to talk. They looked awkward, self-conscious, and there followed a silence at last broken by Jean.

"Madame, I am sorry, but we cannot reach Ville Marie tonight."

"I thought that might happen."

"You don't mind?"

"Why mind what cannot be helped? I have a feeling that we were meant to be here, haven't you?"

He looked startled, gazed about. "Perhaps you're right, there is something about the house that--well...."

"It is now your house."

He brightened at once: "I had forgotten, and Madame is very welcome; she always will be, eh my turtle dove, none in New France so welcome."

"Madame knows that; she will come often."

"I am afraid not, Marie: tonight I am glad to be here, but tomorrow I say goodbye to the farm. I'll often think of you in Castellon. You'll make a fine home of this place."

Jean took out his pipe, rubbed its bowl thoughtfully, caught a sharp look from Marie, and stuffed it away.

"It is difficult to say what is in my heart: there has been so much. We shall certainly be happy and in a few years at our ease, but I would be still happier to work for my patron all my life if that were ... tsch! tsch! listen!! someone lost in the fog."

Jacqueline held her breath: the fire crumbled softly, Jean's brows were pulled down; for a second they heard nothing, then, distinctly, a step that seemed of someone pausing outside. A faint sound as though something, it might have been a man's shoulder, brushed the rough bark of the outer wall. Another pause. Next, a little creak at the back door, and Jean knew that the inner bar was slid open. His scalp prickled and he stared at them in turn.

"That bar!" he whispered, "that bar! who knows the trick now but me?"

"I do," said a quiet voice, and Paul's great figure moved into the light.

— — II — —

Day in Ville Marie, and the old Onontio sat in council in the Governor's house, having pushed his way up river against slabs of drifting ice.

It was his third visit since arrival in Quebec the previous October with de Callières before winter snows shrouded the black ruins of Lachine, and with them came the Iroquois chief Oureouhare, whom Denonville had taken by treachery, and shipped as a gift to His most potent Majesty, Louis XIV. Frontenac, who fought hard but fair, and knew the Iroquois as Denonville never knew them, had insisted on this. Now it stood him in good stead. The repatriated exile sat smoking in his wigwam, and so far that year had not followed the war path.

Frontenac's tall figure was still straight, his hawkish eye still bright. At seventy years of age he had returned to New France to work and die, but he rejoiced in his labour, and, handing him the commission, Louis had said: "Your Excellency, I send you back to Canada where I expect that you will serve me as well as you have already. I ask nothing more than that." At Versailles, Seignelay and Louvois were behind him: in Quebec he found Champigny now freed from the sacerdotal shadow of Denonville, while here in Ville Marie he sat surrounded by men in whom he had faith, men who had proved themselves. In their faces he read the resolution that marked his own dominant features.

De Callières was there and in good spirit, for had not Louis promised him the Governorship of New York so soon as the English colonies were defeated: Vaudreuil, acting Lieutenant Governor of Canada, a man of lofty stature with highly arched brows, bland, wide-open eyes that always held a faint look of surprise, and large firm mouth whose corners betrayed a provocative tilt: Louvigny, Governor of Trois Rivières: Nicholas Perrot, restless, daring, knowing the wilderness and its stealthy tribes as did few other sons of Old France, black-haired, black-eyed, ever athirst for adventure: three le Moynes, sons of the Sieur de Longueil; these were Francis, Ste Hélène and young Bienville who was doomed to die next year under the Iroquois knife: here sat the huge bulk of Dollier de Casson; he was thinking of the history that grew a little every night in his firm, fine script, and here around him was history in the making: Catalogne, the engineer, frowning over an outbreak of scurvy at Fort Frontenac: de Mantet, who had hurried off with a heavy heart the previous autumn, wondering if he could reach Fort Frontenac before

Denonville's orders of destruction had been carried out:--these and others of the fighting noblesse of New France sat at the long table with the old Onontio, and amongst them a great figure in civilian clothes, one Paul de Lorimier, farmer of Lachine.

"Gentlemen," Frontenac was saying, "it is good to be amongst you again: together we have been through a hard winter, and thanks to your efforts New France stands in a less dangerous state than a year ago. Monsieur de Sainte Hélène, you with Monsieur de Mantet have ravished Schenectady, giving the Dutch something to think about. As one result, the Dutch are urging the English to attack Quebec by sea, which," here he smiled grimly, "I should welcome.

"In January, Monsieur Hertel set out for the settlement of Salmon Falls, reaching it at the end of March, and destroyed it. On the way back he encountered my third war party under Captain Portneuf. Last week, I am informed, they surrounded Fort Royal, which should soon be in our hands, this giving the English something to think about, so with this winter's work we may feel content. But we are not yet secure; our efforts must continue, and your counsel in this matter is invited."

At once came a burst of talk, the quick surge of suggestion, in which Paul took no part. Voiceless, he had been watching the old Onontio, on whose straight, square shoulders rested the destiny of New France: he saw the shrewd, penetrating eyes travel slowly from man to man till they met his own, and in them moved a touch of curiosity.

There was much to discuss, much to settle. William of Orange was on the throne of the fugitive James; this had stiffened the Protestants of New

England: also he had declared war on France, and Louis was loath to weaken himself at home by sending further forces across the seas. Sir Edmund Andros, Governor of New York, had, it was feared, instructed Admiral Sir William Phipps to relieve the investment of Fort Royal, so little time could be lost there. If he succeeded, he would certainly attack Quebec. The Iroquois had had a lesson, but still hung about the skirts of every French settlement like the mosquitoes that emerged from rotten logs in early summer. Far west, there was trouble on the Island of Michilimacinac. Everywhere food ran short, for the settlers dared spend but short hours in the fields, labouring with anxious eyes swerving to the forest palisade.

Paul, knowing all this, sat marvelling at the confidence of the men around him, wondering why he himself was there: he had come at the urging of de Bienville, with whom existed a queer rather silent friendship, for that winter the farmer of Lachine had forgotten his farm and given himself to revenge-- revenge for Jules--revenge for the blistering spectacle of last August.

With Bienville he journeyed to Schenectady, tramping leagues of snow softened by a winter thaw till the sinews of his legs were hot wires. It took a month of this to reach the doomed outpost, where, so safe had the Dutch deemed themselves, that instead of sentries the war party found sentinels of snow mounting guard at the barricade gates. Then the surprise at midnight-- the war whoop of Huron fighting men--massacre of the innocents. Paul had killed neither Dutch nor English--he could not--they were farmers like himself--but took toll for Jules amongst their Iroquois allies, and tramped back unscratched.

Later, he fought at Trois Rivières with de

Ramezay, and stood at the end, an arrow through his shoulder, the centre of a ring of twitching brown bodies over whose oily crowns the Hurons wielded their scalping knives.

But with the coming of spring a sort of nostalgia of death seized on him: in the tender shoots of stricken fields he found a rebuke. He questioned the whole trend of life. Through bitter months, while Ville Marie stood on watch, he had hardly seen Jacqueline. Rarely he encountered her as he returned from some bloody foray, head hooded, gun slung, with hatchet, bullet pouch and knife, face frostbitten, cheeks gaunt, eyes sunken with exposure, snowshoes on his back. Once or twice he had seen her in the Place on some errand of mercy, or else she was trailed by children who now regarded her as they did Marguerite Bourgeoys, and on those occasions she seemed to shrink from his formidable aspect. He was the agent of death--she the angel of life, so what, he would ask himself, had they left in common? He longed for her, ached for her, but here, marooned in New France, they were further apart than in Castellon.

Now the old Onontio was in the saddle again, and Paul listened to the dry, incisive voice.

"Gentlemen, with much that you advise, I agree, but not all. First we will deal with Michilimacinac. I have a despatch from Monsieur la Durantaye, also information through the Jesuit Father Carheil that the tribes are on the point of revolt. Captain Louvigny, with a hundred and fifty Canadians you will proceed there, accompanied by you, Monsieur Perrot, taking these orders I have written. Study them at your leisure, and beware of that crafty Huron called The Rat, under whose skin moves the devil himself. Inform Monsieur la Durantaye that I desire his presence at Quebec.

"You, Monsieur Catalogne, will conduct a relief party to Fort Frontenac. I am glad to learn that in spite of--of--" the old man hesitated a moment, "the misguided instructions of my predecessor much of the fortifications still stand. It is your duty to make them good. Holding that point, we secure safe passage of peltries from the west. Monsieur Vaudreuil, of you and Messieurs le Moyne I will shortly ask an opinion as to the further protection of Ville Marie, Chambly, la Chesnaye and Longueil. Now gentlemen, I thank you for your presence, and tomorrow we meet again at the same time. Monsieur de Lorimier," he fixed his eyes on Paul, "I will be glad to speak with you privately. Pray remain."

There was a shuffling of feet: Paul felt a shooting of sharp glances, but no man spoke: in a moment they were alone, the blood climbed to his tanned temples while he met a gaze that seemed to weigh and appraise him, well content with what it found. But what had he to do with the leader of New France?

"Monsieur," began Frontenac quietly, "I have wished to talk with you because of reports that have reached me from different sources. The colour of these may be judged by the fact that you sat at this table today. First, I would learn from you exactly what happened when last August you went in pursuit of Oguntwae, The Hairy One."

Paul breathed deeply: he was not prepared for this, but the old eyes looked friendly. He had tried to put that episode out of his mind, but the thing had gone too deep, being linked with the vision of the woman he loved: it was still vivid, and now, almost without knowing it, he began to talk as though to himself till the keen face of Frontenac grew indistinct under its dark peruke, and the camp of The Hairy One displaced the

371

log cabins of Ville Marie. It was all like yesterday. Curt words he gave that stabbed like knives, and the tale was scarce begun when Frontenac perceived that here was a man after his own heart. As Paul finished, there fell a little silence.

"A brave officer, this Captain Vicotte," said the Governor, nodding. "We met once at Versailles, when I offered him a post in Canada, but he declined; then even before I sailed he had crossed the sea. Perhaps you can tell me why?"

"Your Excellency, I can tell you nothing."

"I understand that you saved his lady's life at Lachine?"

"There being nothing else I could do," grunted Paul.

"Precisely. And this pursuit of yours that cost us so many deaths--you were aware that you violated the orders of Monsieur Vaudreuil?"

"Your Excellency--" it came in a stammer, "I had seen too much to do otherwise. If you yourself...."

"I can read your mind, sir, but the blood of many men--and not only men--being part of the price we pay for His Majesty's new kingdom, we must be sparing of it, while not grudging when necessary. In this case it was not necessary. At the same time were we not ready to pay, we should not be here, and the end is not yet. Those who come after us will not know what we have endured, but I pray that on the soil we buy so dearly other generations will live in security and comfort. This is the only reward we can hope for."

The old man gave an unconscious sigh: he was feeling his years, wondering in secret whether the burden so eagerly and proudly re-shouldered might not soon prove too heavy to be borne. So much that only he could do for New France. And, listening, Paul felt the gulf between their rank and age bridged by mutual love for this mocking, perilous land, while there came a glimpse of the sudden, profound loneliness of spirits that are truly great.

Then in a flash the lined face looked younger: Frontenac approved of Paul's reticence, had only been testing the loyalty of this gruff-spoken giant, for had not de Maintenon herself, relenting a little for the sake of an innocent girl, sent for him privately on the eve of his departure for Rochelle. There, in the accustomed alcove, tapestry frame across her lap, she bade him keep a friendly eye on one Captain Vicotte, late of His Majesty's Bodyguard, and particularly his wife. Also she told him of a brave coward from Castellon, whose country honesty lately impressed her not a little. La Solidité had found pleasure in the talk, and sent the old man off with a twinkle in his eye.

"Well, monsieur, to return to the lady you saved," he went on smoothly, "after a conversation with Soeur Bourgeoys I propose to send Madame Vicotte to pursue her excellent work in Quebec. Life will be easier for her there, with more friends of her own quality. Should she wish to return to France, I have no doubt that His Majesty will consent, subject," he added significantly "to the approval of someone else."

Paul stiffened; the news struck him like a blow, but presently for some reason he was not surprised; it was like learning that a possibility secretly harboured and feared, had become a fact. And it explained much. Now there surged over him the old clumsy moodiness of other days, and his brain was floundering when Frontenac went on:

"My responsibility is for the women as well as the men of New France and you can decide which is the more difficult to discharge. As to yourself and the affair of Oguntwae, did you hear amongst his people any talk of Kondiaronk, The Rat, the renegade Huron who led the Marquis de Denonville far astray?"

"Yes, there was much of it. I garnered that the business at Lachine was the outcome of a conference the previous year between the two."

"I thought as much: you will tell Monsieur Louvigny of all you heard. Now, sir, His Majesty has need at this hour of men with your experience, your courage and knowledge of savage tongues. I offer you a commission in the regiment of Carignan. Your promotion should be rapid, your future secure, and you will be companioned by gentlemen with whom you have recently fought. What do you say?"

Paul gazed at him blankly. "I am no soldier, your Excellency, but a farmer."

"You are too big a man for the settlement of Lachine."

"Is any man too big for the land he lives on?" countered Paul boldly.

Frontenac looked faintly astonished, less faintly displeased.

"A farmer who sows the forest with Iroquois dead! Sir, my task in this new country is not an easy one; it needs the support of those like yourself. I do not offer commissions to those who have not earned them, nor am I accustomed to have the offer declined when made, so--" his long lean fingers drummed the table, touching his lips with a lace-bordered handkerchief he gave a dry smile, "since the matter seems to need thought, I suggest that you wait on me again before I leave for Quebec. Then I anticipate your acceptance."

Paul shook his great head; his face like granite:

"There is no need for thought. I cannot accept. I love the land of this country; that I understand and nothing else. There is no soldiering in my blood, only the soil of Brittany. Were I again to confront the Dutch or English, my sword would have no point, they being farmers too. I am at your service to defend Lachine or--or--" he began to stammer, choking with earnestness, "or Ville Marie, but beyond that leave me to my land. I am at home with growing grain, not amongst dying men. New France needs food as much as gunpowder. Believe me, sir, it is the farmer no less than the soldier who will decide the future, and one acre here is worth ten in Brittany. I have proved it. Let me plant my seed and reap my crops and fight but to defend them."

It was the longest speech he had ever made, but in that moment his soul came unsealed, from his soul he spoke, and Frontenac, listening, his first resentment softening, discerned that here was a man removed from most others. His bravery was proven, his value as an officer without question, but it was borne upon the aging Governor that if the present crisis might be met it would be the farmer and not the army that in the long run would best secure New France to his royal master. Food? it was true that Louis had been infuriated when de Denonville pleaded that corn be shipped from the old country to the new, and one could vision far off days when the sons of that old land would till uncounted acres it was his duty to win from gloomy forests where naked pagans now whetted their scalping knives under birch bark roofs.

So, looking hard at Paul, measuring the stony resolution in the deep-set eyes, marking the formidable proportions, Frontenac was privately rejoiced that men of his ilk should choose Canada, and set about planting their roots deep in its virgin soil.

"Monsieur de Lorimier," he said evenly, "not often have I been addressed like this, and I credit you with another kind of courage. You will consider my offer withdrawn; you will in fact forget it was ever made. Do you know Monsieur Francois Hertel?"

"Of Chambly? we have met, sir."

"No better subject in Canada today! I have seen his letters on bark written to his mother when prisoner of the Iroquois; saved and adopted by an old Mohawk widow. He speaks their tongue like his own. Get him to tell you the rest of it. He has a great seigneury, monsieur, at a strategical point--the mouth of the Richelieu, down which most of our trouble floats from the Champlain district. I desire to strengthen that point, and offer you as many acres as you wish, higher up the river. You and he are of--shall we say--the same disposition, and should mix well. What is your answer now?"

Paul took a long breath: here was high compliment from a high source and he had already mixed with Hertel to their mutual satisfaction in a sanguinary affair with the Mohawks the previous winter. But he said nothing of that. Now, grinning, he sensed that in some queer fashion he began to know Frontenac almost intimately, that here was one to whom he could speak as only to those who are large of purpose. Marking the lines in the strong face, he reverenced the fearless soul in so indomitable a body.

"That too, Your Excellency, needs thought: there is much to do at Lachine; the settlement to be restored, survivors encouraged, while those who still live know but little of the soil and what it can produce. If all is well there, we should soon be able to feed Ville Marie. With permission I would stay yet a while, and later...."

"In so great a bulk I had not expected so agile a pleader. Let it be as you will. I shall count on hearing from you when--" here he smiled again, "you will doubtless inform me of your wishes. I wish you well. Now seek out Monsieur Louvigny in the matter of Kondiaronk, The Rat."

He stalked towards the door, long loose bootlegs flopping against thin shanks, but halted on the threshold with a backward glance of wrinkled roguishness:

"On one thing however I must insist: you will not under any circumstance throw any of my officers into the River St. Lawrence. As yet there are no lily ponds in New France."

*   *   *   *   *

Jean, leaning on his spade, spat three times for luck:

"The soil is just right, not too much moisture with abundance of sun. We shall have a good year, my little muskrat."

He was in a field near the house talking to Marie

377

who stood, arms crossed, her figure displaying a maternal curve. From east, north and west came the kloop-kloop of axes, the sharp singing note of whipsaws as men toiled to raise a new Lachine: the day was cloudless; Lake St. Louis lay in flat, brilliant blue; at the forest edge one could see tall trees toppling with a cushioned crash; wagons creaked along the river road, the air smelled fragrant, and on Paul's farm young corn already pricked the brown earth with tender green.

Marie gave a sigh of satisfaction. "It is good to watch all these young things after so much death. I thought the winter would never end."

"Nor did your husband! how strange a winter it was, and with so little of our patron. After last autumn I guessed he would remain in Ville Marie near madame."

"Instead of which he sought the forest, and seemingly bathed in savage blood. They tell me he killed by the score. So often do I remember the rattle of that door latch the night he returned."

"And his talk--how quiet that was!" Jean scraped his boot on the spade, "I still hardly believe it, and took him at first for a ghost. But he ate a good meal nevertheless."

"And what he said about Eri--you never understood that part of it--she never meant to kill him; she was with child by him--or thought she was--which brought her in the dark with the knife. The rest was only a bit of spite."

"Perhaps, my ptarmigan, I understand better than you imagine. It was not spite, but fear that the old squaws would get at him first, so she filled out the time with a little friendly torture--but not too much. A young

378

woman," he chuckled, "will do anything to keep the man she loves out of the hands of older ones."

"Since when did you know so much of woman, you--you great mule?"

"Long before I met my pouter pigeon: yes, you begin to resemble those overnourished birds that sunned themselves on the gables of the Curé's house at Vitré. When will it be?"

"In September, and God grant it be a son. Jean, tell me how did m'sieu so weak and hungry travel hundreds of miles alone, then find his way across Lake St. Louis in a fog?"

"How does the wild swan travel a thousand leagues to last year's nest?--simply because it is his home."

"But he flies not alone," she said gently, "and that is what I deplore for our patron: his face is changing, also his manner: he is still hungry, and we know why."

"Does madame never speak of him?"

"Hardly a word, though sometimes her eyes betray her: the last time we met it was all of Sister Marguerite and the children, white and savage."

"Then she loves him?"

"Has loved him long without knowing it."

"While certainly he loves her."

"Better, I think, than his life; but he is the same,

always the same: she turned from him once in Castellon, now he will never speak. Since that night he returned they have met but three times, the day he made deposition to Monsieur Vaudreuil of how the Captain died, the day of our wedding, and once at Notre Dame as he left the confessional. It is all against nature. Jean, what do you think it meant when he was summoned yesterday by the Comte Frontenac?"

"He has said not one word. It might mean much, for the Comte--God be thanked he is back again-- wastes no time on trifles: it will be some affair of state or the army."

"Alors, I have an idea."

"More than an idea, mon ange, by that figure. What is it?"

"There they are, to whom we owe so much, in love with each other, yet nothing between them but silence. Being a woman, she will not speak, and our patron is too proud. Is it no possible that we--we--" she broke off, lips compressed, furrowing a smooth brow, "we do something in the matter?"

"What point in telling them what they already know?"

"That is not what I meant, but if--perhaps--" she gave her head a shake, "think of something--think!"

"If perhaps they thought that--Nom de Grâce! what could they think?"

"My husband has all but the ears of a mule," she snapped. "Jean, gardez-vous--here he comes."

Paul was at the house door; he stood looking over his fields like one whose eyes perceive more than what lies before them. His face was grave, for that night he had passed the gates of decision. He loved this place, but the cost of remaining came too high, for here he had saved what he could not keep. All night he had pondered, then with the dawn made up his mind. For the summer at any rate he would stay in Lachine and garner his crops. Perhaps the world would be easier with Jacqueline in Quebec.

He did not question the wisdom of Frontenac's plan: she would kill herself in Ville Marie, and evidently it was only work that she thought of. She owed him nothing: what he had done had been done for any woman that desperate night. She knew this, and he was aware that she knew. He must see her, and bid goodbye, and say that now as always he wished her well, but no more than this. In Quebec she would find friends of her own quality and a less driven life. Frontenac was right.

For the rest of it, when the grain was in, he would consider the seigneury. Hertel was a man to make a good neighbour. As for this house, he would not sell, he loved it too much to sell, but put in a tenant on share partnership. For Jean there was already another plan.

The thing was crystal clear as he came forward; nothing in his expression suggested that he had been through hell.

"Well, Jean, the soil steams in friendly fashion: when are you putting in the tobacco?"

"Tomorrow, m'sieu; it is all ready."

"One should do well with that; also I am thinking of barley--the market asks for it."

Jean scratched his head. "Barley, m'sieu! but where? Going on like this we shall certainly need more land."

"I had thought of that: not less than the same amount, eh?"

"Yes, the same, but you and I cannot...."

"It is not exactly for myself," smiled Paul, "and might be worked by a neighbour. I need one since Pierre Barbarin died."

Jean glanced over the fence where Pierre's house so lately the abode of children and laughter was but a flat, black patch, the barn a tangle of charred timber, eyesore of bitter memory: the land ran down to the lakeside, and the dead Pierre had not done so badly.

"Oh--that place!"

"You approve?"

"There is no better in Lachine."

"A pity to have it yield nothing this year--that is what you feel?"

"Exactly, m'sieu."

"Also an important bit of land to me," went on Paul thoughtfully, "with direct access to the lake in case of attack."

"A safeguard much to be considered in these

days," nodded Jean.

"Well, it will be worked, at least I hope so, by a certain person. Yesterday I conferred with the Abbé Belmont, also notary Bénigne Basset. To make the story short, I have already bought that farm."

"Mon Dieu! is it true?"

"But disposed of it within the hour."

"At a profit, I hope," creaked Jean, quite confused, his master being no speculator.

"I am well content, and pitched on the new owner without difficulty. Monsieur Basset is now recording it in the new name with the Abbé, and," here the grey eyes twinkled, "do you think you will like it, Marie? there is a nice strip of sand beach where children might play in safety."

This brought a stupefied silence; Marie's lips began to tremble, she was bewildered, frightened; Jean's eyes grew round, bulging, roving uncertainly from his patron to his woman, having no words for this: she began to cry, so before the outburst came Paul turned on his heel, striding off down the side road. It had been a good moment.

Presently Jean trotted beside him. "M'sieu means this?" he faltered.

"Why not?"

"But--but--"

"My friend," Paul laid a big hand on his shoulder, "if it pleases you both, it pleases me. The rest is forgotten. We have been through much, you and I, but after this summer we shall not meet so often. At the desire of the Governor, I am thinking of a seigneury above Chambly."

Jean looked troubled. "That is a bad country for anyone."

"It will not always be bad: the soil is good."

"But, m'sieu, that is the country of the Iroquois! I should go with you."

"Perhaps I have something still to settle. I will not be alone--there will be plenty of other men, but no married ones. No, you will stay where you are. Later, I shall expect to see some 'petits Prud'hommes' playing on that sand beach, perhaps a small naked Paul amongst them. Eh, how does that sound?"

"M'sieu may count on us, we shall do our best, but--" he stammered, "what about madame? she will be devastated--does she not know? has m'sieu not told her?"

"Madame, my friend, is shortly going to Quebec, thence she may return to Castellon. I learned that yesterday from the Governor himself."

Jean gaped, choked, shook his head, then went slowly back to where Marie still stood in a daze: he put his arm round her: there sounded a torrent of words, and when Paul moved on towards the lake shore their eyes followed him.

*　　*　　*　　*　　*

Jacqueline sat with Marguerite Bourgeoys in the

house of the Sisters of the Congregation: it faced the Place; through the small window they saw half naked children, white and brown, playing in the dusty earth; a squaw tramped by with a papoose on her back, packed in moss, strapped flat to a short wooden frame; a pair of Jesuits paced in the sunlight, eyes downcast, reading breviaries as they paced; men in uniform went in and out of de Callières' house where a sentry with white leggings and oiled pigtail mounted guard; two Iroquois captives were digging a ditch that drained the Place; came a creak of windlass where women filled buckets at the central well, and hung about, chatting, arms akimbo, this spot making for them the social centre of Ville Marie; on a platform along the inner face of the palisade other sentries walked slowly, muskets over their shoulders, eyes exploring the western distance and faint blue shore of Longueil. The air was mild, the sun bright, a breath of early summer pervaded the settlement so lately banked with ridges of melting snow.

Marguerite Bourgeoys, daughter of Abraham, the candlemaker of Troyes, was now seventy, with half her selfless years spent in New France. Her youthful beauty had long since been tempered by work and exposure, but she was still striking, with firm, pointed chin, lips that retained something of a girlish curve, dark eyes set far apart under benignant brows. Jacqueline, drawn to so gallant and tender a soul, loved her deeply.

It had been a hard winter with shortage of food and clothing, with the Iroquois never far off, a winter of watchfulness and alarms, so now that spring came they were thankful. The children needed less care. But with lengthening days a weariness had crept over the younger woman, noted by the other, whose glance perceived more than she revealed. And, thought Marguerite, here was one not destined to live and die for the Congregation. God meant her for motherhood.

They had talked long and earnestly when Marguerite said:

"The Governor came to see me yesterday and spoke of you."

"But why?"

"He has ideas, that man: one that there is need to organise our labours in Quebec; also in late June there will be an arrival of Filles du Roi who certainly must be cared for; also a new Orphelinage is to be built in the Upper Town. It seems no end of things are in his head, so first he proposed that I move to Quebec. Bishop St. Vallier approves."

"What did you say?"

"That while I appreciated the confidence of His Excellency and the bishop," here she gave a little nod of decision, "my duty was still here. Then I ventured to suggest that as well as the Ursulines there were enough young women in the families of officers in Quebec who might well forget their fripperies and flirtations and apply themselves to something more sensible."

"What did he say to that?"

"He laughed and agreed, with the comment that he found women more difficult to influence than men; but I surmise there are surprises in store for some of those fine ladies. He is a brave man, the Governor."

"Was that all?"

"Not quite--then he spoke of you. Of course he is

aware of the death of your husband, whom he said he had met at Versailles."

"Yes, I know: Jules told me about it, but we never dreamed that...."

"He was all sympathy and the next idea was that you go to Quebec in my place under his escort when he leaves in about a week. Later he said you might return to France should you desire it. I thought that might be wise."

"Wise! Sister, I cannot leave you!"

"Yet we must part for all time before long. I am seventy, my child, and have not far to go. God has been very good to me. I shall have much to remember--elsewhere: my welcome when I arrived here with one hundred and two new settlers just thirty seven years ago; it was Monsieur Maisonneuve who brought us all the way from Saint-Nazaire, and not a single soul took the scurvy--how we opened the first school, it is now thirty three years old, long before you were born--the coming of those first Filles du Roi--how those young virgins gabbled when they came ashore and saw the Outawa savages! There is so much--so much! It seems but yesterday when the Minister Colbert aided to send out my first six novices--when Monsieur le Baron Foncamp gave me that crucifix and the miraculous image, calling it La Vierge de Notre Dame de Bonsecours. You notice that sometimes the holy eyes seem to move. Ah, well, what have I to complain of?"

Her voice faltered a little, then with habitual cheerfulness:

"With you, my child, it will be different; for one so young you have been through enough, though Ville

Marie is now quite advanced from what I found, almost modern. Should you not consider the work in Quebec? Those fine ladies will receive you as one of themselves being an officer's wife, they will listen and labour with you, while at the daughter of a candlemaker in Troyes they might look askance. What do you say? Is there any reason," the wise old woman picked her words, "why you should not go?"

The honest grave eyes were hard to meet: Jacqueline was oscillating between the vision of Jules, dead in the camp of The Hairy One, and a square log house six miles away where she loaded muskets, choked with the stink of blood and burned powder, heard the Iroquois scream when a grim-faced man fired through a loophole.

Then she felt shame for herself: that was Paul's way of reprisal for the wound she had inflicted: deep in her heart she was now forced to admit that she loved him, deeply she knew that always he would love her, serving in silence to the very end. And when might that not be?

Against it, against life with Paul on a Lachine farm, and shamed again in her own weary spirit, she put Quebec with women of her own sort, the gay terrace parade after the Governor's soirées, youth, laughter, attention, something of Old France in the New, ships beating up the Gulf, ships from France, white wings spread on the way to France, security, comfort. Nothing of this since she set foot in Ville Marie. Something fluttered in her breast, then became still.

"I know not what to answer," she said in a low tone.

"While I cannot answer for you. Think it over,

and--"

A shadow fell in the doorway where a Huron girl stood like a slim, brown statue.

"A woman is here, a woman of Lachine, to see madame."

Marguerite nodded. "There is no hurry; it will be as you decide." She went out. A moment later Marie appeared, breathless.

"Come in, Marie; sit down."

Having covered the distance in two hours, she was glad to sit, gazing about at bare walls and pallet bed. It was a tiny room with a pigmy fireplace. Crossing herself before Virgin and crucifix, she put her red hands on plump knees, smiling a little nervously.

"It is many weeks, madame, since I saw you: how thin you are!"

"This warm season will cure that. And Jean?"

"Busy as six men over the land where things seem to rush out of the earth. Madame, I have great news!"

"Of what?"

"Monsieur Paul has given us the farm of Pierre Barbarin for our own," she bleated, "and there is a sand beach: he did it in a few words like brushing off a mosquito, and would take no thanks, and I am here to tell you."

"That is splendid, and very like him. You will be

neighbours."

"But, no! this is what grieves us--he will not be there long."

"What has happened, Marie?"

"Just that the Governor invites him to take a seigneury on the Richelieu which is, so to speak, the backyard of the Iroquois."

"But--but does he desert his own place?" her pulses stirred "no, he will not go--why should he?"

"That is what we ask, Jean and I, but who can say why our patron does this or that?"

"Marie, you must be mistaken."

"No--m'sieu left us in no doubt, and puts in some tenant instead. Believe me it is not done without purpose--and the Richelieu--you know what that means!"

"When did he tell you this?"

"Just after midday; in the same breath he gave us the farm. For some reason, madame, he desires that house no longer, but perhaps," here the voice hardened a shade, "perhaps you can tell me. Also he told us that the Governor had invited you to live in Quebec. Is that so?"

Jacqueline nodded.

"When do you go?"

"It--it is uncertain, nothing is settled yet. How did

Monsieur Paul hear about that?"

"Yesterday, from the Governor himself, and there is our patron with his mind made up, so it seems that we of Castellon will soon be divided, and--" she took a quick breath with the dawning of a new idea, "and in this business of Chambly I think there is something I have not whispered even to Jean."

"Well?" said the girl distantly.

"Madame remembers the girl, Eri?"

"What of her?"

"She loved him, no doubt of that; also it is true she has done for him more than any other woman, though a savage. She saved his life, and when that happens one is generally very grateful--is it not so?-- and it came over me that the country of Eri's father, the old chief Oguntwae, is not so far south of Chambly, so it is possible that--oh madame! it has happened too often, and will happen again, for in this strange land it is not natural for a man like m'sieu to live alone."

Thus delivered, she broke off, aghast at her own audacity, clapping a hand over her mouth. Jacqueline said no word, her face a mask. Her glance wavered, avoiding what she read in the face of this breathless woman. Eri!--she had never forgotten Eri, nor the domestic scene at which Jules had laughed so mockingly--the country wife! Then Paul had made her an offer of Eri, so there could be nothing--nothing in that. Later, Paul lying bound--Eri's brown hand in the darkness with the knife--severed thongs--liberty! What man could dismiss that without repayment as she had dismissed Paul? But Paul could--of all the men she knew he the most likely. Why?

She stared at the image of the Virgin over Marguerite's bed, and it seemed that slowly the mild, holy eyes did move to meet her own, and the blessed face changed to something like her own, and the Child too was softly changed till she appeared to be watching an image of herself with her own babe on her breast while over them towered the great protecting shape of the man who had led her past the gates of death and expected naught for his reward.

"What a strange story you tell, Marie," said she in a small voice.

"I tell you nothing but what I know; he stays till the grain is in--no longer. Ah, madame, we--that is Jean and I--we--"

"Speak, I listen."

"Alors, I will speak! Our hearts are very full of happiness for what will happen to me, full of our new farm and the years together, full of our patron and you. It is now twenty-three years since you came to my breast, but you are still part of my life. It will always be like that, so I talk as to my own child. Our patron loves you with all his lonely soul; he has not ceased to love, though you gave him small cause for that. He will die rather than speak, so he goes in silence. He is not afraid to go, but you--" she burst out with sudden harsh bitterness, "--you are afraid to stay. He does not know I am here, but that is what I return to tell him!"

* * * * *

Paul dug his fingers into the clean sand, trying to sort out a troubled mind. The decision once made, he reckoned that life would go more placidly, but here was mistaken: the glow of a good deed had passed and left

392

him cold. Now he looked out over Lake St. Louis, pictured himself hacking out new land up the Richelieu, but, strangely, that had lost point, while behind him the dark forest palisade signalled its voiceless mockery at the efforts of puny men. What was he and others like him against that immortal growth? Thousands of millions of trees were shooting sunward faster than millions of French could fell them.

Chambly? he knew what he would find there, having come that way when he fled the camp of Oguntwae, christening his trail with his own blood. Eri? his finger touched the white scar, but that meant nothing now. Castellon? Castellon seemed dim, and should Jacqueline return to France, the place would be uninhabitable by him. Nor could he doubt that Frontenac, with many another, knew what had brought him to New France, knew all of it; and though the Governor, speaking more than fair, offered a commission, Paul found no comfort in this.

Hours passed. Brooding, discontent, lonely, undirected, he did not stir: the hour grew on to evening, the sun dipped over the molten sheet of Lake St. Louis; his eyes followed the great coppery disc to a watery grave, and as the disc kissed the horizon there came from his hot heart a conception that quickened his blood.

There was one thing he could do, one he had not yet tried.

During la Durantaye's last visit to Ville Marie, Paul had heard much about the island of Michilimacinac, that distant outpost called by the savages The Isle of the Turtle on account of its great rounded hump. Thither journeyed tribes from western hunting grounds with their peltries, there fighting men of the Illinois,

Outogamis, Chippawas and Mascoutins gathered with Ottawas and Saulteaux, there the traders of New France stored their goods and liquor, there the Jesuit Engelran prayed and preached, there Kondiaronk, The Rat, hatched his schemes of treachery.

Beyond Michilimacinac flowed the Ste Marie carrying flood waters from the greatest lake of all, more than a hundred leagues in length, into whose deadly waters--so ran the tale--no man might fall and survive. Beyond that again lay without limit a strange country where no trees grew, and wild men rode naked on wild horses shooting arrows into longhaired black beasts bigger than the biggest bull. This land, it was said, ended where snow-capped mountains assailed the heaven. On the other side must open the China Seas. La Salle, from the very shore where he now sat, had gone forth to find these seas, and never returned.

There, decided Paul, was the solution: he would select a picked company of coureurs des bois, outfit them as no band of adventurers had ever been equipped, start by way of Fort Frontenac, Aniagara and Michilimacinac, and travel on by snowshoe when winter caught them. Should he find nothing but himself, the thing was worth doing.

It was taking shape when a cart jolted along the road from Ville Marie, drawn by an old piebald horse very familiar to the settlement, driven by an old man in a long rusty coat. This was the servant of Marguerite Bourgeoys. Beside him on the cross plank perched two women, one Marie, the other not Marguerite but taller, more slender. They turned up the side road, and Jacqueline got down first.

He had not expected this, but for some reason was not altogether surprised: his senses seemed to be growing a sort of protective covering: already he was trying not to think of her, or at least not with the old speechless hunger; trying to merge her into a delicate picture that would remain to the end. That, he had assured himself, was how it must ever be, but now, of a sudden the sight of her set up once more all his baffled inarticulate longing; he slipped the new found moorings, his breast thumped.

Watching with resentment, he saw the women greeted by Jean, who seemed to have been awaiting them: Jean was gesticulating, waving his arms: one could not miss what it meant when Marie pointed to where her patron sat half hidden from the road, and Jacqueline came slowly towards him. He saw that her face was pale, her large eyes unnaturally bright.

"Well, Paul, I am glad for once that you are not working."

"And you--from all I hear you are the one who overworks."

"I am well, but a little tired," she admitted, then, with a faint smile, "we have seen little of each other of late: I fear you were too occupied with the Iroquois."

"We met--on occasions."

"And yesterday the Comte Frontenac gave you audience! Ville Marie buzzes over what may have passed between you."

"Also I understand His Excellency is much occupied with your welfare, proposing a change of air. Perhaps it is more healthy down at Quebec?"

"Perhaps," she sent him a sidelong look "also I

learn that you contemplate a seigneury on the Richelieu nearer your friends the Iroquois. I did not realise you were so popular there--except for one reason."

Paul glowered at her. "Madame has no doubt made her plans, while certainly mine are concluded. Why have I the honour of this visit? it was in September that madame was last here."

That went home: again she saw the fog-buried cabin, the crumbling fire, Jean's start at the creak of a door latch slid open, she sensed a wave of damp air, saw a huge figure step into the light. But the moment was not yet.

"You are sorry I came?" she asked quietly.

"I thank you."

"Is there anything I can do for you?"

"I am not accustomed to having much done for me," said he, subduing a hot surge of blood.

"No, that is true. Listen, Paul! Yesterday it was possible that I left for Quebec--now I do not go."

"Why?"

Her lips curved a little. "That is perhaps difficult to explain--there is enough work where--where I am-- also today Marie asked if I were afraid to remain--well-- I am not afraid."

"No," he conceded, "you were never afraid."

"Thank you, Paul. Is there anything more? what is in your mind in not taking that seigneury--do you ever get letters from Castellon--where you are quite a hero?"

"Me, a hero!"

"Of course: I wrote about what happened last August, also your return in September. Didn't you write?"

"No."

"But why?" her eyes held a faint twinkle.

"There was none to write to, that is of any importance."

"I see: is that what you feel about Castellon, really? you are content with New France, always?"

"Yes, always: I understand this country while my own didn't understand me."

That hurt: it was the only time he had ever hurt her.

"But," she persisted, "if you won't live on here, and won't take the seigneury, what will you do?"

Paul could not stand much more of this, he heaved himself up: it was not so long ago that a black-eyed, brown-skinned bitch had tortured him with glowing brands, but in the end was merciful, while in this girl he had loved all his life was no mercy.

"Listen!" he growled, "I am staying here till the crop is in, then start in search of the China Seas. How long that will take I do not know, but it will serve. Once I would not have thought of it. There are some things I did not understand till today--when they are clear. Always I have been a fool, and always will be. Most farmers are fools. All they know is the soil. Perhaps, later, I shall go farming again--somewhere--not here. You owe me nothing--nothing, but since that night in August you said you would ever pray for me--well--I thank you for your prayers, and wish you well."

"Paul," she quavered, "is it so very very important that you find the China Seas--they sound so far away?"

"I should like to be the first. It is getting dark, so better that you start for home."

"Stay a minute! Paul, I'd like to find them too; won't you take me with you?"

His mouth opened, he stared and stared. "What are you talking about?"

"You and me. Paul I have no home--but yours!" Her arms went round his neck, holding him close. "Oh, my dear one, dearest of all men, can't you see for yourself? always yours, you mine, always, always!"

An hour later the old driver made an impatient gesture towards the lake. "We are late, late, and I do not like it: I go to fetch my lady."

"Mon vieux," chuckled Prud'homme, "you are either very brave or a great fool: do you put so little value on your neck?"

www.ingramcontent.com/pod-product-compliance
Lightning Source LLC
Chambersburg PA
CBHW050902250626
47155CB00001B/65